HEART SONG

DENISE KAHN

Copyright © 2021 Denise Kahn - Published by 4Agapi

978-0-9978231-6-5 (Paperback)
978-1-7379183-0-1 (E-Book)
978-1-7379183-1-8 (Audiobook)

Publisher's Cataloging-In-Publication Data
(Prepared by The Donohue Group, Inc.)

Names: Kahn, Denise, author.
Title: Heart song / Denise Kahn.
Description: [Albuquerque, New Mexico] : 4Agapi, [2021]
Identifiers: ISBN 9780997823165 (paperback) | ISBN
    9781737918301 (ebook)
Subjects: LCSH: Women singers--Fiction. | Music fans--
    Fiction. | Hijacking of aircraft--Fiction. | Horsemen
    and horsewomen--Fiction. | Man-woman
    relationships--Fiction. | LCGFT: Romance fiction. |
    Thrillers (Fiction)
Classification: LCC PS3611.A43 H43 2021 (print) | LCC
    PS3611.A43 (ebook) | DDC 813/.6--dc23

DeniseKahnBooks.com / DeniseKahnVoices.com

Books by Denise Kahn

Novels
Peace of Music
Obsession of the Heart
Warrior Music
Music trilogy
Guitar Woman (Novella)
Split-Second Lifetime
Hot Air
Enchanted Football
Heart Song

Travel Tales
(Short travel stories)
We were 12 at 12:12 on 12/12/12 (Mexico)
Entertained by the Gods (Greece)
Sai Baba's Ashram Rendezvous (India)
Gstaad Grace (Switzerland)
Thanksgiving in 24 Hours (Mexico)
Olympic Honor (Italy)

Short Stories
Miraculous Moments;
True Stories Affirming that Life goes on,
By Elissa Al-Chokhachy

Photo Book
Around the World in 80 Quotes on Photos

Children's
Violet's Voyages (Series):
Switzerland: The St. Bernard Adventure
Greece: The Dolphin Adventure

KKO *Keeping Kids Occupied (and adults too)*

Praise for Denise Kahn

Peace of Music

What a thrill this novel is, especially for me, since I am Greek and a singer and have lived in many of the places in the book. It portrays beautifully the history of my country, some of which I lived through. Most of all, I truly love the way music is intertwined in the story. Musicians will not be able to put this book down, nor anyone else who appreciates a good novel.
Nana Mouskouri, Opera and contemporary singer,
UNICEF Ambassador, Author

Music to Your Eyes. This magnificent work of literary art spans four continents and the lives of the unforgettable and colorful characters.
Jada Ryker, Bestselling Author

Obsession of the Heart

This tale is centred around a singing diva called Davina. From the first page the story whisks the reader along, from one crisis to another as we meet many other colourful characters along the way. This is very much an adventure story with love, deception and loyalty thrown into the mixture.
The pace is quick as the action travels from country to country in a world of super stardom, yet very real human emotions. Hold onto your seats in this roller coaster of a journey!
Sonya C. Dodd, Author

Warrior Music

Denise Kahn wrote a masterpiece directly imagined from her heart as her own son, a U.S. Marine was in Iraq in harm's way… My hat is off to the author and most respectfully to her son and to all that serve in the United States Military. A must read for anyone looking for a love story with non-stop action.
Marc A. DiGiacomo, Multi-award Bestselling Author,
Law Enforcement Officer

Just an incredible read for me and brought back memories of my 20 + years in the military. Most highly recommended with additional Hoo-Rahs and a Bravo Zulu to this author.
A Navy Vet/#1 Hall of Fame Top Amazon Reviewer

It will soon be categorized as a historical novel because it superbly chronicles the life of a soldier in the desert of Iraq, post 9/11… Ms. Kahn's son is a veteran of the Iraq War, and this novel is her love song to him. Her pride of him and all veterans shines through in this novel of love, war, and music.
P.A. McAlister, Author

The Music Trilogy

This is an exquisite saga. A beautifully woven tale covering several generations of one family whose paths are intertwined with an amazing Chinese vase. Although the story begins in China, the plot covers a range of countries and continents as well as several centuries as the magic of the vase touches the lives of the family to whom it belongs. The writing is beautiful, the characters are rich and varied and the pace changes from the smooth to the rough of World War. Be prepared to lose yourself in an amazing world of music, laughter and intrigue as you follow the vase from thirteenth century China to modern day Europe.
This novel will not fail to capture the imagination of the reader.
Sonya C. Dodd, Author

Split-Second Lifetime

This book will become a classic! Isabel Allende, Paulo Coelho, Denise Kahn. What do they have in common? They are all amazing writers and storytellers with a touch of mysticism. Ms. Kahn's writing is fluid and elegant. The characters are original and compassionate, the story is intriguing and fascinating, and the settings are international and exotic. Unique scenes will stay in the back of your mind for a long time. Each one of these authors has a specialty or unique ingredient that puts them in a class of their own.
Denise Kahn's 'Split-Second Lifetime', like 'House of Spirits' and 'the Alchemist', is bound to become a classic.
Racquel, Amazon Reviewer

A Beautiful Quilting of Sounds and Images. The author took on a panoramic project with her book and did a magnificent job. I learned more about other cultures and ways of thinking. At the same time, the writing style was lyrical, entertaining, and brought together images, sounds, flavors, and sensations. The book even encompasses humor. The entertaining and unexpected puns made me laugh out loud. Jada Ryker, Bestselling Author

Denise Kahn's writing is highly sensual. "Dodi's words were music to my ears and a symphony in my heart." Her work is further enriched by her exposure to different nations, as she describes details from foreign settings and cultures.
Uvi Posnansky, Bestselling Author

Guitar Woman

A novella full of passion that covers art, music and the sensuous side of human nature. The manner in which the reader is drawn into the sights, sounds and smells of Athens is indeed magical. The food at the tavern made my mouth water! The description of the uniforms of the select few guarding the Tomb of the Unknown Soldier are indeed memorable.
Serenity, Amazon Hall of Fame Top 10 Reviewer

Hot Air

This is my first ride with Ms. Kahn and it won't be my last... with a host of elegantly drawn characters in an array of beautifully described scenarios. Denise Kahn has a wonderful, comfortable writing style and her novel Hot Air is fun, exciting, informed and intelligently rendered.
Sean Costello, Bestselling Author

The story is powerful, as they are in all of Denise Kahn's books (this is not my first by this author, and definitely not last). Her characters come alive. The half Navajo half Irish hot air balloon pilot and elite Pararescueman, his Greek playboy buddy, the Canadian world skiers and the Afghan extremist are but some of the personalities that cross paths that will keep you on the edge of your seat.
Helen A., Amazon reader

Enchanted Football

Solid plot, good laughs, strong characters. Well done to the author for this 'play'. A truly enjoyable read.
MJ from VT - #1 Hall of Fame Top Amazon Reviewer

Around the World in 80 Quotes on Photos

As I sit here in the frozen tundra of New England, I can say that I truly appreciated this photographic journey around the world, especially to warmer places! The quotes added a certain serenity to the experience, and I can honestly say the author has rekindled my desire to travel!
James Tredeau, Professor of French

HEART SONG

Denise Kahn

DEDICATION

To all Artists and Entertainers,

especially my mother,
opera singer extraordinaire,
whose glorious voice singing to me was
my very first memory of life.

Thank you all for sharing your talent.
You fill our hearts with your gift
and give us peace.
We in turn very much appreciate,
love and cherish you.

Music is the divine way to tell beautiful,
poetic things to the heart.
Pablo Casals

He moved like a dancer,
which is not surprising;
a horse is a beautiful animal,
but it is perhaps most remarkable
because it moves as if it always hears music.
Mark Helprin

PROLOGUE

2022 – SOUTH FLORIDA

JAXON

Jaxon Logan enjoyed the workouts with Almea. They ran through fields of mainly wild poppies and daisies, and practiced different step exercises. By the time they finished they were both breathing hard and happy with their drills. They went back to the ranch and Almea stayed at the stables while Jax went to the house to take a shower. He took his time and let the water flow over his body to alleviate the soreness from the workout. When he finished, he stepped out of the wet cubicle, dried off with a towel and tied it around his waist. Some parts of his tall frame, especially his chest and sculpted stomach were still a little wet, but he didn't mind. He would be dry in a few moments. He hand-combed his hair and checked the sides of his winsome face. He preferred to be clean shaven, although a beard looked good on him. As he walked into his bedroom, he heard music from the television and was curious as to what was playing. The Aegean blue eyes looked at the screen and his heart skipped a beat as he stared at the most beautiful woman he had ever seen. He pushed the info button and learned her name was Alina; she was a singer, and this was her concert. Jax watched in awe as she epitomized stunning Latin beauties, such as the magnificent Colombian actress and producer Carolina Gomez of Ms. Universe fame.

Jax sat in a comfortable armchair and examined every inch of the singer as she held the microphone firmly yet delicately, as if it were made of exquisite crystal. As she sang, she moved to the exotic rhythms, her wavy dark hair flowing behind her as her hips made her body gyrate with hot, sexy moves. But she had something else, Jax insisted. After watching a little longer, he realized what it was. Yes, she was of course sexy, but it was more than that. It was a natural, sensual elegance mixed with a kindness that came through her gestures and her entire being. The ensemble made her incredibly attractive.

Jax sat up straighter in his chair and really studied her. Alina's teeth were naturally straight and, oh, those lips! He was sure they would be as tasty as an exquisite wine and were begging to be kissed. He wanted to pass his fingers over them, press his mouth to hers and inhale the magic of her essence. And of course, the smile—a smile every woman would kill for, a casual and natural movement of facial muscles that drove the crowd to an adoring frenzy. Each member of her audience was sure that smile had been meant for them individually. And so did Jax. He kept staring at the screen. Alina moved like a jaguar, sleek and graceful. She was a natural born model, tall and sensual, a woman who could go from a tiny bikini, and make it look sophisticated, to a red carpet designer gown. She could pull it all off effortlessly. Jax thought God must have enjoyed spending a little extra time in creating this woman, and even added a voice of a contralta with a range to rival any opera great.

The amber eyes in the heart-shaped face stared at Jax from inside the television. She smiled again, that endearing I-really-care-about-you smile. When she slightly lifted the lips on one side of her mouth it became a grin that plainly said 'I'm in command here, you are under my spell and you love it'. That did it. The man was hooked. He was falling for her, as he was sure every hot-blooded human was. He was going down fast and hard.

Jax stared blankly, an entranced gaze visualizing the thoughts in the depths of his mind. This woman would become his—the love of his life, his lover, his wife, the mother of their children and the one he wanted to grow old with. He would find out everything there was to know about her. He would become an expert in anything Alina. He would make her his... Jax stopped daydreaming. What the hell had gotten into him? He was aggravated at his own reaction, this strange fanatical obsession he didn't know he possessed. But even this realization didn't stop him. His mind was set on his quest.

Jax was financially very well off, and quite the ladies' man. He enjoyed their company immensely and was grateful for their times together, but never had such a reaction to a woman invade him so forcefully. In the days to come he would be thinking or dreaming about Alina every minute of every hour, from the moment he woke up, throughout the day and into his dreams at night. She became his life's priority and he started planning how he would get close to her and make her exclusively his.

Jax stayed home for a solid week trying to find out everything about Alina. He was the boss of his own business and could come and go as he pleased. His staff ran the enterprise smoothly. If they needed anything they could call and Jax would usually find a solution to any problem very quickly. He loved his work and was passionate about it, but right now he was infatuated with Alina. How was it he hadn't heard of her before? How had he not known of her existence? Yet there was something familiar about the woman. Perhaps he had seen her on a magazine cover. The more he searched the more captivated he became with her. His favorite was her smile. He wanted to stare at it twenty-four hours a day, and touch and kiss her lips continuously. No matter what he did or how he tried to stay occupied he just couldn't get her out his mind. He would see the arch of a chair and think of her delicious curves. He would look at the dark sky and imagine his fingers running through her hair. When the stars winked at him he would see her eyes, the amber shining just as brightly. What was wrong with him? Why was he acting like an adolescent boy with a first crush? What was this fanatical fixation? He had known many women in his life and with his good looks there never was a lack of a beauty parading on his arm, or craving his attention. But Alina was different. Was this love at first sight? Did that phenomenon or cliché even exist? Did this really happen to men? But it must, he insisted to himself, because *he* had fallen into such a predicament. He wanted her. Oh, how he wanted her! He longed to caress every inch of her superb figure, to gently kiss her mesmerizing face and every inch of her body. He wanted to become one with her and pleasure her to heights she could only dream of. He could hardly fathom the deliciousness he would enjoy as well. He craved the woman, but he also wanted to know everything about the person behind the beauty. He was sure her life and background would be fascinating.

Jax had no doubt Alina would be in a relationship.

He could picture hundreds standing in line vying for her attention. He would find out. If she was tied to someone, he would find a way to break that liaison and make her his.

Jax watched every video he could find of her, followed every move, the way her hand caressed a singing partner's cheek during their duet, caring and sensual at the same time. And the hugs she gave so freely and sincerely to her colleagues, band members, friends and even fans left him longing for the same affection. It was a very European and Latin form of endearment and he knew she meant it. He searched through YouTube's inventory, watched every interview and was amazed at her international repertoire of songs and her dexterity to sing in different languages. She was a world class entertainer and her interviews ranged from countries in Europe, the Americas, the Middle East and Asia. She was a global star. Jax was also delighted to find out she was smart and sharp, with quick answers and a fun sense of humor she conveyed during those interviews. He found clips of her as she vacationed on a yacht, other celebrities she hung out with, pieces of concerts or entire shows. And then Jax saw the last piece of the puzzle confirming that Alina was the woman he was meant to be with, the twin soul to his being—she was riding a horse. A small clip showed her as an *Amazona* at the Feria of Seville when she was a little girl and recently galloping across fields surrounded by sunflowers on an Andalusian. The man jumped out of his chair screaming: "YES! YES! YES!"

Alina was perfection. She was his soul mate and they belonged together. Jax had absolutely no doubt about that. How could he meet her? There had to be somebody, who knew somebody, who knew somebody. Right? He had to find a way to connect with her and make her fall in love with him. Alina would be his. His eyes stared blankly as his mind worked incessantly on how to achieve his goal.

Jax decided to take a break and have some lunch. After some food he would start making phone calls to any and all of his contacts if he had to. He went to one of his favorite hangouts in Miami Beach and ordered a Cuban burger, a spicy beef and chorizo patty topped with shoestring fries. He accompanied the food with a mojito. Beautiful women in tiny bikinis lazily walked along the street in front of him but his gaze was far away, his mind focused on his goal. While he waited for his meal, he started devising a plan. Even when his order arrived, he kept concentrating on his vision. Jax enjoyed his lunch and drink, or at least he thought he had. Once finished he headed out, still thinking on how he would achieve his undertaking. One thing he knew for sure: he wouldn't let anything, or anyone, get in his way.

Jax absentmindedly stepped down from the sidewalk, his mind fixated on his mission. Out of the corner of his eye he thought he saw Alina, his constant thought, at the wheel of a classic Dino Ferrari. Or had he just imagined her? The car, however, was very real and charged at him as if it were a bull wrapped in a red cape.

That was the last thing Jaxon Logan remembered.

♫

CHAPTER 1

1990 – GULF WAR, IRAQ

ALEJANDRO

When Alejandro Alonso was a child he wanted to be a bird so he could soar through the infinite sky just like they did. He would watch the colorful little flyers take off from their perches in the almond trees, or follow them through the forests of cork oaks commonly found in his southwestern Spanish homeland. His young mind marveled at their wings, so strong and flexible yet even delicate. Alejandro also loved medicine, so he combined his two passions. He followed his dream, became a helicopter rescue pilot and served with pride in the Spanish Air Force, which helped achieve his goals.

Alejandro's prowess was well-known among the international military community. When a mission needed an elusive and creative flyer to land a chopper in the most dangerous and remote areas of a war zone, the Spaniard was at the top of their list. That early morning was no exception. Alejandro was on loan and flew with a U.S.

Marine unit. When the alarm sounded they ran to get their orders and were quickly briefed. After just a few minutes the rescue team ran to the Phrog, the nickname the Marines called the CH-46 Sea Knight helicopter. The green tandem-rotor transporter, powered by twin turboshaft engines, stood at attention as each member boarded.

As soon as the helicopter was at one hundred percent Alejandro maneuvered the metal bird up into the azure sky. They headed toward the Zagros mountains to extract a unit of Rangers who had been on a mission for several days. The assignment wasn't a difficult one, but the Iraqi region was treacherous. There was no place to land and the pilot had to be at the top of his game. Alejandro flew the Phrog to the coordinates they had been given.

The co-pilot spoke into the microphone next to his face and alerted the crew they were almost at their destination. He looked at Alejandro and gave him a thumbs up. The Spaniard gave him one back. He was on. They slowed and approached a snow-covered summit above a gorge where the Ranger unit waited for them. The men on the top of the mountain were close to a ledge. There wasn't any room for the helicopter to land and hardly any for the men to stand on. The Rangers went to the edge and held on to the sides of the mountain while the chopper descended, the wind coming off the rotors beating the men with sharp, piercing snow. They dug their fingers deep into any cracks in the rock and held on for their lives. Alejandro listened to his crew guiding him as he quickly, yet gently, reversed until his rear wheels barely touched the snow on the mountain top. It took four of them to coordinate, the two pilots and two crew in back. They hovered just above the ledge, the back door open and waiting for the Rangers. One by one they crawled off their perches and headed into the helicopter. One of them, a little older than the rest of the unit and their leader, spoke to Lieutenant Hendrikson, the Marine standing at the open back door. The Lieutenant listened, nodded and spoke into his mic: "Captain, there are two men in the ravine below us. They need to be rescued. They're injured, not too badly, but they couldn't climb up here. We have to pull them out with ropes."

"Understood," Alejandro answered.

"We don't have room to get low enough, it's too tight," the co-pilot said, having heard the Lieutenant as well. The bird is forty-five feet long and the widest spot I see is about thirty. We'll hit the sides."

"I know, but we can't leave them."

"What do you suggest, Captain?"

"Hendrikson," Alejandro said into his mic, "come forward."

The Marine ran to the cockpit. "Yes, Captain?"

"Lieutenant, I'm going to try something, but I can only do it once. You have to pull up the two guys at the same time."

"We can do that."

"Good. However, they can't come up the usual way. You have to rig the ropes to hang out the back end. Possible?"

"We'll get it done, Sir."

"Good man. I need you to be ready in two minutes."

"Yes, Captain."

Alejandro nodded. "I'll wait for your signal."

"Yes, Sir."

The co-pilot looked at the Spaniard. "What do you have in mind?" he asked, a worried frown forming on his forehead. He knew of Alejandro's prowess, but he also knew his methods weren't always very orthodox.

"We're going to pull them up from the back."

"Yeah, I figured," he groaned. He was getting a picture of what was about to happen. If he was right the Spaniard would be just one of a handful of pilots in the world who would be able to pull off the maneuver.

A few moments later Hendrikson let Alejandro know they were ready.

Alejandro spoke to everyone on board through his microphone. "Okay, everybody, we are going to rescue the guys down there. We can only attempt this once so everything has to be perfect." He explained what he had in mind and what everyone needed to do. The men, some of the toughest special operatives in the military, noticed a trickle of perspiration start to roll down their spines. They all looked at each other. Would this be their last mission? Could the pilot really pull his idea off?

Hendrikson could see the thoughts in the men's eyes. He spoke to his crew as well as the Ranger unit: "Make sure you're strapped in TIGHT! I don't want to lose any of you. Captain Alonso is the best, actually he's better than the best, he's a magician. Let's do our part and we'll be out of here in no time." The Marine hoped he sounded confident.

There was no door between the front and back of the helicopter. Everyone could see everything, from the pilots, the men buckled in, to the door in the back which was open and level. The ropes and harnesses were ready. Now they just needed a miracle, a little of the Alonso magic Hendrikson spoke about.

The Marines and Rangers watched the captain, fascinated at the amazing coordination of the pilot's limbs and hands which moved in unison as smooth as the inner workings of a Swiss swatch—precise, strong, yet delicate.

The Spaniard was putting on quite a show for his fellow teammates. The helicopter hovered above the ravine. Alejandro slowly lifted the nose. As he did the ropes dropped out of the back end and started to lower and then dangle. The pilot continued pulling the front upward until the helicopter was parallel to the side of the mountain, the back rotors toward the ravine, the top ones beating between the fuselage and the side of the rock façade. The distance between the helo and all sides of the jebel was no more than ten feet in any direction.

"Holy shit!" one of the Rangers exclaimed, a sentiment everyone on board shared at that moment. One wrong move and they would be kissing the rock face. They held on tight to their harnesses.

The team behind the cockpit was ready for the two men they were trying to reach. Hendrikson motioned to the rangers below to put on their harnesses and hold tight. How long could they hold this position? He wondered. "HURRY UP!" he yelled to his team over the noise. "MOVE! Get those boys up here!"

The crew was on it, each one hanging from straps around their waists so they wouldn't fly out the open back end. The two men on the ground were incredulous at the image of the helicopter above them, in a move and position they had never seen and probably never would again. They quickly put the harnesses on and were lifted into the Phrog.

"They're on their way up!" Hendrikson announced over his mic.

That was Alejandro's cue. He continued his mastery and made the helicopter move farther up. When they were out of the constraints of the mountain's walls he leveled off at a 45 degree angle and waited for the crew to get the two men in safely. Once they were inside

Alejandro leveled the helicopter and headed back to base. Every man on board clapped and whistled. They had made it out and alive, thanks to the entire crew and Captain 'Magic' Alonso. They slapped each other's backs and praised the main man, the magician, and completely understood why he had acquired the nickname.

Alejandro smiled. Life at that moment was particularly delicious. The Ranger captain went to the cockpit and saluted. "Thank you, Captain, that was the most brilliant thing I've ever seen. I would like to shake your hand, Sir."

"Take over," Alejandro said to his co-pilot. Once switched, he left his seat, stood up and shook the Ranger's hand. "*Fuerza Aérea Española,* Spanish Air Force. *Capitán* Alejandro Alonso, at your service."

"It's an honor, Sir."

"He's a bullfighter as far as I'm concerned, and I dare say he really took this bull-Phrog by the horns today," the co-pilot grinned and laughed at his own joke.

"Yes, Sir!" The Ranger agreed.

"How are your men, Captain?" Alejandro asked.

"All good, Sir, thanks to you."

"It was a team effort. I'm glad you are all okay."

"Yes, Sir."

♫

CHAPTER 2

1995 – COLOMBIA

STACY

When Alejandro finished his military duty he left the service and started HeliEmerg, an emergency medical helicopter service. With the money he saved from his tours he invested in his new company, which consisted of one helicopter and an office-trailer which was based not far from Seville, in southwestern Spain. It was an area where he had grown up as a boy, and he now used a part of the land his parents had left him to start his business. The location was convenient as he could extend his services to Portugal and northern Africa. As with the military, his forte was rescuing patients from the most remote areas where others just couldn't seem to get to. Alejandro had the uncanny knack to figure how to get the emergency transport in tight spots. His crew was not only some of the best medical staff, they were also ex-military and knowledgeable with conflict zones.

In the years that followed Alejandro and his team, which included himself, a co-pilot, an ex-military medic and depending on the situation on the ground, one or two former special ops personnel, would set up a temporary HeliEmerg office in different locations around the globe. If Alejandro thought they should be there permanently he would set up an office. HeliEmerg worked with medical groups and governments and would transport the patients and local medical personnel from some of the most remote locations on earth where planes could not take off or land, but helicopters, with a skillful pilot such as Alejandro, could. He and HeliEmerg had made a name for themselves as they could deliver when others couldn't. They provided emergency evacuation as well as patient transfers and life support. They would stay in that location for a couple months, making sure the business was in good hands and ran smoothly. They would train the staff hard and would make them the best possible. Their lives, as well as the patients', depended on it.

Alejandro also had a reputation as quite the ladies' man. The handsome Spaniard with rugged good looks was also charming. The Hidalgo loved the ladies, but no one had rocked his world yet. Not that he was looking for a permanent partner. He was still young and wasn't thinking about settling down or having a family.

Alejandro didn't mind staying for long periods of time in any particular area as he was unattached and loved his freedom, but when Stacy Taylor walked into his office the man could only stare. The woman was tall, pretty and sophisticated, wearing khaki pants and a loose white t-shirt. The shirt tried its best to hide her lovely feminine curves but wasn't doing it very well, as the perspiration from the eighty percent jungle humidity made it cling to her skin. There was just no way of hiding the exquisite physique with the strawberry blond hair cascading over her shoulders.

"Are you Mr. Alonso?" Stacy asked.

"I am," he answered, immediately getting up from his desk and extending his hand. "How can I help you?"

"Are you the big boss?" She asked casually, smiling.

The smile lit up the room and warmed the Spaniard's heart. "I guess so," he chuckled.

"Are you or aren't you?" The woman asked, wondering what was wrong with the man.

"I am, yes, yes, the big, big boss," Alejandro mumbled. What the hell was happening to him? It was the beautiful American with the hypnotic smile. She was the one doing this to him. How was it women could make the strongest of men become bumbling teenagers? "What can this big boss do for you?" He asked, trying to keep his mumbling witty yet charming.

Stacy chuckled. The guy had a sense of humor and oh, was he ever good looking! She loved how the elegant lines of his jaw on his clean-shaven face came together at his chin to form a slight dimple. And that handsome head with the Moorish eyes was attached to a toned, sculpted body the clingy shirt had as much difficulty in staying dry as her own. He was also much younger than she expected. The man was probably around twenty-five, and the owner and operator of HeliEmerg. Impressive, Stacy thought. "Actually, it's what I can do for you," she said, without skipping a beat.

Alejandro looked at her green eyes and wondered if they were liquid jade. "For me?" He asked, holding his breath. She could do *anything* for him she desired. "Please sit down."

Stacy did, and got right to the point. "My name is Stacy Taylor and I hear you're looking for an assistant."

Alejandro wondered how this drop-dead gorgeous woman wound up in his make-shift trailer-office in the Colombian jungle, in one of the most remote and dangerous areas of the world. "I am, but may I ask why you are here?"

The woman looked at him. Here he goes again, she thought. "To be your assistant." It was almost a question.

"Yes, no, I mean, how are you here in Colombia?"

"I came with *Médecins Sans Frontières*, Doctors Without Borders. They're leaving and I'm without a job."

"Surely they will fly you back to wherever you came from."

"Yes, of course, but I want to stay on the road. I want to see more of the world and help where I can."

She had the same kind of wanderlust he had, Alejandro mused. "I can understand that. May I ask more about your work background?"

"I've been traveling with Doctors for a couple of years. I am an emergency nurse and also have a degree in business. I went to university in Boston and besides English I'm fluent in Spanish and French." Stacy decided to add one more thing and see what he would do with it: "I also play the piano."

"Oh, music very much helps," Alejandro said, keeping up with her and grinning broadly. "We roll out the baby grand on every possible occasion."

Stacy smiled. Good comeback. This man would be easy to work with, perhaps even fun. She would love to discover what other talents he was willing to share. She stared at him for a moment and kept wondering what it was about this guy that unnerved her. She was having a tough time relaxing, but she continued: "I'm a fast learner and I'm told easy to get along with." I really want this job and seeing you every day would be quite pleasant, she wanted to add. "I heard about HeliEmerg and I think we would be a good fit."

Alejandro's breathing abruptly stopped. He would love to 'fit' together. When his lungs decided to come back to life he asked as calmly as possible: "Do you have any problem with strange hours, long days or hard work?"

"No, that's pretty much what I've been doing and I sleep whenever I can."

"Speaking of sleeping, do you mind sharing a room or some absurd and uncomfortable piece of earth with a bunch of men and women if the circumstance warrants it?"

"Not at all. Tough conditions come up all the time. I like to think I can handle any situation I happen to get thrown into."

"You said you had a business degree?"

"I do."

"Accounting and such."

"Certainly."

"Would you be willing to help out with paperwork as well as medical duties?"

"Absolutely."

"Okay, then." he simply said.

"Okay?" Did he mean she had the job?

"Yes, okay. When can you start?"

Holy shit! Seriously? "Uh, right now?" Stacy said as calmly as she could.

"Wonderful. Welcome to the team and HeliEmerg." Alejandro stood up and extended his hand.

Stacy immediately shook it. The tiny particle of electricity between the two hands was undeniable. "Thank you very much, but don't you want to try me out first?" She asked.

Oh, Miss Stacy Taylor, in every way possible. "I like to think I'm a good judge of character. Besides, we'll know if it doesn't work out, but I have a feeling it will."

"I think so too," she said and gave him her lovely smile. Alejandro's dopamine was responding in full force. He tried to keep his mind away from her physique, although he liked her spunk as well. He picked up his walkie-talkie and clicked on the speak button. "Fernando? Can you come in?"

"*Sí, Jefe,* I'll be right there," the man on the other radio answered.

"Fernando is my local contact. Do you have any bags with you?"

"Yes, in the jeep outside. A colleague drove me. He's waiting. "

"Great. Fernando will show you where to put your things. Will that be alright?"

"Perfect. I'm looking forward to starting."

Fernando walked into the office. *"Hola, Capitán."*

"Fernando, this is Stacy. She is, as of right now, working with us and part of our team."

"Ay, bienvenida, welcome, *Señorita."*

"Thank you," Stacy answered.

"Please show her the sleeping quarters and where she can put her things."

"No problem, come," Fernando answered, leading her out of the trailer. He held the door for her and let her leave first. He looked back at his boss. Alejandro's longing features were undeniable. *"Echandole los perros, Jefe?"* He whispered.

Alejandro rolled his eyes to the ceiling and waved him off. Stacy overheard, and although her Spanish was fluent she didn't know what 'throwing the dogs at her' meant. Obviously, it wasn't literal. Stacy learned it was a local colloquial expression for flirting or seducing someone.

Fernando took Stacy to the sleeping quarters, showed her how the team worked and the helicopter where she would do most of her life-saving duties. The American woman checked all the supplies and was impressed. It seemed Alejandro ran everything with military precision. She looked forward to working with this team and their boss. Especially the boss.

♫

CHAPTER 3

Stacy didn't have to wait long for her first mission. They had a rescue the very next morning and she would be going along to observe. She scrambled with the rest of the team and ran to the orange medical helicopter with a white cross depicted on all sides. Alejandro and his co-pilot took their seats in the front. Fernando rushed up to them. "*Jefe*, we have a problem."

Alejandro hated those words. "What is it?"

"Gabriel has been vomiting all night, must have eaten something really nasty. He can't even stand up."

"Okay, so he isn't coming," Alejandro stated.

"*Exacto.*"

"Get me Stacy."

Fernando did as he was asked and Stacy went to the cockpit.

"What's up?" She asked.

"Stacy, trial by fire," he answered. "You have to take charge of the medical side and the patients. Gabriel, our medical guy is sick and won't be with us. Can you handle it?"

"I'll do my best, Captain."

"Good enough. Buckle up!"

Thankfully Fernando had shown her all the necessary steps and what each crew member's duties were, including her own. The one big difference to what she was used to was that she wouldn't be stationary, rather she would be working in a moving, flying box. She hoped she would adapt quickly and wouldn't make any mistakes. She would have liked a practice run but assured herself that she would persevere and do the best she possibly could.

The team included Alejandro, his German co-pilot Hans, Fernando the Colombian liaison, Stacy, and two ex-military guys. The pilots were wearing their flying gear and helmets, Stacy was in a one-piece cover-all. Fernando and the former soldiers wore jungle fatigues. Several weapons hung from their belts. Big Rod and Pierre sported bush hats as worn by the Australian military. Rod really was an Aussie and had given a slouch hat to his French buddy Pierre, who thought the chapeau *très chic*. They all wore patches on their upper arms clearly denoting their country of origin and HeliEmerg's logo depicting they were part of a medical rescue team.

Everyone was buckled in, although Rod and Pierre were sitting on the side of the open helicopter as they scanned for what Stacy hoped weren't any guerillas or paramilitary group members. HeliEmerg's mission was to retrieve two wounded men from somewhere in the vast jungle. They had approximate coordinates, but it would still be difficult to find them. They all searched. The pilots wore NVGs, night vision goggles, to hopefully detect unnatural forms that didn't belong in the dark jungle such as injured humans.

"There!" The co-pilot shouted in his heavy German accent as he watched the fluorescent green shapes through his goggles. "Two bodies. By the way they are moving they are alive but injured."

"Yes, I see them," Alejandro confirmed. He spoke to the other members through the tiny microphone next to his face. They all wore the same device. "Get ready, everybody, we found them."

Alejandro called Pierre to the front. The Frenchman was a specialist with blades, any size, and his mind was as sharp as a combat knife. "Pierre, I can't land in the middle of the jungle. Is there any way you could clear a patch just big enough for me to get in there?"

"It would probably take us a couple of hours, even with machetes the size of the rotors. And then of course we could have unwanted visitors who would like to put a few bullet holes in us, like they did to those two."

"Okay, Pierre, thanks. Go in the back and tell everybody to *really* buckle in."

"*Très bien.*"

Pierre had given Alejandro an idea. Hans watched the man next to him and grinned as he practically saw the light bulb shine through the Spaniard's skull. "*Mein Kapitän,* what are you thinking?" He asked, curious and slightly worried. He knew Alejandro's prowess was truly unique, and sometimes the Spaniard dreamed up *very* strange and unconventional solutions to complete his missions.

"Simple, we're going to clear an area."

"Of course." Hans wasn't sure what that meant.

"HOLD ON!" Alejandro warned everyone through his mic.

Stacy and Fernando were sitting in the back, buckled to their seats. The Colombian knew Alejandro well, and when Stacy saw Fernando crossing himself her eyes opened a little wider. What was it about their boss that he knew and she didn't—yet?

Rod and Pierre grinned and gave each other a high five, their adrenaline pumping a little faster. Their captain never disappointed.

When Hans saw what Alejandro was starting, he could only curse: *"Ah, Scheisse!"*

Alejandro hovered above the jungle near the two wounded men. He slowly descended into an opening in the trees just large enough to fit the body of the helicopter.

Stacy watched from a window. "Oh, I really like bamboo but I'm not too sure about this..." She trailed off.

"Si, guadua," Fernando agreed with half a breath.

"Guadua?" Stacy asked.

"Colombian bamboo, very beautiful, as you can see close up, very very very close." Fernando whimpered, the perspiration running down his back. The nature around him made him think of the beauty of his native land, and how much he adored it. It was rich in natural resources, emeralds, cacao, coffee, fresh-cut flowers and coca leaves. He tried not to think of the violence and displacement of so many of his fellow Colombians, mostly in the countryside, and that 25,000 people had been killed in his country in just one year. He hoped his involvement with HeliEmerg and other beneficial groups would make even a little bit of difference. Fernando came out of his reverie when he realized the back end of the helicopter was higher than the front and his body was pushing forward against the seat belt.

Alejandro used the foot pedals to slightly lift the tail rotor so it was clear and wouldn't hit a branch and spin them out of control. He continued lowering the helicopter at that angle, the blades becoming giant machetes cutting an opening in the jungle canopy.

"*Ja!* This is working!" Hans exclaimed.

The two pilots laughed. "Seems to be," Alejandro answered, "but watch the engine air intakes. We wouldn't want any bamboo pieces clogging them up. And of course, anything shooting at us."

"*Ja, ja,* I'm watching."

The immense blades cut through the branches and Alejandro continued until he had enough room to hover over a small clearing. He couldn't land and kept to a half a foot off the ground. The crew knew. It was time. They were a well-oiled machine. Rod, Pierre and Fernando jumped out. They quickly ran to the wounded, assessed the injuries and nodded to each other. The buddies each picked one of the men and carried them on their shoulders. Fernando watched for any kind of movement in the dense jungle. Rod and Pierre hurried back to the helicopter with their bundles. Fernando walked backwards behind them, his senses heightened to their maximum. Suddenly a burst of machine gun fire made them hit the ground.

"Keep going!" Fernando yelled as he sprayed bullets from his machine gun in the direction the original burst had come from. "I'll cover you!"

Rod and Pierre picked up their loads and almost reached the hovering craft when a bullet found its way into Rod. He fell hard and the wounded man slumped on top of him. Pierre dropped his man into the helicopter and let Stacy pull him in the rest of the way. She quickly assessed the injury, more worried about Rod and the other man. She would have to simultaneously work on three people. She hoped the Aussie wasn't badly hurt. She was also terrified. She hadn't been aware this job would be so dangerous. She had never even been so close to being shot, or maybe killed. Bullets still thundered around them. She would deal with her fear, but not at this moment she insisted with herself. She focused on the wounded.

Pierre lifted the injured man off Rod and carried him to the chopper. Stacy pulled him in while the Frenchman went back for his buddy who was crawling toward him and trying to stand up. Pierre managed to lift the big man and they made the few steps to the helicopter and both men fell into the cabin together. Fernando came running and dove into the helicopter immediately behind them.

Alejandro was watching the events from his window and quickly yet skillfully lifted the collective and the metal bird smoothly climbed out of the jungle. Once cleared he pulled hard on the same lever and banked the helicopter out of danger.

Stacy assessed the cases and immediately started working on her patients. She had three of them and she would need help.

"Pierre, Fernando, come here," she said with authority. "This one with the mustache has a bullet in his shoulder. One of you take this gauze and put pressure on it until I come back."

"I've got it," Fernando said.

Stacy looked at the other man. He was in bad shape. She didn't think he would make it. His shirt was soaked with blood. She frantically cut the material and looked closer. There were several bullets in his chest. "Pierre!" She shouted. "I need you to…" The man's head slumped to his side. Stacy searched for a pulse, but already knew the outcome. She shook her head. "Would you just cover him up please, he's gone."

Pierre nodded and complied with her request.

Stacy hurried over to Rod and quickly inserted

scissors into the hole the bullet had made in his pants. She immediately saw where the blood was coming from. It was in the groin area on the inside of his leg, just below the bottom rim of his underwear. She cut through those as well. She let out a sigh as the wound was not too bad and definitely not life threatening. Without looking up Stacy asked the big man: "Hey, Rod, did you ever want kids?"

The man, already pale, turned sheet white. "What?" He asked in panic.

"It's just a deep graze in the groin area and missed the important parts."

Rod exhaled and the color came back to his face. He smiled at the pretty woman. "Does this mean you need to inspect further up?"

"Already have. I don't foresee any problems, unless I slip while suturing."

"Uh, you won't slip, Miss Florence Nightingale, right?"

"Don't give up on me yet. We are in a moving box and this is my first time."

"Uh, you will be careful?" He wanted to make sure he was getting through to Stacy.

"No worries, mate," she said, smiling at the Australian.

"Aw," Rod groaned at her pun. "Would you be singing "Waltzing Matilda" to me next, darlin'?"

"I could." Stacy kept up with his jokes. It would keep the man's mind off his painful injury, or at least she hoped so.

Rod smiled back, trying not to worry about his family jewels.

"I've put a wad of gauze on the laceration. I need you to hold it in place while I try to fix the other guy. I'll be back soon." She turned to his buddy. "Pierre will help you."

"I can handle it," Rod replied, shooing the Frenchman away.

"I'll be right here in case you need me. I won't touch anything, I promise," Pierre said, grinning.

Stacy went back to the shoulder wound trying very hard to not think about the man she hadn't been able to save—her first patient with HeliEmerg. She had known the chances were impossible, but her nurturing and professional side wanted to prove the contrary. She turned to Mustache Man and started working on his wound. She spoke into her microphone hurriedly. "Alex, how long before we reach a hospital?"

Alejandro liked the way she called him. "What kind of problem do we have?"

"We lost one of the guys, too many bullets. He didn't last more than a couple of minutes. Rod will be fine, just a bad graze that needs suturing. The other guy has a bullet in his shoulder and needs a hospital."

"About fifteen minutes."

"Good enough."

"I'll push a bit."

"Thanks."

"Hey, Stacy."

"Yes?"

"You're doing a fine job."

Stacy smiled and would have sworn a few butterflies were flying around her stomach. "Thanks, Captain." She continued working on the shoulder wound, did as much as she could and patched it up enough to get him to the hospital. She went back to Rod. She took off the gauze and was ready to give him a shot to numb the area.

"Hey, what's that?" The big man asked.

"A needle with…"

"Yes, I know."

Pierre shook his head. "He's a big baby, no, a scared little koala."

Stacy raised her eyebrows. "Seriously? You're scared of a needle? You just got shot!"

"Not the first time. Trust me, you can stitch me up without any needle."

"Do you need someone to sing to you?" Stacy asked as she inserted the needle quickly without Rod having seen it.

"Hey!" Rod growled. "You stuck me!"

"Oh, you *are* a big baby," Stacy laughed. "Now, stay calm while I sew you up."

"You will be careful."

"Of course. As I said, try not to move."

The big man looked around. They were in a *moving* bird. He sat as quietly as he could, a scowl on his face and his genitals exposed for the world to see, until Stacy put a towel over them.

"You almost lost your balls, *mon ami*," Pierre said, chuckling.

"Not funny!" Rod growled again.

Pierre just laughed, ecstatic they hadn't lost his best friend.

Once finished with the suturing Pierre leaned over and looked at Stacy's handywork. "This is a work of art! You are a da Vinci, Mademoiselle."

"Merci, Pierre," Stacy answered.

"Yeah, nice work Leonardo," Rod agreed.

"You'll hardly have a scar."

"Oh, but Stacy, the ladies will love it."

"And the crazy Aussie's back," Pierre sighed.

The cabin was quiet as they flew toward the nearest hospital to deliver Mustache Man. Stacy looked at the men in the cabin. They were relaxing and they also watched her. They reminded her of Cheshire cats, grinning from ear to ear. "What?"

"Captain's right, really nice work and under hellish conditions, Stacy," Rod said. "And thank you for fixing me up."

"You're welcome."

"Great baptism and quite unique. You're one of us now. *Bienvenue!* Welcome to the team!" Pierre added.

"*Eso,* what they said," Fernando confirmed.

"Thank you, gentlemen, I am honored."

♫

CHAPTER 4

It was time to unwind after their long and arduous day. The team had flown to the nearest hospital and dropped off the injured man and returned to their base. They cleaned up and slept for a couple of hours when Fernando announced it was time to eat and drink, especially drink.

"Come on Stacy, we have to show you our bar," Fernando said excitedly.

"Your bar?" She asked.

"Yes, yes, now come on," he said, gently prodding her forward toward the jeep.

Fernando drove. He knew the roads and the area best. He could have driven to the bar in his sleep. Big Rod sat next to him in the passenger's seat. Stacy, Alejandro, Hans and Pierre squeezed together in the back, which wasn't made for four people but accommodated them as Pierre and Hans each let one of their legs dangle over the side. Stacy and Alejandro didn't mind in the slightest that they were sardined together, and Hans and Pierre were just looking forward to the alcohol in the bar. It didn't take very long for them to arrive.

The team walked into *La Tusa Pachorra*, The Sluggish Heartbreak, a local bar in a village close to their base.

Stacy immediately smelled the stale beer lingering in the large, humid room. The cement walls were covered with posters of what she surmised was the owner's favorite Colombian celebrities, most of them beautiful women who had taken part in national and international pageants. A few tables, chairs, the bar and the lampshades hanging from the ceiling were all made with local bamboo and filled the room. Salsa music blared from a jukebox next to a dancing couple. Fernando immediately moved to the rhythm. Stacy's eyes grew wide when she spotted an old upright against one of the walls, the many shades of wood faded and scratched. It had seen better days. "They have a piano!" She exclaimed.

"I told you we rolled out a baby grand whenever possible. Well, this is the bar's version of that," Alejandro chuckled, "and even though it's pretty beat up it actually works."

"Do people play?"

"Yes and no."

"I'm not sure I understand."

"Yes, they try to. No, it's not what I would call playing."

"I see," Stacy grinned.

Pierre and Hans quickly put two tables together.

"Make sure this Koala has a chair, we wouldn't want his sutures to tear," Stacy said.

"Well, I wouldn't mind too much if you wanted to stich me up again, uh, without the damn needle please."

Stacy could play along with the best of them. She knew they were 'breaking her in' and she would always enjoy grown men being boys, at least while they discarded some of the day's heaviness.

Alejandro watched his team. They were a joyous lot, powered by their camaraderie and of course several beers.

Pierre preferred wine, French if possible, but when he was around this bunch of brothers he gladly joined them with beers, preferably Belgian. At the moment he would drink any kind. Alejandro was sure Hans had no problem with any nationality beer, but probably preferred his German ales. What counted was their friendship and their professionalism. They were an international family and intent on celebrating Big Rod being alive. Stacy, he mused, was comfortable with her entourage and he liked her easy demeanor. He had also been impressed with her competence, cool thinking and calmness, especially during his jungle shearing with the helicopter blades. He watched Fernando showing off about his country's riches to Stacy, especially explaining the food as the waiter continuously brought platters from the kitchen with local delicacies.

"Ah, the *pasabocas*," Fernando said.

"You mean tapas," Alejandro interjected.

"This happens every time," Hans said to Stacy. "They fight over words while we enjoy delicious food."

"It looks wonderful and I am starving," she said excitedly.

"Here, try this," Fernando said to her as he explained yet more of the different dishes covering the table. "This is *fritanga* or *picada Colombiana*. There are many variations. The most popular is with *chicharrón*, yucca, chorizo, pork ribs and *patacones* which are fried green plantains. And *papa criolla*, little yellow potatoes."

"And all fried."

"Exactly!" Fernando said enthusiastically, digging into one of the plates. "That's why it is so delicious," he said, licking his fingers. "Have a *pola* to wash it down."

"Is that a beer?" Stacy asked.

"Yes."

"Does pola mean something?"

"It is from Policarpa Salavarreta Ríos, the name of a Colombian heroine who helped gain our independence. They created *La Pola,* a beer in her honor. It doesn't exist anymore, but the name lives on.

Hans had accumulated an enormous amount of food on his plate, especially ribs. The German pilot loved his pork and potatoes. They all enjoyed their food and drinks and Stacy especially appreciated the *plátanos asados,* the ripe plantains stuffed with melted cheese and guava that reminded her of little boats. They ended their meal with *cocadas blancas,* a shredded coconut dessert. Stacy looked around and took in her surroundings. Delicious food, uplifting music and wonderful human beings. She could have been anywhere, but at that instant she was surrounded by a union of peace and human bounty in a beautiful area of the world.

"Would it be okay if I tried the piano out?" Stacy asked.

"Absolutely. I'm sure everyone would love that." Alejandro confirmed. He had been curious about her playing ever since she had mentioned it.

Stacy stood up and went to the upright. The patrons clapped. She opened the cover over the keys and looked at the black and white teeth staring at her. She pushed a couple. She had feared it would be terribly out of tune, but to her joy it actually sounded pretty good. Stacy played a couple of octaves and smiled. She looked at the men watching her. "It's absolutely perfect. How about I play a song by Julio Iglesias that just came out?" She asked. It was in the Spaniard's honor.

"Go for it," Alejandro said, beaming. Who didn't know Spain's greatest musical ambassador?

Stacy played "La Carretera" and left everyone in the

bar with their mouths open. She was an amazing pianist, and although her singing was good, her hands were her forte.

"Play another, please," Rod begged after she had finished.

"Okay, Koala, this one's for you, the bush ballad I promised you." Stacy started playing "Waltzing Matilda", the unofficial Australian anthem dating back from 1895 by Banjo Patterson.

"Oh, you remembered. You little ripper."

"Little ripper? I thought she sewed you up, not ripped." Pierre said.

"No, mate, it means 'that's fantastic'."

"You really are a strange man," Pierre added, but Rod wasn't listening, rather he was standing next to the piano, singing along with Stacy, his arm resting on the top of the instrument.

The gang chimed in and sang along. When the song was over everyone in the bar clapped.

"So, Rod, what does the song mean?" Fernando asked the Australian.

"It's about this swagman waltzing with his matilda who makes a billy tea and captures a jumbuck. When the squatter and three troopers chase him he swears they'll never catch him alive. He drowns himself in a billabong and then his ghost haunts the site."

Fernando scrunched his eyes and asked: "Was that English?"

They all laughed as they thought the same way.

"Would you mind translating for us?" Stacy asked the big man from the land down under.

"Sure, a swagman is an itinerant worker. Waltzing is walking, matilda is a bedroll, jumbuck is a sheep, a squatter is a landowner and billabong is a watering hole."

"Well why didn't you say so in the first place?" Hans asked.

"*Encore une?* One more?" Pierre asked Stacy.

"Sure. Any special request?"

"Something French?"

Stacy nodded and started playing "La Mer" by the great chansonnier Charles Trenet, a song from the 1940's, so popular it had been translated into half a dozen languages and recorded by over thirty different artists. By the time Stacy pushed the third key Pierre's eyes were closed and his lips were smiling as he pictured himself in his homeland. As the song dictated she slowly came in with her voice and everyone who knew the tune joined her, in whatever language they knew the lyrics in.

When Stacy finished the piece they clapped loudly and shouted, as if they had been at a concert. Her team members were as proud as peacocks and gathered around her and the piano. They of course flirted with her. It was all in good fun, although Alejandro didn't quite see it that way. His jealous side was getting aggravated. He saw the usual looks of carnal desire by the men's eyes and body language, as well as slightly off-color remarks. He loved his team, but he was on his way to confront them. He was going to teach each one of them a lesson. That one extra beer fogged his mind a bit.

Rod saw his Captain and friend from the corner of his eye and slipped over to him. He seemed to be able to read his thoughts. He discreetly held Alejandro back. "Relax, mate. We're just having a bit of fun; she is part of the team you know. We're just breaking your Stacy in.

The Spaniard stopped trying to push the big man out of his way. *His* Stacy?

"Yes, we all know she's yours and we would never cross that line. But she is also part of the family now and well, we're just being us with a new member. Now, settle down, matador."

"How do you know? What do you mean?"

Big Rod laughed. "Look at her eyes, man."

"What about them?"

"They're very beautiful of course, but they don't shine."

"What does that mean?" Alejandro asked, totally confused.

"Only when they look at you, my man. That's when they glow." Rod explained, a little tipsy but very serious.

"Really?"

"Really," the Aussie answered, grinning and happy for his captain. "You can always tell who a girl fancies by the shine in her eyes."

Fernando only had a couple of polas, making sure he could safely drive the team back to the base. On the way they sang more songs, stood up in the jeep several times and almost lost Hans when they hit a pothole. Thankfully Alejandro grabbed him just in time.

"Tolles Bursche bist du," Hans slurred. "You're a great guy."

They continued singing and laughing until they arrived at their little camp. Rod, who had consumed more beers than any one of them, but could also hold his liquor best, helped Hans and Pierre into the sleeping quarters. They each had an arm around the big man as Rod held them up, until he dropped them on their bunks. They immediately fell asleep. Rod went to his cot and did the exact same thing.

Fernando said goodnight to Alejandro and Stacy and left. He was looking forward to his bed, it had been a long day. The Spaniard looked deep into the American woman's eyes. Alejandro wanted her so badly, he wanted to hold her and never let her go. He wanted to kiss her, right then and there, but he didn't dare. It was too soon, too fast, and he was her boss.

Stacy returned his gaze and read his eyes. "Aren't you going to throw any dogs at me, Alex?"

The man's eyebrows flew up. "You heard that?" He groaned, remembering Fernando's remark during their first meeting.

"I did."

"Oh, no, I'm very sorry."

Stacy wanted to reach out and touch his face, run her fingers through his thick black hair but held herself back. "Oh, I'm not," she said, smiling.

Ah, that smile. Alejandro was quickly sobering up. "Well, let's not waste time," he said and took her in his arms and kissed her. It was long and deep, a confirmation of how much he wanted her. Stacy kissed him back, with more ardor than either one of them expected. Without his mouth leaving her lips Alejandro picked her up and carried her a few more feet to his trailer. He took her to his bed and gently put her down.

"Is this okay?" He asked leaning over her.

Stacy confirmed his question by grinning and pulling his shirt collar toward her until their lips molded together. She rolled on top of him and straddled him. She slowly unbuttoned her shirt. Alejandro slightly trembled with anticipation. He gently helped her undo the rest of the buttons. Their mouths only came apart so that Stacy could take off his shirt. Alejandro removed hers and then slowly pulled her back to him until their lips met. They leaned into each other, discovered each other's bodies, kissed and caressed the most sensitive areas and uncovered the little secrets that gave the other exquisite pleasure. They respected and enjoyed the emotions they were passionately sharing and giving each other. There was anticipation, there was lust, there was discovery, and there was harmony in their love making. They flawlessly melted together and culminated into their euphoric enchantment.

A couple of months later Stacy took a test to confirm her suspicions. She walked into Alejandro's trailer and kissed him. She let a few moments pass before looking deep into his eyes. "Alex, I'm a one-man girl, and always will be."

"I'm very glad to hear that," he answered, not sure where Stacy was going with this.

Alejandro stared at the woman he had fallen deeply in love with and had pictured himself with for the rest of his life. No woman made love like she did unless she adored her partner. Besides, he had learned a valuable lesson from Rod and would never be jealous again. Her eyes only glowed for him.

"I need to tell you something," Stacy said.

Alejandro heard the seriousness in her tone and saw something in her eyes he had never seen before. Why were they different? He wondered. He stared a little longer at the eyes that were always unique when she looked at him, with a love meant only for her man. He noticed a different shine, just as beautiful as the one she had for him, yet gentler, softer. A new meaning, a glorious one. Alejandro immediately knew.

"We created a little human being?" He asked, his own eyes shining with delight.

Stacy didn't miss the slight wetness under his long lashes. "Well, it's probably the size of a cranberry right now."

"But it will grow into the most fantastic little person in the universe!" Alejandro exclaimed. He picked her up and whirled her around the room.

Stacy had been ready for just about anything, but not Alejandro's amazing ecstatic reaction. She wrapped her arms around his neck as he continued twirling her until he stumbled. They started to fall but he held her firmly and gently laid her on the floor next to him. He kissed her lips tenderly and looked into the eyes he adored. He lovingly took her face in his hands and said: "Stacy Taylor, would you marry me? And no, I'm not saying it because of the baby, but because I was going to ask you anyway."

When Stacy first walked into Captain Alonso's trailer a couple of months before she could never have imagined what a turn her life would take. Stacy was now on the floor of that same trailer, on the edge of a jungle in one of the most dangerous places in the world. Alejandro wasn't on one knee and didn't have any kind of speech prepared. Instead, they were sensually lying side by side thinking of a future together. Stacy was certain she was invincible, complete and content. This would always be one of the most special moments of her life.

"*Sí*, Alejandro Alonso, with all my heart and soul."

"*Sí?*"

Stacy reconfirmed by nodding.

Alejandro jumped up and opened one of his desk drawers. He searched for a moment until he found what he wanted. Stacy just watched, curious as to what he was up to.

The Spaniard knelt before her and sing-songed *"sí, sí, sí, sí, my love says sí, sí, sí"*. He took her hand and tied a piece of string around her ring finger. He finished it with a bow. "I will get you a real one soon, *mi amor.*" He would get a Colombian emerald, of course. He would ask

Fernando to help him.

"That would be lovely, but I really, really like this one," she said, admiring the string.

The HeliEmerg team had been on several missions in the last couple of months. Some were more difficult than others and there were injured, mainly by bullets, but none as harrowing as Stacy's first which they lovingly referred to as 'the lawn mower ride'. Since that first night Alejandro shared his trailer and his bed with the love of his life. The other men had known since the first day and they were happy for their captain. They wished someday they too would find a woman for themselves as amazing as their Stacy.

Before leaving Colombia Alejandro and Stacy purchased the engagement ring. It was a special order and in the shape of the string and bow he had given her when he asked her to marry him. Emeralds colored the top and diamonds decorated the loop around the finger.

♫

CHAPTER 5

1996 – FLORIDA

BERNARDO

At six years old Jaxon Logan was a happy youngster. He lived in Florida with his parents in an isolated area between Orlando and Miami. They were horse breeders. They owned and operated a well-established stable where riders, trainers and coaches came from all over the world to find that special specimen they were searching for. They could also board horses they wanted to buy, sell or trade.

One of the greatest assets on the ranch was Bernardo, a man Oliver and Karen Logan discovered in the heart of the Argentinian Pampas. He was a true South American cowboy, a gaucho who knew horses better than anyone. After seeing his prowess the couple was sure he had been a horse in a past life. They recruited him to come live with them at their ranch in Florida. It hadn't been too difficult to convince him as he had just lost his wife to cancer. When Bernardo heard of the offer his eyes began to come alive for the first time since his Maria passed away. He liked the American couple and firmly believed he could help with their endeavors and he would work with the animals he was so passionate about.

Bernardo was a proud gaucho and a silent type. He was honest, strong and very capable of defending one's honor when provoked or needed. He very much looked the part, from his European and Mestizo ancestry to the clothes he proudly sported. He always wore his black beret, a mark of his heritage dating back to his Basque roots. A red scarf around his neck, a poncho, a *chiripa* around his waist and *bombachas*, the long accordion-pleated trousers covering the tops of sturdy leather boots completed the outfit. The only additional accessories were his bolas, the gaucho's lariat, and his *cuchillo*, a knife he used for everything from cutting meat to cleaning hooves. Sometimes the weapons were used for warnings, sometimes to resolve disagreements.

The Logans provided a good salary, all the food Bernardo could ever eat and a small guest house on the property. He and some of the workers often took out a herd of horses for several days. They needed the exercise and he loved the freedom and the hard riding. He cherished the camaraderie with the other men, especially when they built a pit for their dinners of *churrasco*, the beef roasting on spits. When they were ready to turn in for the night the men would leave and go farther away so he could be alone. They understood he liked being on his own as he would put on his Argentinian music he played on his antique cassette player. He would dance a *malambo*, a man's solo dance with improvised footwork, while his land's native music resounded from his old tapes. Sometimes he would dance a tango with an invisible lover, with nostalgia in his eyes in front of red and gold flames from the fire.

Bernardo was comfortable in nature. At night he rested on a blanket with the earth seemingly cradling him. He covered himself with his poncho, used his saddle as a headrest and marveled at the vastness above him. He would stare at the twinkly black canvas and watch for shooting stars. He was sure every time he saw one it was his Maria waving to him.

One night young Jax wandered away from the house and toward Bernardo's fire. He hid behind a bush and watched the older man dancing to his music. When the melody ended Bernardo stopped and turned to where Jax was. He smiled and waved to him.

"*Ven*, come out," he simply said.

"How did you know I was here? I didn't make any noise," Jax asked, puzzled, standing up and going to Bernardo.

"I smelled you."

"What do I smell like?"

"Like an American human boy."

"Oh," Jax said, not sure what an American boy smelled like. "What are you reading?" The youngster asked seeing a book.

"*Coplas.*"

"What are coplas?"

"They are short poems of four verses used in literature and songs."

Jax couldn't quite picture the older man with a face of weathered leather reading poems, but this was Bernardo, a man from the plains of Argentina. "Can you tell me one?"

"Of course. This is one of my favorites," he said. He knew it by heart:

*"Mi caballo y mi mujer
Viajaron para Salta,
El caballo que se vuelva,
Mi mujer que no me hace falta."*

"What does it mean?"

"I will have to teach you Spanish, *gauchito*, little gaucho, and then you will enjoy beautiful works of *literatura* from authors like Jorge Luis Borges, Gabriela Mistral, Federico Garcia Lorca, Miguel de Cervantes, Gabriel Garcia Marquez, Pablo Neruda to name just a few. And songs! The best music and lyrics are in Spanish and the greatest way to learn a language."

Jax wasn't too interested in what Bernardo called *littura* but he wanted to know what that copla was about. "Can you tell me in English?"

"Ah, yes. It says:
*My horse and my woman
Went off to Salta
May the horse return
For I don't need my woman."*

Before Jax had a chance to ask, Bernardo said: "Salta is a city in the north of Argentina."

"I like that poem. And I would rather have the horse too."

Bernardo chuckled. "I had a feeling you would, although when you are older you might feel differently. Now, how about I teach you the copla in Spanish." Bernardo knew the boy would one day gladly give everything for true love when he found it. Oh, how he missed his Maria.

"Okay," Jax said, and thought it would be fun sitting around the fire with Bernardo. It would be like camping.

Bernardo and Jax became an inseparable duo. They spend the afternoons together and sometimes, with Jax's parents' permission, the boy would spend the night at the campfire under the stars. The gaucho was a diligent teacher and became a second father and mentor to Jax. The boy's parents approved of the relationship. The man had many hidden talents and they had known the Argentine for years. They trusted Bernardo implicitly and had watched their interaction. He loved the boy as if he were his own.

Bernardo showed Jax how to tend to the horses, what to do if they were hurt and how to help heal them. He also taught him how to ride in the way of the Gauchos of the Pampas. In the evening they would build a fire in the pit. Once the embers were glowing red hot, they would slowly cook their churrasco on a very hot grill.

Bernardo and Jax were enjoying their meal, a satiated look on their faces.

"Are you happy?" The gaucho asked the boy.

"This is really good!" Jax said between mouthfuls.

"It's the details and the people around you that make living special. Life is a gift and when you wake up in the morning you open a new one every day. Before opening your eyes say thank you seven times and smile the entire time."

"Why seven, Bernardo?"

"Supposedly it is God's favorite number."

"Okay. I like that."

"Good."

"Can I also say it before I go to sleep at night?"

"I don't see why not. Is it because your day was a gift?"

"That's right."

"Even if it wasn't perfect?"

"Yes," the child said.

"You are very smart, *chiquito*, little one, and I think it's a great idea."

Jax nodded. He thought so too.

The next time the two of them were together at the firepit Jax asked Bernardo about the cassette player and the dancing. The older man showed him how his music box worked.

"You like to dance, right?" Jax asked.

"Yes, very much."

"Why?"

"Why? Because dancing makes my mind, heart and body happy."

"How does that work?" The boy asked.

"The music enters my soul and directs my body to move with pleasure. And if you are dancing with someone you love, it is exquisite."

"But I've only seen you dance alone, and sometimes it looks like you're with somebody."

"Yes, there are dances you can do by yourself. And you're right, sometimes I dance with my Maria."

"Your Maria?"

"Yes, she was my wife. We used to dance all the time. We loved each other very much and loved dancing. Unfortunately, she died several years ago, but sometimes I can almost feel her in my arms and I remember the beautiful times when we danced."

"She sounds very special, Bernardo."

"Yes, she was. I'm sure my goddess smiles at me from her special star in the sky."

"Your goddess?"

"That's what she is to me. And you must treat all women with respect and like goddesses."

"I do, uh, I think."

"I'm sure you do, chiquito, but you must always make them feel like they are the most important person in the world, whether you've known them for a minute or a lifetime."

Young Jax had a puzzled look on his face. He wasn't sure what Bernardo meant. How was he supposed to do that, and why? "Uh, okay."

Bernardo chuckled. "Do not worry, I will show you what I mean."

"Okay." The boy didn't know it at that moment, but Bernardo's teachings would take him very far with the ladies when the time came.

The next evening Jax watched Bernardo dance with his invisible Maria. The gaucho waved him over.

"I know, you smelled the American boy," Jax said walking up to him.

Bernardo laughed. "How are you, chiquito?"

"I'm good. What kind of dance was that?"

"That was a tango and it is very special. When people dance it they really connect with each other and become as if one person." He looked at the boy. "You might not think much about that right now but later, when you are a young man, you will see it differently. Come, I can show you some steps. Would you like that?"

"Okay."

The older man showed Jax the basics. The boy was a quick learner and a naturally good dancer. Bernardo could see the youngster was enjoying himself.

When Jax was comfortable with the basics the gaucho showed him new steps. "You're doing very well, chiquito, now let's try some *ganchos* and *saltos*."

"Try what?"

"Ganchos are leg hooks and saltos are jumps."

"Sounds like something horses would do," the boy said.

Bernardo laughed so hard Jax thought the man would fall down.

The next day Jax and his parents were at the corral near the stables. They were very quiet as they watched Bernardo slowly walk up to a new addition, a wild horse everyone thought would be very difficult to tame. Man and beast were one foot apart and they stared at each other until the gaucho slowly lifted his arms. He let the mare smell his torso for as long as she wanted. He lowered his arms back to his body and then slowly lifted one hand and let the horse touch and smell it. She had to decide if she should trust Bernardo or not. She snorted, turned her head and took off galloping around the corral. The gaucho stood immobile, watching but not moving, until the mare came back and smelled him again. Bernardo once again lifted his arm, caressed and lightly patted her neck. The horse snorted and again took off. She circled the enclosure and this time Bernardo ran with her, at the same pace but in a smaller circle, until she stopped. He did too. He walked up and gave her his hand. The horse smelled it and was rewarded with another caress. This went on for about an hour. Jax and his parents watched the pair in awe, marveling at the growing connection. They could also tell how much Bernardo loved what he was doing and how much he cared about this creature.

A few minutes later Bernardo touched several points on the mare with either his index finger or his thumb and held it for about twenty seconds. After every placement she would lower her head.

"What is he doing, Daddy?" Jax whispered to his father.

"I asked him that very same question the first time I saw him doing it too. He is using pressure, acupressure to be exact. Horses have twelve meridians flowing through their bodies, just like humans have."

"What are meridians?"

"Picture them as little thin rivers that flow throughout the body to give it more energy. When you put pressure on certain spots, like Bernardo is doing, it can do a number of different things."

"Like what?"

"It can reduce swelling and pain, strengthen the immune system and mental clarity, or even make you feel like you're getting a massage. I believe that's his strategy right now."

"That's cool!" Jax exclaimed.

"Yes, she probably thinks so too. Do you see her lowering her head after each spot Bernardo touched? I'm pretty sure that's a confirmation."

Bernardo continued until he was able to put a bridle on the horse. The gaucho led her around the corral, slowly at first, and continuously sped up until the horse was galloping and he was running alongside. When they both stopped Bernardo put his arms around the horse's neck and hugged her. They stayed that way for several minutes. Bernardo caressed the mare's face and kissed her just above the nostrils. He also blew air into the same areas. This went on for a while until Bernardo knew what level of trust they were at. When he was satisfied, he put a pad on the mare's back. He stroked her neck and once unafraid of the small blanket Bernardo carefully put a saddle on her. The horse snorted in disagreement until Bernardo caressed her forehead and whispered in her ear.

She snorted again. Was it an agreement, or perhaps pleasure? She let Bernardo tie the saddle to her. The man put a foot in the stirrup and lifted himself up very slowly. She moved, but didn't jerk away. Bernardo stayed standing in that position even though the mare was trotting around. When she stopped the gaucho slowly swung his leg over her back and gently sat in the saddle. She reared up, her front legs waving through the air. Bernardo caressed her neck, leaned forward and whispered into one of her ears. He lifted the reins and gently squeezed his legs. The horse moved forward. He changed the direction of the reins and the mare followed. He slowly pulled them toward him and she stopped. They did this together for quite a while until Bernardo knew it was time. He pulled the reins back and squeezed his legs around her belly. He maneuvered his hands and limbs until he found the sweet spot he was looking for. She walked back a few steps and Bernardo pulled some more until she very slowly went down on her front knees. The back legs followed. When she was almost completely down Bernardo stood up, took his feet out of the stirrups and helped her lie on her side. He stretched out on top of her and caressed her face and neck. She didn't move. He slowly got up, always keeping his closest hand on her and walked to the front of the mare. Bernardo knelt in front of her neck, kissed her cheek and whispered in her ear. He put one hand on her face and lowered his neck onto hers. They both lay there quietly as if they had been sleeping in the same position for hours. Jax held his breath, afraid that if he made a sound the picture in front of him would disappear forever. His parents took in the sight. They had seen Bernardo do this work before and never tired of watching and reliving it. After several minutes Bernardo kissed the mare again and gently pulled on the reins until she was standing. Man and horse were happy together, with a unique understanding between them and a love that would only grow with each passing day.

By the end of the third day Bernardo asked Jax to join them. The boy could hardly contain his joy. Having watched carefully for the past days he had picked up details and quietly walked toward them. Bernardo slowly guided Jax forward until the boy was face to face with the mare.

"Let her smell you. Put your hand out slowly."

Jax did and was rewarded with her muzzle snorting in his hand. He giggled as it tickled. Bernardo pulled out an apple, split it in half with his hands and gave it to Jax. The boy took one of the halves and with an open palm offered it to the mare. She took it and immediately ate it. Jax thought he saw a certain shine in the horse's eyes. Was she thanking him? He hoped so. That would mean she was communicating with him! He gave her the other half.

"It is important horses are happy, whether they are in the wild, a corral, an arena or even a competition. They need to love who they are, and we must understand their needs. If you connect with their heart they will do their best for us. Always watch their ears, nostrils and eyes. That is the way they communicate and both humans and horses must enjoy the interaction. They are loyal and noble and we should strive to be more like them. Violence is never needed, and that is true for everyone not just animals. Do you understand, chiquito?"

"I do."

During the next few days Bernardo would show Jax details and finesses between humans and horses. He taught Jax how to read their bodies and their eyes. When they moved a certain way the horses were sensing the mood of the human standing close to them. They could tell when a person was angry or content. Young Jax found out when he literally touched their hearts. Their rhythms would accelerate when a human was in a bad mood, or beat a little slower when they were happy. How wonderful would it be, he pondered, if humans paid attention to their exceptional animal counterparts and learned from them. Jax was sure horses had a heart song, a melody that connected all living creatures.

By the end of summer young Jax was speaking fluent Spanish and even sported an Argentinian pronunciation. He was extremely passionate about horses and loved helping them through their illness or pain. He wanted to become a veterinarian, specializing in equine health. And he had fallen in love with dancing, especially the tango. Bernardo had been a wonderful teacher.

♫

CHAPTER 6

1996 – 2006 SOUTHWESTERN SPAIN

ALINA

Alejandro and Stacy stayed in Colombia another month before moving permanently to his homestead in Spain. Stacy had no family back in the United States and she was happy anywhere in the world as long as she was with her husband. The wedding had been intimate and performed when they arrived in Spain, with just a few friends and colleagues on a beach with a distant, spectacular view of the shores of North Africa. Guitar players strummed their strings and serenaded them to the tunes of their native Andalucia, and all the love songs their repertoire held. The bride, groom, guests and of course Stacy's team members from Colombia sat at one long table enjoying each other's company and celebrated the happy event. They enjoyed the Spanish culinary delicacies, the music, the ambience, their bare feet in the sand and most of all the love they shared with the people around them.

Fernando's eyes lit up when the appetizers arrived at the table. "The pasabocas have arrived! I am starving. Oh, this looks so good," he exclaimed.

"Tapas!" Alejandro insisted. "This is Spain, so tapas."

"Ah, here we go again, just like Colombia," Hans groaned.

Stacy laughed, the happiest she had ever been in her life. She was surrounded by the men she adored. They were her brothers and Alejandro was part of her soul. She watched their interaction, one big loving family she was grateful to be a part of.

"Hey, Captain, I was right about the glow in the eyes, wasn't I?" Rod asked Alejandro between mouthfuls.

"Most definitely. I thank you, my friend. You played a major role in today's ceremony happening."

"Glad to be of help, mate."

Stacy stood behind the two men and put her arms around their shoulders. "What is big little Koala talking about? Something about eyes?"

Would they divulge their secret?

"I was telling Alex that your eyes shine," Rod said.

"Yes, like liquid jade," Alejandro added, insanely proud of his new wife and totally in love.

"Oh, that's lovely, gentlemen, thank you."

Alejandro's house was a rustic Spanish hacienda that hadn't been lived in since before his parents passed away and they immediately went to work and fixed it up. It was, after all, their love nest. They brought it back to life, made it their own and beautiful. The following months were anything but boring. Alejandro and Stacy both worked on the company goals and took impromptu breaks to make love. Stacy also learned to cook typical

Spanish food from their elderly, portly neighbor down the road who was only too happy to help. She had known Alejandro since he was a boy and had been good friends with his family. She also liked his new wife and firmly believed his parents would have loved her too.

The only other breaks Stacy took was to play the piano. It relaxed her and the music always filled her heart. Her audience was the child she was carrying and for some reason she was sure it would be a girl. She always rubbed her belly before letting her fingers travel along the black and white keys. She sang children's lullabies and every melody she was familiar with. Her favorite was playing Rimsky-Korsakov's Scheherazade and telling the unborn baby her version about a princess held captive and rescued by a dashing prince. The mother-to-be was sure the little one was listening to the adventurous tale and its music.

Stacy was at the piano when her water broke. She called out to Alejandro. By the sound of her voice he knew it was time. True to form he rushed her to the hospital in the helicopter. They arrived in ten minutes. Less than an hour later the little girl was in her parents' arms. It was an easy and uneventful delivery.

As with the birth Alina grew up a quiet and easy child. By the time she was four she preferred books to toys and dolls. Her favorite pastime was playing next to her Mommy on the piano. Even at that young age she loved music and when she attended her first Feria in Seville, she discovered new passions. Little Alina fell in love with the music, especially the guitar players, the flamenco dancers, the horses, the food and the thousands of bright lights illuminating the festival. From little girls to great-grandmothers the majority of them wore the traditional long dresses with ruffles, tasseled shawls and flowers in their hair. Alina was mesmerized by the flamenco dancers and the quick fingers of the guitar players. She watched as the horse-driven carriages paraded in front of her and was enthralled when the men and women, the *Caballeros* and *Amazonas*, performed tricks with their horses and in traditional costumes, especially the youngsters participating as well. She wanted to be just like them and do everything they did. Alina begged her parents to teach her.

"You can't learn too many things at once," Stacy said.

"Why not, Mommy?"

"Well, it's good to know a lot of things, but if you are in an activity you have to try to be really good at it. You might have to drop the others. You usually get really good at just one at a time."

"You'll see, I'll be good at all of them," Alina insisted.

Stacy looked at her daughter with great pride and thought the young girl truly believed she could handle all the different activities. She knew the youngster's heart wanted it, but worried Alina would be overwhelmed. Stacy and Alejandro obliged her by getting her lessons in guitar playing, flamenco dancing and riding. They figured she would eventually choose one over another.

Alina was a natural with the horses and learned quickly to ride and excelled at it. It was the same with the dancing. She would go to her classes and would practice a little at home. When it came to playing the guitar, she was ahead of the game as she had learned solfege, scales and a few melodies from her mother on the piano. She practiced her music the most.

By the time Alina was ten she was accomplished in all three of her passions and had expanded her dancing genres. She had exceeded everyone's expectations and was a happy child. One day she watched her mother play a tune on the piano and realized she knew how to play it on the guitar.

"Oh, I know that song!"

"Well, let's play it together."

"How do you mean, Mommy?"

"I can play it on the piano and you can play it on the guitar."

Alina thought this was the best idea in the world. The duo started playing and when Alina sang along Stacy caught her breath. She never realized how amazing her daughter's singing was. The young girl was completely uninhibited as she let her voice soar. When they finished the piece Stacy asked Alina if she liked to sing.

"Oh, yes! More than anything."

"Even riding and playing the guitar?" Stacy asked, wondering why she hadn't heard Alina's powerful voice before.

Alina thought about her mother's question for a moment. "I think so," she finally said. "But I do love the others too."

"How would you like to take some voice lessons?"

"Why?"

"Well, if you like to sing so much you should be as good as you are with everything else."

"And what do voice lessons do?"

"They teach you how to control your breathing, how to project your voice and how to form your mouth to produce the perfect note. Basically, it makes you sing better."

Alina wasn't exactly sure what her mom meant and

thought, oh, why not? "Okay, let's do it."

"That means more work, more studying."

"No problem," Alina said with the dauntlessness of her age. She really didn't have any idea how much work the singing lessons would entail, but in her young mind she firmly believed she could handle anything.

♫

CHAPTER 7

2000 – FLORIDA

Bernardo woke up because he was coughing. He realized his eyes were stinging and watering. And then he heard it—the most chilling sounds that would ever pierce his heart—horses in mortal danger, squealing in fear for their lives. He wore pajamas yet thought quickly to jump into his boots. He ran outside and his heart skipped several beats as the stables were partly engulfed in fire, the flames rushing toward the black sky.

¡Qué quilombo! What a mess! Bernardo inwardly screamed. He saw Oliver and Karen trying to put out the flames with buckets of water and blankets. They headed deeper into the barn and Bernardo followed them.

"Get the horses out, we'll try to control the fire as much as possible!" Oliver shouted to the gaucho.

Bernardo ran to the horses where the fire was closest and opened the doors to each of their stalls. He slapped their rumps hard and screamed at them to get out. In spite of their fear the horses knew the sound of his voice and obeyed him, galloping as hard as they could for the exit. Jax, who had heard the commotion and saw the fire, ran toward the barn. Karen came out to get more water and yelled at her son: "Whatever you do, don't come in! Promise me!"

"I promise, Mom." At ten years old Jax would listen to his mother, but thought he was old enough to help. "Try to gather the horses that have already come out and keep them together and calm. Can you do that?" Karen knew her son wanted to help, but she wanted to keep him safe and his corralling the horses would be a great support. She would also know where her boy would be and what he was doing.

"Yes, Mom, I will."

Karen ran back into the stables. Oliver was losing the battle against the flames climbing the walls. Bernardo kept releasing more horses. "We've got to get out of here," he screamed to Oliver and Karen.

"Yes! Let's go!" Oliver yelled back. He quickly grabbed his wife's hand and they started running out when one the heavy beams from the ceiling above came crashing down on them.

"NO!" Bernardo screamed. "NO!" He tried to reach them, tried to get as close as he could but the heat and the fire swirled around the fallen bodies. It was too late. The beam had killed them, thankfully before they were engulfed in flames. He looked around. The two last horses didn't make it out either, succumbing to the same ordeal as their masters. He couldn't dwell on the losses and had to get out or he would succumb to the same fate. He immediately thought of young Jax. With the agonizing loss of his parents, the boy would need him. Bernardo picked up a blanket, soaked it in some water from the bucket Karen hadn't had the chance to use. He covered his head and shoulders and zigzagged between the flames that seemed to be everywhere. The heat and the smoke were crushing his chest. He forced himself to keep moving, slowly and carefully, making his way toward the opening, stopping and dodging through the flame-filled death trap. His lungs were in agony and he could barely see. The pain in his eyes was shooting daggers to his brain. Between the unbearable heat and pain Bernardo stumbled. He couldn't control his movements and fell to his knees. He was convinced this was his end. He mustered what will and energy his body and soul still had. Only a few more feet, he coaxed himself. I can do this. I must do this! For Jax! He continued painfully through the embers flying at him in the orange and gray haze.

Jax did as his mother had instructed and corralled the horses. He tied them up and went back to the stables. It looked completely engulfed in fire. His heart skipped a beat. Where were his parents? Where was Bernardo? Were there any more horses coming out? And then he saw a hand on the ground at the entrance. He rushed over and saw Bernardo. He quickly pulled him with every ounce of strength of his little body. It was just enough to save the man's life. A second longer and he would have died with the others as the stables became an inferno completely engulfed with fire.

Bernardo and Jax lay on the ground. The boy jumped up and screamed: "MOM! DAD!" He started running toward the flames.

"NO! STOP!"

Jax wasn't listening.

"STOP! IT'S TOO LATE!" Bernardo screamed as loud as he could.

Jax stopped in his tracks at the same moment flames blew at him from the stables. What did that mean? He whirled toward the man with questioning eyes.

Bernardo lifted himself painfully to his knees and put an arm out to the boy. Jax took it, his eyes begging for something positive, something that would tell him his parents were still alive. The gaucho stood up with great difficulty and held Jax against his body. "I'm sorry," he said, between coughs and trying to catch his breath. "There wasn't anything anyone could do. They didn't suffer." Bernardo knew whatever words he used would never be comforting. "I would have given my life for them. I'm sorry I couldn't."

Jax nodded, tears streaming down his face. He knew what Bernardo said was true, he was that kind of guy. Now that his mom and dad were gone what was he going to do? How could he live without his parents? What kind of world would it be without them?

The sirens of the fire trucks brought Jax out of his stupor. The paramedics checked them out. The boy was fine. They put an oxygen mask on Bernardo and some ointment for the minor burns on his skin. Neighbors who had seen the fire and heard the fire engines came by to see if they could help. They took the horses to keep them in their own barns and stables for as long as was needed. Anything else and they were only a phone call away. The equestrian community was a very tightly knit one. What had just happened to the Logans was everyone's worse nightmare, no matter how careful they were. The ranchers helped with the horses and left for their own estates.

Bernardo and Jax sat on the ground facing the barn for hours, watching the firefighters battle the inferno. The boy didn't want to move. Even after everyone left, they still sat there looking at the burned-out building. Morning came and went. Bernardo just stayed with the youngster, imagining the internal heart-wrenching pain the child was going through. He was just as sad. He had loved the gracious American couple and their special boy. They had been good to him, given him a new spark after his Maria had passed away.

Jax finally stood up. Bernardo did the same. "I can't say thank you seven times anymore. God took away my parents and I'll never smile again!" Jax said angrily.

Bernardo cleared his throat. He knew how much agony and rage was running through the boy's heart, but he also knew he had to help him through what would probably be the most painful event of his life. "Listen, we don't know why any of this happened. Why didn't we die as well? Why are we here? We will never know the answer to so many questions. God has His reasons. Perhaps your parents were needed in Heaven. Maybe God missed them so much He had to have them with Him because they were very special, like my Maria. I think we are alive because we are supposed to do something important for humankind. You already have. You saved me."

"But I couldn't save them. Like you said, no one could."

Bernardo looked at the boy whose life had suddenly completely changed. As stoic and brave as young Jax had been the tears finally burst from behind his eyes, deep and sorrowful. Bernardo caught the boy as he was falling to his knees and took him in his arms. He rocked him and hummed soft melodies for what seemed hours until Jax finally fell asleep. He carried the boy to his room and carefully laid him on the bed. He sat next to the youngster and held his hand until his own tears silently cascaded down his cheeks.

After lengthy investigations the fire was deemed an accident. The only silver lining was the insurance money Jax would receive from the death of his parents and for the building. It would be enough to rebuild a new stable and continue the Logans' work. In their will they wanted Bernardo to be Jax's guardian and help run the ranch. The gaucho thought perhaps that was why he was still alive. Maybe Oliver and Karen, or perhaps Maria, were looking after them and guided Jax to pull him away from the fire.

♫

CHAPTER 8

2005 – FLORIDA

It had been five years since the fire. From the insurance monies Jax and Bernardo rebuilt better and safer stables, and business was once again booming. One of their favorite pastimes was watching a good polo match or any of the world's famous equestrian events. They also enjoyed other sports, whether it was American or European football, a wild game of ice hockey or jai alai, and even lesser known but fun games such as bossaball and underwater hockey. Just two guys enjoying a weekend of athletics. They were both very passionate and Bernardo had been the instigator starting right after the boy's parents died. He wanted to keep Jax's mind occupied and away from negative vices such as drugs and bad influences. Sports brought them even closer and they appreciated the athletes and the games.

Jax and Bernardo sat on the couch in front of the television waiting for the annual equestrian competition. They had prepared a platter of churrasco with chimichurri and a few sides. Through the years the two had become family—a father and son, sometimes brothers and definitely best friends. One was older, the other a fifteen-year-old teenager. There wasn't anything they wouldn't or couldn't talk about, well almost.

"Gauchito, have you had sex yet?

"Bernardo!"

"Well, it's a fair question. At some point it happens, right?"

"A gentleman never tells," Jax said, hoping to end the subject. They had always been close, but his sex life he wanted to keep private.

"Good, that's good. Remember, treat the girls like goddesses."

"Don't worry, I do."

Jax really did. He had learned well and never missed an opportunity to compliment a girl or a woman. What he understood from Bernardo's teachings was to always please the girl and make her feel she was the most important person in the world. The reward was that he took pleasure in their happiness, and yes, of course he had had sex—he was the most sought-after boy in school. The combination of good looks, manners, respect and compliments elevated Jax in everyone's eyes, especially the female population.

"Don't forget to treat them like goddesses in bed too, especially in bed."

"Bernardo!"

"Okay, okay; now tell me, how was the dance the other night?"

"Yeah, it was good. It was fun," Jax answered nonchalantly.

"Any girls?"

Would the man not let up? "Sure."

"Any special one?"

"Maybe," Jax said, as vaguely as possible. He wanted Bernardo to get off the subject of girls and his sex life.

"Maybe I should meet her."

"Maybe not yet."

"Okay, I'll wait for you to tell me when the time is right."

"Of course. Hey, they're about to start. Let's watch," Jax said, trying again to steer Bernardo to a different direction.

"Of course," the older man repeated to his protégé, "let's watch."

The prestigious *Campeonato Ecuestre de Andalucia (CEA)*, the Equestrian Championship of Andalucia in southern Spain was as revered as the Kentucky Derby, the CHIO in Aachen or the Royal Ascot. The venue had similar rules and all the equestrian events of the Olympic games. They included the individual and team competition in eventing, which included jumping, dressage and cross-country. Any medal at the Campeonato was a pathway to the Olympics.

As Jax and Bernardo watched the competitors the youngster wanted to be one of them, to compete and show the world how a human and a magnificent equine could be one. He had been riding for the majority of his young life and he wanted to show off the beauty of a horse and a rider. Jax's heart was pounding hard and fast in his chest. He knew what he wanted and *needed* to do. He quickly turned to the man sitting next to him.

"Bernardo, I want to compete in the Olympic Games."

"Why not, chiquito?" He said, biting into a piece of bread laden with the green chimichurri.

"I'm serious. Will you help me?"

"With what?"

"With the training, the horse, the details, the clothes…"

"Slowly, slowly," Bernardo said, thrilled that Jax had something to focus on other than his parents' tragedy. He had provided anything he could think of to alleviate the pain the boy had endured for years. Now he saw a new spark in the boys' eyes he had never seen before. He would do everything in his power to make them shine even more. "Yes, of course. I will help you wherever I can."

"Thank you," Jax said and hugged the only family he had.

Bernardo held the boy in his arms, as he had done so many times since the day of the fire. He would not let him down. He was an expert in horses and he also knew Jax was an amazing rider and had the heart he needed for this endeavor.

"The Olympic Games in Beijing," Jax murmured.

"That's in three years. It will be a lot of work."

"Of course, and even more to be the best and win a medal!"

"The world and China await!" Bernardo chuckled.

For a solid week Jax and Bernardo gathered information from clubs, equestrian federations, telephone calls, the internet and their neighbors. They learned everything they could about becoming an Olympic equestrian, what qualifications were needed, the different events and the ideal breeds for the grueling workouts and competitions. Bernardo made two more phone calls without Jax's knowledge, one to Puerto Rico, another to England.

A few days later, very early in the morning, Bernardo entered Jax's room, went to his bed and blew into an old-fashioned blowout noisemaker. It rolled out and gently hit Jax in the face. The youngster practically levitated in fast motion up off his mattress.

"Bernardo! What the hell…"

"Happy birthday, chiquito!" The older man said excitedly and gave him an enormous bear hug. Welcome to the beautiful age of sweet sixteen and what is sure to be a great year for you."

"How do you know?" Jax asked, sitting up and rubbing the sleep from his eyes.

Bernardo produced a polaroid picture from his shirt pocket and showed it to Jax. It was a horse.

"Wow, stunning," Jax said.

"You like?"

"Of course. What's this all about?" Jax asked, his curiosity peaking.

"First we eat a good breakfast, which I have prepared and is ready, then we will talk about this horse."

"Okay." Jax was intrigued. What did the gaucho have in mind?

Bernardo and Jax ate all the boy's breakfast favorites. They enjoyed the meal and talked about the Olympics.

"Let's go outside, chiquito, I want to check on the horses."

"What's with the horse in the picture?" Jax asked.

"Ah, I will tell you, but first I need to go to the stables. Accompany me, please."

"Sure."

They walked to the barn and entered. Jax always loved the smell that emanated from the horses, the hay and the leather of the saddles and bridles.

"Over here," Bernardo said as he entered one of the stalls.

Jax followed and came face to face with a horse he had never seen before. She stood about fifteen hands, was a dark chestnut with beige markings which colored her ears, some of her chest and through her thick mane, forelock and tail. Jax's heart skipped a beat when his eyes connected with the horse's. He held his hand out as Bernardo had done so many years before and let her muzzle touch his palm. The nostrils flared and inhaled Jax's scent.

"Happy birthday, chiquito, this is *Almea*, which means dancer. Almea is a Paso Fino and is the beauty in the photograph. She came from Puerto Rico."

Jax looked at his mentor. "Are you saying Almea is mine?"

"All yours, the one you will take to China. Say hello to your new partner."

Jax embraced both the horse's neck and Bernardo's at the same time. He held them next to his face and was sure this was the best day of his life.

Bernardo and Jax led Almea outside and walked her toward the corral. She was strong and refined and when the sun hit her markings they seemed to turn to gold as if wearing earrings and a necklace of several strands of coins on her chest. Her thick auburn mane, forelock and tail had blond highlights as if she had just been coiffed at a very expensive salon. Almea was a handsome horse and her gait indicated she definitely knew how stunning she was.

A man, wearing riding boots and breeches, stood next to the door of the corral. He was lean, tall, distinguished and looked years younger than his sixties. When he saw Jax and Bernardo he smiled.

"Good morning," Bernardo said, "may I introduce you to Jax. Jax, this is Sir Charles Huffton, a man you will be seeing a great deal of."

"How do you do?" Charles said in his sophisticated English accent.

"Please to meet you," Jax replied.

They shook hands and sized each other up. Jax wasn't sure who he was. Bernardo read his mind and said: "Sir Charles is from England. He was a military officer, a colonel, and he is a rider. He is a former Olympian and won several medals for his country. He is also a coach, your coach."

"How do you mean?" Jax asked.

"I hear you are a very good rider and would like to participate in Beijing," Charles said, looking at the youngster.

"Yes, I would really like to."

"Well, that is my specialty. I can get you there, if you'll have me, and if you follow my directions."

Jax looked at Bernardo. The gaucho smiled and slightly nodded his head.

"Really?" Jax asked, excitedly.

"Really, chiquito. I think all together we make a good team."

"Oh, yes, absolutely!" Jax said and hugged Bernardo. He turned and shook Charles' hand. "It would be an honor, Sir Charles."

"Jolly good. Now let's see what our darling Almea has to say about this." The Englishman patted the horse's neck and lifted himself into the saddle. Several jumping logs had been erected inside the large corral and Charles quickly brought Almea to a gallop and guided her over the bars effortlessly, or so he made it look. Jax's eyes were the widest they had ever been. In just that one jump he saw the erectness of the former military man, the discipline of the rider and the love of being one with the horse. What a magnificent image, Jax thought. He hoped Sir Charles could help him reach their caliber, or at lease close to it. He was definitely prepared to put in the work. The Englishman brought Almea to a full stop. Jax watched carefully and barely noticed the movement in the man's legs and hands which made the horse go into a lateral and four-beat gait, extending her stride. It was as fast as a canter or slow gallop. Jax would later learn that the name for that move was a *paso largo*, a large stride. Almea, very appropriately named, was thrilled and in her element. She was dancing and Sir Charles highlighted her delicate footstep and the rapid, piston-like movement.

Jax moaned in pleasure and amazement.

Bernardo's smile was as big as his face. "Is that not the most beautiful thing you have ever seen?"

"Almea is amazing!"

"And Sir Charles, too," Bernardo added.

"This is definitely the best day of my life!" Jax exclaimed.

Sir Charles rode up to them. "Alright, young man, I hear you're a great rider. I would like to see what you can do."

Jax was a little apprehensive, and not at all confident. After seeing the Colonel's prowess he wasn't so sure of his abilities, but he would try his best. He patted Almea's neck. She was warm from the workout with Sir Charles. He put his foot in the stirrup and lifted himself into the saddle. He walked her for a few moments to get her body's feel and then smoothly guided her into a gallop. His heart pumped hard in his chest as they flew over the jumps. He could tell she loved what she was doing. Jax tried to mimic everything the colonel had done, including the dressage steps at the end. He failed miserably. Sir Charles of course expected this.

"Well, Jax, that was good, however…"

Oh, oh, here it comes, Jax thought. "Yes, Sir Charles?"

"You are an excellent, strong and intuitive rider. Your timing on the jumping is good and you are wonderfully in sync with the horse. I'm pleased."

"Really?"

"Yes, however, we are going to make you even better. You will be as one with Almea, who I can tell is already fond of you."

"Oh, and I love her too, Sir Charles."

"Yes, that's perfect. We also need to *really* train you in the dressage, starting with your posture. It has to be smooth and elegant, as a couple dancing a waltz."

"Or maybe a tango?" Bernardo ventured.

Sir Charles raised an eyebrow. "Or even a tango, why not?" He thought Jax already rode like an Argentinian cowboy, now he needed him to be more of an Austrian, one who could ride a Lippizaner and make it look like a Viennese waltz. "Uh, we'll work on that."

Jax was in bed looking at the ceiling above his head. It had been an exquisite day. He couldn't stop smiling thinking about it—his gift of the stunning Almea and the amazing Sir Charles. He looked forward to working with his very own coach, the mare and Bernardo of course. He heard the gaucho walk by and called him. The older man entered and looked inquisitively at the youngster.

"What's up, chiquito?"

"Thank you for being in my life, Bernardo. Thank you for the best day I've had in a very long time. I want you to know how much you mean to me."

"If I had a child, I would want him to be just like you. Thank you, too, gauchito, *te quiero mucho,* I love you very much.”

“Bernardo?”

“Yes?”

“I love you as much as I loved my parents.”

The Argentine knew that, but to hear the boy say it moved him and left him speechless. He hugged him tightly.

“I said thank you seven times and smiled, the first time since…” Jax trailed off.

“I’m glad and very proud of you,” Bernardo said and kissed Jax on his forehead. “Good night, chiquito.”

“Good night.”

The older man closed the door and silently jumped up and down in the hallway. He pumped his hands toward the ceiling as if he had just scored the winning goal for Argentina in a world cup. The man was happier than he had been in a very long time. The boy had finally broken off a piece of his mountain of pain.

♫

CHAPTER 9

2007 – BRAZIL

As a toddler Alina had looked very much like her father with dark hair and dark eyes. Through the years she took on more of her mother's characteristics. At eleven years old she was a combination of both her good-looking parents, with dark hair, hazel eyes and the endearing Stacy smile. Alina was tall for her age and the curves and assets of a young woman were starting to show. There was no doubt she would become a stunning young woman. Alejandro was sure his daughter's tender heart would also care for people, but in a different way; he didn't think she would follow in his footsteps. Alina was very much like him in her tastes. She loved flying and medicine, but she also loved her passions. His profession was a noble one that helped people, especially in critical situations, and the adrenaline rush than ran through both Alejandro and Alina would always be there. However, music, dancing and horses were very much part of her DNA and her beauty would help play an important role in the career she would choose. Alejandro was the proudest a man could be of his child. He never missed the flutters of pride in his heart when men, women and even children stopped in the street to look at the pretty young Alina.

Alejandro and Stacy were relaxing on the sofa in their home in Spain watching their daughter play her guitar in the patio. It seemed every child in Spain knew how to dance and play guitar, but Alina was an extremely passionate young person. She wanted to be the best at everything she did, and she had the drive to achieve it. She excelled rather than just participated, and she was good, really good.

"Can you believe Alina is eleven years old today?" Stacy exclaimed.

Alejandro took his wife's hands and kissed them. "I am the happiest man in the world and have been ever since you walked into the trailer in the jungle in Colombia, Stacy."

"Are you, my love?"

"Yes, and it's thanks to you. I have the most amazing, talented, beautiful wife, and a daughter who takes after her mother in all those qualities."

Stacy smiled in appreciation. She knew he meant every word, and yes, they did have a very special daughter. "She does have the best of her father as well. You make us very happy too, Alex."

"You know, I've been thinking."

"Have you? Should I worry?" She chuckled.

"I don't think so."

"Oh, wait, this actually sounds serious."

"Hear me out," Alejandro said.

"Okay." Stacy wasn't worried, rather she was intrigued. Her husband was a wise and intelligent man, and when he was serious she always waited patiently for him to unravel his ideas.

Since Alejandro started HeliEmerg the business had locations in Spain, Colombia, Lebanon and Brazil. They would travel to their other sites every few months to check on the work their stationary teams performed and help them with anything they needed.

"I believe it's time to show Alina other parts of the world. We have offices in different areas of the globe. We could stay several months in each place. What do you think? Good or bad idea?"

"Brilliant, actually," Stacy said. "There is no better education than to expose her to different cultures and languages. We could spend a school year in each place."

"That's perfect. Let's do it. We can figure out the details and right after summer we could start. Yes?"

"Absolutely."

Alejandro and Stacy knew the secret to a life-long happy marriage. They communicated well, understood each other's needs and wanted to please their partner. There was no subject, big or small, they wouldn't talk about or find a solution for. As with HeliEmerg it was a team effort and they loved working and being together. Stacy gave the man she adored a long, slow kiss. Alejandro responded with the same ardor of their first embrace, and always would.

Alina was excited to go to her new school in Brazil, in the heart of the Amazon. She wasn't worried about the language as she was practically fluent in Portuguese from all her visits to Portugal near her home in Spain, although she did notice some differences in pronunciation. In some ways she found the Brazilian Portuguese more musical as it had longer vowels. She noticed it even more when she listened to the local music, which she immediately fell in love with, especially the rhythms and melodies influenced by southern European and African countries. Alina was of course already learning how to dance the Brazilian samba, forró and lambada, among others. At the same time she watched local musicians playing their songs. She always seemed to find them, whether on a street corner or at the beach, or even among her classmates. Not being shy, she would ask if she could join them, if she could learn from them. The musicians were always eager to share their passion, especially with this lovely young foreign girl. Alina also figured out that she could perfect her Portuguese very quickly by learning the songs.

The HeliEmerg office was strategically located close to Manaus and the Amazon River. As with other sites around the world the local team had been trained by the same original crew, which included Alejandro, Stacy, Rod, Pierre and Hans. Fernando remained as the head of the Colombian station and was very happy, especially when the rescues were successful. He was faithful to his mission: making his country a better place and saving as many lives as he could.

HeliEmerg and the Alonsos were recognized not only for their prowess in emergency rescues, but also in that they had no affiliation with any groups, especially political. Their motto was simple: To help everyone. They were strictly a medical service and were always on call for anyone's emergency. There was an unwritten understanding that HeliEmerg and their people were not to be harmed and would be granted access and passage to wounded or hurt individuals, no matter where they hailed from. Enemies would stand down for HeliEmerg's humanitarian aid. It was a condition Alejandro demanded.

He was in the business of saving lives and when he and his teams were on a mission, they, and the wounded, would be protected. It was a welcome rule benefitting all. There was no reason any rescue had to be mortally dangerous. Due to the casualties on Alejandro's 'lawn mower' mission where one of the injured had been killed and Rod had been wounded, the unwritten decree had been created and enforced.

On their day off from school and work the Alonsos decided to take a quick trip to see some of the unique sites around Manaus. The trio boarded the HeliEmerg chopper and headed out of the city toward the *Encontro das Aguas*, the Meeting of the Waters. Instead of doing a tour on a boat the family took in the unique site from the sky. The dark Rio Negro and the beige Rio Solimões came together, but instead of converging into each other they ran side by side making a dual ribbon for almost four miles.

"How is that possible?" Alina exclaimed, amazed at the site below her.

"Two different speeds of flow and temperatures. The Rio Negro is slower and warmer, whereas the Solimões is quicker and cooler by a few degrees. The lighter comes from the water being full of sediment from the river bed starting from the Andes mountains, the darker takes its color from dead leaves and plants. It has practically no sediment and starts from the hills and jungles of Colombia."

"Oh, *Papá*, I love that you always know everything about everything!"

"I don't know about that, but I do what I can."

Stacy smiled. She always enjoyed the tacit interaction between her husband and their daughter. They were so good together. And yes, Alina was right, Alejandro seemed to always have answers for all his little girl's questions.

They continued flying low and slow when Alina shouted: "Mom, Papá, look! Pink dolphins!"

"Yes, they're river dolphins. Maybe we could swim with them another day," Stacy said.

"Oh, yes, that would be wonderful," Alina answered.

They continued to their destination following the Rio Negro to Tupé beach, home of the Desana tribe. On their way they enjoyed the lush region of flooded forests and wetlands, brimming with monkeys and colorful birds which they could immediately see, as the animals scattered from the noise of the rotors. They were amazed at the flora and fauna, especially the enormous Victoria lilies with a diameter as wide as seven feet. They approached their destination where Alejandro hovered above a river close to the village of around one hundred people. The locals waited as the water pontoons gently touched down and kept the helicopter afloat. An older man wearing a full headdress of brilliant yellow feathers greeted them. The people of the tribe were honored by their presence and welcomed them. Perhaps they thought the Alonsos were gods as they had descended from the sky in the enormous flying insect with strange wings on its head.

Dressed and living as they had for centuries, the tribe preserved their traditions and culture. They were a peaceful people and the men sported tones of blue feathers of different heights from macaw birds, depending on their status in the community. The men wore black underwear covered by long woven loin cloths and women wore hay skirts. All men, women and children wore necklaces, some with flowers, some intricately beaded and some with teeth from dangerous jungle and marine predators such as jaguars and alligators. They were also covered in intricate designs of face and body paint.

The children ran around the newcomers and suddenly some of the adults, who had been sitting around the grass huts, jumped up and started playing maracas and different flutes. Members of the tribe started dancing and the children grabbed Alina's hands and pulled her into their circle. She was in heaven as she followed their gyrations, trying to mimic their dance and their singing. She learned quickly and everyone smiled and clapped at the foreign girl. The adults danced next and Alina and the children took part with percussion instruments. One of the youngsters handed her a *tinamou*. She learned from the kids, as they pointed to the tinamou birds in the trees, that they were the amazing singers she heard through the leaves. The flute had the same characteristics and was very important in Brazilian music. The little ones had no inhibition at all and would just start talking to her. By the end of their 'very important' conversation, even though they understood each other better with hand gestures, Alina embraced them—a hug that projected, they were sure, a rainbow which enveloped all of them in a special bond. Alina had captured their hearts and was presented with a flute, several necklaces and a long tube which mimicked, as the children explained, water falling from the sky—a rain stick.

After the dances and singing the Alonsos were invited to eat cassava and fresh-caught fish which they prepared over a fire. As they waited for the food to cook the children offered their guests a snack. The trio smiled at each other as they ate big black ants from a large pottery bowl. It was better than they anticipated.

The Alonsos were saying goodbye to their hosts,

heading out to the beach to relax, when they heard a shrill scream that made them shudder. A woman came out of the jungle near the river running and shouting and carrying a child close to her chest whose leg was covered in blood. In a matter of seconds, the woman relayed the problem and the village was frantic.

Alejandro caught the arm of the man who spoke a little Portuguese and had been their guide during their visit. "What's happened?"

Stacy had a better view. "I think she's been attacked by an animal; she's bleeding, and bad," she said quickly.

Alejandro's military instinct took command as he immediately instructed the guide to follow him. The young man was right behind him as he explained to the villagers who they were and what they did. Stacy and Alina ran to his side. The guide explained to the frantic mother that they were medics and could help them. Stacy looked at the girl's pale face. She had lost a lot of blood and the crimson liquid was continuously running down one of her thighs. The mother had done a smart and good job plugging the holes with *machimango*, a root found in the jungle she had chewed and turned into a paste. She had dressed the wounds and covered them with leaves. Unfortunately, one of the puncture wounds had found the femoral artery. Stacy could tell as the blood oozed out of the leaf bandage and wasn't stopping.

"Holy shit!" Alejandro swore, "a caiman attacked her."

"If we don't stop the bleeding she'll die," Stacy told him.

"We're taking her to a hospital," Alejandro said to the villagers. He turned to the guide. "I can only take one more person. I would prefer you because of the language. Make it happen."

The guide nodded and explained to the mother and all the others from the family and the village who had gathered around, that these people were their only hope to save her life.

"Let's go," Alejandro ordered.

The mother didn't want to leave her daughter, but living in that part of the world she feared the girl would die without intervention. They had seen these injuries before. Jungle remedies could only do so much. She reluctantly handed her over to the guide and kissed her.

Alejandro started running to the helicopter, as did Stacy and Alina. The guide carried the girl and the mother ran behind, holding her hand until they reached the chopper. The villagers followed as well. Alejandro started the engine. Stacy jumped in quickly, donned her headset with its microphone and held her arms out for the guide to pass the child to her. As he did Alina jumped aboard and immediately held the youngster's hand. She looked at the mother from the village and smiled. She took the little hand and put it to her heart. The woman understood and although the tears were streaming down her face Alina saw the gratitude in the frightened eyes. The guide went into the helicopter as well.

Alejandro gently hovered right above the river, ready to take the helicopter up when a black caiman jumped out from under the water and landed onto one of the pontoons. An immediate shriek rang out from the people in the cabin as well as the villagers. Alina stared at the closest she would ever come to a member of a dinosaur family. She couldn't help but wonder if it was a descendant from the Mesozoic Era. Apparently, he wasn't going to give up that easily and wanted to retrieve his prey. They all watched the frenzied animal try to climb into the cabin. The villagers screamed, threw stones, grabbed his tail and tried to pull him off but the caiman kept slipping through their hands. The guide tried to kick him off from inside. Nothing worked. It was as if the caiman was glued to the floating device. Stacy wanted to start working on the girl, instead, she was calculating how big of a dose and what kind of needle she would need to immobilize the caiman. And then she remembered the missions in Colombia. Stacy shouted to Alina and the guide: "Buckle yourselves in and tight!"

"What about the caiman?" The guide asked.

"Do what I say, right now!"

Alina was already buckled in and pulled tighter on the seatbelt. The guide did as he was told. The girl was tied down. Alina and the guide were waiting, their eyes glued on the caiman who was inching himself into the cabin. Stacy grabbed the handle next to the door being careful not to get too close to the animal, its tail thrashing in anger and to balance itself.

Stacy shouted into the microphone to Alejandro: "ALEX, UP FAST AND BANK HARD LEFT! NOW!"

Alejandro did just that, his reflexes still honed to military speed and acuity. And he completely trusted Stacy. They had been on enough missions to know each other's expertise and competence. They had either lived through the unconventional, or had the skills to resolve any problem. Stacy held on tight as she expected the rough jerk on her shoulders. Even though she anticipated the distressing pain from her body being roughly pulled out of the cabin and into the air her shoulders still screamed in agony. The caiman tried to hold on by snapping at Stacy's dangling foot, but she managed to pull it away just in time.

"Mom!" Alina screamed, more afraid of losing her mother as she had ever been. "Hold on! Hold on!"

"Talk to me!" Alejandro shouted from the front and into the microphone.

"Keep it just the way you are. A few more moments and the damn gator should fall out."

But the tenacious animal held on. Stacy squeezed her hands with every ounce of strength she possessed. If she slipped she would first land on the caiman's open jaw and sharp teeth. She didn't know which was worse—the caiman possibly taking a bite out of her, or flying out of the helicopter and landing hard somewhere the jungle. Either way it was a lose-lose situation. The villagers, Alina, the guide and Alejandro watched in horror at the scene unfolding in front of their eyes.

"I swear if you don't leave, I'm going to make a suitcase out of you!" Stacy screamed, managing to kick the caiman on its snout. It was just enough to loosen the animal's grip on the pontoon. It fell out and plummeted erratically toward the river. The villagers watched the flying alligator, riveted to their spots. It splashed hard into the water. "Later, alligator," Stacy said. "No, not later, make that never!" She turned toward the cockpit: "Okay, Alex, he's gone. Straighten out!" As fast as you can, she wanted to add as her hands were numb and would slide off the handle at any second.

Alejandro heard his wife and did just that. At the same moment she lost her grip on the handle and fell into the cabin against the opposite wall. She gasped and knew her body would produce some profound bruises in the next few days. Stacy was happy to be alive and away from the caiman. She looked at Alina and the guide. "Are you okay?" She asked.

They all looked at each other and nodded.

"We're good. How are *you* doing, Wonder Woman?" Alina asked her mother.

Stacy laughed. "All good. Let's get this girl fixed up as best we can," she said and quickly moved over to her patient.

Alejandro was sheet white with the thought that he could have lost his amazing Stacy. As his color slowly came back he chuckled—his wife had the biggest balls in the world.

Stacy quickly looked around. Everyone was fine and her shoulders were just about back to normal. She started working on the youngster. Alina was by her side and, as before, held the little hand. She started singing an Amazonian song she had just learned in the village. The girl's eyes opened in surprise and managed a smile.

"Mom, if you need anything I'm right here."

"I know, sweetheart. Right now I think I've got this under control and you have the best medicine going. Keep doing what you're doing." Damn, she was proud of her daughter.

They flew as fast as possible to the nearest hospital. Alina watched in awe. Her parents were so good at what they did. They reminded her of musicians: her father at the controls, the maestro of his craft; her mother, working at a furious speed, her fingers smooth and quick as the piano player she was. Stacy didn't need to look anywhere to grab a pad of gauze or any of the life-saving instruments. Everything was placed exactly where she wanted and Stacy was her own little fine-tuned orchestra. Alina was very proud indeed to be part of this family.

Stacy worked furiously on the girl's thigh after giving her a shot to alleviate the pain. She inspected the bleeder and quickly cleaned and disinfected the area. She clipped the artery until it stopped. She was sure the girl now stood a chance. She continued checking, removing damaged tissue as she went. The holes in the leg made by the caiman's conical teeth of his V-shaped snout left symmetrical lines on the thigh reminding Stacy of a flock of flying geese. She repeated the process in each of the cavities. "Hey, Alina, look at this," she said, showing her daughter her discovery.

Alina watched closely as her mother pulled one of the caiman's teeth out of the young girl's thigh. She held it up to the light with the tongs. She cleaned it off, put it in a little plastic bag and gave it to her daughter. "Maybe the girl would like it as a souvenir."

"I don't know, but we can ask her later," Alina answered, wondering how painful the encounter must have been to have a broken tooth in her thigh.

Stacy continued until she was satisfied she had done all she could. They just needed to get to the hospital.

Less than ten minutes later, Alejandro landed gently on the medical helipad where several members of the staff were waiting. They quickly loaded the girl onto a gurney and took her to the operating room. The guide went with them.

The Alonsos sat in the helicopter and took a few deep breaths. "Good call with the hard bank," Alejandro said to his wife.

"It worked beautifully," Stacy said.

"Mom also threatened the caiman she would make him into a suitcase if he didn't let go," Alina added.

Alejandro laughed. Nobody messed with his Stacy, not even a caiman.

"Well, I think today was one of the most amazing days I've ever had," Alina added.

"I quite agree, *amorcito*, my little love. "Only one thing I regret," Alejandro said, turning to his wife.

"And what would that be?" Stacy asked.

"Rod and Pierre. They would have loved this."

"They certainly would have!" Stacy said and laughed good-heartedly, happy with the day's outcome and finally relaxing.

Alina went to the hospital every day until the girl from the Desana tribe was discharged. The operation had been successful and she kept her leg, thanks to everyone's quick thinking. From the mother's machimango paste to 'Wonder Woman's' stunts and medical care, to Captain Alejandro's quick thinking and maneuvering, the girl would make a full recovery. Alina and the girl became friends, even with their limited words, but they had music and taught each other songs during the convalescence. When she was discharged the Alonsos took her back to the village. At first she didn't want to go into the ugly insect with the wings on its head, but after a little coaxing from Alina she finally boarded. When Alejandro lifted off the girl's knuckles turned sheet white from holding on so tight to the edge of her seat, until she realized she wasn't going to fall out of the sky. When she saw the world from above, as the birds did, she wanted to stay up there forever. When they arrived they were welcomed as saviors descending from the sky. The mother of the girl embraced her daughter for a long time, as did other members of her family.

The mother went to Stacy and put a necklace around the American woman's neck. It was decorated with caiman teeth. She was a great warrior. It was the highest reward she could give this person who helped save her daughter's life. The two women looked at each other and Stacy said: "Is this our black caiman?"

The Desana tribeswoman understood Stacy's questioning eyes. She nodded and hugged Stacy. The necklace and the embrace were the most special gift the

American woman could have received. Stacy was most partial to the hug. Alina thought her mother was the real thing—an Amazon in the Amazon jungle.

The villagers went all out with a feast, singing and dancing. The guests enjoyed the meals and entertainment, but Stacy didn't partake in the black ants.

The Alonsos returned to Spain for the summer, richer from their experiences and the sites they visited. Alina was now fluent in Portuguese and had learned wonderful dances and great songs. She had loved and enjoyed Brazil, its people, their traditions, the music and the Amazon with its tribes. Alina, however, always looked forward to her next adventure.

♫

CHAPTER 10

2008 – Beijing, China

RANDY

Randolph Newton III did everything by the book to arrive at the Olympic Games and claim a spot on the U.S. Equestrian team. He grew up in a horse-oriented family who had been championship riders for generations and he was to continue the tradition. As a boy he spent his childhood in riding organizations and entered all the competitions he could. He had been part of high school and college teams and his coach had been with him for many years. His family always bought the best horses and he competed constantly at as many venues as possible. Randy had indeed inherited the family gene and was a very good rider, which brought him to Beijing after years of hard work. His heart, however, was not into it, as the fun and pleasure had been erased. The pressure from his family to bring home the gold was unbearable and his passion had vanished. Bringing home anything less than the top medal would certainly banish him from the family. It had been pummeled into him ever since he could remember. He had been groomed for this event for years. In the next twenty-four hours he would take part in the greatest competition of his life. The expectations were massive and asphyxiating. These, then, were Randy's thoughts as he checked his clothes, his equipment and his horse. For the tenth time.

Jax, who had qualified for the Olympics after working very hard at his goal, accompanied Randy and two women from the U.S. Equestrian team. They went out to eat some authentic Chinese food. They walked out of the Olympic Village and headed for a restaurant someone had suggested. They found it easily and once inside ordered several of the specialties.

While lost in his thoughts and waiting for their food Randy spied a bar in the restaurant. He asked the waiter what he would recommend as far as a good and strong Chinese drink.

"Baijiu," he answered.

Randy gave him a thumb's up.

"Hey, man, you think you should be drinking?" Jax asked.

"Hey, I'm not in gymnastics I'm into horses, remember? And they'll be doing most of the work tomorrow."

"Still, just go easy."

"Yeah, don't worry. I can hold my liquor."

"Right," Jax answered, not too sure about Randy's confidence or how much of the alcohol he could actually consume without dire effects.

When their meals arrived the little group enjoyed the local specialties of Beijing roasted duck, *jiaozi*, Chinese dumplings filled with meat or vegetables and noodles with sauce and tuck. They also tried assorted flavors of the sweet *fulingbing*, also known as tuckahoe pie.

Randy was also diligently emptying the bottle of Baijiu. He did offer to refill his teammates glasses, but they declined after one drink. He stared at the liquid and lost himself in his thoughts. He was so tired of always having to compete to be the best groomed, the richest, the most up to date in fashions and expensive hi-tech gadgets, or having the latest toys of the rich and famous. He had to emulate his parents and be the top at everything, from riding to drinking anyone under the table whenever he was out with company. He probably would have been excessive with drugs had he not been an athlete and been forced to do spontaneous tests. He was exhausted of having to prove he was unsurpassed at everything, that he was filthy-rich and high-class and had to flaunt it. He was a member of a family that either didn't know how to love, or never showed it. Perhaps it was beneath them. Randy just wanted to be 'another guy', someone people actually liked, to maybe love a pretty girl and be loved in return. Unfortunately, Randy didn't know how to be 'normal'. He only knew how to be arrogant, demanding, pushy and make sure he was better than everybody else. He was the finest at being nasty, rude and crude. He was the epitome of the guy nobody wanted to hang around with.

"Hey, which one of you gals wants to come back to my room?" Randy ventured.

"Are you serious?" Jax asked.

"Okay, I'll take both of you."

"Stop it, Randy!" Jax exclaimed.

"What? Jealous?"

"I said stop it. What is wrong with you?"

"What? You don't want to do some fooling around?

These girls are hot, with nice firm muscles."

"Why do you have to be such an ass all the time?" one of the women asked.

"What? I was complimenting you." Randy said as he took another drink.

"You're drunk," she added.

"You don't have to like it," Randy answered.

"You're very right about that, I most certainly do not. Why don't you just take your arrogant ass and leave."

"No, I'm going to finish the bottle first. Maybe *you* should leave."

"Hey, guys, come on," Jax said, "we're in China, taking part at the Olympic Games. We're representing the U.S. and we're members of the equestrian team. We're enjoying a wonderful meal in a beautiful country filled with so much history. Can it get any better than that? Why don't we all take it easy and enjoy our time here. This will never happen to any of us ever again."

"You make a good point, Jax," the other woman said, "but Randy here is just ruining all of it. I'm sorry, I'm going back to the village. I'll see you there."

"I'm coming with you," the other woman said.

They left the guys at the restaurant and headed out.

Randy kept drinking.

"Maybe you should hold off on any more of that firewater."

"Jax, you are a pain in my ass. Why don't you just join me and have another glass."

"No, thanks, I've had enough. What do you say we get out of here?"

"And go where? To the dorms?" Randy said, sarcastically. "Why don't we just go to a nice hotel?"

"Because we're not allowed to. We have to stay at the village. You can tough it out for a few more days."

"Why should I have to?"

"Come on, let's go," Jax said, standing up.

"Oh, fine," Randy said. He tried to stand up, but realized his legs were wobbly.

"Oh, shit!" Jax said as he grabbed his teammate before he fell on the floor. "Hold on."

Randy did, and the two men staggered out of the restaurant.

"What is wrong with you, man?" Jax asked, not happy at all.

"Hey, what's the big deal," Randy slurred.

"This isn't… oh, I don't know, Australia, where the people are fun-loving and could give you a run for your money trying to drink you under the table. A country where everyone loves their barbie, beer and babes. No, you idiot! This is China. *China!*" Jax emphasized, "a really strict country, and a communist one too. Sure, they love to drink like the rest of the world, but their protocols are rigidly enforced. And not to forget we're representing the United States. We're ambassadors here, and we don't always have the best reputation when we're overseas. You've heard of the ugly American tourist? Well, *you*, asshole, fit the bill completely."

"Yeah, that's me," Randy slurred, "the ugly American."

"Get with it, man!" Jax growled, holding up his teammate. "These guys following us are not the nice Chinese people, they are the nasty ones—the local police who would love to throw our asses in jail and lose the keys forever."

"Where is the massage parlor?" Randy wasn't listening to Jax at all. "You know the one with the lovely ladies who give you baths and really nice massages."

"You mean Geishas?"

"That's them."

"Wrong country, moron, that's Japan."

"Well, they must have something similar over here. I mean they've been practicing medicine and weird therapies for years. You know, like acupuncture."

"Yeah, I'd like to stick a million needles into you right now. Maybe that would bring you out of your miserable drunken state."

"Had a couple too many, huh?"

"Ya think?"

"Hey, what was that Chinese vodka called?"

"Baijiu."

"Right, shit's kicking me like a mule. I think my head's gonna fall off."

"Now there's a great idea, maybe I'll try it."

"The Chinese vodka?"

"No, kicking you."

"Oh."

Jax held onto to his teammate and they soon arrived at the dorms. Jax watched the police turn the corner and leave. He let out a sigh of relief and then presented their credentials to the guard at the gate of the Olympic village. The man stared and wondered what was wrong with the American. Was he drunk? That wasn't allowed.

"My friend ate too much duck and too many delicious dumplings. They were very good, but he overdid it." Jax chuckled, trying to lighten the mood.

Just hearing about food made Randy's stomach lurch and his body shudder. Jax held him tighter. "Hold it, man, don't you dare hurl here. We're being watched," he whispered.

"Again?"

"No, continuously."

"Why?" Randy asked.

"Why are we being watched?"

"Uh-huh."

"Because we're at the Olympics, for Christ's sake. This is serious business, man. We're supposed to be on our best behavior and follow the rules.

"Yeah, I followed the rules my whole life. Lots of fun," he said, sarcastically.

"Come on, Randy, our room isn't far. We can do this."

"Yup, if you say so."

As Jax reached the door he unlocked it with one hand and held his buddy with the other. Randy was ready to vomit.

"Oh, no, you don't! Hold on, just another minute." Jax pleaded. He managed, just in time, to get Randy to the bathroom and to place him on his knees in front of the toilet. Randy's stomach immediately released its contents. Jax held the man's forehead. Randy's tears burned his eyes and cheeks. He didn't know if it was from his body's reaction or from the pain in his heart. He believed the man holding his head actually cared enough to be there. He wasn't used to other people acting like that; rather, he was used to being unliked and treated as an outcast.

When Randy was completely empty and spent, Jax helped clean him up. He then half carried him to the bed and dropped him. "You okay, man?" He asked.

Randy grunted and passed out. Jax took off his teammates' shoes and loosened his belt. He covered him with a blanket and went to take a shower. His mind carried him to as far back as he could remember, starting with his parents when he was really small to his best friend and mentor, Bernardo. As he showered he also saw the devastating fire and the blazing stables from where his mother and father never came out. His heart skipped a beat. As much as he loved Bernardo there would always be a little piece missing from his life. Through the water falling from the showerhead Jax's tears ran down his face as well. It had been years since he had missed them so fiercely. He sat on the floor embracing his knees to his chest and let the water pour over him as he cried. He was certain the pain would never go away. Every day the bitterness burned his throat, but thankfully it was less and less frequent. His parents would have been so proud of their little boy, of the man he had become and the way he represented his country. Jax fervently wished they could have been present. He hoped they would be holding hands from their special star in the sky as they watched their son compete with the U.S. equestrian team.

♫

CHAPTER 11

After the school year in Brazil, the Alonsos went back to Spain. They were spending their summer enjoying their vacation before heading out to another HeliEmerg location. Alina seemed to dedicate herself to riding, playing music and dancing. She shared her passions with her friends from the area. One of the highlights that summer was watching the Olympic Games in Beijing. Alina was especially thrilled with the equestrian events. She and several girlfriends were sitting on cushions on the floor in front of the television, enjoying freshly squeezed orange juice and snacks. They waited for the competition to start.

Stacy chuckled when she saw what the girls were eating. It made her remember the first time she and Alejandro went to see a film in the local village. As the movie started she kept hearing strange noises in the dark theater. She looked around and almost burst out laughing when she realized what the sounds were. The theater wasn't filled with popcorn-eating patrons, no, the viewers were eating bags of *pepitas*, sun flower seeds. The noise was coming from teeth biting down gently on the seam of the shell and the spitting out: Crack, fthou, crack, fthou.

Alejandro watched his adorable wife and laughed. He turned to her, pulled out a bag of pepitas and demonstrated the art of removing the kernel: "Hold the seed by the round end between your thumb and forefinger, hold it perpendicular to your teeth and bite gently. When it cracks open remove the seed with your tongue and spit away the shell. Repeat many times."

Stacy grinned. "Only you could make this so sexy," she whispered as the film was starting.

Alejandro moved closer to her. "Which part?"

"Oh, all of it. Well, maybe the tongue part…"

As Stacy watched the girls in front of the television with their pepitas, Alejandro was sure his lovely wife was remembering their first film together. Stacy looked at her husband and winked at him. Yes, they both knew what she was thinking. She went to the sofa and sat next to him. "Pepitas," she simply said.

"Mm, yes, I figured you were back in the theater."

"I was, and I seem to *really* remember the moments after the movie when we came back home."

"That was even more delicious than the pepitas," he grinned.

"Should we go to the bedroom for a while?" Stacy asked.

"I would love to; however, we have a room full of teenage girls who could get curious and could possibly catch us in…"

"…a delicious situation?"

"Exactly. We might have to wait for later."

"Mm, you might be right. Pity," Stacy said, and gave her man a kiss.

"Papá?" Alina interrupted.

"Yes, amorcito?"

"Do you think maybe we could go to the Olympics sometime?"

"You mean the next games?"

"Yes, maybe the opening ceremony."

"That actually sounds like a good idea."

"Hey, everybody, it's starting," Stacy announced.

The girls squealed in delight and watched the television. They giggled as they saw the perfectly groomed riders parading with their horses. The girls were entering that wondrous phase of their lives. No longer were boys yucky, now they were cute.

"Oh, check him out," one of the girls whispered. "He's sooooo handsome!"

They watched the equestrians and thought the American man was quite good looking and looked very sharp in his dark blue riding coat.

On the other side of the world Jax took in the manicured venue of the dressage arena. The spectators, many in country colors and waving flags, anticipated a magnificent show.

Jax liked the fact that the equestrian events weren't divided by men and women, and age didn't matter. They all competed together, the youngsters together with the experienced older athletes. Although youth was usually best in most sports, experience and intuition favored riders. It was the same for the horses. All together they were a beautiful mix of ages, experience and talent.

Jax was one of the youngest riders and was looking forward in acquiring some of the experience other equestrian competitors present had. The oldest was a German woman, much older than any of the others, an Olympian having won several medals in different Olympics. The equestrian competition included individuals and teams in a three-day eventing of dressage, stadium jumping and cross-country.

The riders from the different participating countries were getting ready for the dressage free style, a six-minute choreographed routine incorporating compulsory figures and performed to music. The goal was to make the public, and judges, watch and enjoy the most flawless and synchronized routine possible. Jax remembered how Sir Charles worked tirelessly to make his protégé a sophisticated European rider instead of a South American cowboy. The coach hadn't minded the style when the two of them first met and Sir Charles appreciated the younger man's prowess and unmistakable intuition. He was a good rider and his style came in handy for jumping, especially in the cross-country where horse and rider had to negotiate natural obstacles of hills, logs, streams, ditches, forests and even fences over a four to five kilometer course. The timed event was a grueling trial of skill, endurance, agility and mental and physical challenges.

In the dressage freestyle a set series of movements had to be performed by the horse and rider. Optional actions to increase levels of difficulty and artistic merit, very similar to figure skating, could be added. Fifty percent of the marks came from technical execution and fifty percent from artistic, which included harmony between the rider and the horse, choreography, rhythm, flexibility, creativity and the interpretation of the music.

Sir Charles and other coaches watched their team members. They were doing a good job of controlling their anxiety. They had trained and waited for this moment for years. It was finally time. The trainers looked at their riders and glowed with pride as their protégés were some of the best riders in the world. They had all worked very hard to arrive at this moment in their lives. Sir Charles was sure his heart had grown a little in the last moments as he watched his lad. Jax indeed was the epitome of an elegant rider. His posture was perfect, his riding attire exquisitely tailored. The young man was very handsome in his black top hat, dark blue swallowtail coat, white shirt and tie, white gloves and breeches, and tall black boots. Both men and women sported the same clothes, the only difference were the ties. The women wore scarves with pins. The horses as well were groomed to perfection. Their manes were braided into rosette buttons which helped highlight the horses' toplines. Their tails, brushed for what seemed hours, hung loosely behind their powerful hind legs. They sported a white pad under the leather saddles, the only inscriptions the Olympic logo and their athlete's number.

Jax rode Almea, his beloved Paso Fino. She complemented Jax perfectly, especially when the sun hit her tan spots and turned them to into what seemed gold jewelry. She was a beautiful specimen among the exquisite equines present. Jax looked at Randy's Dutch Warmblood, a magnificent performance breed. He was big, impressive and had a good temperament. Jax couldn't say the same of Randy's mood as he could tell he was fighting a nasty hangover.

Randy looked into the stands at his parents and analyzed them. They were extremely wealthy, hailing from the insurance alliance of both sides of old Connecticut families. Did his parents even love each other? He wasn't sure. Perhaps they were happy, in their own way, with what they had and how they lived. Had their marriage been a business transaction? Randy didn't doubt it. They lived off their name and their lifestyle. They seemed to be just fine in their small world. Their forefathers were descendants of the Mayflower and everyone who knew them, or of them, were well aware of that fact. They seemed a happy couple and stood out, but to Randy the look was fake. Randy could tell his mother's body and face had undergone the seemingly inconspicuous age-related nips and tucks of a plastic surgeon's scalpel. Appearances were everything to the Newtons. How else could they maintain the status others yearned for and were envious of? Randy thought that was the most ridiculous concept of the so-called Rich and Famous. His parents were also recognized for the most expensive toys in the world, from mansions to cars to yachts. And of course, the horses—a collection of the finest equine specimens on the planet, from Arabians to multi-million-dollar thoroughbreds.

The Newtons always wore the most expensive clothes from Chanel or Yves Saint Laurent, Balenciaga or Valentino. The horses had tailor-made designer blankets, saddles and bridles. His mother's jewelry was world famous, stemming from exclusive stores such as Cartier, Lalaounis, Bulgari or Tiffany's. And his father wouldn't be caught dead without his six-figure Rolex. They weren't nouveau-riche gaudy, they came from old money and were very aware that everything they did or wore had to be perfect and elite by rich and famous standards. Nothing but the best the world had to offer would do. That was also the reason for wanting their son to bring them an Olympic gold medal. Anything beside the top prize was unheard of. Randy pictured the 'trophy' room, a large part of the mansion that housed every accolade the Newtons ever received. It seemed every wall was decorated with frames of newspaper stories with the provenance of each honor. Many of the awards were in glass encasements on small tables. There was one new container, an empty one, the one that would house

Randy's gold medal from the Beijing Olympics. Randy looked away from his parents and concentrated on the competition.

Jax was up next. He waited for the officials to give him the signal for him to start. He did one last visualization of every movement of the ride and then leaned forward so that his face was close to the horse's ears. He still smiled every time he saw Almea's 'earrings'.

"We're up next, *guapa*, beautiful. Are you ready?" Jax asked his favorite girl.

The horse felt the lips brush her ear and heard his whisper. She softly snorted back. Yes, she was ready to show the world their dancing skills.

Jax's eyes searched for Bernardo, his mentor, his rock, the father figure who did his best to keep his promise to Oliver and Karen Logan and who loved him just as much as his parents had. The gaucho was the one who had kept him together through his personal challenges and helped him on the path to conquer his painful mountain. Jax loved and respected the only person he considered family, for his amazing teachings, the training they both worked hard at and enjoyed, and to the sweet sixteen birthday gift of Almea. He spotted Bernardo's beret first. He was with Sir Charles and the other coaches. The men were, of course, watching their boy. Jax brought his arm up and saluted them. The Colonel saluted back and the Argentine covered his heart and gave him a thumbs up. His chiquito was living his dream and the gaucho was proud of how far they had both come. The icing on the cake would be a definitely achievable medal. He thanked his Creator and his Maria for the path he was walking. He was sure the Logans were watching their boy as well.

As Jax and Almea stood in silence the rider remembered the road that brought him to this moment. It had started when he and Bernardo watched the equestrian event at the Sydney Olympics the same year the Logans were killed. The Games had taken his young mind off his parents' demise and let him focus on the synchronicity and perfection of horse and rider taking place on the television in front of him. That was when he made himself a promise that one day he would be a competitor as well. With help he had achieved his goal.

The official gave Jax the green light and the duo walked toward the low barriers leading to the twenty by sixty meter arena where they would perform their routine. Jax heard the announcer's voice introducing him and his horse. He raised his right arm, signaling they were starting. They entered the showground with a *passage*, a very slow trot where Almea momentarily suspended her feet after each step between footfalls. As horse and rider arrived at the center of the arena they stopped. Jax bowed his head and extended his right arm toward the ground. It was their moment. Almea stood very still and regal with her natural 'jewelry' and her highlighted forelock and tail.

The music started with a bandoneon, an Argentinian accordion, giving rhythm to the piece. The tango medley, a six-minute mix of very well-known tangos, filtered through the loudspeakers. The crowd almost clapped and wanted to sway their hips as they immediately recognized the music, but they stayed respectfully quiet. Jax had convinced Sir Charles tango music would be perfect, and he also wanted to honor Bernardo. It didn't take too much coaxing as the Britisher immediately agreed.

Jax and Almea began their routine with a similar passage and when the piano came in horse and rider began a slow canter half-pass, where she moved forward and sideways at the same time. Her hooves came down exactly in time to the rhythm. The melody was perfectly suited for dancing and that is exactly what Jax and Almea were doing. As the full orchestra softly entered they continued their movements smoothly into a pirouette where the horse turned on her haunches in several strides. Jax and his partner performed changes of lead where the duo seemed to be skipping nonchalantly along a beach. They followed with a piaffe, a cadenced trot in place and into another piaffe pirouette to the side and middle of the showground.

The music started its crescendo as did the duo. Jax and Almea dazzled the crowd with her breed's specialty of very rapid, piston-like steps, perfectly synchronized to the beat during an extended trot, covering as much ground as possible. The spectators were amazed at the dazzling rapid footwork. From the moment they started, the duo's performance had been smooth, with clean changes of balance and direction. They remained calm, without breaking their rhythm or forward impetus. Almea was in perfect time all the way through. True to her name she was a dancer, and when the music stopped her foot hit the ground on the last beat of the music and stood completely immobile, majestic and proud.

Many of the spectators had tears in their eyes. In Spain, the Alonsos and the girls were completely silent, moved by the perfection they had just witnessed. Alina was sure she had never seen anything more magnificent between a person and a horse. The harmony of the duo's dance, with the music enhancing the performance, would always remain with her.

The crowd applauded profusely at what they were sure was one of the best dressage routines the world had ever witnessed. Jax lowered his right arm toward the ground, signaling the end of the routine and then pumped his fist in the air. He took his hat off and waved to the crowd. When he put it back on he let go of the reins and leaned far forward and hugged Almea's neck. It was almost as if the pair were doing a last move, a dip at the culmination of their tango. Jax knew, and maybe his partner did as well, they had just performed their best ever, and this was the place to have done that. They had gone from rookies to medal finalists in a very short amount of time.

As the spectators, coaches and riders waited for Jax's score their eyes also followed the duo—the man dismounted, hugged Almea's neck again and lovingly caressed and kissed the sides of her face and muzzle. Many of the women would have loved to take the equine's place.

The scores from the judges were finished being tabulated and they announced the result. Jax was in first place! Would he be able to retain it? Other riders still hadn't competed. Randy was among them, and as good as he was, he had to agree Jax's ride had been spectacular. He started to perspire. If he didn't win, his parents were going to be furious and there would be hell to pay. He just didn't how bad it could get. Randy's name was called and horse and rider proceeded to the arena as Jax had done. Their performance was seamless, but not quite enough to beat his teammate. The routine had been technically perfect, but it didn't have the harmony and love everyone recognized between Jax and Almea.

When the competition was over the three medalists rode their horses into the arena where they had competed. The grooms accompanied them and took the reins when the riders dismounted to go stand behind the podium. Randy was on the left, Jax in the middle, and a member of the German team was on the right in the bronze medal spot. She was also the oldest rider among the competitors and she would make Olympic history as she had competed in several Games and won a medal in each of them. In the field in front of the platform members of the Olympic equestrian committee were ready to hand out the medals to the winners. The voice of the announcer on the loudspeaker called the bronze medalist and the rider stepped up. The crowd applauded and cheered, German flags waving throughout the stadium. Randy was next with the silver medal.

Randy looked up into the stands. His parents were staring at him. He knew if their eyes could they would be hurtling daggers at him. His mother and father left the stands and walked out. Randy didn't need to see their eyes or watch their body language to know that a new kind of perdition was about to begin. He had let them down, but he had done his best and did manage to win a medal for his country. He looked at it. It was the wrong damn color. If his parents hadn't made his life miserable Randy would have been ecstatic and proud of his accomplishment. It was an Olympic medal!

"Gold medalist and Olympic champion, representing the United States, Jaxon Logan," the announcer's voice boomed throughout the venue. Jax stepped up onto the winner's place and accepted the medal and congratulations from the committee.

After the ceremony the riders returned to the stables. They were showered by hugs and congratulations from other team members, coaches and in Jax's case Bernardo and Sir Charles. The three men embraced, incredibly proud of each other and their achievements. Randy only received his coach's scowl. He was sure his parents had already gotten to him. Sure enough, the man approached him and without saying a word gave Randy a message from his parents. They were expecting him for dinner. The time, restaurant and its location were the only words on the paper. Randy groaned as if he had been punched. A congratulatory remark about how wonderful it was to win a medal, or how long and hard he had worked for it, would have been nice.

♫

CHAPTER 12

Randy, his parents and his coach were sitting at one of the most expensive restaurants in the city, sipping on tea, as they waited for their dinner to be served. The Olympian listened to the tongue lashing from his parents for his failure in bringing home the gold. It was the worse he had ever received in his life. Silver was for losers. He was silver. He was a disgrace to the family, to his name and to his country. Randy's hands were becoming fists and he visualized them smashing into his father's face. He slowly stood up, threw his own eye daggers at his parents and figured he had a split-second to make up his mind: Either carry out his desire to beat the hell out of his father, or just simply leave. He chose the latter. "Great parents," he mumbled as he turned around and left. They could go to hell as far as he was concerned.

"You'd better win the competition in Spain!" His father shouted after him. Randy heard the older man. They still weren't satisfied and now they wanted him to win the Spanish event. He knew it was the most prestigious among the equine community. He wanted to scream and smash his fists in every wall of the restaurant, but he just headed away from his parents and out the door.

Once outside Randy took several deep breaths. He was proud of himself for not having thrown punches or blowing up, but he did need to release his fury and calm his temper. He continued walking, then started jogging until he was in a full sprint through the streets of the city. He had to release his anger and try to erase his parents' continuous comments and jabs about his worthlessness. He was just so tired of their treatment and expectations. Whatever happened to his childhood and to having fun? He had traveled, seen a great part of the world, had as many women as he wanted, tasted everything the good life could provide and, yet was unhappy. He didn't want to seem ungrateful, but there was something missing. What was it? he wondered. What was missing from his life? He continued running through different neighborhoods at full speed and laughed to himself as he thought of the police possibly following him. Or were they? If they were they probably figured the American was losing it, or was crazy. Randy finally stopped when his lungs were screaming at him. He put his hands on his knees and breathed in great gulps of air. He felt better. He wasn't as angry, but he also knew this wasn't the end of the evening. He started heading back toward the Olympic village and then decided to look for a bar. He decided to get absolutely plastered into oblivion, but on his own. He certainly didn't want company and, although grateful to Jax for his previous help, tonight he would wallow by himself. Besides, the son of a bitch had managed to win the gold from him, which made Jax partly to blame for his problems.

Randy caught a taxi and asked the driver to take him

to a deluxe hotel. They surely would have a western bar with bourbon or whisky. Once there he decided he was going to get very drunk in a nice room instead of the bar where people, especially the local police, could watch him. He didn't want to worry about anything; besides, his Olympics were over. His events had taken place and he only had to attend the farewell ceremony in a few days. He gave the receptionist a credit card. He went to the suite, appreciated the combination of western and Chinese décor and the luxurious amenities. He called room service and ordered a bottle of bourbon, a cheeseburger and some local fried rice. He hadn't really eaten all day and he didn't have any of the dinner he was supposed to share with his parents. His meal and the bottle arrived in just a short while. Randy opened his wallet and the bellboy noticed the wad of yen. The tip was substantial, and the American man asked him for a little entertainment. Randy knew that with money anything was possible.

Randy poured himself a strong drink, enjoyed the familiar liquid and quickly ate his meal. Once finished he removed his sweaty clothes and took a long calming shower in a luxuriously appropriate and convenient bathroom. It was a far cry from the ones at the Olympic village. He came out in the bathrobe provided by the hotel and poured himself another glass of bourbon. In less than ten minutes there was a knock on the door. Randy opened and was delightfully surprised when he saw the two distinguished lovely women he would spend the evening with.

"Hello ladies, please come in. I'm Randy."

They bowed slightly. Randy bowed back.

"I'm Qiang."

"And I'm Yue."

"We are very pleased to meet you," they said together. They greeted him in fluent English, with just the slightest trace of a Chinese tone. They wore similar long evening gowns with exquisite designs of lotus flowers embroidered with gold thread. One of the dresses was red, the other turquoise, with discreet openings at the front for just enough mystery of their hidden assets. The color of their shoes and clutches matched their clothes. They were both about the same height and size and exuded an unmistakable Chinese loveliness and sophistication. Their skin was flawless, their eyebrows shaped to perfectly suit their eyes, and their lips and smiles were endearing. They both wore their black hair back, tied up in a chignon. Randy raised his eyebrows; he was impressed. These ladies were definitely pros—discreet and refined. He was sure they would be exquisite in everything they did. He made a mental note to compliment and compensate the bellboy.

They entered, very at ease with their surroundings.

"Would you ladies like a bourbon? Or maybe something else, perhaps champagne?"

"Champagne would be lovely," Qiang said.

"Yes, thank you," Yue agreed.

Randy picked up the phone and ordered two bottles.

"英俊的男子 *Ying ch-ien da nantzu*, good looking man," Qiang whispered to her partner.

"这可能很有趣 *Ch kana haï ochee*, this could be fun," Yue whispered back in agreement.

In less than five minutes chilled Cristal was delivered to the room. Randy poured each of them a glass. "Cheers, ladies."

"Cheers," they repeated and each drank a sip of the exquisite sparkling liquid.

Randy sat in an armchair and enjoyed the

champagne. Yue found the remote control and put on relaxing Chinese music. The guzheng in the melody immediately filled the entire suite from the living room to the bathroom. The soft plucked zither sent waves of mystery and calmness throughout.

Qiang knelt in front of Randy and started massaging his feet. Yue stood behind him and rubbed his temples. They started from each end; one from the head, the other from the toes on up. They had, of course, realized how tense Randy was, and not just physically. They worked on him until his body finally started relaxing; his muscles released their tension and his stress diminished.

Yue quicky removed her dress. She wasn't wearing anything under her gown. Randy's eyes were closed and didn't noticed. She continued massaging his face with one hand and slowly pulled his bathrobe off his shoulders with her other hand. She continued to his neck, his chest and his stomach. She had to reach from behind him and, as she did, her breasts caressed his cheeks. Randy smiled but kept his eyes closed, savoring the light touch of her chest on his, and the perfume from her skin. Qiang quickly removed her gown and went back to his feet and slowly moved up his calves. She continued massaging and kissing as Yue did the same on his arms, chest and stomach, and inched up to his face. She lightly kissed his lips until Randy responded. Their mouths parted and their tongues danced together until Qiang took his hands. She pulled them and the three of them stood up and looked at each other. Randy was amazed the women had undressed and brought their hair down. Without saying a word the women casually removed his robe and took him to the bedroom. Randy lay in the middle of the bed as Qiang and Yue covered his entire body with sensual strokes. They took turns kissing his lips, one at a time and then together, their tongues intertwining with carnal delight. Randy touched and tasted every inch of them. He kissed and licked and discovered their bodies as they did the same to him.

Qiang and Yue gently pushed, rubbed, kissed, lightly scratched, and sucked every part of Randy's body. They used either their hands, feet or mouth on every pressure point and erotic zone. Randy firmly believed the women had a degree in sexual reflexology, if that even existed. Their night was just beginning. The women moved over Randy's body in perfect unison, pleasuring him over and over to levels he never knew existed or were even possible.

Before their second round of pleasure began Qiang and Yue gave Randy another massage.

"Do your names have a meaning?" Randy asked them.

"Mine is rose," Qiang answered.

"And I am moon."

"Very nice."

The women continued working, one from the head, the other from the feet until they met in the middle. They looked at each other, smiled, nodded and started a different kind of kneading. In an instant Randy moaned and was ready for the next round, which turned out just as exquisite as the first one, with yet more pleasures for Randy. When they were spent the three of them relaxed on the bed and drank more champagne. After a short while Qiang and Yue ran a bath. They led him into the water filled with bubbles and flower petals. Incense filled the room and the lighting was gentle and subdued from the candles around the bathtub. They sat in the large tub, Yue behind Randy, Qiang in front of him; their legs intertangled. The women cuddled closer to Randy until the ménage à trois seemed to be one body. Qiang and Yue washed him with gentle sponges and squeezed their bodies tighter into him. Randy would discover even more in round three, among the bubbles and petals.

Qiang and Yue left in the early hours of the morning while Randy was sleeping. It had been a good night for all three of them.

♫

CHAPTER 13

2008 - LEBANON

After their summer vacation in Spain, the Alonsos spent the next school year at the furthest eastern point of the Mediterranean. The HeliEmerg location in Lebanon was just outside Beirut.

Alina and Naila, a friend from her new school, were riding exquisite Arabians, galloping at full speed on a pristine deserted beach. There were no other people, just the two of them and the horses. The girls' parents were good friends and colleagues and were waiting for them at one end of the beach. They watched their daughters and believed in their maturity. They were good girls and quite advanced for their age, but they always kept an eye on them.

Alina and Naila rode a while longer until they were tired and wanted to give the horses a break. They were also hungry. They went to where their parents were relaxing, enjoying the sun and the shade from the palm trees at the edge of the beach. The girls dismounted and tied the horses to the trunks. They gave them carrots and apples, and a bucket of fresh water; and a lot of love. Alina knew how special these creatures were. Horses made her want to sing.

"Come, girls!" Zoona, Naila's mother said, taking food out of a cooler. "Come, eat."

The girls didn't need any coaxing, they were at her side in seconds.

"What did you make for us, *Umii*?" Naila asked her mom.

Zoona offered open-faced meat pies to everyone present.

"Ooh, *sfeeha*, my favorite," Naila exclaimed.

"Looks delicious!" Alina added.

Stacy helped and brought out hummus, cheese, pita bread and salad. Alejandro and Waleed, the dads, helped as well and put rice pilaf and kofta kebabs on the picnic table. They gathered around on beach chairs and enjoyed the meal and the company. Waleed also played local popular tunes on the MP3.

"You have outdone yourself, Zoona, this is delicious! Thank you," Alejandro said.

"I'll second that," Stacy added.

"Yes, thank you very much. It's so good!" Alina also chimed in. She had really enjoyed it.

"Oh, Alina, you have to try the *ma'amoul*," Naila said excitedly.

"Looks beautiful. Are they cookies?"

"Yes, filled with dates and different nuts," Naila explained of the dome shaped desert.

"Girls, would you like some tea with the ma'amoul?" Zoona asked. "It goes very well together."

"Oh, yes, *shukran*, thank you," Alina said.

"Hey, Waleed, what happened to the music?" Stacy asked.

"Oh, give me a moment, I'll put some on." He started the player and belly dancing music blared from the little machine.

Alina discovered the local music and loved it. It reminded her quite a bit of Southern Spanish songs with their Northern African influence. As with most things, her young mind was thirsty for knowledge. Alina learned as much as she could from the Lebanese people she had come to cherish. They were warm and extremely hospitable, always welcomed anyone with open arms and retained the tradition of being well educated. Alina loved that almost everyone in the country spoke three languages—Arabic, French and English. She had a talent for languages as she spoke fluent English, Spanish and Portuguese. Always pushing herself in her learning, Alina decided she would learn both Arabic and French. By the end of the academic year, she had achieved her goal and managed the languages well. She learned a great deal in school, and by living in Lebanon where she was immersed in the local language and mannerisms. Her best teachers had been her friends. They didn't make fun of her when she didn't know something or mispronounced words. On the contrary, they helped her out. They were actually proud that someone who wasn't Lebanese wanted to learn so much of their ways. One of their favorite pastimes was going to the movies and seeing classic films. The movies were always shown in their original language, mainly English, as many were either American or English. Alina was especially happy as they were subtitled in both Arabic and French. It was a wonderful way to learn the languages. Some of the girls from school went to belly dancing classes. Some did it for the love of dance, others to exercise with music. Alina loved anything that had to do with dance and joined her schoolmates, moving to the gyrations of the local Middle Eastern rhythms.

Naila, who had finished her lunch, immediately jumped up and started dancing. "Come on, Alina, let's show them."

"Okay," Alina said, always excited to dance and wanting to show her parents how much she had learned.

The adults smiled as they watched their young daughters' excitement. They were very proud indeed.

The two families enjoyed the magnificent sunset over the Mediterranean before heading out. The picnic and riding had been part of a goodbye celebration as the Alonsos were heading back to Spain for the summer. After a couple of months, they would spend another school year in a different area of the world as part of Alina's exposure to other cultures.

The house the Alonsos had rented was on the outskirts of Beirut, close to the HeliEmerg Lebanese branch of the business where the helicopter was parked. They unpacked the company car and headed into their temporary abode. As soon as the family was inside, three men with black bandanas covering their faces grabbed them. Alejandro and his girls struggled hard, but it was useless. They had been taken by surprise in the dark. The masked men tied them up and made them sit on the floor. The Alonsos wondered what was going on and what the intruders would do to them. Alejandro was concerned for his family. They were hostages and he knew the only way they would survive was to think fast.

"What do you want from us?" He asked.

One of the men, wearing a white shirt, backhanded him hard across the face. Alejandro winced. Stacy and Alina screamed for him to stop.

All three carried small machine guns, Uzis perhaps, made by their Israeli neighbors. They held them a little tighter.

"You will all be quiet!" White Shirt threatened. "You will speak only if we ask you. Is that clear?"

They nodded back. Stacy detected a slight accent with the Arabic intonation when the man spoke English, the kind acquired when learning a foreign language as a teenager. Perhaps he had studied in England. Alejandro was also analyzing the men and wondering if he and his family were to be used for a cause, but why them? How would they be useful? They weren't political and had no affiliation with any warring groups. And then Alejandro remembered the helicopter. Of course! Their captors could make such good use of it. The man cringed as his mind tried to find a solution to their predicament.

The three abductors were similar in body size. The black bandanas across the bottom of their faces covered their features. Only their dark eyes were visible. They wore similar khaki pants. The only difference was the color of their shirts. One was white, the other blue, and the third man wore green. White Shirt seemed to be the leader, just by the way he acted. He was also the one who hit Alejandro. He gave orders to the other two, who promptly lifted the Spaniard to his feet. They searched him and found his keys. One of them opened the area to where the helicopter was parked. The two men left the house and went to a van they had concealed. They drove to the helicopter, unloaded a barrel, and carried it to the quiet metal bird. They groaned as they carefully loaded it into the medical aircraft. They left it inside, behind the open side door, and went back to the house.

White Shirt saw them coming in and asked them if the bomb was on board. Alina's eyes grew very wide as she understood. "You!" The leader said to Alejandro, "I want you to fly us out of here."

"Why would I do that?"

White Shirt took a gun from the back of his pants and pointed it at Alejandro; thought about it, and aimed it at Alina instead. "Any more questions?"

Alejandro shook his head, his anger visible in his clenched jaw.

Stacy had to keep calm. She remembered how many dangerous missions she and Alejandro had been on and knew they would get through this calamity as well. They always did, but this time they had Alina with them.

The kidnappers took them out of the house and drove them to the helicopter. The Alonsos were on the floor of the van, huddled together.

"Listen to me," Alejandro whispered to Stacy and Alina. They did. "No matter what, always stay tightly buckled in. Got it?" They nodded back in agreement. "I love you both very much. We'll get out of this, I promise."

They arrived at the helicopter and the hostages were roughly pulled out of the van.

"I'll do whatever you want. Please leave my family out of this," Alejandro begged.

White Shirt laughed. "A man will do anything to keep his loved ones safe," he answered. "The women come with us."

That was Alejandro's fear. The bastard had leverage, and he was right. He would do anything for Stacy and Alina. They were pushed into the helicopter. Alejandro and White Shirt went up front to the cockpit. The others stayed in the back. The kidnappers kept close to the door and the barrel. Stacy and Alina buckled themselves into their seats. They remembered Alejandro's instructions.

The Spaniard started up the helicopter. He spoke into the microphone and asked the tower for permission to take off. He was immediately cleared. HeliEmerg was well known and the only time they flew was for emergencies. Alejandro thanked them and immediately lifted off. "I need to know where we're going," he said to White Shirt.

The man gave him a piece of paper with coordinates.

Alejandro looked at it. It wasn't far, maybe fifteen minutes. He gently directed the chopper off the ground and headed out.

The two kidnappers in the back were talking to each other.

"We're going to give it right back to those bastards," Green Shirt said.

"Yeah, a taste of their own medicine," Blue Shirt replied.

"May I ask who and what it is they did?" Alina said quietly in Arabic, having overheard them.

The two men looked at her, surprised she spoke their language. They looked at each other and grinned, an unspoken sign that once they finished their mission they would kill her. Maybe they would first take turns with her as well. She was a pretty young thing. Stacy, who wasn't as fluent as her daughter, picked up more from their smirks and their body language than from their words. A shiver ran through her body. She knew what they were talking about. She refused to believe her entire family would be obliterated by malicious murderers.

Green Shirt figured the foreigners would be dead very soon. There was no danger in telling them what they were up to. Besides, they would see it in just a short while. "We are going to drop this barrel on an enemy safe house, just like they bombed ours a few days ago."

"And killed some of our family members," Blue Shirt added angrily.

"I'm sorry to hear that, but it sounds like an eye for an eye. If both sides continue to do this, it will never stop," Alina said in her young and innocent outlook of world political statistics.

"That's just the way it is," Green Shirt said.

"And will always be," Blue Shirt added.

"That's ridiculous. You'll always be at war."

"Wouldn't it be nice if we could eliminate all of them?" Green Shirt said, laughing raucously.

"That's no solution. Why can't you learn to forgive and live together?" the youngster asked.

Stacy slightly smiled. She was proud of her daughter and couldn't help but appreciate her innocence. She also knew, however, that the girl was treading into a dangerous subject. She hoped the men wouldn't take their anger out on her.

"Forgive?" Green Shirt yelled. "How can I forgive when most of my family has been killed, for decades now!"

Alina looked at them. She felt bad, but she always wanted a solution to every problem, or at least try to find one. "I have an idea," she said.

"About what?" Green Shirt asked.

"About peace, how everyone can be happy."

"Oh, really? What makes you think you're so smart?" Green Shirt smirked.

"Yeah, you know the solution for world peace, huh?" Blue Shirt added, cackling.

"No, I don't think I'm any smarter than anyone else, and I don't have a solution for world peace. As I said, it's just an idea."

"Alright, let's hear it, smarty pants," Green Shirt said.

"Let me ask you a question first. You say this has been going on for generations, right?" Alina asked.

"Right."

"And your families have been killing each other for centuries."

"That's about right."

Stacy was amazed her daughter was just 'chatting' with these two bastards who were going to kill them. How much time did they have left? What could she do to prevent their intended outcome? She listened to Alina as she tried to figure a way out of their predicament.

"Well, how about this: Stop the eye for an eye for two generations, starting with the present one. The second generation will know not to kill anymore and will settle things more peacefully. Besides, they wouldn't know who killed whom decades before."

The adults looked at her. Stacy was impressed. The other two just laughed.

"That would never work," Green Shirt said.

"Well, you won't know until you've tried," Alina said with finality.

White Shirt left the co-pilot's seat and went to the back. They were close to their destination. He told his men to get ready and went to help release the barrel out the open door and onto their target. As the three started to push, Alejandro shouted in Spanish: "HOLD ON! CAIMAN!" Stacy and Alina did, grateful they were buckled in and knew exactly what he was doing, just like he had in Brazil. They held on as best they could as Alejandro moved his lever very fast and banked left hard. The three kidnappers who were aligning the barrel into position to drop it out in the next few minutes were suddenly thrown from the chopper, along with the lethal explosives. They plummeted through the air toward the desert below them, their arms spinning in their own version of an erratic windmill. As White Shirt fell toward the earth he was able to aim his gun at the cockpit and fired as many shots as he could before plummeting to his death. Only two bullets managed to do any damage—they found their way into the front cabin and lodged themselves forcefully into Alejandro's shoulder and leg. The pain seared through him as if ember-hot spears had been roughly shoved through his skin and muscles. He yelled out in agony and still managed to make the helicopter swerve fast to the right, away from the explosion. Alejandro was still in control as he, Stacy and Alina watched the kidnappers and the barrel hit the desert floor. On impact the explosion sent shrapnel and sand into a macabre and deafening cloud.

Alejandro was able to level off and Stacy immediately unbuckled herself and closed the door. Alina was just as quick and went to the cockpit. She saw her father bleeding on his left side. From his shoulder to his foot he was covered in the flowing crimson liquid.

"Papá! Papá!" She turned to the back and shouted for her mother. "Mom! Papá's been shot! He's bleeding really bad!"

Stacy was at her side in a split-second. She cringed when she saw her husband. "Alex, how badly are you hurt?" she asked.

Alejandro could only groan.

"Can you fly back alright?"

He tried to answer but suddenly his head slumped forward.

"Alex!" Stacy shouted. The man was unconscious. She felt for a pulse and, to her great relief found it, albeit faint. "Alina, can you hold the chopper steady?" Stacy asked, hoping her daughter would remember everything she had ever seen Alejandro do with a helicopter.

"Yes, I think so."

"Good. Get in the other seat and take over." Stacy was worried out of her mind. Her entire family was on that flight. Would they make it? she wondered.

Alina had watched her daddy for many years, just like she had watched him drive a car. The man had shown her little tricks and even let her hold the controls. Alina had no doubt in her young mind that she could do it; besides, every time they had gone up in a helicopter Alejandro would explain what he was doing and what each instrument or lever was for. Thankfully her young mind didn't think of disastrous consequences, rather she concentrated on the challenge and buckled herself in.

Stacy hurried to get medical supplies and went back to Alejandro. Suddenly the helicopter swerved right and then left. She hit one side of her body against the door frame and then the other side. "What's wrong?" She asked her daughter, ignoring as best she could the sudden pulsing pain from the hard hits.

"I don't know, it's like everything is stuck. I can't get anything to move," Alina moaned. She looked at her father's hands and feet. "He still has control!" She screeched.

"Yes, I see the problem," Stacy said. "Hold on, Alina." She tried to take her husband's hand off the lever but it was frozen tight. She couldn't pry it loose. It was a death grip, from somewhere deep in the man's subconscious he was protecting his family. Stacy found the nerves in his wrist and squeezed hard. It was enough to unfreeze his fingers. She moved his hand away from the instruments and pulled him to the back of the chair. "Try it now," Stacy said to her daughter.

Alina did. "Got it!" She said, as the helicopter

obeyed her. The twelve year old girl kept the metal bird as steady as possible.

Stacy quickly assessed her husband's wounds. She put tourniquets on his leg and arm, which was no easy feat as there was hardly any space for her to work. The bullets were still lodged in his body and she didn't dare move him to the back. She couldn't chance a heavy blood flow and she wanted to be all together. If either Alina or Alejandro needed her she would be there. She gave him shots of pain killers and patched him up as best she could. She waved smelling salts under his nose. Alejandro came to and moaned.

"Alex, stay as still as possible, you've been shot."

He nodded and looked around, trying to assess the situation. He saw Alina in the co-pilot's seat. "Are you flying?" he whispered.

"Yes, Papá, just like you showed me." Alejandro looked at her, not quite sure what his brain was registering. "I always watch what you do when we're flying together," Alina answered.

The man was sure he was in the middle of a nasty nightmare, one where he was supposed to be in control but couldn't be. The left side of his body was completely numb, and hurt and burned like hell itself. His mind was getting clearer. He focused harder. "We can do this together, amorcito," Alejandro whispered. He tried to sound positive for his girl, and swore he wouldn't let anything happen to his family.

"Yes, Papá."

As if Stacy had read his mind she gently squeezed his good shoulder and kissed his cheek. "I have no doubt the two of you will pull this off," she affirmed.

Alejandro nodded, clicked his mic and spoke to the tower. He gave them their coordinates, relayed what had transpired, what their predicament was, and requested an ambulance upon arrival. The air traffic controller confirmed and scrambled his people as soon as they disconnected.

"Alina?"

"Yes, Papá?"

"I know you can do this. Make sure you keep your headset on in case you need to talk to the tower and I can't."

"Okay."

Alejandro wanted to take control but he didn't trust himself. He'd already passed out once, and he and his daughter had been on enough flights together to where he was pretty confident of her capabilities. "Remember everything we ever discussed. I trust you, amorcito."

"*Sí*, Papá, don't worry."

"Stacy..." Alejandro passed out again before he could say anything.

Stacy immediately passed the smelling salts under his nose. She didn't know how long she could keep him conscious. "Alex, you're back again. What do you need?"

"Alina, remember, the collective will make the helicopter go up and down. The cyclic lever makes the bird go left and right and the nose go up and down, faster or slower. Don't try to hover before landing, just set up your approach. Make an imaginary line from the nose of the aircraft down to the spot where you're landing. Gradually slow your speed down..." Alejandro was fading fast. "Watch the windsock..." he managed to say before blacking out.

"Alex?" She knew he had to get to a hospital fast.

"Is he alright, Mom?" Alina asked.

"How much longer?"

"I can see the airport now. The tower just cleared us.

Is he… is he…" Alina couldn't bring herself to say *dead*.

"No, he's very much alive, but really weak. You can do this. I know you can." Stacy had to sound as positive as possible for her young daughter.

"Yes, Mom, I'm going to bring us in." Alina was pretty confident she could, but for the first time she was scared. What if she made a mistake? What if she crashed? Would she kill her parents, and even herself? She took a deep breath and tried to stay calm. *I can do this.* She had seen her father land dozens of times and remembered his smooth movements.

Alina first looked for the windsock. Thankfully it was almost flat to the pole so winds wouldn't be a problem. In her mind she heard her father's instructions and visualized his maneuvers. She pictured an imaginary line from the nose of the helicopter to the spot where she wanted to land. Next, she watched her speed. She was at 75 knots and almost at the airport. The tower told her she was clear and asked if she needed help.

"Under control, thank you," Alina said, making her voice as calm and mature as possible.

Stacy raised an eyebrow. Was her daughter that sure of herself? She certainly hoped so. "You good?"

"I am, Mom." *I am. I am. Right?*

Stacy was between her husband and her child. She kept a hand on each of their shoulders and braced herself. She wouldn't move from that spot until they landed.

Alina watched the needle decreasing from 75 to 60, her hand controlling the speed. She kept the helicopter as level as possible and started lowering the collective. 50 knots. She pushed forward on the cyclic and lowered the lever some more. *Almost, almost, I can do this*, she kept repeating to herself.

Stacy watched every movement her daughter was

making. She, too, was an old hand in helicopter missions and she knew the girl was trying her hardest. She instinctively held on to Alejandro as the helicopter was almost on the ground. It was getting closer, closer still. Would it be smooth, or…? The landing gear hit the ground a little sooner than expected and they bounced, but thankfully not too hard. Stacy held on tight to her husband. She wanted to prevent as much shaking as possible. At least they were down and alive.

"You did it! Oh, Alina, I'm so proud of you!"

"Thanks, Mom. A little rough, I know. Sorry about that. Did that hurt Papá?"

"No, you were perfect. Your father would be very proud of you too. He'll be fine."

"Let's get him to the hospital," Alina said, as she turned off the switches. The helicopter was quieting down as the paramedics, who had been watching and waiting, rushed inside. They took Alejandro out of his seat and carried him to the ambulance. Stacy and Alina were right behind them and jumped in. The medical team immediately started working on him. Stacy wanted to help, but the pros were doing everything they were supposed to and she let them work.

Once at the hospital Alejandro was rushed to the operating room where the doctors removed the bullets. He would make a full recovery with the help of the medical staff and, most especially, his adoring family.

♫

CHAPTER 14

2009 – SOUTHWESTERN SPAIN

Jax was caressing Almea's muzzle and checking the equipment one last time. He was looking forward to the competition. He loved the equestrian events and everything leading up to the rides, and after his Olympic medal he most definitely acquired a taste for winning. This was his first time in the Iberian Peninsula and the CEA, the Campeonato Ecuestre de Andalucia. He was also excited to see where the famed Andalusians, also known as the PRE, the *Pura Raza Española,* originated from. At the moment, though, he was concentrating on the next event, the jumping.

Randy watched Jax and Almea. She was a pretty horse, and although not as big as his own Dutch Warmblood, he knew she was quick and powerful. The rivalry between the riders was certainly no friendly one, and although the two were pretty well matched, Jax was just a little better. He had that uncanny ability to communicate with the horses. Randy couldn't take the chance of losing to him again. That bastard Jax had stolen the gold medal from him, unleashing a monster in his father. This event was just as prestigious as the Olympics, as far as equestrian events, and he wanted that gold. He *had* to win the competition. Nothing and no one would stand in his way. He would get that medal! Anything else was worthless as far as he was concerned. Besides, he overheard Jax talking with another teammate, saying that just being present and winning any kind of medal was fine by him. Well, he could have everything but the top prize. Randy waited for Jax to leave Almea. When he did, Randy quickly went to the Paso Fino. He looked around. They were alone. He patted her neck, then bent down and lifted her front hoof.

After their year in Lebanon the Alonsos stayed in Spain for the summer. They boarded the HeliEmerg helicopter as passengers on their way to enjoy the CEA. They arrived at the venue and landed at the far end of the field. Alejandro waved to his girls. "I'll see you in a little while, just need to talk to the crew for a few minutes."

"Okay," Stacy said, "we'll see you in the stands, Alex."

"See you soon, Papá."

Stacy and Alina took off and went to the bleachers. They waited for Alejandro and the competition to begin. The HeliEmerg crew was working the venue and was double-checking every last detail. They knew if there was an emergency it would be serious. Such a case could be a rider being badly hurt, or perhaps a spectator with a bad fainting spell from the heat or even a heart attack. They hoped everything would be fine and Alejandro wouldn't be called and could just enjoy the event as a family.

Alejandro went to his family and turned to his daughter: "I know you wanted to go to the upcoming

Olympics, but that's a couple of years away. Until then we have this," he said, motioning in front of him.

"Oh, Papá, you're the best! This is perfect! Thank you."

"My pleasure, amorcito."

"Look, they're coming out," Stacy exclaimed.

"Oh, everything is so gorgeous," Alina murmured, very much in awe of the riders and the pristine event. As much as the young girl had enjoyed the Olympic games, it didn't compare to being at a venue in person. They watched the jumping competition. Randy Newton was next. His routine was a flawless ride, save for one mistake on the very last jump. The horse nicked the log just enough for it to fall. Although they were in first place, they lost valuable points on the knockdown. There were only two riders left. Jax was next. As Randy watched his teammate start his slow gallop, he thought he detected a slight deviation in Almea's steps. Jax didn't see it but felt it. Something wasn't quite right; her stride was just a little off. Horse and rider were lined up perfectly for the first jump. The steps seemed to be calculated and choreographed as the duo harmoniously hurdled over the first obstacle of bars, although Almea whinnied when she landed on her front hooves. They continued toward the second set of obstacles, a double jump. When they were just in front of it, Jax squeezed his heels and the two of them lifted off. When Almea landed, her weight, along with Jax's, entirely centered on the one hoof causing her foot to buckle. She bucked crazily, especially every time her hoof touched the ground. Jax had never experienced this reaction from his beloved horse. She was in such pain that she couldn't control her feet, and her entire body landed violently into the second set of the jump. Jax was still in the saddle when they went down. One of his legs caught between two logs. As horse and rider fell, Jax's limb did not follow his body. It forcefully snapped and shattered as if invisible giant hands were breaking a chopstick. The crowd gasped en masse, certain of the pain the rider was in. They knew the damage would be intense.

The medical team was immediately on the scene, as well as one of the trainers who reached Almea and calmed her down as he carefully led her back to the stables. She was limping badly and snorting with pain. Some blood was seeping out from the bottom of her foot.

Jax could hear Almea's cries. "Take care of her, don't put her down!" He shouted as loudly as he could to anyone around, although it was barely a whisper. "You're going to be okay, you're going to be okay," he kept repeating to her, praying his words would be true. He fervently hoped she wasn't hurt too badly. "I don't understand what happened," Jax moaned over and over.

The staff helped the medics with Jax. They removed the logs as carefully as possible as his leg was still wedged between two of them. The man screamed. Never had such pain invaded his body. Jax was put on a stretcher and lifted into the ambulance that had made its way into the arena. They immediately took him to the HeliEmerg helicopter.

"This is bad," Alejandro exclaimed to his family. "I'm going with them."

"Do you want me to help?" Stacy asked, ready as always for any medical emergency.

"No, you stay here with Alina and enjoy the rest of the day."

"Okay, don't worry about us. Keep in touch."

"I will," he said, and ran toward the helicopter.

When he reached his crew, he saw they were already working on the rider and were ready to take off. "I'm coming with you," Alejandro announced as he jumped into the chopper. "Let's go!" He watched his team as they worked furiously to contain the bleeding and save his leg. He looked at Jax. The man was mumbling incoherently. Alejandro caught the name of the horse and watched the tears running down the young face. The equestrian needed more than being transported to the hospital and receiving medical attention. Aside from being physically fragile, Alejandro could sense that something was breaking in his mind and in his heart.

Jax's gaze was glazed over as they worked on him in the helicopter. He worried about Almea and saw a flash of his parents and Bernardo before passing out. He came back when Alejandro held his hand. He pulled the Spaniard's arm toward his chest with the last ounce of strength he possessed. Alejandro held him as a father would cradle a scared child.

"Please," Jax begged, his voice just a whisper over the din of the rotors. "Please, I don't want to lose my leg. Please don't let them amputate."

"You have the best medical team in the world working on you, *Amigo*. This is not their first *corrida*. You say rodeo, yes?" Alejandro was trying to keep Jax's mind occupied, as he prayed fervently his crew would come through for the athlete. His leg looked bad. Alejandro hoped they wouldn't have any serious complications on their way to the surgeons.

"Yes, that's right, rodeo," Jax mumbled. "Now I know how those cowboys feel when the bull gets them."

"They are tough, your American cowboys, and you are too. We will take good care of you. Now try to relax."

Jax never felt so alone. The closest companions in

his life had been his teammates and, of course, Bernardo; who wasn't with him on this trip. At this moment Alejandro Alonso was the dearest person in the world to him.

"My wife is American," Alejandro said.

"She must be very special," Jax replied, moaning in pain.

"Of course, and you are too. Now hold on for me, we'll be at our destination in just a few minutes."

Jax nodded. He was scared and delirious, but just coherent enough to be grateful for Alejandro and believe in him.

The HeliEmerg helicopter hovered above the hospital landing pad at the top of the medical facility, and gently touched down. As they transferred Jax to the waiting medical staff one of the crew hollered out the numbers of his vitals and explained the case: "He's from the CEA, equestrian, thrown from his horse and landed on the jumping bars. Multiple breaks in his right leg."

Alejandro held Jax's hand until the hospital staff pushed him into the operating room.

Randy continued watching the riding event. He overheard some of the staff saying that they might have to amputate Jax's leg. A pang of guilt rang through his body. Randy just wanted him to have a 'normal' fall and not win. Getting hurt as bad as he had was not his intention, and he hoped he wouldn't lose the leg. He knew Almea would be alright.

The last rider was from Pakistan and his routine was flawless. He would take the gold, Randy another silver.

♫

CHAPTER 15

The morning after the competition and Jax's fall, Randy and his parents were eating breakfast at their hotel restaurant. Randy was thinking about Jax. He felt bad for his teammate. He didn't deserve to have his leg messed up that badly, and was glad he wouldn't lose it.

The Spanish police and the venue security officers walked into the restaurant and went up to the Newtons' table. "*Señor* Newton," the lieutenant from the Guardia Civil said, looking at Randy, "we would like you to please come with us, with no fuss."

"What? What for?" Randy asked, turning very pale.

"What is the meaning of this?" The older Newton said.

"Señor Newton is being arrested for attempted murder of Señor Jaxon Logan," the lieutenant answered.

"Don't be ridiculous! That's total bullshit!" Randy exclaimed.

"We have reviewed the footage, especially the hoof of the horse, and thoroughly checked it out. I will ask you one last time to please come quietly. It is the best way."

The recording revealed Randy tampering with

Almea's foot. He had inserted a pin on the side of the frog, the triangle in the middle of the bottom of the foot. The more she stepped on it the deeper it went in. When she landed after the first part of the second jump the pin hit a nerve and the horse's pain disoriented her.

"I'll have my lawyers check this out. Just go," Randy's father said.

Randy stood up and was immediately handcuffed.

"Is that really necessary?" the older Newton asked.

"I'm sorry, Señor, it is."

Randy didn't think his father did it for his son, he believed it was just for appearances. The police escorted him out of the building and drove him to the police station.

By the end of the day Randy's lawyer, a local Spanish defense attorney who had been appointed to him, gave his client the news: "It was not easy, but I was able to get your very long sentence of attempted murder reduced to attempted manslaughter. You will only serve two years, amigo."

"Are you crazy? I'm going to spend two years of my life here, in a Spanish prison?"

"Yes, that is correct. Oh, and the equestrian federation has banned you for life and rescinded your medal. You can no longer compete."

Randy and other new inmates went through the rough initiation of the first day in prison. Before being given an orange jumpsuit with the prison's initials they first had to go through painful pressurized spray-downs, de-licing and cavity searches. The prisoners were each assigned a cell they would share with three other inmates. They made sure Randy knew their rules.

Randy didn't sleep that night. He was sure he would

be stabbed in his sleep. He stayed vigilant, ready to defend himself, although he figured he didn't stand a chance against three of them. He wondered if he would be killed during the night, or whether they would wait a couple of days.

In the morning the inmates went to the cafeteria, stood in line, had their trays filled, and went to sit down to eat breakfast. Randy followed suit, grateful, albeit surprised he was still alive; and did exactly what he was told. He placed his tray on an empty table and sat down. Five prisoners sat down next to him.

"Are you going to eat your roll?" one of them asked.

"Oh, I'll have anything on *your* menu, handsome," another said.

"You can have the roll," Randy answered.

"What about the eggs?" the first one asked.

"You can have those too." Randy figured he would just go along with everything and keep the peace as much as possible. He was sure his life depended on it.

Needless to say, the American didn't have any breakfast, was bullied, hit on, and smacked around. Just enough so the guards wouldn't bother them.

Six men, one of which was a leader in the prison, cornered Randy in the showers. As much as he tried to defend himself, he was no match for that many attackers. They beat him mercilessly and had their way with him. When they were finished they left him unconscious on the shower floor, blood oozing out of several orifices of his body.

The guards found Randy and took him to the infirmary. The doctor and the nurse worked on him for quite a while. They gave him fluids, stitched up the cuts, bandaged his torso and all other spots that needed covering. They also put ointment on the areas that had been torn.

Randy woke up after two days. When he opened his eyes it took him a while to figure out where he was. The doctor noticed and pulled up a stool next to the bed.

"Back to the land of the living," the doctor stated.

Sharp pain flooded Randy's body and he moaned. The doctor gave him a shot. Randy quickly felt better. He tried to say something but realized he couldn't move his mouth.

"You were severely beaten, Randy. Most of your ribs are broken, your spleen is bruised, and your body will be black and blue and swollen from the blows for quite a few days. Especially your face. We also stitched up your cuts. They will hardly be visible."

Randy nodded.

"Also…"

Randy wondered why people always left the worst for last.

"There was no internal bleeding, but you were violated and it was vicious. There were tears and we repaired where it was needed."

Randy remembered the violent attack and swore he would somehow get back at each one of the bastards.

"There's one more thing, Randy," the doctor continued.

Here it comes, the coup de grâce, Randy thought. What else?

"Your genitals were damaged."

Randy had a million questions and just as many worries.

The physician continued: "The good news…"

What good news? Was this guy serious?

"… you won't need an operation, but you will need

time and patience. Lots of patience."

Randy was dying to ask, but he couldn't speak. *Come on, doc, will I be able to use it and can I have children? Just answer those two. Please.*

"I know you have questions, but as I said only time will tell. I figure it will take six to eight months for normal function to return. Whatever you do, don't force it. It will be painful to urinate for a while. Also, keep your guy very, very dormant. Understand?"

Randy nodded.

"Alright, I'll see you later," the doctor said as he left to check on other patients.

Randy lifted an arm in thanks. The physician nodded. As Randy lay in the infirmary's bed his hatred for Jax and his father grew. It was their fault, Jax for beating him out of the gold and his father with his overbearing and ridiculous expectations. After a couple of days Randy was able to speak and made conversation with Ramirez, the inmate in the bed next to him. He was a middle-aged man who talked to him, even when he was unconscious, and tried to cheer him up as much as possible. He had terminal cancer. Randy learned a great deal about the men who attacked him and the ways of the prison. The information would come in handy if he was going to survive the next two years, and that was without any problems. If he was caught going after the men his sentence would be extended. The one good part of being laid up was that Randy could concoct his revenge in relative peace and quiet.

After ten days Randy was able to leave his bed and carefully move around. A guard came to get him. He led him to a small room where a middle-aged man in a suit waited for him. There was a table and an empty chair.

The guard told Randy to sit down, handcuffed him to a bar on the table and left.

"You've looked better," the man said as Randy sat across from him. He was sure his mother wouldn't have recognized him, but then again she wasn't going to see him anyway.

Randy stared. "Do we know each other?"

"We've met. I'm your father's lawyer."

"What does he want now?" Randy hissed.

"Listen, boy, you should be grateful," the lawyer said roughly.

"Yeah? Why?"

"Because you're getting out as soon as the doctor says you can."

Randy's temper flared. "Is this a fucking joke?" He knew he had to suffer two years in this place and wasn't sure he would survive it, if the last beating was any indication.

"No, it's true. Your father pulled a few strings, found the best local lawyer in town and was able to clear you of all charges. The tape wasn't that clear. They couldn't prove you did anything to that horse's hoof." Randy wondered if the footage had been tampered with. Randolph Newton II knew how to use his wealth, including getting his son out of jail. The lawyer put a briefcase on the table, opened it and pulled out a sealed envelope. He handed it to Randy. "I'm here to get you out."

"What took him so long? Why didn't he get me out sooner? Surely he could have gotten me out before they beat the shit out of me!"

The lawyer was pretty much ignoring him. "I'm also here to tell you there is a check in here for a substantial amount to get you on your feet. It will be the last amount of money you will ever get from your father. He doesn't ever want to see you again."

"Are you saying he's disowning me?"

"Call it anything you like."

"And you say I should be grateful?"

"Yes. You're getting out of this place with enough money to start a new life."

Randy took the envelope and was ready to tear it up when he stopped himself. He knew his father. He never backed off anything he committed to, or firmly believed in. Disowning him was just his modus operandi for a problem. Randy remembered the look on his father's face in Beijing, and again when the police arrested him for what he did to fix the last competition. He didn't tolerate failure or embarrassment, and Randy was guilty of both. The older man didn't care he was kicking out his son, his own blood. Randy knew there was no solution. He was out. He didn't belong to this family anymore. Period. It was his way to make his son suffer for his failure and the disappointment caused. He didn't want anything to do with him. Trying to reason with his father wouldn't be possible. He knew his guards wouldn't even let him get close enough to talk to the son of a bitch.

"Fine," Randy said, holding back his temper. "I only need one more thing."

"What would that be?" The lawyer asked.

"I need ten thousand euros, in cash."

"What for?"

"Look, it's the last thing I'll ever ask my father. Hell! I can give it back from the check you gave me when I get out."

"What do you need that much for?" The attorney asked again.

"To stay alive until I get out, damn it!"

The attorney stared at him and then said: "I'll get it to you by tomorrow."

"Thanks."

The lawyer left and Randy was taken back to the infirmary.

"Hey, *Americano*," Ramirez said, "how did it go?"

"Well, my father disowned me, but he did give me some money to survive for a while."

"Eh, better than nothing, but he's still a moron. *Familia* is everything."

"You're right, amigo, but he doesn't understand that. Anyway, I've been thinking."

"*Ah, si?*"

"Yes. Here is what I need," Randy said to his only friend. "I know you have a wife and two children, and I would like us to help each other."

"What do you mean?"

"I'm getting out in the next few days, as soon as the doctor says okay, but I want those bastards to pay for what they did to me."

"Ah, I understand."

"Can you help me with that?"

"Well, amigo, if my body wasn't being eaten away I would do it myself."

"I know that, thank you."

"I have some connections, but it will take money."

"I figured. Tomorrow I will have ten thousand euros which will be yours. Use them for your family and for, uh, justice. I will give you another ten thousand once I'm out. I will send it directly to your wife. I give you my word. Would that be okay?"

"You would do this for me? For my family?"

"It's the least I can do, Ramirez. You have been a great friend; more like a brother and even as a father. I wish my own father could have been more like you. You were there when I needed someone, and I will never forget you."

"Thank you, amigo, I won't ever forget you either. Don't worry about anything. Those bastards will feel your wrath."

The next day Randy received an envelope from the lawyer with ten thousand euros inside. He immediately handed it over to Ramirez when he saw him.

By sunset of the same day the six inmates were rushed to the infirmary. Three of them were in critical condition, two others would probably never be able to eat food like they used to, and one of them died. Randy didn't have any kind of remorse, which he considered odd. But when the pain shot through his body, all he thought about was that justice had been done.

Randy was released two days later from the foul prison. He wanted to disappear and just be alone. He had to figure out how to survive on the amount of money his father had given him, and how to move forward with a disgraced life. He had gone to university for a couple of years and learned a little about several things, but nothing he could rely on as far as a career. He knew he would eventually have to find a way to support himself. Until then, he would find a cheap place to live, lock himself in, let his body heal and drink himself into oblivion.

Randy found the cheapest plane ticket back to the States. It was a flight to Atlanta, Georgia. He made his way to the airport, and before going to his gate he dropped the envelope for Ramirez's wife in a mailbox. As he walked through the door of the aircraft, he absent-mindedly went left to the first-class compartment. The flight attendant looked at his ticket and directed him to the economy section. It was another eye-opener of his new life. He realized he had never been in the 'back' before. His temper flared, but he kept cool and quietly took his seat. It was also the next rung of his hate ladder toward his father and Jax. The more he thought about them the more furious he became. He would make their lives miserable and inflict his revenge over and over again. He swore their world would turn very dark indeed.

♫

CHAPTER 16

Alejandro went to visit Jax at the hospital the morning after the surgery. Although he had been kept up to date by the staff, he had taken a liking to the young equestrian and wanted to see for himself. He entered Jax's room carrying a box of chocolates. The patient's eyes lit up at the sight of the man who held him together the day before, not just medically with his incredible staff but also emotionally.

Alejandro saw the many rods and screws around Jax's leg. They were surely holding everything in place after the surgery. He knew the doctors had worked long and hard inserting pins and cutting bones, picking out fragments, building new parts and putting it all back together. Their science was also an art and they were very skilled at it. "Looks like scaffolding. I can picture kittens and puppies climbing all over," Alejandro chuckled, pointing to the bars and screws around the equestrian's limb.

"Oh, don't make me laugh, ribs hurt!" Jax gasped.

"Sorry. Hey, I'm told you're going to be fine."

"Yes, thanks to you and your guys. Thank you so

much for saving my leg."

"Are you ready for quite a bit of therapy, Amigo?"

"I am. I'm just so grateful I still have my leg. I have no doubt it's going to be painful and a lot of work, but I'm willing to put the effort into it."

"Bravo! That's the spirit. Remember that when you think you're done and firmly believe you can't go on."

"I will. Thanks. Uh, are those chocolates for me?"

Alejandro was still holding the box. "Oh, yes!" He said, handing them over.

"Come on, let's have some. There's nothing wrong with my stomach. Problem is much lower, you know, toward the foot."

"Okay," he chuckled. He handed them over to Jax. "By the way, Almea is doing fine. Just a few bruises and her foot will heal nicely."

"Oh, thank God. Do you know what happened?" Jax asked.

"Apparently a pin got inserted into her foot and when she came down hard on that jump, well, it literally hit a nerve."

"Oh, my poor girl."

"Yes, but they're taking care of her and she'll be fine. They'll be flying her back to the States where your man will take over."

"Bernardo?"

"That's right."

The men talked for a couple of hours until Alejandro left. He would return every day until the patient was released. The Spaniard found out that Jax couldn't fly for at least another week and insisted the younger man stay at the Alonso hacienda for the duration. They had become good friends and Jax was grateful for Alejandro's presence in his life. He hadn't realized that even after all the years since his father's death the emptiness of an older male figure still left him numb. Bernardo had been just as loving and protective as an uncle or a parent and Jax, of course, adored the gaucho and missed him very much. He was anxious to see him, but right at the moment he was thankful for Alejandro and Stacy. They made him a member of the household and were happy they could help.

That evening Stacy came out of the kitchen with a beautifully decorated paella and placed it on the table in the patio. The rice cooked with saffron constituted a perfect yellow background under the shrimp and mussels. The appetizing national dish could have been a picture on the cover of a food magazine.

"Ah, in your honor Jax," Alejandro said. "Stacy made my favorite dish and I must tell you she makes it even better than the locals."

"Now there's a compliment," she said kissing her *caballero* lightly on the lips.

The smile and loving look on Alejandro's face told Jax this was the epitome of true love. He hoped one day he would find an amazing woman he could share love and life with, as wonderfully as this couple did.

"I'm the luckiest man in the world, Amigo."

"Yes, you are, my friend." Jax turned to his compatriot: "Stacy, you have outdone yourself. This is absolutely beautiful!"

"You better try it first, Jax," she replied.

"Oh, I have no doubt it will be perfection! Oh, and the smell! I can hardly wait."

Stacy served the men at her table. Alejandro lifted a glass of local wine: *"Salud!"*

"Salud!" They all said and toasted each other.

"Oh, Alex, you're right! This paella is exquisite," Jax said between mouthfuls. "Bravo, Stacy! You've raised the bar even for the Spanish ladies."

"Why, thank you, Jax. I'm glad you like it," Stacy said, putting more on his plate.

"Don't mind if I do, thank you."

Alejandro and Stacy smiled. The young man was doing well with his leg, and his appetite was definitely back.

"I'm sorry you missed Alina," Alejandro said.

"She sure is a busy young lady," Jax agreed. "You mentioned she loves to ride, play the guitar, and dance. Sounds like a full schedule. Is she at some lesson today?"

"No, she and some friends went to the beach in the Algarve," Alejandro said.

"In Portugal?"

"Yes, it's not that far. A group of them and some of the parents are spending the week camping out there before starting school next week. They left early this morning."

Jax looked at a family photo. Alejandro and Stacy were on either side of Alina smiling, with one of their hands on the girl's shoulder. "How old is she?"

"Just turned twelve, going on thirty."

"Mature, is she?"

"Like no one you've ever met. She amazes me."

"She must be very special. I hope to meet her one day."

"Of course, you will. Without a doubt."

"Unfortunately, it won't be during this trip. I have to get back to the States."

"We'll be sorry to see you go," Alejandro said, really meaning it. He had grown very fond of Jax.

"You're leaving?" Stacy asked, having just reentered the room with some fresh squeezed orange juice.

"Yes, back to the States in a couple of days and then more rehab."

"You don't have to go back, Jax. You can stay with us and we could help you," Alejandro emphasized.

"Yes, absolutely, for as long as you want," Stacy agreed. She liked the young wounded man as well.

"You are both the best. I don't know what I would have done without you. You must know that I will always be grateful." Jax turned to Stacy. "I will especially miss *Señora* Stacy's paellas. However, I must get back and take care of some business and figure out what I'm going to do with the rest of my life."

"Any thoughts? Something with horses?"

"I'm not sure. I think I need to stay away from them for a while," Jax answered. He hadn't told Alejandro or Stacy about the recurring nightmares where horses continuously tried to kill him. They would attack him like a pack of wolves, corner him until he was surrounded, and kick him mercilessly until he was bleeding and writhing on the ground. Thankfully Jax always woke up before the final hoof met his screaming face and killed him. "By the way, if you ever consider opening a HeliEmerg office in the States, you should look into Florida. There are some great places that not very expensive in my area, between Orlando and Miami. You should check it out."

"That does sound interesting. I'll definitely give you a call and come see you."

"I would love that, and it would also give me a chance to pay you back in kind."

"Just having you in our lives gives us joy. That's payment enough."

"Do you have someone to take care of you?" Stacy asked.

"Yes, I do, actually." Jax grinned thinking of Bernardo. He missed the older man.

Alejandro saw the smile on the younger man's face. "Ah, a *señorita* perhaps?"

Jax laughed. "No, not at all. More like a tough, older leather-faced Argentine."

"Oh, my," Stacy laughed, "not what I pictured at all. I was actually thinking a little gentler."

"Oh, the gaucho is actually very gentle in many ways, and rather good at most everything. He's also quite the philosopher. He's the one who took care of me when my parents died. He taught me so much about horses, dancing, and literature."

"Literature?" Stacy asked, not quite visualizing an Argentinian cowboy with his nose in a book.

"Oh, yes, he especially loves Pablo Neruda and Julia Alvarez. One of my fondest memories was listening to him read to me around a campfire waiting for the churrasco.

"Interesting man," Alejandro said.

"And quite the gentleman. He has these rules of how a man should act, especially around women."

"Really?" Stacy asked, intrigued. "Can you give us an example?"

"Sure. Always carry two handkerchiefs. One for yourself in your back pocket, and one for the ladies in your breast pocket, close to your heart; clean, of course."

"Oh, I like this guy," Stacy exclaimed.

"Uh-huh. And you should see what he does with animals, especially horses. He's a horse whisperer."

"Oh, Alina should be here!" Alejandro said.

"The way he cares for wounded animals is just

amazing."

Alejandro laughed and said: "Well, I guess he will be performing his magic on the two-legged version."

"Oh, you are so funny, Alex," Stacy said. She turned to Jax. "Don't pay any attention to him."

"I've actually been wondering what Bernardo has up his sleeve. You never know with that guy. When you come visit you'll meet him and I'm sure you'll love him."

"He sounds like quite the character," Stacy said.

"That he is. Please come, sooner rather than later. And bring your daughter so I can finally meet her."

"Sounds like she would love him too," Stacy added.

"She definitely would. I'll be expecting all of you. We have a couple of small guest houses. There's plenty of room for you to stay for as long as you want. As a matter of fact, if you really are planning to set up a HeliEmerg office in the area I insist you stay with me."

"It's a plan, Jax," Alejandro said.

♫

CHAPTER 17

2009 – COLUMBUS, GEORGIA

Randy walked out of Atlanta's Hartsfield International and into the humid air surrounding the airport. He spent the last few hours on the flight trying to figure out what he would do with his life, where he would live and what jobs he could find. He came up with nothing and decided to just spend a few days in some motel trying to think. All he needed was some food and a couple of bottles of alcohol. As he was walking he spotted some guys in military fatigues. They probably knew of a motel somewhere. He was going to ask them until he saw them getting on a bus. Randy decided to get on as well.

"Hey, guys," Randy said, taking a seat across from two soldiers. "Do you know how long it takes to…" He realized he didn't even know where they were driving to.

"Columbus is about an hour and half away," one of them answered.

"Great, thanks."

"We're going to Ft. Benning. Are you in the

military?"

"No, I'm not, but I sure appreciate you guys."

"Thanks."

Randy and the soldiers talked the entire way and quickly became buddies. He learned a lot from them. Ft. Benning was home to the Army's elite shooters, the snipers.

By the time they arrived at the Columbus bus terminal Randy knew he wanted to learn how to protect and defend himself, and about snipers and their rifles. The soldiers had suggested a cheap motel and told him the name of a bar where many of the military hung out. Randy was starting to form an idea. He checked into the motel, bought beers and local bourbon and drank until he passed out.

The next morning Randy woke up with the worse headache and hangover of his life. He went to the shower, stood under the water for a very long time letting it numb the pain from the beating. His ribs were healing as was his spleen. The bruises and cuts on his face were almost gone as well. When he felt a little better he got out, dried himself and carefully put on some clothes. His body was still very sore and his recovery would take weeks. He would tear up every time he urinated, the pain sending fire to his genitals. He looked around the room and cringed. He had trashed the place. He hadn't remembered doing it. No wonder he was even more sore than the day before. He went to the manager, explained that he received a phone call with bad news—his parents had died in an unexpected car accident and he became very upset as he was very close to them. He figured it was as good a lie as any. He told the man to bill him for the damage and add an extra thousand dollars for himself. He promised not to break anything in the new room he requested. The manager was understanding and accommodating.

Randy started putting his plan together. It consisted in learning how to defend himself and to becoming an expert shot. He went to the bar the guys on the bus had mentioned, and met up with them. It didn't take long to get answers and to find just the man he needed after buying a couple rounds. With money anything could be bought and he still had the majority of what his father's lawyer had given him. It would last him for a while, until he met up with his parents again, whether they wanted to or not. He hired the man, a trainer at the military post who was an expert in self-defense, small arms weapons and knives. He was also an instructor to the sharpshooters.

Randy purchased a laptop and a rusty pickup to get around. He was being careful with the money. That was all he had. His days consisted of waking up with a hangover, going to practice with the trainer and returning to his motel. He would do searches on the internet and get all the information he could on his parents as well as Jax. He kept up to date with everything they were doing. By the end of the day he would drink until he passed out. He followed this pattern until his trainer told him he was ready enough. This had taken several months. His wounds had healed, his face didn't show any scarring, and although his genitals still occasionally hurt he found that everything still functioned.

Randy was lying on a sweat-soaked crinkled sheet on the bed of the fleabag motel room he had been staying in. His hair was long and disheveled and the once white t-shirt and shorts were a filthy dirty gray. The man didn't care about his appearance, but he did focus on getting back at Jax. He wanted his former teammate to suffer, physically as well as psychology. He stared at the ceiling and pictured how Jax would lose everything, including friends, community and family. Randy wanted Jax's pain to run deep in his body, mind and heart. He wanted him dead. For months he worked hard toward his goal and he swore he would not fail. Randy would first try to get back with his parents.

♫

CHAPTER 18

2009 – FLORIDA

Alejandro and Stacy drove Jax to Seville to catch his flight. After saying their goodbyes, the airport staff took over and wheeled the wounded equestrian to his departure gate. They brought him down the jet way and the flight crew helped him into the aircraft. He could manage getting to his seat with crutches. The man was miserable and depressed. His equestrian career was finished and he didn't even want to focus on any other dreams or projects. The goal of performing at the Olympics was achieved, but his first Games would also be his last. He could maybe teach or be a coach, but that pull wasn't strong enough and, with his fear of horses, that was definitely out of the question. He was just numb.

Jax dozed off and his recurrent nightmare since the fall took hold of him. He was shaking uncontrollably until one of the flight attendants touched his shoulder.

"Are you alright, sir?" she asked.

Jax opened his eyes and stared at her. When he finally realized where he was, he nodded. "Yes, thank you.

Could I have some water, please?"

"Of course."

The rest of the trip was, thankfully, uneventful.

Bernardo entered the airport wearing his traditional beret, shirt, waistband, pants and boots. The knife and bolas stayed in the car. He was quite a sight. People looked at him and thought him unusual yet distinguished and admired the pride of his tradition. The Argentine was used to looks and stares. He would never apologize for who he was and what he wore. He was proud of his heritage. People could take him or leave him; it was their choice.

Bernardo waited for his boy to arrive and, as tough as the man was, he didn't expect to see Jax in a wheelchair being pushed toward him by an airport worker. He turned pale but kept it together. He welcomed his chiquito with open arms. They hugged for a good moment and then Bernardo helped him to the pickup. They drove to the ranch and were silent for quite a while until the gaucho finally said: "Almea is back and doing fine. She's been quiet and wasn't really hurt in the fall. Her foot is almost healed. I'm sure she's anxious to see you."

"Um, yes, right," Jax said absentmindedly. The perspiration running down his spine was confirming the fear of facing horses, even his beloved Almea. How could he tell Bernardo of his phobia, of being killed by them, just like in his nightmares?

"Okay, gauchito, what are you hiding from me?"

"Nothing at all. What would I hide from you?" Jax asked, amazed that Bernardo had already picked up on a problem.

"I've known you since you were little. I can tell."

"I said nothing's wrong!" Jax said angrily.

"Okay, that's fine." Bernardo knew there was a problem and he would definitely get to it, but at the moment he would let Jax cool down. He would find out when the time was right, whether it was from Jax himself or through his own gentle probing. He understood the boy was angry, and hurt; in more ways than one. He had been betrayed by his teammate, almost lost a leg, had surgery done, started painful physical therapy; and there was more he would have to endure. Bernardo wondered if his mind was the most afflicted. He would help him out and be there for him.

Just picturing a horse would almost bring Jax to his knees. As they saw horses in a pasture along the road the terror was only too real. He immediately started hyperventilating. He suppressed it as best he could. He didn't want Bernardo to know what was going on or what he was experiencing. The older man, however, instantly picked up on it, but didn't let on. He would treat Jax like any wounded horse; with love, patience and understanding.

They arrived at the ranch and Jax looked around. It wasn't the same as when he left for the competition, but he couldn't figure out what was different. Everything looked the same. Was he losing his mind?

"Come, chiquito, let's go into the house. I'll bring your bags."

"Okay," Jax said, as he limped into his home with the crutches.

"How about we go to the pit later and eat some of your favorites?" Bernardo asked.

"No, not today. I'm really not hungry."

"Okay. Why don't you go lie down for a while? You're probably tired from the trip."

"Yes, I will."

"You let me know if you need anything, *si?*"

"Yes, thanks for picking me up."

Jax went to his room and fell on the bed. He immediately fell asleep. Bernardo looked in a little while later, said a prayer for his boy and covered him with a blanket. Jax slept through the evening and most of the night until the nightmare was back. It was getting worse. The horses practically killed him this time. Jax started screaming in pain and anguish. Bernardo was at his side in moments and calmed him down. He held him in his arms the same way he had when his parents were killed.

"Shhh, everything is going to be alright, chiquito."

Tears ran down Jax's face until he finally fell asleep, just as he had that fateful night. Bernardo stayed with him until the rays of the sun came trickling through the window. He went to the kitchen and prepared breakfast, every one of Jax's favorites. He knew his gauchito would be hungry.

When Jax woke up he didn't know if it was because of the sun coming through his window or the smells wafting in from the kitchen. He smiled. Bernardo had surely prepared a feast. Jax took his crutches and followed his nose to the food. He smiled from ear to ear. He was right, the gaucho had gone all out and was humming as he cooked.

"Smells divine," Jax said.

"Good. Have a seat. Orange juice is on the table. Freshly squeezed, of course. Help yourself."

"Thank you. And thank you for last night."

"No problem. That's what I'm here for."

"How do you mean?"

"*Ay,* chiquito, you are my life. I love you like a son. You weren't killed in the fire and I was spared to protect you like a father. I wouldn't have minded being with my

Maria, but being with you is my path in life and it gives me great joy. And you know what? It's good and noble."

"You are an amazing man, Bernardo, and I'm very grateful you are part of my life. I love you like a father, and I thank you for all you do and for your big heart. I want you to know that."

"I do, chiquito, I do. Now, eat a good breakfast. You have much to do today."

"I do?"

"Yes, I received instructions for your physical therapy, and you must do what the doctors say."

"Oh, no, I thought I could get a few days off."

"No, not yet, but I will help you."

"You mean you'll be a slave master."

"Whatever gave you such an idea?"

"I know you."

Bernardo just laughed.

Jax groaned. Not only would he have to endure the grueling physical therapy, he would also have to contend with Bernardo's 'gaucho rehabilitation'.

The two men enjoyed their breakfast and thought of the day ahead of them.

"I have a favor to ask you, chiquito."

"What do you need?"

"Do you remember little Cecilia?"

"Yes, of course. From Edward and Irma's ranch."

"Well, she was hit by a car when you were in Spain."

"Oh, no! Is she alright?"

"Thankfully nothing broken, and she is doing much better. She's in some pain, of course. I'm on my way to see her. I would appreciate it if you came with me. Would you?"

"Of course." Jax was only too happy to get away for a while. A change of scenery and seeing friends would be perfect.

Bernardo pulled up the pickup and helped Jax in. He put the crutches in the bed. "Ready?"

"Let's do it."

After a few miles Bernardo put a hand on Jax's knee. "Do you want to talk about last night?"

"What about it?"

"The nightmare?"

Jax didn't say anything and the gaucho didn't ask again. He knew when the time was right the boy would open up.

"I'm afraid," Jax said a few minutes later.

Bernardo knew the time was at that very moment. He pulled over to the side of the road. "Of what, chiquito?"

"Of… of horses," Jax whimpered.

This was worse than Bernardo could imagine. Horses and Jax were practically the same race. "In what way?"

"Just thinking of getting close to one…"

"What do you think would happen?"

"They want to kill me… just like in the dreams."

"Do they kill you in your dreams? Can you tell me what you see?"

"I'm in the middle of an open field, just standing and enjoying nature around me, smelling the air. I can tell somewhere nearby there are flowers and trees by their aromas. Then I smell something else—horses, dozens of them." Jax remembered how much he had loved their scent, but just thinking about it churned his stomach. "And then they come galloping toward me at full speed. I know they're going to knock me over and kick me to death. I fall on the ground and stay in a fetal position, trying to protect myself. They've formed a circle around me, screeching like the night of the fire, but not in agony," Jax said, and shuddered. "All of them are angry with me and want revenge. I've hurt them somehow, and even Almea is there; pissed off and wanting payback for what I did to her."

"But you didn't do anything to her. And she knows that," Bernardo said.

"How do you know?"

"Because it was that bastard Randy Newton. Tell me more of the dream."

"I'm lying on the ground, covering my face and watching them through my arms. They're standing on their hind legs, their front hooves in the air ready to come down on me hard, ready to kick me to death." Jax stopped. He couldn't breathe. He grabbed the console in front of him and gripped it with every ounce of strength he had left. His knuckles turned white with the effort. He dropped his head and Bernardo grabbed him. He held him up in the seat and kept repeating: "Breathe! Breathe!"

"What's happening? What's wrong with me?" Jax managed to ask.

"It will pass, chiquito, now breathe deep!"

Jax took in as much air as he could. His breathing slowly came back to normal. "What happened?" He asked as soon as he could.

"Panic attack."

"Oh, that's just great."

"It's okay, this happens. Now, tell me, do you ever die in your dreams? Do the horses ever kill you?"

"No, I always wake up just before they do."

"Perfect."

"What's perfect?" Jax asked.

"In any dream, if you don't die then that is not the way you are going to die in real life."

"And just how do you know that?"

"Ah, everybody knows that," Bernardo answered.

Jax smiled. He knew that was the gaucho's standard response when he knew something for sure but couldn't remember how or where he learned it. Most likely from a book, or perhaps from personal experience.

"I think everything will be okay, chiquito, it will just take a little time. Besides, horses are your friends, your brothers and sisters. They wouldn't hurt you."

"How do you know?"

"Ah, everybody knows that too."

There he goes again, Jax thought.

Bernardo started the pickup and headed toward their friends' ranch. When they arrived, they were greeted by Irma and Edward, little Cecilia's parents. They mainly talked about Jax and Cecilia, who were both on the road to recovery.

"Would it be alright if I gave this to Cecilia?" Bernardo asked.

"Of course," the parents answered.

"They are very light and won't make any damage or hurt her."

The gaucho gave Cecilia the bolas he made for her. They were made of felt and filled with cotton, all held together by woolen strings. He showed her how to use them. Cecilia clapped as the bolas wrapped themselves around a chair leg.

"Me, me, I want to try!" The little girl exclaimed.

"Okay. Give me your hand and hold it like this," Bernardo explained as he showed her what to do.

"The worse that could happen with the bolas is make a fly swerve from his trajectory," Jax chuckled.

The adults looked on, pleased with Cecilia's happiness.

"Let's get a cool drink on the patio," Irma said.

"Sounds good," Jax said, following them out.

The adults sat around drinking iced tea and fresh lemonade as Bernardo continued playing with little Cecilia. Jax was nervous. He hadn't realized how close the patio was to the corral. After a little while Edward stood up and went to the stable. He brought a horse out and led it into the enclosure. Another man walked beside them. Jax thought he might pass out. Every muscle in his body was as taunt as a rubber band ready to be released.

"It's for Cecilia. It's the best therapy in the world," Irma said.

"How do you mean?" Jax asked.

"Watch. It's impressive."

Cecilia saw the horse and squealed in delight. "I get to go riding!" She announced to Bernardo and Jax.

"That's wonderful, chiquita!" Bernardo said.

Irma took her daughter's hand and helped her walk to the corral. It was slow and painful for the little girl, but her goal was to ride. Just the anticipation made her feel better. Her brow furrowed as she endured the pain. When Cecilia was next to the horse, she rubbed its muzzle and kissed it. The horse affectionately snorted back and looked at the little person with the gentlest eyes Jax had ever seen.

"Is there anything more special than that kind of communication?" Bernardo asked, beaming.

Jax didn't answer, whether the question was intended for him or not.

The man, who had come out of the stable with Edward and the horse, was the trainer. He lifted himself into the saddle. Edward carefully raised his daughter up to the man who accommodated Cecilia in front of him. She needed strengthening in her little body after the accident. The walking movement of the horse mimicked human movement as it moved her hips, her spinal column and her shoulders the same way it would in a normal walk. Simply by sitting on the horse Cecilia was emulating walking without the physical pain. The length of time she sat on the horse was equivalent to time she would have been walking. The trainer also stood the youngster on her feet and held her in front of him so she could get back a better feel for balance. Jax and Bernardo could see the girl's joy and pleasure from the big smile on her face.

"The hippotherapy has been amazing," Edward said. "She started not being able to move at all to walking on her own. What you are watching is the best therapy in the world, not just for this kind of injury but for many kinds, including mental."

"She truly is doing so much better!" Bernardo agreed.

"You should try it," Irma suggested to Jax.

"I'll, uh, think about it. Thanks," Jax answered.

Cecilia and the horse were close to the barrier. "Oh, Jax, come pet the horsy," she pleaded.

"Maybe some other time."

"Pretty pleeeease."

"Uh, I'm a little sore right now."

"You should get on the horsy too, you'll feel so much better."

"Yes, I'm sure. You're doing great. Keep it up."

"I know, and I want you to be all better too. Come on, Jax, pleeeease."

Jax wanted to escape but he didn't know how. One thing he was sure: he couldn't bring himself to get close to the horse, or any horse. Would he ever be able to? Would he ever want to?

Bernardo switched to Spanish so as not to embarrass

Jax. "Gauchito, you'll never find a gentler horse than this one. I know it's tough for you and I promise you I will always stand by you and protect you with my life. I will never let anything harm you, especially horses. Your nightmares are just terrible dreams. It is your brain's way of releasing the anxiety caused by the injury. Don't let your mind destroy the passion and the love you have for these creatures. They are your friends, your siblings. Give them a chance to show you their heart song."

"You want me to go up to the horse?"

"Yes, please. I will walk next to you."

"I can't, Bernardo," Jax whispered.

"I know it is difficult, but I also know that you can do this. Together we can do anything, chiquito."

Jax was practically in tears. Somewhere in his soul he wanted everything to be perfect, just like before the injury. He would love to pet the horse and even maybe ride him, but he was scared out of his mind. "I can't! I just can't."

Bernardo was hopeful. At least Jax was listening and not getting angry. "Let's slowly walk up to the horse, together. I promise the horse will not harm you in any way, *hijo mio*, my son."

Jax stared at Bernardo. Never had the gaucho called him his son before. The older man's eyes were filling up fast. Never had he seen the toughest man in the world shed a tear. "I should say yes before you let your eyes overflow," Jax said, trying to keep the mood light. Bernardo only stared. "I can't right now, but I promise I will try soon, with Almea."

"I accept, chiquito," the Argentine said and held out his hand. Jax shook it and gave him a hug.

For the next couple of weeks Jax worked hard with

his physical therapist. It was tedious and painful, but Jax wanted to get back to his old self. He wanted to be the athlete he once was and not worry about his body. Bernardo helped with the therapy as well, and even used acupressure in a comparable way he did with the horses. Jax was amazed how much it helped. He kept thinking of the hippotherapy with little Cecilia and the incredible success. He wanted similar results, but his fear was still very real.

When Jax was exhausted, they called it a day. "Bernardo, today was very good. Thank you for everything."

"Yes, it was. Now go get some rest. Tomorrow you have more therapy, chiquito."

"Yes, slave master."

Bernardo chuckled.

The next morning the gaucho was preparing breakfast. Jax walked into the kitchen and sat at the table.

"You know, chiquito, I think it is time to see Almea. She needs to know you love her and don't blame her."

"She understands that?"

"She is special, that one, as are you. The two of you are familia."

"I don't know, Bernardo, I'm still…"

"Scared? Of horses?"

Jax nodded.

"Now you listen to me. Yes, you had a fall and it was bad. You were hurt, but you are so much better and improving every day. You are strong, chiquito, and you will soon be back to your old self. And you are passionate, about life, about horses. You are also intelligent, and you know so much about these animals. It is time to reconnect. You know in your heart you will be fine. Let's start today."

Jax looked at the man he adored. "Today?" He asked, almost inaudibly, the perspiration starting to form over his skin.

Bernardo nodded. "Right after breakfast."

Jax and Bernardo walked toward Almea's stall. He slowly hobbled closer to the half door. When Jax saw her, he almost cried. Oh, how he loved her. Her rump was toward him and Jax appreciated her tail's beautiful highlights. Almea smelled him before she saw him. She whinnied, her voice welcoming him as she turned around and walked up to the man she had missed and shared so much with. Jax hadn't been this close to a horse since his fall. He apprehensively put his hand over the door. His fingers trembled as Almea came up to him and gently put her muzzle under his hand. Jax's tears rolled down his face as he caressed her. He leaned in a little more over the half door and hugged her neck. He just held it as his tears ran down his cheeks. She rubbed her face against his. She was so happy to see him.

"Hello, beautiful. How's my favorite girl?" Jax whispered close to her ear.

Almea answered back by softly snorting, her nostril and ears pointed toward him.

"I'm sorry, I'm so very sorry."

Almea rubbed her face against his again, as if apologizing too.

Bernardo smiled. Jax and Almea were together once more, their love intact and stronger than ever; attesting to the vanishing of Jax's fear of horses.

Jax spent the better part of six months in therapy and got his leg back in shape. It had, as he expected, been tough and painful, but he was proud of himself and his results. No repercussions from his fall were noticeable other than a large scar on his leg. He could still walk, dance and exercise, but his competitive riding days were over, at least Jax thought so. Bernardo would eventually remind him of the older athletes who still competed in the equestrian events at the Olympics and other prestigious venues. That was the beauty of it, riders could ride indefinitely. When the time was right, he would bring the subject up. He knew Jax thought he physically couldn't compete, but Bernardo was sure he would heal to the point where he would still be able to take part.

What brought Jax out of his depression was the therapy he received. He knew it wasn't so much the physical side but the mental rehabilitation he needed most, and his reconnection with the horses, especially Almea. As he grew stronger he realized he had found a new passion. It was in great part thanks to Bernardo and to the visit with little Cecilia.

After a long day Bernardo and Jax went to their rooms. Jax lay on his bed and looked at the ceiling. His eyes started seeing what his mind was creating and he knew for sure he had found his calling. He would do everything possible to make his dreams a reality, and make a better place for humans and horses. A new world had just opened to him. Jax didn't sleep that night. His mind was too busy focusing on his plan. When the sun started to lighten up the room he went to find Bernardo. The older man was in the kitchen already preparing a healthy breakfast.

"What is it, chiquito?"

"We have to talk about something very important."

"Is everything alright?"

"Very alright."

Jax told Bernardo his plans. He wanted to build a center for hippotherapy. It seemed logical having his parents' ranch and his deep connection with horses, so much so he was sure he could communicate with them. He had learned so much from both Bernardo and the animals about their behaviors and subtleties not found in textbooks.

Bernardo listened attentively.

Jax continued: "I also want to have a place where horses can retire to, where older unwanted horses wouldn't be euthanized due to their age or their inability to produce results for their owners, such as racehorses or stallions. They could just roam freely and graze. They would be provided with food, grooming and medical needs until they pass away."

"That's wonderful, chiquito. Horse owners everywhere would be thrilled knowing a place existed where they could leave the horses they had loved so much, that they would be taken care of and would be able to live out their days. Many times it is difficult and too expensive for the owners to just keep them around, but with your idea the horses could be happy here."

"I also want the center to help veterans. I know the horses would be wonderful for them."

"You are absolutely right. You have a beautiful dream, gauchito."

Jax looked at Bernardo. "What do you think?" he asked.

"I believe everything that has happened to you was for a reason."

Jax nodded. "What is that expression you always say?"

"The ancient Greek one?"

"Yes."

"One of my favorites: 'Every obstacle brings something better.'"

"That's the one."

The two men looked at each other and smiled. It had been a great day.

"Well?" Bernardo asked.

"Well, now that we know exactly what we want we just have to figure out the details and the finances."

"Let's make it happen."

"Indeed."

Jax and Bernardo gave each other a big hug and proceeded to work on their endeavor. They had been at it all day and were exhausted. They retired to their bedrooms.

Bernardo stood alone in his room and pondered on the day's events. Jax's passion for horses was back, not that he had ever really lost it. Fear had eclipsed that love for a little while, but now everything just seemed to flow back into normalcy. The gaucho silently jumped up and down, and pumped his hands toward the ceiling as he had done so many years ago after Jax had started conquering the pain from his parents' demise. He marveled at God's infinite wisdom and the path humans followed, sometimes with painful and unexpected bumps and holes along the way. At that moment Jax's path looked pretty smooth; Bernardo was ecstatic.

♫

CHAPTER 19

2010 – CONNECTICUT

Randy left the fleabag motel and headed north on I-85 to Virginia and continued on I-95 toward Greenwich, Connecticut. The thousand-mile drive took him fifteen hours. He did it in two days as he was worried the pickup wouldn't hold up. He stopped about mid-way at a motel on the highway. Randy knew the old truck was on its last legs, but he only needed it for one last trip. If he was lucky it would take him to his destination. Over the last months he had grown fond of the rust bucket as he understood at some point that it hadn't hurt him, as everyone else in his life had. On the contrary, the pickup had taken him everywhere he wanted to go. It had been a faithful companion, the one and only. Randy had given the jalopy a name, Rusty, in honor of the rust everywhere. He knew it wasn't very original, but it suited the old heap.

On the afternoon of the second day Randy walked into a barber shop, had his long unkempt hair cut and his beard trimmed. He looked like a new man. His good looks were more prominent, although this was the first time his parents would see him with facial hair. It suited him. Randy wanted to look presentable and not like a hippy gone wild. He believed it would help his cause.

Randy drove up to the gate of his parents' mansion. The guard came out of his shack and took one look at the pickup. He had no idea who Randy was.

"Are you lost?" The security man asked in a condescending tone.

Randy glared at him and held back his temper. "I'm here to see the Newtons."

"Do you have an appointment?"

"No, I don't." He balled up his fist, ready to let his hand fly into the man's face. Instead, he just whispered: "Just tell them it's Randy."

"Randy who?"

"Their son, Randolph Newton III," he answered angrily.

The guard, taken aback, looked at the pickup and said: "I'll be right back."

"You do that."

It took the guard quite a while before he buzzed the door open. While Randy was waiting, he wondered if his parents were debating on whether or not to let him in. He drove in and gave the man a dirty look. If he wasn't so focused on seeing his parents he might have punched the son of a bitch, maybe even more than once.

Randy stopped in front of the stately home just as faithful Rusty emitted a loud sound from its tailpipe; the type of sound that could have come from a firearm. Like an old soldier, Rusty had given a last hurrah before dying. Randy looked at the mélange of rust, metal and bolts, patted the side of the door a couple of times in thanks and headed to the mansion he once called home.

A housekeeper opened the main door, a woman he

had never seen before, who told him his mother was waiting for him in the library. As he entered the room he looked around. Everything was exactly as it had been the last time he was in the house. His mother was sitting on a couch looking at him. She didn't get up or hug her son, she just sat there staring.

"What is it you want? Why are you here?"

"Mom, seriously? Not even a 'Hello, how are you?'"

"What do you want, Randy?"

"Don't you know?"

"Your father isn't here, but he'll be home soon."

"Is that why it took so long to open the gate for me? You had to call to get his permission?"

"You know me better than that."

Randy's mother was colder than he remembered. The woman didn't seem happy, not because of Randy's visit but because that's the way she'd been her whole life. At least since he could remember. Was the life of the rich and famous not as magnificent as claimed? Or was his father being particularly despicable?

"Okay, then you called him to try to figure out what to do with me."

Randy's mother didn't answer.

"Well, aren't you going to say anything to me?"

"Like what?"

"Oh, I don't know, something like 'I missed you, son. How are you? Do you need anything?' You know, things that a mother usually wants to know about the child she loves… supposedly," Randy retorted irritably. He waited for an answer, but still she didn't say anything, which was only making him angrier by the minute.

"Then how about: 'How bad was it in prison? How often did they beat you up? Did they rape you? How many times did they try to end you with a shiv?' Or how about 'How long were you recuperating in the hospital?'

"That's enough!" Randy's father shouted from behind him, having just arrived and hearing the last of questions. "Leave your mother alone. She doesn't deserve to be spoken to like that."

"Oh, and what would you know about who deserves what? Just like you did with me. You threw me out like a dirty old rag."

"Hardly. I gave you enough money to start a new life. Why are you here?" His father demanded.

"You know, I'm not sure anymore. I thought maybe my parents would be glad to see me after all this time." Randy turned to his mother. "I thought maybe you would actually give your son a hug, Mom. I mean, after all, you are the woman who brought me into this world. Isn't there some sort of maternal connection, some invisible cord that unites a mother and her child? Or perhaps you lost your heart along the way and the cord went with it." Randy took a breath to calm himself down. He still wanted to make amends, to belong to this family, but he never expected the brick wall, better known as his parents, would continue to hit him this hard. "And you, Dad, was winning a medal more important than having a son? Really?"

"I want you out of this house," the older man said.

"Well, I'm not leaving. I came in good faith, trying to mend things up with you. Why can't we try?"

"Randy," his mother said, "I think it's better if you left."

Randy could hear the disgust in his mother's voice and her words hit him hard. Was it his clothes? The way he looked? He couldn't believe his mother didn't want him around. "But why?" He asked, almost a whimper.

"Do as you mother says."

"Or what, Dad?"

"Or I'll call the police."

"You would actually do that to your own son?"

"I don't have a son. He died in China, and then again in Spain."

"It's all about fucking trophies?"

"I said get out, or I'll throw you out myself," his father menaced.

Randy laughed. His old man had no idea what he had been doing for the past few months. He could kill him in a second. "Yeah, right, Dad."

"Stop it, both of you! Randy, please leave."

"But Mom, come on, let's be a family again."

"You'll never be part of this household, never!" his father yelled, slapping Randy hard across his face.

The housekeeper, who had been behind the closed door of the library, heard the arguing between the parents and the son. She was frightened something bad would happen and called the security guard, who, in turn, called the police.

"You shouldn't have done that, Dad," Randy said.

"Oh, why not? Are you going to grow a pair and hit me back?"

If only his father knew how long and how much that 'pair' had suffered. He had been in constant pain, and it had taken quite a while before his genitals weren't in agony and started functioning properly. The alcohol had helped, but by the time the evenings rolled in Randy was on his way to drinking himself into a stupor.

"Dad, please, for the last time, I'm asking you to give us a chance at being a family again."

"I told you!" the older man yelled, "I don't have a son! I don't ever want to see you in this house, in my life or in front of my eyes ever again. If you see me on the street, turn the other way."

"Dad, please…" Randy tried once more, but it was in vain as his father threw a punch that landed forcefully on his nose. He heard it crack as he stumbled backwards and fell to the floor.

"You want more?" the father asked menacingly, his fist balled and ready to hit the man who was lying at his feet, the son he had disowned.

"I asked you nicely, I begged you!" Randy said, standing up. He looked at his father, his nose gushing with blood and running down his neck and shirt. "All I wanted was a little boy's dream, something every child is entitled to—just a little love from you and Mom and to know you had my back. But no, you abandoned me instead. If anyone should be ashamed, it's you two," Randy said, and he pushed his father hard. The older man didn't expect the speed his son came at him and lost his footing. He fell on a hard wooden coffee table. The police rushed in just as the older man hit his head. Randy was immediately handcuffed and taken to the police station. They booked him for first degree assault and was given twelve years in the correctional institution. Randy's saving grace was that his father didn't die and recovered quickly, but neither he nor his mother tried to help him. It would not have taken too much effort to just tell the police that it was a petty family disagreement and that everything was fine. He could have been free. Instead, they made sure he would do the full time. Randy was once again on his own. He had never been more bitter, disappointed, angry or more determined to avenge himself on those who had put him in the position he was in. They had ruined his life. He would make them pay.

Right at the moment he was grateful and pleased with the months of training in Columbus. He was skilled in arm-to-arm combat, small arms, knives and long range high-precision rifles. It would serve him well while he was in prison, and keep him from any similar predicaments to his last incarceration. His proficiency commanded respect, and the inmates stayed away from him after they witnessed what Randy could do with his bare hands if he needed to.

♫

CHAPTER 20

2010 – FLORIDA

Jax and Bernardo had organized their thoughts about Hippo-Camp, and hired specialists to make the dream a reality. Even though Jax had received a sizable settlement from the lawsuit the Equestrian Federation had insisted on against Randy Newton and his family, there wasn't enough for the three different parts of the camp. They had, however, started the first phase. They waited for a bank loan to come through, but it was proving lengthy and difficult.

As the two men pondered on their endeavor, they prepared snacks to nibble on while waiting for the FIFA world cup game to start between the Netherlands and Uruguay, being played in South Africa. They were passionate about their sports, and they watched and enjoyed games together. Once the match was underway, they followed the event and munched on their food. They were regaled with five goals, three for the Dutch and two for the South Americans.

After a fun afternoon the phone rang. Jax answered

it. "Hello?"

"Mr. Logan? Mr. Jax Logan?" The voice on the other end said.

"Speaking. Who's calling, please?"

"Mr. Logan, my name is Theo Goodwin and I'm an agent from New York. Could you spare me a few minutes? I promise to get straight to the point and not waste any of your time. This call could possibly be very important to you. I hope so."

Jax was intrigued. The guy wasn't pushy and didn't sound like a telemarketer. He was a professional in his field, and Jax could sense something interesting coming his way. "Go ahead, Mr. Goodwin, you've made me curious."

"Thank you, Mr. Logan…"

By the end of the conversation Jax turned to Bernardo and, as calmly as possible, told his favorite gaucho that a few people from New York were going to stop by for a meeting in two days.

"From New York? What kind of meeting?"

"You know how I was trying to figure out where to get large amounts of money for Hippo-Camp?"

"Yes, I remember." Bernardo was waiting. He could tell Jax was just about ready to jump out of skin. "And these people have answers for you?"

"YES!" Jax said, doing a few dance steps around the room.

"Oh, somebody seems very happy. Tell me, chiquito, why are you so excited?"

"This guy, Theo, is an agent from New York. He will be coming with a couple of other people. And do you know what they want to do? They want to give me a lot of money."

"Why?" Bernardo asked, concerned this deal might

be shady.

"Well, Theo would be doing all the negotiations, for which he would get his cut, as he would be doing most of the work. But I would always have the last say on everything."

"You still haven't told me what this is about," Bernardo said, growing impatient. Was it really good news?

"Theo is bringing a clothes designer."

Bernardo stared blankly at Jax. The most he knew about clothes were the ones he wore on his back, and the same style he had worn since forever. "And?" The man had absolutely no idea where this was going.

"Bernardo," Jax said, sitting next to him, "they want to use my name on a new collection, a clothing line that would look like riding clothes; along with hats and boots. And there would be a second line with real riding gear and accessories for riders and horses as well."

"Why?"

"Why what?

"Why do they want to use your name, and why do they want to create clothes with it?"

"This is what Theo said: Because I'm a world-famous Olympic champion, and because I have a feel-good survivor story. A kind of phoenix, if you will."

"Ah, coming back from the ashes."

"Something like that. Oh, and he said I have a pretty face."

"Okay." The pretty face Bernardo could understand, and agree with, but the rest was possibly the farthest from Bernardo's world as the man could get.

"And the amount to be made is astronomical!" Jax continued, "more money than we could have ever imagined or even hoped for. Not only are we going to be very rich, but the best part is that we can build everything we wanted, and even more and better."

Bernardo wasn't quite sure about what this collection stuff was about, but he saw the joy in the younger man and how he could help others in need. He was happy for him. "That's wonderful, yes?"

"Yes! Very wonderful!" Jax answered as he lifted Bernardo off the couch and whirled him around the room.

Theo Goodwin showed up with Siyavash, the designer, along with one assistant each. They introduced themselves and, Jax, who had googled not just the agent but the fashionista, couldn't help being reminded of a tall and thin Dutchman but with an ethnic nose and a Middle Eastern tan. He also sported Scandinavian blond, impeccably dyed hair. Siyavash, of course, was dressed perfectly in designer shirt and pants, and the ensemble made him distinguished and rather intriguing. His English was the Queen's, with a trace of a Persian accent and nuances. Theo on the other hand, was short, balding, with glasses and a goatee. He also sported a substantial girth that showed his love for bagels and potato latkes. His clothes were expensive and quintessential New York. There was no doubt that with his metropolitan accent the man was born and bred in the Big Apple.

Theo explained the details, Siyavash showed them some of his designs, the assistants took notes and helped out. Jax asked questions. Bernardo just listened.

"Siyavash, does your name mean anything?" Jax asked.

"Oh, you'll like this," Theo said.

"Yes," the designer answered, "it is from ancient Persia. In the epic poem 'Shahnameh' there is a prince and that is his name. It also means 'owner of black stallions', hence my love and curiosity for horses ever since I was a child. I've incorporated this passion in my work and I try to give my art an equine influence and elegance." Jax liked the answer. Bernardo even more so. It was a sign. How could it not be with someone who was named Prince of Horses, or something like that.

Siyavash continued about his designs, the horses and his ideas. The Iranian was passionate, which was the reason for his success, but Jax feared the man would talk for hours.

"How about we take a lunch break?" Jax asked quickly.

"I must make *tahdig*," Siyavash blurted out.

"Now?" Theo asked.

"Right now, Teo." There was no *th* sound in Farsi.

"What is that?" Bernardo asked.

"Rice. Persian rice, a specialty."

"I have a specialty too."

"Yes?" Siyavash asked.

"Churrasco," the gaucho said proudly.

"Oh, of course, from the Pampas."

"How did you know I was from Argentina?"

Siyavash answered with a wave of his hand toward the gaucho's attire. "I make clothes for a living, remember?"

"Of course. Do you like churrasco?"

"Love it!"

"I have a special place where I cook. It is outdoors and over a fire pit. Would you like to cook together? What do you need for your..."

"Tahdig."

"Yes, that."

"I have the rice and saffron with me. All I need is a

big pot with a lid, butter, salt and a clean kitchen towel."

"No problem. Shall we cook everything outside?"

"Oh, yes, that would be perfect and will make the dish even more delicious."

"Okay, let's go, Horse Prince."

"Right behind you, Mr. Gaucho. I see you were listening."

"I may not speak too much, but I learn many things."

"Yes, you do."

Jax, Theo and the two assistants grinned at the unusual pair and watched them gather the materials they needed.

"Those two will be busy for a while. Bernardo will call me when everything is ready and we'll join them. We could bring them a salad."

"We'll make it," the assistants volunteered. They knew what their bosses liked.

"Sounds good. Everything you need is in the kitchen," Jax said.

Bernardo and Siyavash headed outside and went to the stables.

"We will be riding there. I'm pretty sure you are a rider and you would enjoy that," Bernardo said.

"Hey, my energy comes from my name. Of course, I would love to ride. I miss it. I can't really do too much of that in New York City now, can I?"

"Well, anytime you want to come to the ranch you are most welcome."

"Thank you, Bernardo, that's very kind of you." The Iranian man knew he meant it. In the Persian culture hospitality was enormously important. The entire Middle East was well known for their generosity, and would go to extreme lengths to prove it. It wasn't just good manners; it genuinely came from the heart and was a way to prove to the guests how special they were. This is the way Siyavash saw Jax and Bernardo, and that was one of the reasons he wanted to make them the rice dish. The other reason was the fastest way to make a man happy was through his stomach, and Siyavash truly wanted this deal to go through. He really wished to design a line that did justice to the amazing equines. It would be unique and would put him at the top of the elite fashionistas of the world.

Bernardo made a fire and prepared the meat. Once the embers were hot Siyavash started his tahdig.

"Tell me about yourself, Mr. Gaucho. How did you come to live in Florida with Jax?"

Bernardo talked about himself, Maria and the Logans. He also relayed how he and Jax were all the family either one of them had.

"Well, now you have me and Teo. Your family is growing, my friend."

Bernardo and Siyavash, two men of incredibly different backgrounds, other than their love of horses, were fast becoming good buddies.

"Thank you, Amigo, that means a lot. Now, your turn, tell me about yourself."

"As you know I come from Iran. My grandfather was well off and owned vast lands. My best memories were going to visit him. He was a rugged man with a sense of humor and a brilliant mind for investments. It is from him that I have a love for horses."

"From your grandfather? How so?" Bernardo asked.

"Yes, he was passionate about the animals, not only because they are exquisite and unique, but because they are living history."

"How do you mean?"

"There are many amazing horse breeds in that part of the world. For example, there is the beautiful Asil, an Iranian breed and incredibly pure strain of the Arabian. And then you have the Caspian, the oldest breed in the world, even older than the Arabian. It is a smaller horse, usually about 10-12 hands and is a great jumper with tough hooves. I can picture the Mongols on them."

"That is fascinating!" Bernardo was truly captivated and enjoying every moment of the conversation.

"And there are others, like the Bakhtiari from southern Iran; the exquisite Dareshoori with its silky coat, a wonderful horse, friendly, courageous and fun to ride. There are several more, all rare breeds and pure animals only found in Iran."

"You grew up around them?"

"Yes. I used to love to ride them, accompanied by my grandfather who would tell me stories about them." Siyavash took a breath. "And then it all stopped."

"How do you mean?"

"The revolution happened. The Shah was overthrown and my parents had to flee. I was only six, but I remember every moment of that time, especially with my grandfather. As I mentioned, he was a smart man. He had purchased a building in London as an investment and when he insisted we leave Iran, we had a home and income from the other apartments. The old man's insistence and his fear we might be killed, because the family was wealthy, made us survive."

"Did he leave as well?"

"No. Unfortunately he stayed. They took all his land and possessions, including the horses. He died of a broken heart a few months later."

"I'm sorry to hear that."

"Yes, he was a good man, kindhearted. Maybe one day when the political regime is no longer hostile, especially to people like me, I would love to go back, rediscover the ancient horse breeds and ride them in the beautiful lands of my grandfather."

"That would be wonderful."

"And you should join me, Mr. Gaucho."

"It would be my great pleasure. Just tell me when."

"I will."

"What did you mean when you said 'people like me'?"

"I'm a little too exotic for them."

Bernardo laughed as he always pictured Iran as exotic. "Their loss, my friend."

"Absolutely."

"Hey, Siyavash, are you married?"

"No, I don't think I'll ever marry."

"Why not?"

"I'm too independent, and I love the human body too much."

"Ah, you must have many ladies chasing you, *si?*"

"And men."

"Of course." Bernardo wasn't sure what to make of that statement, and did find the designer a little eccentric. He quite enjoyed the man with his pleasant, charming and even mysterious ways. And from his sketches Bernardo could tell he very much loved what he did and, even more importantly, he adored horses. That was sacred to both of them, and the Argentine would help wherever he could.

Siyavash added saffron to the basmati rice as Bernardo prepared the meat for the grill.

Jax answered his phone, nodded and hung up. "Bernardo just called," he announced to his guests, "the food will be ready in ten minutes. Why don't we head out and join them?"

"Sounds good," Theo said, his stomach starting to growl. The man worked hard, didn't complain as he loved his job, but he also loved food. Besides, it wasn't every day Siyavash prepared his delicious crusty rice.

"The guys took a couple of horses, but we'll take the van," Jax said.

"That sounds very good, Jax," Theo agreed. He wasn't exactly the athletic type and there was no way he would get on a horse. The closest he had ever been to one of the beasts was seeing them around Central Park, pulling lovers or tourists in a carriage. Even as a boy he had no desire to ride the animals. How he had gotten this equine gig was still a bit of a mystery, but he liked the people associated with the endeavor and firmly believed they would all have a good time, and definitely reap its benefits. He was excited, and when he got that way the results were superb.

They drove out to the firepit as Bernardo was taking the meat off the grill, and Siyavash was unmolding the rice from the pot onto a platter. When he pulled the cooking utensil off, the golden crust on top of the rice glistened from the butter and everyone clapped. Tahdig was not the easiest rice dish to prepare. As Siyavash would insist, it was an art.

"Here you are, my friends, the bottom of the pot," the Iranian announced.

"How do you mean?" It was a question Bernardo seemed to keep asking Siyavash.

"Tahdig, that's what it means. It is an old Persian word.

Jax looked at Bernardo and Siyavash. The two men were completely different. One was tall, refined and eccentric. The other was shorter, a beret-wearing gaucho and very down to earth. He wondered what they could have been talking about, other than horses of course.

"How are you two doing?" Jax asked them.

"Very well indeed. This chap is absolutely lovely," Siyavash answered.

Jax raised his eyebrows and almost laughed. He could never have pictured Bernardo as 'lovely'.

"Yes, Siyavash was telling me about magnificent ancient horse breeds in Iran."

"And we also got into a great discussion about Rumi, Gibran and Silvina Ocampo."

"Ah, yes, Bernardo loves great poets."

The group enjoyed their meal, and by the time they were finished Jax pulled out a bottle of champagne from the cooler housing the drinks. "I believe this calls for a toast as we seal the deal on…"

"*JAX* by Siyavash," Theo said.

"To the Jaxon Logan lines," they repeated together and cheered.

The next six months were a whirlwind of activity as Siyavash and his team created exquisite designs for the clothing and accessory lines. The agents, designers and manufacturers practically worked around the clock. They had to get the lines ready and had to move fast as Jax, the athletic novelty, would only be remembered for so long. But that was Theo's expertise—the promotion and the publicity. When the moment was right, Jaxon Logan and *JAX* would become world famous. Siyavash and his crew were pulling long days and crazy hours, but even with exhaustion hanging over them their passion fueled the energy they needed to keep going.

Jax, Theo and Siyavash spent hours conversing via

their computers until the collection and details were complete. All they needed now was to film a commercial.

Theo Goodwin was well known in the fashion industry. Every fashionista, established or trying to make it big in the business, had their eyes on the premier agent. At the moment he focused all his energy and worked on the *JAX* endeavor; then he received news that Jax didn't want to star in his own commercial. Theo thought about it for a moment and knew that if Jax wasn't in it, after they had worked so hard for the line to be a success, it would all be for naught. The work would be pushed back months, or even years. Jax was the key. He had to get through to the man. He had to convince Jax. That was what Theo Goodwin, agent extraordinaire, did. That was his forte, the reason he was so successful—he knew how to convince people. His mind worked like a chess player's, strategizing, knowing the opponent's move and beating him to the punch, all with diplomacy and insight. Theo knew he could talk to Siyavash, who could speak to Bernardo since they were good buddies, who in turn would know how to convince Jax. Theo could take many avenues to accomplish his goals, but decided to call Jax himself. He picked up the phone and dialed.

"Jax, my boy, how are you?..." Theo asked in his very New York way.

The conversation ended with Theo convincing Jax to be in it. After all, it was his story and it would play out in the commercial. Jax was the star of the show, and in so many ways.

The New York gang flew to Florida. In addition to Theo, Siyavash and their assistants, a film crew assembled the necessary equipment, some of which they easily found and rented in Miami. It didn't take long for them to be ready to do the shoot.

Siyavash and his team had worked very hard on the designs, and although they had shown them to Jax through their respective computers, Jax was duly impressed with the clothes and accessories when he saw and tried some of the pieces. They were comfortable and made him look sharp, as any good design should. They ran from casual to eveningwear, for both men and women, manufactured with exquisite materials and still affordable to the general public. Jax had insisted on that. He didn't want the clothes to be for a select few, but for everyone who wanted items from the collection. The riding line was exquisite and unique, with designs which were elegant while still conforming to the needs of the riders, which included jackets, vests, breeches, boots and hats.

The film crew used Jax's ranch and house for their needs. The dressers and make-up artists used his bedroom to get him ready. They used another of the house's bedrooms for the female model who would be filming with him. Once finished, Jax went outside where the director was waiting for him. He looked around. The 'set' was part of the ranch. Tripods, cameras, lights, reflectors and an enormous fan stood at attention. Experts in their field were ready and waiting to start.

The director saw Jax and greeted him. "Okay, in you go," he said.

Jax looked at the car the director wanted him to get into. It was a beautiful classic metallic beige Austin Healey 3000 with brown leather interior. He looked at the front of the car and smiled. The grill was definitely grinning at him. Jax sat down in the driver's seat and waited for instructions. He caressed the lacquered wooden steering wheel and gear shift knob, quickly falling in love with the exquisite driving machine.

"Jax, we're going to start up the air machine in a moment," the director said. "Just be casual, move the steering wheel right and left a little as if you were driving and enjoy the air flowing through your hair. Smile. Life is good. Just be yourself. Okay?"

"I think so." Jax thought he could actually do that. He had been nervous, even though Theo had assured him the director was the best at what he did and he could get anybody, especially nonprofessionals, to produce perfection.

The film crew worked for three days. When they finished, they all gathered in Jax's living room to watch the commercial on his large TV screen. They were spread out on the couches and the floor, as excited as children going to a movie. While they had been filming Jax didn't quite understand everything he was doing, as it seemed to him the process was being made in pieces. However, he knew the best pros in the business surrounded him and he followed their direction. Theo had even mentioned that the director and his company had quite a few Clios, the advertising equivalent of the Oscars.

"Okay, everybody ready?" The director asked, looking around the room at the people and his crew. Each one was a specialist in their respective field. Some of the production staff included the producer, cinematographer, editor, sound mixer, lighting specialists, makeup artist and each of their assistants.

"Yes!" They all shouted enthusiastically. They wanted to see the end product and the magic everyone had had a hand in to make this project unique and beautiful.

"Hit it."

The camera panned to Jax sitting in the car, the breeze slightly blowing in his hair as he drove down the road, until he veered off into a field of wildflowers and red poppies. After a few moments the car stopped and Jax got out. He wore casual, yet elegant clothes from the *JAX* line. A 1960's Land Rover with a horse trailer hitched to the back was parked in the field of flowers, with a stylish model leaning against it. She wore a lovely dress and matching scarf from the designer line. Jax walked over to her, embraced her, sensually kissed each cheek and took her by the hand. Jax didn't need any help from the director for that screen moment. The model was a pretty woman who truly brought glamor and beauty to the project, and the camera loved her. She looked stunning in the *JAX* clothes. They entered the horse trailer and the next shot was of both of them, now in clothes from the *JAX* riders' line; with beige breeches and brown riding boots that matched the colors of the classic car. The couple came down the ramp of the trailer. The model sported a bolero hat, very typical of Spanish women riders, and a different scarf around her neck waved in the breeze. They were both good looking, with athletic bodies, and made a very distinguished romantic couple. They pulled the reins of the two horses that followed them out of the trailer. Almea was one of them, the other a stallion from the stables on the property. Jax helped the model up into the saddle and then mounted Almea. One of the model's talents, and also one of the reasons she was picked, was for her expertise as a rider. The horses were just as elegant and regal as their human counterparts, especially when the riders gently pushed them into a cantor and then a gallop through the field of flowers. After a few moments they slowed to a stop. Jax continued on his own with Almea and did a few steps from his Olympics dressage routine, including the tango music in the background which played throughout the commercial. The sun was just waning in the horizon, and Jax stopped Almea in front of the model and did a signature move where the mare kneeled. The next shot was of Jax and the model in eveningwear in the dark of night, illuminated by only Bernardo's fire pit. They held hands as they walked toward the flames and Jax elegantly turned the model and guided her in an elegant tango around the pit. They did a few steps and the last move of the dance was a dip where Jax held the model and smiled at her. They looked into each other's eyes with a subtle yet clear sensual intention. Almea did her move with the bent knee again and snorted to the stallion next to her. Both Jax and his beloved horse were putting on their moves for their counterparts. The clip ended with the collections' line and logo: *JAX, life is a ride.'*

Everyone in the room clapped and hollered. They were proud of their work. It was done well, with subtle nuances and without a word spoken. It was the kind of commercial where you wanted to follow the lives of the people on the screen and, in this case, the horses as well. They congratulated each other and popped a few champagne corks.

The next evening when everyone had left, Jax and Bernardo rode out to the firepit. They threw around some ideas for the Hippo-Camp and reminisced about the olden days. When the stars came out they watched the sky. A shooting star streaked above them.

"Hi Maria!" They both shouted, a ritual they did ever since Bernardo had told young Jax he was sure his wife was saying hello.

"You know, Bernardo, even on my worst days I will

still, and always, say thank you seven times."

"What makes you say that?"

"It seems something good always happens to me after a catastrophe, or at least it seems that way."

"How do you mean?"

"Well, if I hadn't fallen, I never would have discovered the hippo therapies and become rich with a clothing collection through which I am now able to build the center where everyone who needs it can come for free. Look at how much I've accomplished so far in my life, Bernardo."

"It is wonderful, but a little empty if you don't share it with someone you love."

"I do. I have you."

"No, you need a good woman by your side."

"Bernardo, don't worry, I have no problems getting ladies."

"No, chiquito, a woman you are in love with and who loves you the same way."

"Ah, maybe later, in a few years."

"You'll remember me when you find her."

"Okay, I'll let you know," Jax said, trying to change the subject. Why couldn't Bernardo understand that he was still young and wanted to enjoy his youth before settling down?

♫

CHAPTER 21

2012 – MIAMI

The Alonsos lived in Spain but that year they decided to open a new location in Florida, in an area between Orlando and Miami. Alejandro had kept in touch with Jax, who was thrilled with the news and that they would be neighbors. Alejandro came over by himself to set everything up and Jax helped the Spaniard with whatever he required and gave him the guest house for as long as he needed. It didn't take very long to get the venture up and running. Alejandro was pleased to find out that opening a business in the States was easier than in most other countries. With the right preparation, paperwork and funds, the permits were fairly easy to acquire. Besides, this wasn't his first office; HeliEmerg in Spain was home base, and the other locations were in Colombia, Brazil, Lebanon and now in the States. Stacy flew out to visit a couple of times to help. She couldn't leave her Hidalgo for more than ten days at a time. Alina stayed with friends as they didn't want her to miss any classes. At the end of the school year they would move to their new location in Florida.

The Alonsos settled in nicely and Alina went to a new school. She was used to big changes, geographical as well as social, and adapted easily to her surroundings. She was popular, and as in other places around the world, made new friends quickly. The boys thought she was hot, and the girls looked up to her. She was world-traveled and had grown up differently, but they liked that about her and loved her stories.

When the young girls found out that Latin heartthrob Diego Molina would be in South Florida, they begged their families to take them to the concert. It wasn't too hard to convince them, as they too liked the famous singer.

Alina and three of her friends, with their respective mothers, went on a girls' weekend to Miami. Stacy rented a van large enough for all of them to ride together and drove to the city. They would spend their Saturday shopping, go to the concert that night and sleep at a hotel after the show. On Sunday they would relax at the beach before driving back home in the evening.

The drive was about two hours. The Moms sat in the front of the van, the girls in the back. Everyone was excited. They were going to lovely stores, always a treat, and then going to watch Diego Molina, a favorite singer who attracted all ages with his romantic songs.

The group was enjoying the concert and when Diego ended his song the audience exploded into applause. At the same moment he spotted Alina in the crowd in front of him. He wasn't sure why his eyes fell on this lovely young woman. He motioned to her and she waved back. "Come up here!" Diego shouted.

Alina's friends screamed in delight and pushed her toward the stage. Two of the beefy security agents came forward and each took one of her arms and effortlessly lifted her onto the platform. Diego reached out to her. He took her hand, brought it to his face and kissed it. He did the same on one of her cheeks. More screams from her friends and the crowd applauded profusely. "What's your name?" He asked.

"Alina."

Diego strummed the first notes of a song on his guitar. "Do you know it?" He asked.

"I do."

"Can you sing?"

"I think so," she answered shyly.

"Perfect." Diego wasn't worried about her singing prowess. He and his band could cover up anything terrible. He was more interested in her personality. Being a decent reader of body language, he was usually right on. He would alternate between audience members in each show, one of his trademarks. In one performance it could be an older woman who for sure knew all his songs, or a young pretty girl like Alina. It always made for a good show. "Would you accompany me?"

Alina nodded.

In the crowd Stacy just grinned. She knew, and soon others would too. As would her daughter. The youngster was too modest, or perhaps it was the age that didn't allow her to see how talented she really was.

Diego started humming into the microphone in front of him and when he sang the first words Alina walked up closer and joined in. No one expected the exquisiteness unfolding before them. The young woman's contralto voice was haunting, charismatic and as smooth as warm honey. She delivered the mesmerizing controlled notes emanating from behind the endearing smile with the finesse of a professional entertainer. Alina also possessed a natural stage personality that couldn't be learned. Every person in the theater was excited and firmly believed she was part of the show. Her girlfriends stared open-mouthed. They didn't know their friend could sing so well! Diego was captivated at the amazing young woman next to him. Their faces were close together and he could see from the glow in her eyes how alive they had just become, for this passion which she perhaps was still unaware. He knew the syndrome; it had been the same for him. Her soul was hungry, ready to savor the awakening feast Diego was sure would be the musical path of her life.

Alina truly loved her activities, especially the horses, music and dancing. As she stood on the stage in front of the microphone, giving joy to the people listening and watching, she suddenly realized her greatest passion was not just in music, but in singing. This was what she wanted to dedicate her life to doing. An enormous shiver enveloped her entire body in blissful affirmation as she held a note and tried to concentrate on the song and her singing partner.

Diego and Alina's duet was enchanting and when they ended he asked her simply: "Are you a professional singer?"

The audience anxiously awaited her response. Was she someone famous they weren't aware of?

Alina giggled and answered: "I'm a diva in the car and in the shower."

Diego and the crowd laughed. They liked the young woman.

"May I ask how old you are?"

"Sure. Fourteen."

The audience gasped. She looked older. Her lovely curves belonged to a woman's body, and her voice certainly had the maturity of a seasoned singer.

Diego really liked her, but she was so damn young and he was twenty years older. She was pretty and he knew that in the next few years she would be a spectacular beauty who would undoubtedly break many, many hearts. But he wasn't willing to wait for her to 'grow up', rather he saw himself more of an older brother, a protector who wanted to take care of his protégée. He gave her a hug, kept one of his arms around her shoulders and with the other raised it to the lights. He turned to the audience. "Ladies and gentlemen," he shouted into the microphone, "the world of music has a new star!" The spectators agreed and clapped hard. Diego kissed one of her cheeks and quickly whispered in her ear. "I will wait for you backstage after the show. My people will expect you. Please do not take this any way other than I believe you are truly a talent and I would like to help you."

Alina didn't give anything away, rather she was calm and collected. "Thank you, I will see you then," she whispered back. "This was fun."

Alina was right, Diego thought. It had been fun, for both of them. This was how it was supposed to be. Music wasn't a job, rather it was a passion that came from the depths of one's soul. He was grateful to her for reminding him. He led her to the edge of the stage and the security men lifted her as easily as they had the first time and set her gently on the floor. She smiled and thanked them. Diego watched Alina go back to her friends and waved. Alina immediately told her mother about the invitation and although Stacy hadn't been invited—they really didn't know about her—she had complete confidence in her daughter and wasn't worried about Diego or his people. Perhaps it was her mother's intuition, maybe a musician's, or quite simply she had faith in her child and her talent. She would wait for Alina with the other friends at the designated area and would be there if she was needed. For the moment she would let her daughter step into this new world on her own.

After the show Alina went backstage. As promised one of the entertainer's staff waited for her and she was ushered to a large room. There were so many people she could barely make Diego out. When she finally reached him, he was very pleased to see her.

"Ah, Alina, you made it."

"I did. Wow, this place is packed. Aren't you supposed to be relaxing?"

"Oh, I don't mind. A few minutes with some special fans is good public relations and always fun. It makes them happy and gives me the satisfaction they still like me."

"They will always like you."

"What makes you say that?" Diego asked, intrigued.

"You're a good guy with big talent. You will have fans forever, unless you do drugs and too much alcohol," Alina said with the typical sincerity of her age.

Diego raised his eyebrows. "How old did you say you were?"

"Fourteen."

"Going on forty."

Alina giggled. "My father says that."

"He's right. Now, I want you to meet Miguel. He's my manager and my right hand. You two need to talk. I've already spoken to him about you."

Diego introduced the two. Miguel was in his late

thirties, wearing a light summer suit of pastel peaches with an iridescent scarf around his neck. He was a sharp dresser and wore it perfectly in the South Florida atmosphere.

"Alina, come, let's go where there's less noise," Miguel said.

"Okay, lead the way."

Miguel noticed that the girl had no fear, spoke her mind and could probably take care of herself, both verbally as well as physically. Her stride was athletic and her self-assuredness made him think she had perhaps some martial arts under her belt. He knew he would enjoy getting to know her. "I have a room across the hall," he said, heading to his suite. They entered and Miguel motioned for her to sit down. Alina did. He left the door open.

"Well, this is a little quieter," Alina said.

"You think?" Miguel chuckled. He went to a little refrigerator. "Would you like something to drink?"

"Water would be perfect," Alina answered.

"Yes, I'll have the same." Miguel produced two bottles and gave her one of them.

"Thank you, uh, Mr. ..."

"Miguel, call me Miguel."

"Okay."

Alina noticed that Miguel's eyes didn't shine the same way other men's did when they met her, until another man walked in the room. The man was big, really big. He and Miguel stared at each other. No words were uttered, just a loving smile for each other.

"Alina, this is Santiago, our guitar player from Spain. Santi is also my husband," Miguel said, introducing them. "Santi, this is Alina."

"Hola, *guapa,*" hello, beautiful, Santiago said and

kissed Alina on both cheeks as if they had known each other forever. Alina could see the attraction. Santiago immediately exuded warmth and kindness. She had no doubt this pair was a loving, doting couple who could be an example to many. He was also one of the biggest men Alina had ever seen. He reminded her of a giant teddy bear, sweet and cuddly, but was sure no one messed with him. She remembered him from the musicians as his instrument was the classical guitar which was one of her favorites and the one she loved to play. She was even more in awe of his delicate fingers as she hadn't realized how big the man was.

"Mucho gusto," Alina answered and gave him a big smile.

"Now that's a million-dollar smile!" Santiago said.

"Make that many million!" Miguel answered back.

"Ah, this smells like a business meeting."

"You're right, Santi. Diego thinks we have a budding star here."

"Diego is absolutely right. I heard you sing, young lady, you were terrific!" Santiago complimented her. "And you are a very pretty girl. Sounds like a perfect package to me."

"Thank you," Alina said, glowing and excited from all the compliments, especially from such musicians as Diego and Santiago.

The big man left the room dancing, heading to where there was more noise and especially music, food and drinks.

During the meeting Miguel learned of Stacy's existence and had of course invited her. She was prepared and told her friends that if she was called, to leave with the van. She and Alina would find a way to the hotel. She was ushered to the room where Miguel and Alina waited for her. After they were introduced, he answered every one of their questions and gave them a rough outline of what he could do for Alina and her musical career, if she wanted to go ahead with it.

Diego and Santiago walked into the room all excited.

"Guess what?" Santiago shouted.

"What?" Miguel asked.

Santiago could hardly contain himself. "The Diego-Alina duet from the concert was posted on social media. It's a phenomenon! Even the late news channels are talking about it! The morning shows are sure to run it too!"

Diego turned to the Alina and said: "Well, rising star, are you ready to…" He noticed the other woman in the room. "Oh, hello," he said to Stacy. Now this was more his age bracket, and the lady was a knockout. He realized this must be Alina's mother as he recognized several traits.

"Hello," she said, extending her hand to Diego, "I'm Stacy, also known as the mom."

Diego gave her a very Latin kiss on the back of her hand. "I gathered. And also the reason for all the beauty in the room," he answered, already smitten.

"Alina definitely has Mommy to thank for her good looks," Santiago said.

"Is Daddy beautiful as well?" Miguel asked.

"He's a drop-dead gorgeous Spanish Hidalgo," Stacy said proudly, knowing the husbands would appreciate her compliment. She also quickly, albeit gently, put a pin in Diego's balloon.

"Does your husband know how lucky he is?" Diego asked.

Alina watched her mother. She was seeing her in new

light, in a way she had never seen her before. Diego was actually flirting with her. What would her mom do? The girl wondered.

"Actually, I'm the lucky one," Stacy answered.

Alina grinned.

Diego understood and appreciated the devotion. Stacy was obviously happy with her marriage. He knew there wouldn't be anything he could do about how much he would have liked a relationship with this lady. Diego deflated as fast as he had inflated. He changed the subject and asked Alina: "Well? Ready to make this a full-time job?"

"It's hard work, it really is," Santiago added, speaking from first-hand experience.

"That's true," Miguel added, "but I think you have a strong personality with a sharp mind and won't be easily awed so as to deviate from your path. From what you and your mom told me about your background you're very well rounded and traveled, especially for your age. That's a great asset for you to have."

The more time they all spent together the more they warmed up to each other. They laughed good-heartedly and had interesting conversations. The meeting had been easy going and professional.

"Well, I think you need to take some time and, of course, speak to your father," Diego said. "Let us know what you decide."

"We're here for you, Alina," Miguel added.

"We will. Thank you all very much," Stacy said, standing up.

The others followed suit and the customary kisses and hugs ended the meeting.

HEART SONG

♫

CHAPTER 22

For the next several years Miguel worked incredibly hard to launch Alina's career and introduced her to the international musical community. He did his job so well he catapulted Alina to superstardom. He booked her on every talk show possible, not only in the U.S but in Latin America and as far east as New Zealand and Japan. When she started to take off and was becoming well known, thanks to her manager as much as her talent, Miguel booked performances at major venues. He also arranged her appearances not to interfere with her schooling so that she could graduate and even attend a couple years of university.

In seven years Alina became one of the biggest stars in the world. Miguel remembered their first meeting, impressed by young Alina's talent and self-assuredness. Her mother Stacy had been a big help, as a mentor and a financial advisor. Her business degree had come in handy and mother and daughter oversaw the transactions and remained vigilant of the financial negotiations. It wasn't that they didn't trust the people working for them, rather it was to keep everyone on their toes, including themselves. They double checked every expense and had a say in what Alina would do, where she could sing and what she could do with her earnings. A percentage of each concert and royalties was put in a separate account for charities. From the travels with her parents in impoverished areas, Alina wanted to help and do some good.

Through the years Alina became more and more passionate about her charitable contributions. Her main focus was on health, which included medicine, purifying water and growing food. She always managed to get the top people of pharmaceutical companies to donate a small percentage of their medicine for free, to all corners of the globe, including to the needs of Médecins Sans Frontières. She did the same with water purifying and agricultural companies.

Another of Alina's charitable passions was education. She firmly believed that if everyone had rounded general knowledge, learned a trade or continued higher education, especially women, people could progress. Having traveled extensively and lived in different areas of the world Alina was well aware that poverty and desperation only brought negative results such as misery, hopelessness and crime. Stability brought peace, hope and joy. Her dream was to see and to live in such a world. She wanted to help make that vision into a reality.

Preservation of national treasures, whether manmade or natural wonders, was another area where she was generous with her money and her time. People came and went, but their heritage and history needed to survive in order to keep their identity forever alive.

In return, several times a year, Alina would give free concerts for the employees of the companies and the sponsors helping, wherever in the world their enterprises were. It was a winning situation for everyone.

After each show Alina worked the room. She remembered Diego's concert and what a wonderful experience it had been for the artist, and more so for the fans. She continued the tradition.

One of the painful aspects of being famous were the bad gossip and the lies. Alina read an article in one of the newspapers that was known for demeaning celebrities. She couldn't believe what they were saying about her. How could they report she was making out with two different men in a club she had never even heard of?

"People will say unkind things no matter how perfect you are," Miguel responded. "Human nature includes fear, hate and jealousy. As hard as you try you can never please everybody. Don't let it affect you. Brush it off with a little humor or forget about it completely. In the meantime, I'll take care of that rag and threaten to sue them."

"It doesn't matter. What's done is done," Alina said, anger now taking over the sadness and disappointment.

"I know, but it will make them think twice before printing any more garbage about you."

♫

CHAPTER 23

2019 – MIAMI BEACH

Seven years after that first time on stage, Alina, at the tender age of twenty-one, was a famous international sensation and a very wealthy young woman. She loved the good life and fun, expensive toys. One of her favorites was her red vintage Dino Ferrari. She also loved good wine and food and had an affinity for ethnic specialties. Her travels at a young age had been the impetus. On her world tours, which always included dozens of foreign countries, she was very often invited to the most succulent meals a country's representative would provide, but she preferred putting on a big hat and going incognito to where the locals hung out. She loved asking the policeman on a corner where he would take his mother to eat and when the answer came with a proud smile, she would go to the recommended eatery. It was almost always the best meal.

Alina could buy anything she wanted, but most important in her life was the love of family. Her parents meant everything to her. They had given her a global education, lived in different countries around the world where she learned languages and the importance of traditions such as music, food, a way of life and beliefs. She realized that no matter what country, religion or background, every person in the world longed for the same thing—to love and be loved, to be happy and at peace which was a form of love as well. She firmly believed in giving back, as she knew how incredibly lucky she was. She provided funds and supplies to charities around the globe and never bragged about it or advertised it.

Alina loved being a citizen of the world, as she referred herself, but she needed a base, a pied-à-terre. She wanted a place to call home and Miami seemed to be the right city in the best geographic location for her needs. It was a perfect crossroad between the Americas and the European continent. Besides, she loved the bustling metropolis. It had its modern amenities, yet it had distinct traditional values. It was international with a great culinary scene, a hopping nightlife and great beaches. It was a fun place to live.

Alina called a real estate agent her manager suggested.

The round building, also known as the Vinyl, stood out on Miami Beach's skyline and enhanced its beauty. As Alina looked up at the circular building it reminded her of a stack of records, hence its nickname. How appropriate for a singer, she thought. The imposing building seemed to be made of dark glass and towered toward the heavens. It was very exclusive, with each floor an enormous single apartment with a magnificent 360-degree view of the ocean and the beaches from north to south as well as the city of Miami and its environs. The roof sported a helipad with service to Miami International, Opa Locka, Ft. Lauderdale-Hollywood International, or any other airport in the surrounding area a tenant would wish to catch a plane from, commercial or private. In addition to the immense outdoor pool and bar, twenty-four-hour amenities included small more intimate pools, both indoor and outdoor, a spa, beauty salon, gym, a laid-back piano lounge, a dance club and several restaurants that included American as well as international delicacies by the most celebrated chefs from around the world. Three of the lower floors were converted into a private mall solely for the Vinyl occupants. Different stores carried exclusive merchandise and famous clothing designers added their mark to the prestige of the building. Housekeeping services were always available, as well as personal assistants who could probably find or get anything a resident desired, day or night. In addition, there were master carpenters and staff on site who could make special furniture as the building commanded beautiful and unique rounded pieces. There was also a small clinic for minor injuries or emergencies, such as heart attacks. If needed the resident helicopter could take a patient to the nearest hospital.

When Alina purchased her apartment, which was located in about the middle of the building, there were several features she fell in love with. One of them was the windows. They were clear to enjoy the magnificent views and brought in wonderful light, but from the outside they were tinted very dark. She could run around completely naked and no one could see her, although no other buildings were really close enough, but as a celebrity it was nice to feel protected from the eyes of fans. Alina also loved the elevator that opened directly into the apartment. If a resident expected guests one of the concierges would accompany the visitors.

Another state-of-the-art feature was the uniqueness of its own small police department, not just regular guards. The security systems were the best in the world, from vibrational motion detectors to canines walking the grounds. Specialists watched the grounds and building from a room full of screens receiving data from surveillance cameras and 24-hour whisper-silent drones.

The Vinyl boasted some of the most expensive real estate in the world and the inhabitants were of the wealthiest and well-known on the planet. Miami was a Mecca for celebrities, especially Latin American stars. And then of course, South Florida prided itself with prodigious business opportunities, which included the fashion industry and modern studios for film and music. It didn't matter where you came from in the world, all nationalities were welcomed and made to feel at ease. Alina was one of those celebrities and was proud to call Miami home.

One of Alina's favorite areas in the apartment, which she called her music room, housed delightful and unusual instruments collected from around the world. Some of her favorite pieces were from Latin America, especially the rain stick and the tinamou flute made from beautiful exotic *ipe* wood also known as Brazilian walnut. They were gifts from the Desana tribe in the heart of the Amazon. Never would Alina forget the villagers, especially the wounded young girl and the harrowing escape from the black caiman.

From the Far East Alina picked up several music makers, such as a *yi-wu* from China, its two strings and bow connecting with the sound box covered with snakeskin. One of her favorites was the gopichand which she had seen when she sneaked off with Santiago, her main man to have fun with, whether it was dancing or going to unusual places like a concert or a gathering of local musicians. The big man also doubled as her bodyguard. As incognito as possible, Alina and Santiago had attended a performance by a group of mystic minstrels who mixed elements of Sufism and Sahaja from the Bengal region. Alina was fascinated by the instrument they played, its design a piece of bamboo split in half with one steel string tied to a peg at the top and fastened at the bottom of a bowl. She bought two and gave one to a friend who had a Bengal cat and swore it sounded exactly like the miniature leopard kitty.

From Australia she couldn't help but accept an amazing didgeridoo from a group of Aborigines performing in the outback. They also gave her a coveted bullroarer, an instrument used in ceremonies such as initiations, burials and to ward off evil spirits. It was decorated with local Aboriginal drawings and wasn't much larger than a man's hand. It was in the shape of a surfboard, with a hole in the back and a string running through it so it could be whirled. When it spun through the air, it made a low-pitched sound which traveled quite a distance.

From the central coastal state of Maharashtra in India Alina picked up a brass decorated dotar, *do* and *tar* meaning two and string in Hindi. The soundboard was goat skin stretched over a pumpkin gourd body. She also picked up an Afghan jaw harp.

The room also housed many music makers from the Middle East including a variety of drums, string instruments such as a Turkish zither, a tanbur, a saz and an oud. From Israel Alina learned to use a shofar by putting her lips against the mouthpiece to force air through. In the beginning she would laugh as it vibrated her lips and made them tickle. The vendor explained the horns usually came from rams or kudu antelopes and would be used to announce events such as Yom Kippur. Alina's collection also included bouzoukis from Greece.

Among the African instruments there were assortments of exquisite drums, flutes, zithers and thumb pianos. One of the more unusual instruments was a rattle from the Hopis in Arizona. It was made of a sun-dried antelope scrotum filled with sand.

Alina also had a recording studio built in her apartment which housed the consoles behind the glass where Alina and her musicians produced their melodies. Like the rest of the residence, it had unique views and she adored sitting at the piano or playing the guitar as she composed with the exquisite vistas around her. She also enjoyed her gym room with some favorite equipment she used as faithfully as possible. After a grueling workout she thoroughly appreciated the marble bathroom with yet more views, a television, music and a phone, all with a voice control system while soaking in the massage bathtub. Sometimes she sipped some chilled champagne or a lovely, tepid Cognac. She didn't like getting drunk as she believed it stripped away the character of the person, and really didn't like the morning-after effects and the abuse on the body. As far as drugs she had absolutely no use for them and didn't tolerate them around her. She loved letting loose, but still liked being in control of her faculties. Her natural highs came from her passions and the pleasures of nature, music and people. As she soaked in the bathtub, she dreamed of finding a twin soul to share her life with. Alina wondered if she would ever find a love as profound as her parents had.

Another of her pleasures at the Vinyl was that she could walk around the shops and restaurants and feel safe and wouldn't be bombarded by adoring fans. All the residents were famous, for one reason or another, and when they saw each other it wasn't a novelty. Another perk was she could wear comfortable sweats, or an exquisite long gown. Although everyone discretely paid attention, they did the same and no one cared. Alina loved that unique freedom and privacy.

♫

CHAPTER 24

2022 – MIAMI BEACH

Jax watched the newest Alina interview. It had been taped in her home, and although the crew did a very good job to not reveal the exact location, Jax caught a reflection from a window. It told him exactly where she lived. She was in the Vinyl! Of course, absolutely appropriate for a singer to live in a building that looked like a stack of records. Jax's mind was racing. Now that he knew where she lived, he had to find a way to meet her there. He obviously couldn't just knock on her door, even if he got that far. He was sure there was some sort of incredible security everywhere. Jax studied the building from every angle, googled everything he could find about the property and the apartment. An idea came to him. He checked the realtors that carried the listing for the Vinyl. He studied their faces and decided on Lucy, a middle-aged woman with a happy smile. He immediately called her. As expected, she was very receptive and professional. Jax gave her the information she requested and when she discovered who he was, she was eager to meet her prospective client. They made an appointment to see one of the apartments.

The next day Jax and Lucy parked their cars at the entrance to the grounds of the skyscraper. Jax drove up in an Austin Healy similar to the one in the JAX commercial. It had been love at first sight, and when the first large funds came in, he thought he deserved to splurge on the sports car and made the purchase. Jax wore a polo shirt and perfectly fitted jeans from his collection. Lucy liked the look and appreciated the handsome man wearing the clothes.

"Jax?"

"Yes, hi, you must be Lucy," Jax said, recognizing her from her picture on the website. "Nice to meet you," he said as they shook hands.

"Nice to meet you too." This guy is gorgeous, Lucy thought, and no ring. He probably had a girlfriend, but she knew how to get information out of him and even more. "Ready to see the apartment?"

"Absolutely. I can hardly wait!" If you only knew how much, dearest Lucy. With each step Jax was getting closer to Alina.

"Great. One of the guards will drive us to the building's entrance in one of their carts."

"Sounds good. Security must be tight here."

"Oh, yes, it is. In addition to security, they have their own police force."

"Considering it's the most expensive building in south Florida."

"That's true, Jax, many VIPs live here. This building and the amenities rival anything in Monte Carlo or Dubai. Worth every penny."

"Lucy, as you say many celebrities live here, including

Alina. I need to ask you what floor she lives on." He waited a few moments before adding: "Because I wouldn't want to be above or below her." Just without clothes, he thought to himself.

"That's an interesting question. May I ask why?"

"Because being a singer I'm sure there are loud parties and maybe even recording sessions." He knew she had a studio in her apartment from an interview he had seen and of course he knew it would be soundproof, but he needed the information.

"Oh, that won't be a problem, the entire building is soundproof. She could be using a megaphone or giving a concert from her apartment and you wouldn't hear it even if you had your ear glued to the wall. Unless of course the party is outside on the balcony. I must tell you up front there are only a couple of apartments available and that is several floors away from her. Would that be too close?"

"I think that would be okay," he said nonchalantly.

"Okay, let's check them out."

"Sounds good, Lucy, thank you."

The security guard drove up in a golf cart and they promptly took off. Lucy explained the amenities as they headed toward the building. Once they passed more guards and police officers, they stopped in front of an imposing lobby and headed inside. Lucy was right. The Vinyl was as exquisite as any building the rich and famous called home. Although Jax had been around the world for elite equestrian competitions and had been privy to some unique grandeurs, the Vinyl impressed him. But he kept it low key. "It's nice," he said, almost with a yawn.

Nice? Lucy thought to herself. Was he one of those rich, pompous asses? She hoped not. She had researched his background. His financials seemed sound, and he was the famous Jaxon Logan from the *JAX* lines, but she would keep an eye on him.

Jax of course would have loved an apartment in the Vinyl, and he was well off, but this was financially out of his league, at least for the time being.

The concierge led them to the elevator and took them to the floor they would visit. They quickly arrived and the door opened directly into the apartment. It was exquisite. Jax had expected it would be, but it truly took his breath away. "This is very nice," he said slowly.

This *nice* shit again, Lucy thought. "It is rather lovely and truly unique. Shall we see the other one?"

"Yes, please."

They headed to the other apartment. Lucy had to get closer to her client. She wanted to make a sale. Her return would be substantial. "Alina's place is two floors below us," Lucy whispered. "Please don't tell anyone I said that."

Jax's heart jumped a beat. Perfect! "I didn't hear a thing. Don't worry, and thank you, Lucy."

"Remember, there are others wanting to see these apartments."

"Yes, I'm sure."

"Would you be living here alone, or perhaps with Mrs. Logan?"

"No, just me." Jax knew what she was doing. He wasn't a rookie with the ladies and knew she was fishing. "I think I like this one more than the other one. I know they are similar, but I like the view better."

"Okay. Jax, listen I'm not trying to be pushy, but these are in great demand."

"I understand. I'll let you know in the next couple of days."

"Sounds good."

The concierge escorted them back out.

♫

224

CHAPTER 25

Back at the ranch the sun was setting. Jax and Bernardo rode out to the firepit the gaucho had built so many years ago. There were many wonderful memories since that first time young Jax started asking the older man questions. Now they were riding side by side, looking forward to a churrasco and a night under the stars.

When they finished dinner Jax said goodnight and went to his makeshift bed, a saddle he used as a pillow and a blanket he threw over himself. Before falling asleep he watched Bernardo dancing a tango with his invisible Maria. As Jax listened to the music he slowly drifted off. Once asleep he dreamed of Alina. He watched himself checking his computer, searching websites and fan clubs, but wasn't getting anywhere or any answers in how to reach her. His dream continued into a meeting between himself and a private investigator. Now he was getting somewhere. The P.I. found information on upcoming concerts, TV shows, interviews and all of their locations. He also had information on *Global Songster*, her yacht, and the apartment building where she lived. Jax followed the clues. The first was that Alina would be relaxing on her pleasure vessel before heading out on a grueling world tour. The Private Investigator had managed to find out the location. She was headed to Key West. Alina and a few of her closest friends sailed through the turquoise waters of the Florida Keys to the most southern point of the United States. Jax was driving over the seven-mile bridge toward the same destination. He loved the bridge as he imagined he was rolling on the surface of the water. The drive took him approximately three hours. He found the yacht moored away from the marina and went towards it. He could see the people on board having drinks and eating appetizers as they enjoyed the party. He recognized some celebrities.

Jax continued watching himself in a diver's suit swim under the anchored yacht. He was going to the party as well. Why didn't he walk up the gangplank like the other invited guests? *Because you aren't invited, stupid.* Jax continued swimming until he was almost at the back of the boat. He heard the powerful engines of the yacht start up. *Oh, no!* The voice in his head screamed. He watched the anchor being pulled up and suddenly he was being pulled toward the boat at a very fast pace. Jax struggled to swim away, but it was in vain. The intake was too powerful. When he saw one of the propellers just inches from his body he started to scream. He immediately woke up.

Jax was soaked in perspiration, so much so he thought maybe he really had been under the yacht. He shook his head, chastised himself for the ridiculous dream and covered himself up. He was soon fast asleep again. This time his dream took him to the Vinyl, Alina's apartment building. He watched the meeting between himself and Lucy and remembered details of the structure. He knew exactly how he was going to meet Alina.

The moon was hidden behind some clouds and Jax stood on the roof of the tall edifice. He was dressed all in black, from his shirt to his shoes, and wore a black helmet. Jax smiled in his dream. He was just as handsome, sophisticated and creative as James Bond. He was also a suave Cary Grant on the French Riviera and Alina was his Grace Kelly. But Jax wasn't chasing bad guys or stealing jewels, no, he was going to present the greatest gift possible to Alina—himself. Jax lifted a rope from a black backpack, attached it to a carabiner and onto a post on the roof. He went to the ledge, threw the rope over and started rappelling down the side of the building. Inside the helmet Jax's eyes were looking into the night vision goggles. He could have been an enormous four-legged insect from outer space with glowing green eyes. As he continued down, he could see green silhouettes of people in their apartments living their lives. One was jumping up and down, exercising on a mini trampoline. Another was taking a round green item out of a very large glowing green box. Jax assumed it was a pizza from an oven. On a lower level a couple was making love. Jax continued until he was on Alina's floor. He could see her green silhouette and his breath caught in his throat. He was closer than he had ever been to her. He watched what she was doing and smiled as he could tell she was enjoying playing something on her guitar.

Jax wanted to rush in and have sex, to satisfy the carnal need of an aching teenager, but his heart and his mind held him back. No, he wanted to be the most magnificent lover Alina could ever imagine or desire. As she saw him on the balcony she grinned and stood up. She went up to him and held out her hand. His heart melted as he read the longing in her eyes and the happiness in her smile. She was delighted to see him. He took her hand and climb over the railing. Jax tenderly cradled her face between his hands and kissed her lips, slowly at first then hungrily. Oh, had he ever been right! Those were the sweetest, most luscious lips in the world. Her hands moved slowly over his chest, lingering along his torso. Jax could feel every nerve ending coming to attention. Suddenly she stopped and turned around. The move was so fast and so unexpected that it took Jax by surprise and he lost his footing. He started falling over the railing and tried to grab the rope. He missed and tumbled over the top of the balcony and headed fast toward the ground. He landed in a large swimming pool with a colossal splash.

Jax woke up. He took a deep breath and shook his head. *The most wonderful kiss in my life on the way to the best love making ever was a fucking dream? Seriously!? Not very 007 of you, moron.*

♫

CHAPTER 26

2022 – CONNECTICUT

After twelve years Randy walked out of the gates of the prison he had spent more than a decade of his life in. No one waited anxiously to give him a loving embrace or to take him to eat a nice meal. Not that he expected anyone. His parents definitely were not there. In the beginning, for the first two years he was incarcerated, Randy had a glimmer of hope his parents might come visit, maybe even just his mother, but they never did. He even wrote to them, but the letters always came back, unopened and just as lifeless as Randy's heart was. He even hoped they could get him released, as they had in the Spanish prison. His parents never asked about him or sent a lawyer. They kept their word and never saw their son or tried to contact him again. Randy wondered if they ever missed him, or even thought about their only child. Well, the Newtons would see their son one more time. They would pay, and it would be painful.

Randy caught a bus to the nearest town on the ocean. He needed to smell the air coming off the water, that delicious combination of salt and freshness, a subconscious rejuvenation and peacefulness. He sat on a bench and watched the waves gently crashing on the edge of the beach and the foam caressing the sand. He didn't move for over an hour and took in the sea air, the birds singing and the quiet. It was the beginning of the year and the bitter cold kept other people away. Randy didn't care. He welcomed the peace and his new-found freedom.

When the cold started turning him numb, he walked toward the center of the town. He looked into store windows and found what he was looking for. He bought a tablet. He was amazed at how much the technology had advanced in the last decade. He went to a diner and studied the menu. Comfort food. He was free. It started dawning on him that he could do anything he wanted, he could eat whatever pleased him and he didn't have to answer to anyone. A waitress came by his table. She wore an apron over her uniform and held a little notepad and a pen. She was in her early thirties and gave him a warm smile as she welcomed him. Randy almost didn't know what to do. No one had smiled at him in such a long time, especially not a woman. She was cute, with a kind demeanor. She had natural Nordic blond hair and soft blue eyes. Randy was sure she was a descendent from Vikings. She had a lovely mouth with nice, straight teeth and a soothing smile. He pictured clearing the table, laying her on it and having sex with her. He hadn't touched a woman in years.

"Hi," she said joyfully, "do you know what you would like to eat?"

'Normal' conversation. That was a novelty, too. Randy looked at her and realized he could still smile. "Yes, I do." He ordered enough food for two people.

"Oh, you're a hungry boy!" She giggled.

"I am."

"Good. I'll bring it out as soon as it's ready."

"Thank you."

While Randy waited for his food, he absentmindedly watched the television on a wall in the diner. A commercial came on and he immediately recognized Jax. His former teammate was with a model, both were on horses, galloping through a field of wildflowers wearing clothes from the JAX collections. Randy recognized Almea and his blood seemed to boil in his veins. He heard the tango music from the dressage competitions Jax used. If that wasn't infuriating enough, Jax had his own line of clothing, including an exclusive one for riders. Randy had been holding a glass and he desperately wanted to throw it at the television. His heart pumped faster and his blood pressure skyrocketed making his face turn an ugly crimson. If *he* had won the gold medal at the Olympics, *he* would've been in Jax's shoes and living that life, and not the one he had endured for more than a decade. Randy started trembling as his rage soared. The waitress walked by and saw him shaking.

"Are you cold?"

"What? Uh, no, I'm fine," Randy said, fighting hard to control his temper.

She put a hand on his arm. "You're sure now?"

Randy shuddered. He hadn't been touched in years, at least not in a caring way and certainly not by a woman. He nodded that he was okay.

"The food will be here in a couple of minutes," she said, "that'll warm you right up."

"Thank you."

True to her word the waitress brought out Randy's meal. It took her two trips. She wondered if the man actually could eat everything he ordered. She looked over every once in a while, curious about him. He didn't seem homeless and he was a decent looking guy, but there was something weighing him down, a clear emptiness and sadness in his eyes. He looked tired, as if he had been on a long trip. When Randy was almost finished, she went up to him.

"How was it?

"Really good, thanks."

"Would you like some dessert? How about a homemade hot apple pie? We make them from scratch every day."

"Sure, why not?"

"Vanilla ice cream on top?"

"Absolutely."

"Well, alright," she said jovially, "coming right up." She left to get the order and came back a couple of minutes later. She put the plate on the table in front of Randy. "Here you go, enjoy."

"Wow, it looks great. Thanks."

"Tastes even better."

Randy tried it and looked up at her. "You're right, it's delicious."

"Great! Glad you like it."

"Definitely. Uh, may I ask your name?"

"Of course, it's Darla. You can call me Dar if you want, everybody does."

"Okay, Dar," he said, smiling to her. "I'm new in town. Do you know of a motel somewhere, something not too expensive?"

"Oh, sure, there's one not far down the street. Tell them I sent you and they'll give you discount."

"That's very kind, thanks."

"My pleasure. Anything else I can get for you?"

Randy immediately thought of one particular thing.

He would have loved to take her to the motel room, instead he asked for the check.

Randy walked to the motel, checked in and went to his room. It was the usual cheap one-night rest stop, but to Randy it was a real mattress and a private bathroom, luxuries he hadn't enjoyed in years. He took a shower that lasted almost an hour. As he let the water rain on him, he started thinking about his plans for Jax and his parents. When he finished he flopped on the bed and passed out, a combination of having eaten such a large meal and the psychological freedom his brain had craved for so long.

The next morning Randy opened his tablet and checked for any new updates concerning Jax and his father. First, he googled Jax, his parents would be next. A list of information about Jaxon Logan immediately popped up. The more information he read the angrier he became. He learned that Jax had a clothing collection, which he understood from the commercial, and the man had opened an equestrian center in Florida. Jax was wealthy, a model citizen and praised for his philanthropy.

Randy listened to his stomach growling, telling him that it was hungry again. He decided to go back to the diner for breakfast. It seemed the early morning rush was over and people were leaving to go to their jobs.

"Hey, how are you?" Dar asked, recognizing him. She was carrying a tray of dirty dishes.

Randy smiled. "Good. Hungry."

"Great! Have a seat wherever you like and I'll be right over," she said, taking the tray to the kitchen.

Randy nodded and found a table in a corner. He liked the quietness. He picked up a breakfast menu and realized what a treat it was to hold a menu and order anything printed on the pages. When Dar came around she poured him a cup of coffee. He thanked her and ordered the 'super special', a sampling of everything and enough for two people. When it was ready she brought the food and put it on the table.

"I brought you some syrup and extra butter," she announced.

"Great, thank you."

"By the way, how was the motel?"

"Oh, just fine, thanks, and the guy gave me a discount."

"Oh, good. Are you passing through, or are you hanging around for a while?"

Randy looked at her. "You know, I'm not sure yet, but if I do hang around, I'll definitely come to eat here."

"You're always welcome. Well, enjoy."

"Thank you, I will."

When Randy finished, and there wasn't a crumb left anywhere, Dar smiled and removed the plates. "You sure were hungry again," she giggled.

"I was, and I enjoyed the meal very much."

"Well good, another satisfied customer."

"Uh, Dar, do you ever take a break?" Randy asked.

"As a matter of fact my shift ends in about ten minutes. Did you need anything?"

"Well, I wanted to ask you a couple of things about the area, if you don't mind."

"Oh, sure, I'll come back as soon as I'm off."

Randy checked his finances and realized he still had quite a chunk from when the lawyer gave him the check in Spain. Basically, his father buying him out of his life. He hadn't touched much of it, even in Columbus, and the interest accumulated in the years he was incarcerated amounted to a significant sum. He could easily live on the funds for quite a while.

In less than a quarter of an hour Dar was dressed in casual clothes. She went to Randy and sat across from him at the table.

"Hey, I like the civilian look," Randy said.

"Yeah? No uniform, right?"

"Right."

"Okay, so what did you need? Something about the area?"

Randy and Darla spent the next hour talking. It seemed both people needed someone they could talk to. Darla relayed her life story, how she was born and raised in the area, her alcoholic parents and how she and her brother had run away. The youngsters had been teenagers, sixteen and seventeen, Darla being the oldest. They couldn't stand the smell of the stale alcohol, the filth in their home and their parents' indifference toward their kids and life in general. They wondered how long it would take them to realize their children had left. But no one ever looked for them, not their parents, nor the authorities. They lived on the streets for a while until Darla found a job waitressing at the diner. She had been there ever since.

Darla's story moved Randy and he couldn't help but think that some people should never be parents, probably even his own. "What about your brother?" He asked.

Randy saw the shadow forming over Darla's eyes. "I think he was just too overwhelmed by my parents and the misery of our life. After we left, he fell in with a bad crowd from the streets, became a junkie and started dealing. He was caught by the police and since he wasn't quite eighteen they gave him a choice—jail or the army. He went into the service and was sent to Afghanistan."

"Oh, no."

"Yeah, and unfortunately he stayed there."

"How do you mean? Was he…"

"IED. It killed him."

"Oh, Dar, I'm so sorry."

"Yeah, thanks. Maybe he's in a better place. I keep thinking, if I had done something differently, he would still be alive."

"Hey, I'm sure you did everything you could. You can't blame yourself; besides, if it's anybody's fault it would be your damn parents!" Randy said angrily, his voice rising. "Oh, I'm sorry, I didn't mean to shout."

"I have a feeling you have a parent issue as well."

Randy decided to tell Dar everything, from his upbringing to his incarceration. He was sure she would understand and oh, did it ever feel good to be able to talk to someone about it. Darla definitely was understanding. She took his hands in hers and squeezed them. "I'm sorry your parents were such asses. Your life could have been very different. Sounds like you were a prince with all the luck in the world and they failed you. Well, their loss is my gain."

"How do you mean?" Randy asked.

"If they hadn't been such idiots, they would have realized what a nice son they have."

Randy laughed. It was the very first time anyone had *ever* called him 'nice'. "How do you know?"

"I work in the hospitality business," Darla said with panache, "I'm really good at reading people."

Randy chuckled. He liked her, she was fun and had an easy manner around him. She was nice to look at too and she wasn't afraid of him. He sensed she was enjoying their talk as much as he was. "I see. And what is your gain?"

"Why, that I met you, silly."

Randy and Darla spoke for another half hour, holding hands the entire time. Neither one wanted to let go. They hadn't had any kind of caring physical contact with another person in a very long time. Randy lifted himself up from the bench in the diner and kissed her across the table. Darla didn't stop him. When their lips parted, she smiled.

Darla drove Randy to the motel in her old car. When he asked her to come in, she did. It only took moments for them to embrace. They held each other for a few minutes until he cradled her face and kissed her gently and then with much more enthusiasm. Darla went right along with him. She needed him as much as he needed her. They made love. Although Randy hadn't been with a woman for years, and had dreamed about a moment like this, he took his time and respected the woman that was showing him kindness. She had been good to him at the diner and now her heart and body were being just as compassionate. Randy and Darla stayed together through the night. They talked, made love, talked some more, and continued throughout the night until she had to go to work.

After two weeks Randy moved in with Darla.

"It's not the Taj, but its home."

"I think it's lovely."

"Yeah?"

"Yes, I do. It's cozy and inviting. You've done a nice job with the place."

"Thanks, Randy. I worked hard to call this my home. It's not big and fancy, but it's mine and I'm proud of how far I've come."

"You should be. You're a fighter, with a kind and caring heart."

Darla made him feel 'normal'. Randy worked very hard to keep his temper away from her. She only deserved to be treated well and he was careful around her. He also didn't drink, for two reasons. The first one was he was sure Dar hated anything connected with alcohol, which probably brought back painful memories of her parents. The second one was he didn't want to fall back into the alcoholic oblivion of his time in Columbus. He liked their relationship and was comfortable in their daily routine. He had grown very fond of Darla and he dared to think maybe he had even fallen in love. Perhaps it was her kindness and her understanding. He was also attracted to her pretty face and figure, and their love life was thrilling and satisfying.

"Dar, listen, I like you very much. Well, even more than that."

"I do too, Randy." Where was he going with this? she wondered. Was he leaving her?

"I have something I need to take care of. I have to leave tomorrow. It will probably take me a few weeks, or maybe a little longer. When I finish, I would like to come back and see you, be with you, if that's okay."

"I'd like that, Randy. I know we come from very different backgrounds, but I think we're good for each other. I'm sure you and I would work. I'm willing to wait for you."

Randy hugged her and kept her close to him. "I'm sorry I can't tell you more, but it's better for you."

"I understand. But can I ask if you really need to do whatever it is you want to do?"

"I really do." Randy had been preparing for years.

"You know, revenge and hate will only ravage your heart and soul."

Randy stared at her. He knew Darla was smart and

had she had the chance in her younger years she would have certainly excelled in a different career or an entrepreneurial endeavor. She also had good common sense and read him very well.

"Alright, I won't ask again. I would have preferred you stay here with me, but I understand it's something you think you need to do. Just be careful, please," she said.

"I will."

"Please come back to me, Randy."

He looked into her eyes. They were very wet and fiercely held back the tears that were just about to run down her cheeks. "That's my intention, believe me."

Darla nodded and Randy held her tightly. When she left for work, he wrote her a letter.

Dear Dar,

If you are reading this, I'm in a place, where admittedly I put myself, and will probably never be released or be my own person ever again. Perhaps I even died. You are the only one who was ever really kind, listened and truly cared for me. Words cannot express how much you and your love mean. If I am still alive, I will carry you and your love in my heart. I know it will keep me going. You are the only person I truly love. Please know that I am grateful for the time we had and maybe, if things had gone my way, we might have stayed together. Since they didn't, I want you to forget about me and move on with your life, find someone to love and who loves you back the way you deserve. Maybe have kids if you want them. I know you would be a good mother. How do I know? Yeah, I know something about people too and you have a big heart. Never change that.

I've enclosed a check since I won't be needing any money anymore. Use it any way you want. I hope this helps make your life a little easier.

(Signed) Randy

Randy folded the letter, put in a check for fifty thousand dollars and enclosed the papers in an envelope. He still had another ten thousand and figured he would probably spend around that amount in the next phase. He wrote her name and address, attached stamps, folded it and put it in his wallet. If he was caught and thrown back in jail, which would probably be for life this time, the letter would be ready to mail.

♫

CHAPTER 27

2022 – CALI, COLOMBIA

Alina's world tour was close to ending after six months on the road. She and her team had performed in twenty-five countries, throughout the United States, Europe, Latin America and for hundreds of thousands of spectators. The last venues were in Rio de Janeiro, Sao Paulo, Bogota and Cali. Her final one in a few days would be in Miami, but before returning to the States she wanted to really unwind and have some fun. The music and rhythm of the city awaited her.

Alina had no doubt that from the northern Mexican border to the tip of Cape Horn every person on the continent and in the Caribbean was alive with rhythm from the moment they woke up. No one lived without music and dancing. From the Mariachis of Mexico to the cueca dance of Chile, the sambas in Brazil, the merengue from the Dominican Republic, the Cuban mambo and everywhere in between, the impetus to move to a beat and shake hips was deeply rooted in their DNA. Since Alina was conceived in Colombia, perhaps the love of rhythm was insentiently in her as well. And maybe just the reason she had to put on a short blond wig, a loose t-shirt, jeans and sturdy dancing shoes. She added very red lipstick, which so many Latin women loved, and looked at herself in the mirror. She marveled at the difference and hoped she wouldn't be recognized. She wasn't the Alina people knew. She would pass as a pretty girl among other pretty girls.

Alina rehearsed constantly and danced hard on stage, but tonight she was ready to just let go and have a good time among the locals. She wanted to experience the love and pride of the Colombians for the dances they shared with the world. She especially wanted to check out the seductive and sensual champeta from the Caribbean coast, the vallenato from the Guajira peninsula, and the smooth native cumbia. Cali and her inhabitants were famous for their dancing and Alina was sure she would find a club where she could watch and maybe learn some of the steps.

Santiago accompanied her. Not only did he want to have fun and dance the night away, but he also wanted to be there for Alina. She was a fellow musician and he loved her as much as he would a little sister. She was family in many ways. And oh, could the girl dance! The other reason Santiago accompanied her was that the man was as big as a door and no one in their right mind would mess with him. No matter how independent Alina was, and how many adoring fans she had, there was always a danger element. She could be accidently hurt, or even forcefully kidnapped. He would protect her with his life.

Alina and Santiago discreetly headed out of the hotel and hailed down a taxi. They told the driver to take them to the *Juanchito* neighborhood where all the hottest salsa nightclubs would be blaring their *pachangueros*, the happy-salsa-dancing-partying songs of the city.

They arrived in the hopping *barrio*. In every corner, from every club, music boomed into the street.

"Santi, we're definitely in the right place," Alina said excitedly as they exited the cab.

"Got that!" Santiago confirmed, already moving his hips to the rhythm.

Alina grabbed his hand and entered the first club in front of her. The Afro-pacific music native to Cali and its surrounding area pulled her in. They would try this one first. As they entered, some couples, possibly professionals or from one of the many local dance schools, were practicing their love of the insanely fast and sexy Colombian salsa. To them dancing was a beautiful addiction they couldn't get enough of. They loved showing off their ability and the spectators encouraged their amazing impromptu shows. Salsa was born in Cuba, but the Colombians were famous for their own lightning-fast version, especially the *Caleños'* sizzling feet which were as fast as blurring drumsticks.

Alina wasn't sure what she loved so much about Colombia. She couldn't get enough of the food, history and love for life, and was fascinated by the music and different dances. She found the people incredibly attractive, especially the women. They seemed to range from pretty to beautiful to stunning. Or perhaps it was the stories her parents had told her about how they met and fell in love in the jungle. Maybe it was simply that she was conceived in this country and somehow a 'I love Colombia' cell found its way into her DNA. Interesting concept, she thought, and wondered giddily if she would have a penchant for Antarctica if Alejandro and Stacy had lived there.

Alina and Santiago listened to the salsa music and

watched for a few moments before taking the floor. They danced to their hearts' content. The big man was surprisingly light on his feet and complemented Alina wonderfully. The singer cut loose. She let the love of music and dance fill her as she moved to the exotic and enticing rhythms. Alina and Santiago took a few breaks in between dances to hydrate, sometimes with water, sometimes with a local mezcal. They became friends with a cute couple who showed them intricate footsteps of the dances Alina had been interested in. She also thought Santiago would have been an amazing boxer as he was so light on his feet. After a little while, they heard a scream.

"*¡Ayyyy, es Alina!* It's Alina!" A fan shouted, recognizing her, delighted to see her idol in a club in her hometown barrio.

Santiago pulled her closer to him. "Time for us to disappear, you've been discovered."

"Yes, I heard, and I also see a group coming our way."

"Stay behind me and hold on to my belt. Whatever you do, don't let go."

Alina stepped behind him, grabbed a handful of the leather band and top of his pants and hung on. She was ready for the ride. She loved her fans and communicated with them via social media as much as she could. She understood and appreciated their adoration and respected them in return, but sometimes it became overwhelming. As it was in this instance. The big man moved quickly, faster than anyone expected. Alina was practically glued to him and made herself as small as possible, not always easy with her height. She towered over all the women and even some of the men. Santiago pushed toward the front exit when the mob, which had grown exponentially, suddenly moved in on them. Crazed fans were going after their favorite celebrity, others perhaps wanted a piece of her. He looked at their eyes to see which it could be. He didn't detect any danger, just adoration, but that could get out of hand. Fans grabbing a star to get a souvenir, such as a piece of clothing, wasn't unheard of. The mob was getting too close. Between the music and the screaming, the noise was deafening. At any moment the fans would be on them and they would be trapped. Alina could possibly talk her way out, at least for a few minutes, but Santiago didn't want to chance it, especially when he saw hands and arms close to grabbing his protégée. He whirled around, picked her up and threw her over his shoulder. "We're out of here," he yelled.

"Like this? Seriously?" Alina asked.

Santiago didn't answer. He was focused on getting her out safely. He leaned forward and into the direction of the crowd. They, in turn, saw the giant coming at them as if he were a linebacker for a professional NFL team, charging at them with his unusual and coveted 'football'. The crowd actually moved out of his way and the big man carried his bundle out the door. Once outside, he lifted Alina off his shoulder and put her on the ground. They ran to the nearest taxi, quickly entered and locked the doors as some fans tried to open them. They told the driver to immediately hit the gas pedal, and hard, and would tell him where to go in a moment.

"Well, Santi, that was interesting. Thanks for getting us out. By the way, where did you learn those moves?"

"I watch the Dolphins," he chuckled.

"As in the football team?"

"Uh, huh."

Alina nodded. "Well done. Maybe you'd like to join them? I'm sure you'd be their star player."

Santiago laughed. "No, I already play, with my

fingers on a beautiful guitar."

"That's true. And no other musician could replace you, my friend."

"Not to mention Miguel would kill me," he groaned.

"Oh, he'd kill both of us."

They laughed good-heartedly, pleased with their fun-filled evening and their escape. They told the driver to head to the hotel. Alina and Santiago had enjoyed their dancing and the entertainment and, even crazed as they were, the adoring fans.

♫

CHAPTER 28

2022 – CONNECTICUT

With the help of the investigator tracking Jax, Randy could now organize himself and finalize his revenge. His parents were first though, and they would pay dearly. How sweet it would be. He had planned and waited so long; the time had finally arrived.

Randy rented a pickup truck, went to a thrift store and bought an old bicycle that worked pretty well. He put it in the bed. Late that night he drove toward his parents' house. He went to a twenty-four-hour truck stop parking lot and left the pickup as far away from the lights as possible. Traffic was minimal and the moon was well hidden behind some clouds. Randy took the bike and started riding the two miles to his parents' house. When he arrived, he left it hidden under a tree and climbed the wall. Since he had grown up in the house, he knew all its little secrets and how to get in undetected. He jumped off and ran to the mansion. He was dressed all in black, including the ski mask, hoodie and gloves. The clothes were a couple sizes too large and that's what he wanted. It took away the details of the body and distorted the size and shape. Randy disconnected the alarm and climbed up a trellis attached to one of the mansion's walls. At the top he stepped over to a balcony and entered his father's den. It was dark, but there was just enough light from the street and he knew where everything was. He went to a Vermeer painting and pulled on one corner of the frame. Behind it was a safe. He pushed the numbers on the keypad. It opened. Randy had been ready to spend some time to decipher the combination but shook his head as he couldn't believe his father hadn't changed the combination—the month, day and year the company had gone public. He opened the door and pulled out what he was looking for, a Smith and Wesson .45. He didn't touch the clips storing the bullets next to it. The papers and cash in the safe didn't interest him. He checked out the pistol. It wasn't loaded and that's the way he wanted it. Randy left the door to the safe open just a crack and closed the painting. He put on black sunglasses. The Newtons would only be able to see an undistinguishable body all in black. He pulled out a common stenographer's notebook tucked in his pants, opened it to the first page and headed to his parents' bedroom. He carefully opened the door. They were asleep in the king size bed. He stared at them a few moments. His father's hair had turned salt and pepper and the skin on his face had acquired quite a few wrinkles in the last decade. His mother's face looked even more plastic from several additional lifting surgeries. Randy had been curious about his reaction when he saw them again. He wasn't surprised when there was only emptiness and hatred, a loathing for the injustice and indifference for their only child. These people were strangers, but they were also enemies and they would pay dearly. In prison Randy had dreamed up ways of how he would kill them. He thought of poisons, weapons, anything from a knife to a sniper rifle; a car accident or plane crash, but that was too easy, too quick. No, they had to suffer, not so much physically but psychologically. That would hurt more. Randy pictured himself on that bunk in prison and saw the smile on his face when he finally figured out how he would hurt his parents.

The moment was now. Randy put the gun on his father's forehead and tapped it until the older man woke up. When he did Randy, slapped him hard and put a gloved finger to his own lips. Damn, that felt good! He had dreamed about that as well. The older man was ready to scream, but instead put his hands up and kept quiet. Randy held up the steno pad. The writing, in thick marker, read:

WAKE HER UP.

The older man looked at the notebook and nodded. He didn't recognize the writing as Randy had spent several hours practicing with his left hand. He shook his wife until she woke up.

"What is it?" she asked, grumpily.

"You need to wake up and pay attention," her husband said.

She looked at him. He pointed to the man in black. She gasped and covered her mouth as she saw the gun pointed towards her.

Randy turned the page.

GO TO THE DEN. QUICKLY!

The Newtons obeyed and went to the room down the hall in their designer pajamas. Randy pointed to the chair and his mother sat down. He directed his father to his desk. He flipped another page.

OPEN YOUR COMPUTER.

"Why?"

Randy pointed the gun next to his mother's face.
"Okay, fine."
Randy turned to the next page.
DON'T THINK YOU CAN FOOL ME!

FOLLOW THESE INSTRUCTIONS:
GO TO THE FIRST ACCOUNT, WITHDRAW
$1,999,000,000 AND TRANSFER TO THE
OTHER ACCOUNT.

Randy had written down both account numbers.
"That's almost two billion dollars."
Randy pointed the gun toward the laptop and then to the older man's face.

"Fine." The older Newton wondered about the amount as that was more or less what his own fortune was worth.

Randy's father had no idea that earlier that evening his son had paid his accountant a visit, where, with the same steno pad method, he made the logistics man combine the entire Newton wealth into a new account. He could have made the accountant do what his father was now doing, but he wanted to see the older man's reaction when he realized what was going on. Randy had left the accountant tied and gagged to a chair and took his laptop. The man wouldn't have a way to track or prove anything he had just done, either to his father or the police. Randy knew the man's wife would be home the next day from a business trip. He would just have to wait until she found her husband. By then Randy would be long gone. It had all been meticulously planned, down to the timing of all the people involved.

Randy stood behind his father, the gun pointed at the back of his head. He lifted a finger to his lips. His mother nodded. He looked over the older man's shoulder and saw the confirmation of the transaction of the funds to his offshore account in the Cayman Island.

Randy flipped another page and showed it to his parents.

GO TO THE KITCHEN.

They looked at him questioningly. Randy waved the pistol toward the door. They hurried out and went downstairs. They stood in the middle of the kitchen and Randy looked around as if he had never been there before, but he knew exactly where everything was. He waved the gun toward a pantry.

"Who are you? What was this all about?" His father asked.

Randy shoved his parents in the pantry. The older man slipped and fell to the floor. His mother was by his side until she realized he was fine. She sat next to him.

"Please don't kill us," she pleaded.

Randy stared. It would be so easy to kill them. He hadn't made one sound and he really wanted to tell his parents what assholes they were, but he held back. That momentary pleasure could land him back in jail for the rest of his life, something he swore to himself he would never go through again. Instead, he turned to the last written page of the steno pad.

IF YOU'RE WONDERING WHAT THIS WAS ALL ABOUT IT'S SIMPLE.

YOUR ENTIRE FORTUNE WAS TRANSFERRED EARLIER TO THE FIRST ACCOUNT.

JUST NOW YOU TRANSFERRED THAT AMOUNT, LESS 1 MILLION, TO THE OTHER ACCOUNT.

ALTHOUGH YOUR WEALTH IS GONE DON'T CRY TOO MUCH. YOU STILL HAVE 1 MILLION.

Randy watched the color drain from their faces as the realization hit them. He had waited for this moment for years. All the pain and suffering had almost been worth it, and the young man had become an instantaneous yet unknown billionaire. He looked at his parents one last time. As far as he was concerned there were no emotions, no family feelings that tied any of them together. Anything he ever felt for them had long died. He knew he would never see them again and he was fine with that. He would try to erase them totally from his mind. Randy shut the door and wedged the back of a chair under the handle. The cleaning lady would be coming around in a couple of hours and would let them out. He quickly shoved the notepad in his pants and ran up to the den. He put the gun back in the safe and closed it. He heard his father scream as he realized his entire fortune had been taken away, and he was the one who had transferred the money. He could hear his parents yelling at each other. He pushed the painting back in place and left the way he came. He quickly reconnected the security system and went to the hidden bicycle. He pedaled to the pickup, threw the bike in the back and started driving toward Hartford.

Randy stopped at a gas station on the highway. He went to the bathroom and removed the oversized clothes he wore over a pair of jeans and t-shirt and threw them in the large garbage bin. He took the bicycle from the pickup and left it next to a dumpster. Maybe someone would be able to use it. Randy went to the drive-through and picked up breakfast. He stopped in the parking lot and enjoyed his freedom. Before his incarceration never did Randy think twice about the pleasure of sitting in a car and eating a fast-food meal. Once finished he headed toward the airport. He returned the rented vehicle and went to the terminal and his gate for the flight to Miami.

As Randy sat in the back of the commercial aircraft, he knew the next flight he would take would be in first class or maybe in his own private jet. In the meantime, he was happy with the smooth and profitable results of the first phase of his plans. The next one would be with Jax. With the help of a private investigator Randy had learned everything he needed about his former teammate's whereabouts.

The Newtons decided not to call the police. What could they tell them? That a man, dressed in all black, from his head to his shoes and with dollar store black glasses, and never saying a word pointed a gun and gave them directions via a steno pad, had broken into their home? They had no idea of his age or even the color of his skin. As far as his size they couldn't even be sure about that as his clothes were baggy. He was probably about six feet tall, which was no help as eighty or ninety percent of the population was that height. No, he hadn't taken anything, other than their entire fortune. And no, there was no way of tracking any of it. Waste of time and major embarrassment.

"Who would do such a thing?" the older man asked, trying to visualize which business enemies could have done this.

"Did you ever think of your son?"

"Don't be ridiculous. That dimwit wouldn't have the brains to pull something like this off."

Randy's mother just lifted an eyebrow and would

always wonder. If it had been her son, she might, in a strange way, have been proud.

Other than the accountant and the maid, who were paid well to keep silent, no one ever found out about the incident, but the blow was a major one. The Newtons sold everything they had as the business went into bankruptcy. They went to live in a small house in an area where no one knew them. They were miserable. More than once they contemplated suicide. They were nothing without their wealth. They didn't know how to be happy without their fortune. Randy had been right. The payback was the worst they could have received.

♫

CHAPTER 29

2022 – MIAMI

Jax watched every one of Alina's world tour concerts. He knew what song would come on at what moment, and in what language. He knew the musical sequences, the dancers' moves, the musicians' cues, the wardrobe changes. Jax knew the entire show by heart. At first he thought he would follow her to each venue, but he figured she would never see him in the crowd, no matter how many shows he attended. He stayed home instead and focused on his goal of how to meet her. However, this was the last concert and he didn't have to travel far. He definitely would be present to see her *live*. Jax had been anxious for weeks before the Miami show and couldn't wait for the day to arrive.

The audience clapped, whistled and waited with great anticipation for the show to begin in Miami's enormous venue. Alina's concert, the last of her world tour, would be starting at any moment. Everything was ready. Her staff, who put this show on for the past months, did so with military precision—the stage, lights and instruments seemed to stand at attention. The musicians were anxious as well. They were all proud of their work and never tired of the pleasure and success as they watched their accomplishments unfold and come together. From the reviews and from their own witnessing they knew their audience felt the same way. They were a close-knit group and were more of a family than co-workers. It was in great part due to Miguel's guidance and Alina's demeanor. The manager was the consummate professional. He always had time for any one of the staff and made sure he had a solution to any problem. Alina was just as much the boss and the group loved her as well. She was, of course, lovely to look at, but they appreciated her heart more than anything. She knew every person who made up the entire staff and cherished them. Each was the best in their field; whether they were musicians or technicians, she respected their professionalism. She made sure everyone had what they needed as far as equipment, meals and sleeping accommodations when they were out of town, and she paid them well. She never failed to compliment them and always showed them, usually with a genuine hug, how much each one meant to her. She honestly loved them and was grateful for their expertise, devotion, passion and mutual sentiments toward her.

While waiting for her entrance cue Alina reminisced about the first time she stood on this same stage with Diego Molina, the man who empowered the first steps of her career. That had been ten years ago. As she waited, she remembered her goals and ambitions. She wanted to be the best she could be—passionate, unique and creative. The audience needed to be mesmerized by the show with the music, singing and dancing. She wanted them to take away an evening of pure talent, entertainment and perhaps even a little edification as she sang not only modern popular songs, but old ballads. She wanted to keep these traditional melodies from around the world alive and thriving, as the great musicians and songwriters had done decades earlier. She respected tradition while blending a fun, young energy into her music and added electric and classical guitars accompanied by sassy Latin horns. She incorporated exciting and sometimes unusual indigenous instruments. Santiago, who had become her maestro since she first started, loved sitting down with Alina and working on the arrangements with her. Whether it was old established melodies or a new composition she had just written, Santiago loved her creativity and the way she incorporated native instruments. The result was successful as the audience could not stand still. They had to move to the rhythms and let the melodies envelope them.

Alina waited with the usual before-the-show excitement. She stood in the wings of the dark theater, waiting for her cue. The audience was anxious and curious as they could only see the giant red curtain in front of the stage, hiding what they presumed were the musicians and their instruments. And then the lights in the venue completely dimmed. The show was beginning. The curtain parted in two and disappeared into each side of the stage. In the background an enormous screen started playing a film showing planet Earth from space and continuing toward the continents. A deep, warm male voice could be heard throughout the venue: "Before anything, there was sound". A symphony played, accompanying the reel, reminiscent of the soundtracks of space themes. The crowd clapped and followed the camera's point of view as it continued from space to the Amazon River and its jungle. The focus landed deep into the rainforest on a lone tinamou. The bird was relaxing on a tree branch. The music faded and the little songster opened its mouth. A few notes from one of the musicians playing a wooden tinamou rang out into the theater, perfectly synchronized with the bird on the screen. It was accompanied by a rain stick as the film showed the sudden typical diluvian rains of the jungle. Thunder was added with the help of a *halilintar*, an Indonesian spring drum. The film showcased the sounds of the forest by the talented musicians on the dark stage. Other 'nature' instruments followed with maracas and gourd-rattles, adding rhythm to the composition. The reel left the jungle and headed to the ocean where dolphins and whales swam deep and squealed their sounds, replicated on stage by a waterphone.

The film continued from the depths of the ocean and rolled toward the pebble-strewn shore. The camera zoomed in on the stones and then cut to several musicians' hands on stage, illuminated by spotlights, holding the same kind of stones. They hit them together and followed the music of the soundtrack, producing a louder rhythm. "Perhaps this was how the first 'rock' concert began," the original voice from the screen related. The film and the stage slowly faded to black and the spectators applauded. They had enjoyed the piece and anticipated the continuation with enthusiasm. The audience was once again bathed in darkness.

After a few moments a lone spotlight illuminated part of a beautiful rosewood marimba. Out of the dark a mallet hit one of the tone bars of the large instrument. The sound was gentle, mellow. More notes rang out from more mallets and produced what seemed like a cascade of melodic, sonorous bubbles. Congas could be heard coming in and lights appeared only on the hands beating the tall drums. Immediately people in the theater started to tap their feet and move to the rhythm. Synthesizers followed and then the entire ensemble of musicians and their instruments joined in as well. Additional spotlights highlighted the newcomers and when the piece seemed to be winding down, a classical Spanish guitar, played by Santiago, rang out alone throughout the venue. The big man was sitting on a stool in the middle of the stage, lit by a solitary light. Out of the darkness a hand appeared on his shoulder and then lovingly caressed the side of his face. The man smiled and looked up as Alina entered the spotlight's radius. She held the microphone delicately and slightly tilted her chin up as the first notes came out of her mouth, crystal-clear, powerful and silky. The audience applauded profusely as their star sang to them, the circle of light gradually growing wider until all of her physique was visible.

Alina wore a flowing multicolored muumuu, each diaphanous layer a different color, which gave the impression of a rainbow moving in slow motion. As with the universal concept of her concert this too was part of the nature theme. Her hair was pulled back giving an unobstructed view of her face.

Jax watched from one of the front rows, completely mesmerized by Alina's presence. He was in the same space as she, breathing the same air, living the same moments together. Jax's heart fluttered as he watched her. He knew every city and venue she had performed in and on what day, but tonight he was *with* her in Miami, close to the stage. She was exquisite in every way possible, from her gestures to her attire. Her enchanting smile melted everyone's heart and Jax stared at the lips that held the perfect notes. He wondered what it would be like to meld his mouth to the one producing such passionate and magical sounds.

When Alina finished projecting the song with her rich, powerful voice, the light engineers faded the venue to black giving the hall an enigmatic impression. The lights came back on a few seconds later and the spectators clapped in approval. Alina no longer was in the rainbow dress but now wore a simple thin-strapped red flamenco gown with a narrow waist which then flared down to the floor. It was modern and fun, not the classic cascading ruffle-filled gown. It was simple and graceful and emphasized the allure of her body. The cleavage was cut just low enough to reveal a little of the mysteries behind the material. Her accessories included dark shoes and a large red flower in her hair which now flowed down her shoulders. Alina was at the tip of a V formation of the group of dancers who wore the same outfits and stood ready in a beginning flamenco pose. Alina also wore a face microphone as she wanted both hands free for the dance.

Jax stared at the image in front of him. He took in every inch of her physique and believed he had never seen anything more feminine or sensual in his life. His breath caught in his chest and he didn't know if he would ever breathe right again.

"GOOD EVENING, MIAMI!" Alina shouted to the crowd.

The spectators answered back. "GOOD EVENING, ALINA!" They loved being part of the show.

"It is so wonderful to be in this amazing city!"

The audience clapped. They completely agreed.

Jax watched Alina and the dancers. Even though he had watched the show several times on television it didn't compare to being live at the concert. The dancers' hands were raised above their heads and were highlighted by the spotlights. They were also projected on the immense screen at the back of the stage. Santiago's hands on the guitar playing the music associated with southern Spain and the Gypsies, were beginning to superimpose on the dancers' hands as he strummed the instrument. The performers started clapping and double clapping with the music and when Alina entered with her voice the troupe slowly lifted their arms in a classic flirtatious move. They inflated their chests and slightly moved their hips, making sensuous curves from their shoulders to their feet. Alina danced right along with them and as the rhythm picked up so did the speed of the dancers. They twirled their bodies and their flared skirts followed, giving the audience the sensation of whirling dervishes. The dramatic art form of flamenco was perfectly portrayed through their body language and the love of their craft. They showed the public the power of women as they slightly raised their chin, one arm and twirled, perfectly in command and synchronized. When the music stopped for a moment, the dancers did as well, but they did it on pointe and in flamenco shoes. The audience was duly impressed. At the end of the elegant and sensual dance Alina smiled, as did the other women behind her. It was the perfect final touch.

As before, the lights dimmed to black and when they came back on, the dancers had changed in just a few seconds. They had shed their shoes and their flamenco dress. An almost transparent red scarf was attached to their hips and flowed toward their feet and the dancers started shaking the gold coins on their red bustiers. They sultrily articulated their hips as their bare feet followed the belly dancing music. Jax watched in delight at the seductive scantily covered bodies. Alina was his favorite.

Alina had asked Naila, her school friend from Beirut who had become a leading expert in Middle Eastern dances, to help with the music medley and the choreography the dancers and Alina were now performing. Their movements were continuous and flowing, accented by staccato beats of the hips, chest and shoulders, showing off the control of their abdominal muscles. The dancers made their bustiers shimmy and their waists rotate. Alina not only danced but sang.

At the end of the medley the lights dimmed again, as before. In the dark the dancers quickly left the platform and one of the stagehands helped Alina change. When the lights came up, she was wearing a high-waisted dark palazzo pants and a large white shirt with the ends tied in front of her stomach. It was simple, yet elegant and left the crowd at ease. Jax was reminded of the Andalusian women riders. All she needed was a bolero hat. How he would love to go riding with her on the ranch, side by side, maybe holding hands, or even both riding the same horse. He groaned as he visualized her sitting in front of him, her back nestled into his chest. His dream was interrupted as Alina started to speak.

"Ladies and gentlemen, as you know the music we play and our shows are very international. The reason is that music is universal. It doesn't belong to one nation; it belongs to everyone. Each country produces beautiful songs that sometimes are big hits and become legendary classics, but the magic is that this music can be heard and enjoyed by everyone all over the world. I have the privilege to be part of a group of amazing people I lovingly call our own little United Nations. We are from all corners of our planet. We are of every color and faith, and most importantly, even though in our hearts we are all the same, we are each unique individuals. Every one of us speaks English, but at any one time you could hear us conversing in one of around twenty languages. However, let me tell you a secret." The audience waited attentively. "Every single one of us in this venue and around the globe understands, and is fluent, in the most universal language there is: Music." Alina looked at her audience and said: "There are seven tones in the universe which give us infinite possibilities of combinations. There is always a way to create a melody, and as far as I am concerned if everyone treated peace like their music, imagine the communication and understanding between all people on earth."

The audience clapped.

"As you might know I am American and Spanish; my right-hand man and manager, Miguel, is Cuban-American and a Miami local." The crowd applauded their home boy.

Alina continued: "My personal assistants who help me with scheduling, clothing, make-up and basically keep me organized and looking my best are from New Zealand, Malta and Israel. My brilliant stage, light and sound engineers are American and Canadian, ranging from Ontario, Alaska, Hawaii, Maine and several states in between." Alina blew a kiss to the invisible people in the sound and light booth high up in the theater. In response the light engineer played with the lights, making crazy patterns of white and colored bursts throughout the venue.

"My amazing musicians are from everywhere," Alina continued. "It is my pleasure and my honor to present them to you." Alina went toward Santiago and waved her hand in his direction and reintroduced him. "My maestro and classical guitar player, Santiago, from Spain." The Spaniard nodded to the crowd as his fingers strummed a few notes performing difficult chords and glissandos. The audience clapped, the loudest from Spaniards. Santiago kept playing, segueing into a ballad.

Alina walked a few steps to Joao, from Brazil. She introduced him and his lightning-fast fingers took off on the bongos and gave the song a beat. Two of the dancers, lovely Brazilian women, were dressed in carnival costumes as if parading in Rio de Janeiro. They walked toward the middle of the stage and started shaking and dancing to Joao's rhythm. The audience moved right along with the women.

"From Australia we have Waru," Alina said about a young man, "who is a beautiful and proud Aborigine. He plays the indigenous didgeridoo made from a eucalyptus tree. He is also an expert with the bullroarer. Waru is fluent in, and I love pronouncing this word, Pitjantjatjara, an Aboriginal language." Waru grinned and gave her a thumb's up. He then blew hard into the didgeridoo and at the same time started spinning the bullroarer. The spectators were fascinated by both the uniqueness and the sounds being produced, while enjoying the melody and the rhythm. They loved Alina and had come for her, her music and her voice, but they never expected these interesting moments during her show. They appreciated her pride and respect for her team. They understood she wanted to make sure they were given the accolades they deserved. They also enjoyed learning about each individual and their specialty.

Alina continued. "We have the divine Ukaleq from Finland, surrounded by what we love to call 'the toys'." The Finnish woman was encircled by a triangle, a glockenspiel and tubular bells. She delighted the crowd as her hands seemed to play all the instruments at the same time. The audience clapped loudly, impressed by her dexterity.

"This is Stavros. He is Greek and plays the bouzouki, the Cretan lyra, the oud and several other Middle Eastern instruments." The man plucked the bouzouki, delighting the crowd with the quick chord changes and the unique sound.

"On the piano and synthesizer, we have Max from the Alps of Switzerland, as perfect as a Swiss watch and as lovable as a great St. Bernard. He also speaks French, Italian, Romansh and Schwiizerdütsch." Max smiled and pushed the ebony and ivory keys of the classy instrument and grinned as Alina sat next to him. They played together à quatre mains, enhancing the song the band had been performing since Alina first started introducing her team. After about a minute she left Max playing the piano.

"Our wind boys include Charlie from New Orleans and Juan from Havana. I swear they must each have a gene from Louis Armstrong and Arturo Sandoval. Charlie also speaks Yat and Creole French. Together they play different trumpets, saxophones, trombones and flutes. Charlie is always telling everybody to *Laissez les bons temps rouler!* Let the good times roll! He definitely knows how to let go and get everybody in a great mood." The two men blew into their trumpets and highlighted their prowess. Charlie's tunes were more Dixieland, also known as New Orleans Hot jazz, and Juan had a more Afro-Cuban and Latin jazz vibe to his playing. The audience was mesmerized. Alina's musicians were amazing.

"And here is Kemuel from Trinidad and speaks his island's Creole. He plays the steelpan and the scratcher." Kemuel tapped the mallet in the steel drum with one hand and let the pleasantly tinny, hollow sounds reverberate throughout the theater. With the other hand he held a comb and scratched the cylindrical aluminum sheet that had hundreds of tiny holes punched into it.

Alina moved to the next artist.

"Sata is from Madagascar and plays the Djembe drum from Ghana, the Zimbabwean mbira, the ferrinho from Cape Verde and the rattle made from his native island's unique baobab tree's fruit and seeds. He represents the continent of Africa and its surrounding islands and speaks Malagasy." Sata quickly moved his fingers up and down the mbira. The crowd was fascinated.

"Jairo is from Colombia and is an expert in Afro-pacific music. His specialties are native to Cali and the surrounding area, and he plays the marimba de chonta, which is from a tropical palm tree wood. He amazes us with a *curulao*, a rhythm on the marimba and also plays the *guasa*, a shaker, and the *bombo* and *kounouno* drums." Jairo played a few moments on each instrument, accompanying the other musicians.

Alina continued to the next musician and went closer to him. "Ladies and gentlemen, last but definitely not least, the very special Andres from Venezuela. When this wonderful musician is not touring with us, he is a professor of Latin American ethnomusicology at the university in Caracas. Once a teacher always a teacher, and we love teachers! One of the most noble and important professions in the world. Pythagoras use to say, 'educate the children and it won't be necessary to punish the men'." The crowd applauded, liking the maxim. Alina went over to her musician and as the camera followed it also picked up the different instruments around Andres and projected them on the large screen. "All these beautiful instruments are authentic, indigenous music makers from different parts of Latin America," Alina explained. "Andres, would you tell us about them?" This was also a chance for Alina to take a breather.

"It would be my pleasure." This was one of the professor's favorite moments of the show, a combination of music and teaching. He picked up each instrument and explained their provenance, all in less than two minutes. "There are more than sixty different instruments native to Latin American. Some are native to each country, some cross borders. For example, these *chajchas*," Andres said lifting his arm, "are made of goat hooves and originated in the Central Andes." He showed the audience the bracelet around each wrist and shook them. "Don't they sound like wind and rain?" He asked the crowd as if they were his students.

"YES!" They shouted back at the fun professor.

Andres picked up another instrument. The spectators thought it was a toy or a very large tobacco pipe. Andres held it up so everyone could see and the screen projected it as well. "This is an Andean saxophone. It can be made of wood or bamboo and the range is approximately two octaves." He blew into it and the audience was surprised to hear how true the sound was.

"Good?" Andres asked.

"YES!" The crowd answered back.

"Finally, we have *la antara* which originated in the ancient Nasca and Paracas cultures of Peru. You may know this better as a pan flute." He blew into the small tubes and the audience listened to Andres accompanying the melody that had been playing throughout the introduction. Alina joined her musicians with her own instrument, her voice, and after about a minute they ended the song. The audience clapped profusely. They had enjoyed the musicians, the unusual instruments, the piece of music and even the edification. The performers covered the globe and highlighted each continent.

"Ladies and gentlemen, please give our own little United Nations, these unique and incredible musicians, another hand. We are one big family and we love playing for you." The audience clapped and whistled as all the members, including Alina, bowed to them.

The musicians hadn't stopped playing, but when Alina, as she did in all her shows, started talking to the audience the band went silent and gave them a break.

"I had a dream that I was stranded on a small, deserted island."

"I'LL COME RESCUE YOU!" A man's voice shouted from the crowd. The audience laughed. Jax completely related.

"Very kind of you," Alina answered back and blew a kiss in the direction of the voice. She continued with her story. "I realized there wasn't any music or instruments I could play on this island. What would I do without music? I listened to the sounds around me. I heard a bird." In the background a flute produced a few notes. "I also heard leaves rustling and saw bamboo trees." A cymbal being scratched by a wire brush replicated the sound of the leaves. Another musician added a beat by tapping two bamboo pieces together. They kept at it, as did the flute. "And the ocean and the waves." Andres rattled the chajchas reproducing the sounds. A melody was forming. "Of course, there was one instrument that is always with me. She lifted her hands toward her neck. "My voice." The audience applauded. "This is the song that came from that dream," Alina said and continued the melody, a gentle ballad she had written from that initial idea. It made the audience wave their arms from side to side above their heads. They knew all the words to the song Alina had composed. She didn't expect the crowd, however, to sing the song they knew by heart to *her*. They continued along even when Alina's voice completely stopped. She was overwhelmed. She had never witnessed so much love coming from what seemed every single person in front of her in the enormous theater. Yes, they cherished her and her music. They were showing her how much they appreciated her. They continued singing and waving their arms en masse from right to left with the rhythm, making waves throughout the venue. Alina's tears ran down her cheeks and she brought a hand to her heart. She still couldn't sing. Her voice wasn't obeying her mind's commands. She would, however, be honest with her fans as hardly any sound came out of her mouth. "I'm sorry," she kept saying to the crowd. They screamed in solidarity, understanding her speechlessness and empathizing with her. "You are all so amazing! Thank you, thank you!" Alina whispered. "You have moved me so much. I loved you before and now I love you even more, if that's even possible." Alina focused, took several deep breaths and her voice, low at first, joined the fans still singing. They sang together. They were one family, united by love and music. They were there for Alina, one of their favorite singers and celebrities, whose professionalism and melodies never disappointed and always gave them great pleasure. When the people, together with Alina, finished the song she crossed her hands to her chest and bowed to the audience in gratitude. They in turn clapped back, as did Jax, more infatuated with Alina than ever.

"I have a theory," Alina continued. "I haven't checked it scientifically or medically, but I'm pretty sure that if you love music and dancing then just sing and dance to your heart's content. Especially Latin rhythms. You don't have to be at a party, you can be on your own, in your house or in front of a mirror. I do this professionally and by myself in my home. It gives me fun and soothing energy, alleviates stress and envelopes me in a great vibe. Just enjoy and do it for yourself. I believe we'll be happier and even live longer. And if you're getting sleepy in the car, sing as if you are rehearsing for your upcoming concert. Maybe it's a duet you and I would perform together." Alina looked at the audience. "Uh, don't dance in the car." The crowd laughed. Just mentioning the little car trick could possibly prevent accidents and save lives. Jax was picturing a slightly different duet.

Alina ended another song and noticed a young boy in the first row next to a couple she presumed were his parents. She went to the edge of the stage and waved to the youngster. He smiled and waved back.

"Do you like the show?" Alina asked.

"Yes," the boy answered.

"What's your name?"

"Brody."

"Hi Brody," Alina said and gave him an endearing smile. Her crew, some of the best in the business, was right on the ball and projected their interaction on the enormous screen above the stage, in addition to the live feed to the television channel. "Do you know any of my songs?"

"I do."

"I love this young man! He must be my youngest fan," Alina exclaimed to the crowd. She turned back to the boy. "How old are you, Brody?"

"Five," he said and held up a hand with all fingers

stretched as far as they could go.

The spectators *awwwwed.*

"Is there a song you know really well?"

"The one my Mommy sings all the time."

More clapping from the audience.

Alina nodded and laughed. It was the most endearing sound Jax had ever heard. It was warm and winsome. He wanted to listen to it for hours, or at least have it as a recording and play it whenever he wanted.

The singer blew the mother a kiss. "Thank you, Brody's mommy! Young man, would you like to sing it with me? Up here on the stage?" The crowd clapped hard, anticipating a unique moment. "Mom, would that be alright?" The boy's mother nodded back.

Jax stared, mesmerized. *The mother of my children loves kids too.* He kept watching the show.

One of the theater's security guards lifted Brody out the chair as if he were a mere feather and sat him on the edge of the stage. Alina sat down next to him. Their legs dangled toward the floor. She took his little hand in hers and asked him: "Are you ready?"

Brody nodded and began to sing the first notes of the song a cappella. He had taken off on his own with no inhibitions whatsoever. He hadn't waited for the diva or her musicians. Alina raised her eyebrows and watched little Brody belt out the melody of her song. The crowd had a difficult time trying to keep silent. Alina quickly put the microphone close to his face so everyone could hear him. She saw his eyes light up in surprise as his voiced carried throughout the theater. Alina noticed he was having a good time. He kept singing on his own until Alina gently came in and accompanied him, making sure she did not overshadow him. The unusual duet was one of the hits of the evening. Brody knew the entire song and sang most of it on his own. Alina let the spectators enjoy the boy and his singing of her music.

When the duo finished the crowd went wild and Alina gave Brody an enormous hug and congratulated him. "Brody, that was absolutely wonderful!" She turned to the audience. "Don't you agree? Ladies and gentlemen, please give another big applause to this amazing young man!" They didn't hesitate. It had been a treat.

The security guard lifted Brody off the stage and the boy waved to the spectators. The guard held him up in the air for a few extra seconds as if he were a trophy. After all, when would this little guy ever have such a celebrity moment? The crowd waved back and applauded. Some even shouted his name. It would be a souvenir and a memory little Brody would always cherish. The guard put him gently back in his seat and nodded to his parents as they thanked him.

"She's magical," Jax said to no one in particular. He wanted to swim in her essence and discover every part of her being. He was also a little jealous of young Brody.

Alina finished the three-hour show with an amazing dance, each of the dancers wearing a costume from their home country. They were the best of the best and for their final number they performed a medley of many dances from around the world, with steps from classical and modern dances alike. The members of the troupe were brilliant, their movements clean and crisp as they showed off their prowess and the love for their profession.

The concert had been filled with world rhythms, from Latin America, the Middle East, Oceania to popular modern American and European tunes. There was something for everyone and the spectators enjoyed

Alina's music, both the traditional classics and her own international compositions.

Alina performed the last song, as she had the entire evening, with her entire being, with her voice, her body, and the depths of her passion. That was her talent, her forte and her gift to the world. The audience couldn't get enough of her. The men wanted to protect her, make love to her, or both. The women wanted to be her friend. They wanted to be a part of her uniqueness. She had touched them all. Many eyes were wet, as Alina's were. She could sense how much love the audience projected toward her and she loved them back as well.

As the show came to an end she thanked the crowd, bowed deeply and exited the stage. The spectators were all standing, clapping profusely. They wouldn't leave and begged for an encore until Alina came back out. She thanked her fans again and announced that the song she was about to sing was entitled "Our World" and was a new composition. It was an honor to introduce it to the world with the Miami audience. The spectators were ecstatic and shouted their enthusiasm. Alina did not disappoint. The song was exquisite and the people approved. Miguel had suggested to Alina to introduce the song during her last show and at the very end of her performance. It was the tune the audience would walk away with. As always, he was right. In the next few days, the entertainment world and the social networks made it a global hit.

After the show Alina went to her dressing room. She was pulling on a pair of jeans when Miguel knocked on the door. "Are you decent?" He yelled through the door.

"I've been known to be," Alina answered, chuckling. She loved having fun with her manager.

"Does that mean I can come in?"

"It does."

Miguel opened the door as Alina was zipping up her jeans under an oversized shirt. He went over and hugged the young woman. "You were magnificent tonight!" Miguel beamed.

"Thank you, but I couldn't have done any of it without every single person on that stage, our team and you, of course." She returned the hug and gave him a kiss on the cheek.

"Heading home?" Miguel asked.

"I am, but first I'm going to Tina's to get a gyro. I'm starving. Then a relaxing soak and a long sleep in my oversized bed."

"Just make sure you don't fall asleep soaking."

"No worries. Do you and Santi want to eat?"

"No, we're good but a little tired. We're heading home.

"Okay."

"Well, that's the last concert of your world tour and it all went without a hitch. We can talk tomorrow."

"I'll call you, probably late morning. Right now, all I can think about is food, so let's get out of here." Alina covered her head and face with a large hat.

Miguel nodded and escorted her out to the waiting inconspicuous SUV. The chauffeur drove her to a corner on Miami Beach where Tina's, her favorite Greek food truck, was serving its clientele.

"The usual?" The driver asked.

"Yes, please, and get whatever you want."

"Will do. Thank you."

The chauffeur ordered and came back with Alina's dinner, or was it a midnight snack? Either way she started devouring the gyro and French fries. For dessert she had *loukoumades*, the Greek version of beignets with honey. Had Alina looked up she would have seen a handsome man ordering from the same food truck. Had Jaxon known Alina was just an arm's length away he would have melted into the pavement.

Once finished, Alina and the driver headed to the Vinyl where she already pictured herself soaking in the bathtub and enjoying the view of the Miami lights.

♫

CHAPTER 30

2022 – MIAMI BEACH

Alina and Miguel came out of the television building where she had been recording an interview for an upcoming special.

"Done for the day," Miguel said. "Drop me off at my place?"

"Of course," Alina answered.

"Great, thanks."

They went to her sports car and got in.

"Well, that went well," Miguel commented as they leisurely drove down the avenue on Miami Beach.

At the same time Randy watched Jax leaving the restaurant from his parked rental car. His former teammate seemed to be in a daze, staring in the distance. Although Randy had developed several scenarios that would devastate Jax, it wouldn't be as easy as his parents' intervention. The Newtons were still alive because he knew the predicament he left them in was worse than death. Jax, however, would not be left alive.

Jax finished his lunch and left the restaurant. He

smiled as he was sure he was dreaming that Alina was in the car coming toward him. Nice classic Ferrari with the signature *rosso corsa*, racing red, he thought. He saw her signature smile and loved the way her face beamed with happiness. He absentmindedly stepped down from the sidewalk, lost in his reverie, when an agonizing pain suddenly tore through him. He gasped as invisible internal flames seemed to sear his body. The only other time he had gone through such extreme pain was at the competition in Spain when his leg had shattered.

"Yes, Miguel, everything went very smoothl…" Alina never saw the man walk in front of her car, but she certainly felt the impact of his body against the bumper. He flew back and landed awkwardly a couple of feet ahead of the Dino. She slammed on the brakes so hard that Miguel almost hit the windshield. Thankfully her reactions were quick, and she swerved just enough not to hit him again, or even run over him.

Randy didn't know what to do. Should he run to Jax and try to help so that he could have the satisfaction of killing him later? Should he just let him bleed to death and not get his hands dirty? He decided not to do anything and watch the events unfold. If Jax died, well, that would be it, although he would regret he hadn't had the pleasure of inflicting the pain and the final coup de grâce. If the man didn't die, then he would devise a plan and make his death a reality.

Alina and Miguel jumped out of the car and ran toward the body on the road. Miguel noticed the front of the Ferrari and was amazed that the classic hardly had a scratch on it. He grimaced, though, at the sight of the crimson gushing from the man's face. Jax lay on the pavement unconscious and bloody. His clothes and the road were covered with thick rivulets of red. Alina subconsciously thanked her parents for everything they had taught her about emergency medicine and immediately checked for a pulse and found it. He was alive! She gently probed the back of his neck with her fingers. Everything normal there as well. She quickly looked over the body lying on the pavement. She didn't see any limbs in strange, unnatural positions. Hopefully no bones were broken, although x-rays would confirm what couldn't be seen with the naked eye. There was, however, an alarming amount of blood splattered on his polo shirt, neck and especially his face. Broken nose at the very least, she thought. Noses always bled a lot. Was he young? Older? Was he handsome? She couldn't really tell as more blood kept streaming out of his nose and several deep cuts on his face which masked his features. She did surmise from the rest of his body that he was probably in his late twenties or early thirties. The warm red liquid ran into his mouth and he started choking.

"Get me the first aid kit out of the car," Alina cried out to Miguel.

Miguel ran to the trunk and tried to find a case. No luck. He ran back to Alina kneeling next to the bleeding man. "Sorry, no kit."

"Seriously? You could buy a damn pharmacy with the money that car costs."

"Very true. We'll have to get a kit for next time," Miguel said. Alina threw him a dirty look. "Uh, not next time, I meant we need to get one for the car."

Even though unconscious Jax coughed, spraying out blood from his mouth. More trickled out from his nose. Alina grumbled, hoping it wasn't from anything internal.

"Miguel, take off your shirt," Alina ordered.

"What? Why?"

"Just do it!"

The manager took off his shirt, grateful he was wearing an undershirt and they weren't in Siberia.

"Tear off a sleeve!"

"What? Oh, never mind." Miguel tore one off his designer shirt and handed it to Alina. He watched her tie the sleeve around Jax's face, trying to hold back the flow of blood. He looked at the guy and finally asked Alina: "Is he breathing? I don't see his chest moving."

Alina had noticed it too and Miguel's question made her heart skip several beats. She immediately put her ear to the man's torso. "Shit," she whimpered. She carefully turned Jax's head to the side, stuffed the rest of the shirt under his face and opened his mouth. With a couple of fingers she scooped out the blood that had coagulated into globs and let it fall onto the asphalt. She put her hand on his chest and pushed slightly. The man coughed out more small pieces and he started breathing. Alina and Miguel let out a sigh of relief as did the crowd that had gathered. And of course, the proverbial cell phone recording was in full force, especially when someone screamed: "Hey, that's Alina! Wow, she just saved that man's life!"

Randy watched from the sidewalk with the rest of the onlookers. Jax was still alive thanks to this woman. He wondered who this Alina was. He made a mental note to check it out.

Alina was busy wiping the injured face with Miguel's shirt. She was gentle and tried to see his features, but the blood had painted and caked over on his skin.

Jax came to when he heard the name the onlooker had screamed and tried to focus his mind. He was sure he was still in his dream, but he needed to be certain. He slowly opened his eyes but couldn't see much. Blood had found its way over them and his vision was blurry. He saw a woman's face hovering over his. He wasn't sure what she was doing and then he recognized her. It was Alina! Damn it! Would this dream ever stop? Obviously, the great Alina was not the one leaning over him. He cursed internally. He looked at the stunning face of the love of his life. It really was her! Jax could only smile before passing out again.

Alina heard the ambulance siren. It was close and she was glad. She tried to do as much as she could for the man she hit. She looked at his face and almost laughed as he had one the happiest smiles she had ever seen. She couldn't understand why as she was sure he was in pain, at least when he had been conscious. She also spotted a small tattoo on his forearm with Olympic rings, although they weren't round but in the shape of horseshoes. Was this man an Olympian? Perhaps an equestrian? Her curiosity and love for horses piqued.

The ambulance arrived. Alina silently thanked whoever had called the emergency services. The paramedics quickly checked the injured man and then lifted him onto the stretcher trolley. Jax came to again and saw Alina. Hey, she was still there, he thought groggily. She hadn't left his dream yet. He lifted a shaky hand toward the woman he adored. Alina took it into hers and held it. Jax almost screamed. She *held* it! After all he had been through to connect with her was this really how they were meeting? Was she really in front of him? Or was this just another part of his obsessive dream? And if per chance this wasn't a dream, was he really hurt? Was it bad? Was he dying? The pain running through his body suggested it was definitely real.

Jax wanted her to be as real as his pain. "If you let go of my hand I will die," he whimpered.

The man's words penetrated Alina's skin and invaded

every nerve in her body. He couldn't die! She wouldn't dream of letting go of his hand. She quickly walked beside the paramedics pushing the stretcher toward the ambulance and started to get in. The EMTs just stared at her. They of course knew who she was.

"Alina, what are you doing? Where are you going?" Her manager screeched running up to her.

"Miguel, for heaven's sake, I hit this man! I'm going with him to the hospital. I want to make sure he's alright. Take the car and meet me there."

"The paramedics have it under control, Alina. That's why we have phones. We can check on the guy that way," Miguel pleaded. Alina wasn't paying attention. He knew it was no use. Once she made up her mind about something there was no way to deter her. He would talk to the police, who were now at the scene, and when they were all finished he would join her at the hospital. But first he would stop by his apartment, which was close, get a new shirt and quickly wash up. Miguel hated rushing and not being clean.

Randy had been one of many in the crowd watching the events following a car versus a pedestrian accident. Since the woman, who left in the ambulance with Jax, was apparently a well-known celebrity, most of the fans followed her to the hospital. Randy went along. He quickly started his car and smiled, a deep satisfying smile that seemed to emanate from the core of his being. His revenge might prove much easier than he anticipated. His mind started piecing together a myriad of possibilities he could concoct in a hospital. He stayed close enough to the ambulance to see which hospital they were taking Jax. He parked his rental and mingled with the crowd of fans outside the main entrance. Security had been called and the guards kept the devotees at bay and peaceful.

Randy mixed himself in with the people gathered. It was a good way to be inconspicuous and find information he could use to get to his nemesis. "What's happening?" He asked an older woman.

"Oh, Alina is here. She saved a man's life, but she ran over him first," she giggled.

"Really?"

"Uh, huh."

"An out-of-control fan?" Randy asked, keeping the mood light.

"Naw, I think he just wasn't paying attention. Maybe he saw her driving her car and was dumbstruck."

The woman was right. That was exactly what happened. Randy had seen it. "Are you a fan of this uh, Alina?"

"Oh, yes! She's the best! Her full name is Alina Alonso, but as a singer she only goes by Alina."

"She's a good singer?"

"Oh, yes, beautiful voice, and range. Haven't you heard any of her music?"

"I'm not sure." Randy didn't think he had. With a dozen years in a prison he certainly didn't have much choice in the matter.

"You probably have. The girl's music is very international. She can go from pop hits to hot Latin rhythms to Middle Eastern tunes, even sings in different languages."

"Really."

"Yes, and of course she's a very pretty young woman."

"I did notice that. Well, I have to go. Pleasure talking to you."

"You too, young man, take care. And make sure you

check out her music."

"Will do."

Randy drove to a restaurant near the hospital, ordered a steak and a vodka and enjoyed his dinner. He let almost an hour go by before finishing his meal. By then Jax would have been checked out, given different tests, patched up and taken to his room, unless he needed some sort of surgery.

Randy took the steak knife and the glass and slid them under the table. He poured the remaining alcohol in the bottom of the glass over the blade, wrapped a paper napkin around it and hid it in his pocket. Randy looked around. No one was watching. He asked for the bill and watched the Miami sunset melt over the horizon, giving way to the upcoming darkness.

Randy went back to his car, drove into one of the emergency parking spaces in the hospital garage, took the knife and cut his forearm. He groaned as it was a little more painful than he expected. It wasn't too deep, just enough to make a bloody mess and require stitches. He wrapped his arm with a towel he had in the trunk and walked over to the emergency room entrance. The security guard, seeing the injury and the blood seeping through the white towel, rushed him in. A nurse quickly assessed the wound and went to get some bandages and a kit for suturing. While she was away Randy quickly went to the nurses' station, which at the moment was empty, and took a look at the computer. He found out what room Jax was occupying. He also quickly read the medical report. His injuries hadn't been life-threatening. He rushed back to his room.

The nurse returned and took care of his arm. Randy watched her and made small talk. When she was finished, he was discharged. Instead of leaving, Randy walked the floors and the stairs above and below the one where Jax's room was. He made mental notes of where supply closets were, nurses' stations, security cameras, employee rooms, elevators and stairways. He watched the comings and goings of the staff, and when a nurse left a cart in the hallway and went into a patient's room Randy went to the cart, made sure his back was to the security camera, looked through the drawers, found a syringe and quickly put it in his pocket.

Randy had all the information he needed to get to Jax. His plan was coming together. He left the hospital, but he would be back the next night for that coup de grâce.

♫

CHAPTER 31

Jax groaned and had a difficult time breathing. He lifted an arm and touched his face. It was wrapped in gauze. Only his eyes and lips were uncovered. He mumbled something incoherently. And why was his face covered like a mummy's? Man, it throbbed. Did I die and come back? I didn't see any tunnel with any light, he mused. He slowly opened his eyes. "Where am..." Jax tried.

"Welcome back to the land of the living," Alina said, smiling. The doctor had given her a prognosis for a full recovery.

Damn it! Jax was getting tired and very aggravated. That fucking dream was getting more and more real. Maybe he should find a shrink. But wait, that *was* Alina's voice, he knew it so well! He would recognize it anywhere.

"You're in the hospital. You've had an accident," Alina said.

She spoke! Again! "Really?" He whispered. Maybe this wasn't a fantasy. "Is this for real... or is it a dream?" He still wasn't sure.

Alina took his hand. "I'm afraid this is as real as it gets. I'm sorry. I hit you with my car, although you did just step off the sidewalk without looking. There was no way I could avoid hitting you. Uh, you didn't do it on purpose, did you?" Alina asked, wondering if maybe he had and what the man's state of mind was.

"Uh, uh, no."

She was glad to hear that. "My name is Alina."

Holy shit, this wasn't a dream! And the love of his life was holding his hand! "I'm Jax."

"Yes, I know."

"You do?" She knew his name!

"Yes, they checked your wallet and told me."

"Am I… am I okay?" He asked, not knowing what else to say.

"Yes, you will be. You had a concussion, a broken nose and some really deep cuts. Minor bruises over parts of your body. Your face took the majority of the impact." Alina realized she didn't know what the guy looked like, although he had great Aegean blue eyes and his lips hadn't been hurt at all. They looked pretty good too. Was he a good kisser? *Where did that come from?* She wondered. "But everything should heal nicely and no real noticeable scars the doctor said," she continued, trying to focus.

It was all worth it, even if the cliché of 'love hurts' truly applied in this case, Jax mused. He promptly fell asleep from the medicine running from the I.V. into his arm. His hand, still in Alina's, went limp. He had a smile on his face. Alina immediately rang for a nurse who quickly showed up. "I think he fell asleep," she said, a little worried.

The nurse, a portly middle-aged black woman, checked him out. She was all business and the consummate professional. She turned to Alina and smiled, a smile so warm it could lift any patient's or visitor's spirits. "Yes, you're right, Sugar," she said with a lovely southern drawl. "He's sleeping. Best thing for him right now. He probably won't wake up for hours. You should go home and get some rest." She stared at her patient.

"What is it?" Alina asked, a little worried that the nurse wasn't moving or doing anything.

The hospital specialist giggled. "Look," she simply said, pointing to his face.

"I know, I almost killed the poor guy," Alina said with a pang of guilt.

"No, no, his smile. Even in his pain this boy is very happy about something."

"Seems a little strange. Have you been able to contact any family member?" Alina asked.

"We did check his wallet, but apparently there isn't anyone."

"Alright, I'll come back later," Alina said.

"May I suggest you come back tomorrow, Sugar? He'll be in and out through the night, more out than in."

"I'll do that. Thank you for everything."

"No, thank you. What you did was great."

Alina groaned. "I ran into the poor man. Actually, he ran into me. Oh, never mind, the least I could do is make sure he was alright."

"He'll be fine," he chuckled. The nurse took out a paper from her pocket and scribbled on it. "Here's my number if you need to call. Also, when you come tomorrow call me first and I'll take you through a back way far from the crowd."

"You know who I am?"

"Does a bear love honey? I most certainly do, and I'm quite a fan."

"That's very kind, thank you. Uh, are they outside?"

"Paparazzi locusts," the nurse hissed.

"Damn." The downside of being famous—no privacy.

"You know what Ms. Alonso, I'll take you the back way right now."

"That would be great, and please call me Alina."

The nurse nodded and smiled. Alina reached for her cell phone and dialed Miguel. "Where are you?" She asked.

"In the hospital parking under the building. I figured it would be a bitch trying to get you out from the front entrance and this would be the best area."

The nurse nodded and showed her to the door. She motioned for her to follow. The two women headed out.

"You're right. I'm actually with a wonderful nurse who's taking me through what I'm sure is a labyrinth it would take me two weeks to figure out," Alina said to her manager. She turned to the nurse. "Where should I tell him to meet us?"

"Where is he?"

"In the parking lot below the building."

"Perfect. By space 215."

"Did you hear?"

"I did. Heading there right now," Miguel answered.

The women and the manager arrived at about the same time. The nurse went out the door from the stairs, looked around first and then let Alina out. "You're good. No one's around. Go."

"Thanks, uh…" She realized she didn't know the nurse's name.

"Grace."

"Yes, you most certainly are. Thank you again."

"My pleasure, Sugar. May I suggest you come back

right here tomorrow morning at ten o'clock? I'll wait for you. If you don't show I'll understand, although you do have my number if you need anything before then."

"Thank you, Grace, I like your plan. I'll see you in the morning," Alina said and gave the nurse a big hug.

The hospital worker was thrilled. That embrace meant the world to her. The young woman was lovely in every way.

♫

CHAPTER 32

The next morning Alina drove to the hospital in a non-descript typical black SUV she borrowed from the Vinyl's carpool. She left the Dino in the apartment building's garage. She headed toward the designated area where Grace was waiting for her. They were both right on time. The nurse waved and Alina parked. She reached over to the passenger seat, picked up a large purse and a box. There were several CDs inside she had signed to Grace.

"Good morning, Sugar."

"Good morning to you, Grace," Alina answered and gave the older woman a hug. It was very Latin and Alina loved the tradition, especially when she really meant it. She certainly did appreciate Grace.

The nurse returned the gesture with pleasure.

"This is for you. Not much really, but the next time I have a show in town I'll get you tickets and a backstage pass for you and three others. Would that be alright?"

"Does a dolphin like water? That would be mighty nice, thank you so much!"

"My pleasure. Now, tell me, how's the patient?"

"He's doing much better. He'll probably get discharged tomorrow, maybe even today."

"Oh, that's great."

The two women arrived at Jax's room and Alina gasped. She had of course seen people who had been severely hurt, just like the girl with the caiman in Brazil, and even her father's gunshot wounds in Lebanon, but she hadn't been prepared to see what *she* had done to this man. Jax lay on the bed without bandages, a caricature of what she believed could possibly be a handsome face. It was puffy and swollen with black, purple, blue and yellow marks over most of his skin. There was tape across his nose and quite a few stitches on each of the large cuts on his face. She went up to the bed and touched his arm. "Oh, I am so sorry." Alina was practically in tears. She kept thinking she had done this to the poor man.

"He's going to be just fine, Sweet Pea," Grace said quickly, seeing the grief on the young woman's face.

"Don't worry. It will heal. I'm sure it looks worse than it is," Jax added, speaking slowly and carefully, thrilled Alina had come to see him.

"You're right, Sugar," Grace piped in as she went up to him. "You're going to be just fine. It'll just take a little time to heal." The nurse looked over the cuts and put some salve on a couple of them. "Did you need anything else?"

"No, I'm good. Thank you."

"You're welcome. I'll come back later." Grace picked up her box, smiled at Alina and nodded her thanks. She left the room.

"I'm really glad you came to see me," Jax said.

"It's the least I could do. Oh, I'm sorry, I haven't introduced myself, I'm Alina." Did he know who she was?

"Pleased to meet you, uh, I think." He started laughing, but quickly stopped as his bruised ribs seemed to scream. If this magnificent woman only knew how ecstatic he was to meet her. "Oh, laughing is definitely not good yet," he grimaced, holding the side of his torso.

"I'll remember not to make you laugh." Alina put her hand out. Jax took it and shook it. He would have sworn some electric charge had just gone up his arm and through his body. "I'm Jaxon. Call me Jax."

"Okay, Jax." She opened her large purse and brought out a gift. "It's a book I thought you might like. It's about horses."

Jax lifted an eyebrow. "Horses?"

"Uh, I noticed your tattoo." She wondered if he had any others she couldn't see.

As if reading her mind, he answered: "The one and only. I'm not a great fan of tattoos, but I had to get this one. It means a lot, something special in my life."

"Most tattoos usually do. I saw the rings and shaped in a horseshoe design. I thought maybe you were an Olympian, perhaps an equestrian."

"Very good. And yes, on both counts, very perceptive." He knew the girl was sharp.

"Would I have seen you at the Olympics?" Alina asked.

"Beijing."

"Of course! You won the gold!" She exclaimed. "I'll never forget your dressage routine with the tango."

"Wow, I'm impressed you remembered. That was quite a few years ago."

"It was, and it was one of those immortal moments like the 'miracle on ice' hockey game, or Abebe Bikila's barefoot marathon win, or Torvill and Dean's ice dancing routine with their Ravel's bolero; or even Greg Louganis,

Mary Lou Retton, Ingemar Stenmark and of course, the immortal Jesse Owens. I could go on forever."

"I see you're quite the Olympics aficionado," Jax said listening to Alina's excitement.

"Oh, absolutely. People and athletes at their best and making an impression that stays with you a lifetime."

"Well, I'm flattered you would put me in such a group."

"Completely deserved," Alina answered. As much as tried she couldn't picture his face and she certainly couldn't distinguish his traits the way he was banged up. She was fairly positive the equestrian team had all been good looking. She remembered giggling with the girlfriends at the house in Spain.

Jax wanted to change the subject. He wanted to know more about her, to listen to that glorious voice— the one that drew her to him, the one who sang in different languages, the one that made his body quiver. "Thank you for the book. Can't have enough of them, especially if the theme is related to horses." He looked at his present. It wasn't new, although extremely well preserved. It was a collector's book on Orientalist horse paintings. Jax was impressed. "This is magnificent!" He exclaimed after looking at several pages.

"You like it?"

"Are you kidding? This is really special. Is it yours?"

"Yes, I've had it since I was a youngster. I picked it up in Beirut, in my favorite bookstore in the world."

"Why was it your favorite?"

"The Lebanese have always been famous for their diversity and education. Almost everyone in the country usually speaks Arabic, French and English so the bookstore had all these unusual books in different languages, real gems! I would spend hours in there.

"Thank you, Alina, I will cherish it with all my heart."

"I'm glad it's going to a home where it will be loved as much as I loved it."

"Absolutely. It seems to me you have a love for horses too."

"Most definitely."

"Would you mind telling me? I think you are just as much of a horse person as I am."

"I would love to; I don't get to talk horses too often."

Yes! She was going to hang around a bit longer. Jax wondered if she knew that he knew who she was. "You don't mind staying a little while?"

"No, not at all. I don't have anything urgent to do today, just a dinner tonight."

Jax's heart skipped a beat. "Ah, husband? Boyfriend?" He asked charmingly, finding the right opening for his query.

Alina looked at him and grinned. Did he know who she was? They hadn't really talked about her background. "No, and no. I'm much too busy. Crazy lifestyle, you know."

"Oh?"

"Yeah, I'm on the road a lot."

"You're a truck driver?"

The singer laughed out loud, a boisterous fun laugh that made Jax's heart grow in his chest. He started laughing with her until the pain in his face and ribs made him groan. "I guess you're not. Oh, please, don't make me laugh," he pleaded.

"Oh, I'm sorry. I just never thought of being a truck driver and it seemed funny to me, although I'm sure I put at least as many miles behind me, if not more."

"Really?"

"Uh, Jax, you do know who I am, right?"

"You mean besides a very beautiful woman with a killer smile and a heart of gold who loves horses?" She was also thoughtful and caring, and fun to talk to you. He wanted to gently caress her face with the back of his hand, take her in his arms and just hold her. Jax stared at her. She truly was magnificent. She was stunning on stage and in pictures but sitting in front of him just took his breath away.

"I thank you, kind sir."

"Could I ask you for a favor?" Jax asked, still not giving her a straight answer.

"Sure, do you need anything? Should I call the nurse?"

"Actually, if you wouldn't mind putting some salve on my face? The AC is drying it up pretty quickly and the stiches are pulling."

"Of course," she said as she went over to the table next to the bed and picked up a tube and a swab. She leaned against the mattress. She looked at the stitches and cuts and a pang of guilt invaded her body again. "I'm so sorry, Jax."

"Hey, it's okay. To be honest I'm enjoying our time together."

"I am too."

"It was worth every stitch."

"Stop that, don't be such a gentleman."

"Really, Alina, it's fine. This will all heal and go away."

Alina carefully cupped one side of his head with her hand. She slowly brought her lips to his face and gently kissed his cheek. Jax was sure every cell in his body was tingling. He had waited so long to get together with her and now she had just put her lips on his skin. He shuddered.

"Are you cold?" Alina asked

"Uh, no, I'm good."

Alina's cell phone rang. It was her father. "Oh, excuse me, I have to take this."

"Of course," Jax said, cursing whoever was on the line who had interrupted the moment they were having.

Alina left the room and spoke to her dad. She explained what had transpired in the last couple of days. As always Alejandro listened attentively to his little girl. When she finished, he asked her what the name of the man was.

"Jaxon."

"I see."

"You do? And what is it you see?"

"I'm pretty sure it's Jaxon Logan. He's the guy that owns and runs Hippo-Camp down the road."

"Really? I've always wanted to check the place out, but never got a chance."

"Sounds like a timing thing. Anyway, tell him we'll fly him home. What are neighbors for?"

"Thank you, Papá, you're the best. Kiss Mom for me."

"I'll do more than that."

"Papá!"

Alina heard her father laugh before the phone clicked off. She venerated how in love her parents were, even after more than two decades of being together.

Interesting, Alejandro thought, Alina finally met Jax. After missing each other for the last ten years they ran into one another, literally. Alejandro laughed at his own pun. As promised, the Spaniard set everything up to fly Jax and his daughter home.

Alina called Miguel and told him she would be at her father's place for a few days, maybe more. She asked him to cancel that night's dinner and have the borrowed car picked up from the hospital garage. She went back to the room and spoke to Jax. "I talked to this man Alejandro from HeliEmerg. He says he knows you and insisted on sending a helicopter to pick you up to take you to your ranch," Alina announced.

"Really? Wow, that's fantastic. Alex is the best."

"You've known him a while?"

"Years."

"You know the family too?"

"I know his wife, Stacy, absolutely lovely woman, but I never met their daughter."

Grace walked into the room. "Well, young man, as soon as the doctor checks you out you will be free to go.

"That's great news!" Alina exclaimed. "What time do you think he can leave?"

"Probably between an hour or two."

"Okay, thanks."

Alina called her father and told him what time they would be ready. She turned to Jax. "Alejandro mentioned you were the owner of Hippo-Camp."

"That's right."

It suddenly hit her. "You're Jaxon Logan from the JAX clothes lines!"

"That would be me," Jax grinned.

"And what an exquisite collection. I have quite a few of your pieces. How is it I didn't connect all of this earlier?"

"You were worried about me."

"I think you're right. I'm sorry," she said again.

"Oh, please, don't be. It was my fault. I wasn't paying attention. I was thinking of this beautiful woman."

"Really?"

"Uh-huh. An amazing singer."

"Seriously?" Alina knew where he was going, but she didn't know if he really was serious or making the story up as they went along.

"Seriously."

"You know who I am then."

"I do, and I'm a big fan. As a matter of fact that's why I was in town, I went to your concert."

"You were there?"

"Absolutely, front of the theater."

"I'm sorry I didn't see you."

"Too many people."

"Yes, it's difficult to try to just see one face at a time."

"I can imagine."

"What did you think of the show?" Alina asked. She always liked getting feedback from her fans.

"Best show in the world. You were magnificent."

"You're not just saying that?"

"No, I would tell you the truth, but I'm serious, you were absolutely perfect. The show, the singing, the dancing, your musicians and your compositions are truly special."

"Thank you, Jax, that means a lot. I must be doing something right."

"Most definitely."

About an hour and a half later Grace walked in again. "Jax, Sugar, you are free to go. You have been discharged," Grace said, pushing a wheelchair. She gave him a little bag. "I put in enough salve in here for several days and some pills for the swelling and some extra ones if you have pain."

"Thank you very much," Jax said.

"Right. In you go, Sugar."

"I don't need the chair."

"Now, don't give me any trouble. Hospital rules."

"But, Grace…" Jax sing-songed.

"Sit!"

"Better do as she says," Alina advised. "She's the boss."

"Fine." Jax sat in the wheelchair.

Alina followed Grace as she wheeled her patient to the elevator which would take them to the top floor of the building. She had been told how they would leave. Once outside they were met by the crew of the helicopter waiting for them on the hospital's helipad. Alina knew them well and hugged the two men. Jax watched from the wheelchair and wasn't so sure he liked how friendly she was with these strange men.

"We're ready if you are," one of the men said to them.

"He's all yours," Grace said. She turned to her patient: "Up you go, Jax, uh, literally."

Jax stood up and hugged his nurse. "Thank you for everything, Gracie. I hope I see you again, but not as a patient."

"Sounds like a plan. Now get in that metal bird." She looked at the helicopter and the blades whirling above the body. "Reminds me of somebody beating eggs. You'll never catch me in one of those things."

Alina laughed. In the back of her mind she thought Grace would actually enjoy a ride. Maybe she would set it up.

Jax did as his nurse told him and walked a few steps toward the helicopter with a little help from the crew.

"Grace, thank you for everything. When we have a

concert in town I'll have tickets for you," Alina said, embracing her.

"Thank you, Sweet Pea, now you go and take care of Jax," Grace said and winked at the younger woman.

The singer looked at her fan. What did the wise woman know that Alina didn't?

"I will. Thank you again for all your care."

"My pleasure," Grace said waving.

They climbed into the chopper. Once installed with seatbelts and headphones Jax just had to ask Alina: "Do you always hug or kiss strange men?" It was gnawing at him.

Alina almost laughed. She managed to only let a smile show. Jax was jealous, she mused. She had known this crew for years and they were like family. "As much as possible," she answered, giggling.

Jax knew she was having fun with him but was still uneasy with her comportment. He turned toward the window and enjoyed the sites of the amazing city.

What Jax couldn't see was Randy in his hotel room having a temper tantrum. Randy had gone to the hospital, went to Jax's room, ready to inject bleach from the supply closet into the I.V. bag, and would add some air into the line for good measure. If Jax was asleep maybe he would just smother him with a pillow. But the room was empty. He went to the nurses' station and asked about him. He found out that Jax had already been discharged. They had let him go! Of course, no one would tell him where he was. Randy went to his hotel, ready to break everything he could lay his hands on. Instead, he decided to get very drunk. He ordered a bottle from room service and proceeded to drink himself into oblivion. In the morning he would call the private investigator and find out everything he needed about Jax's whereabouts.

♫

CHAPTER 33

Jax remembered the other time he was in a HeliEmerg flight and how Alejandro had stayed with him in the helicopter and came to visit at the hospital. The man had kept him together, literally and psychologically. He knew his life would not have been the same without the Spaniard's caring.

"Alejandro is a friend of mine, he's the best. Do you know him?"

"Is he a good guy?" Alina figured Jax didn't know her relationship with the head of HeliEmerg.

"He really is. I hope he's around. I'd love to see him and introduce you."

They took off from the hospital's helipad and took in the amazing sights of the beach and the city. The flight lasted less than an hour. It didn't take long to arrive at HeliEmerg's compound.

Alejandro was near the helicopter landing area ready to greet them. He waved as the door of the chopper opened and Alina and Jax came out. Alejandro went to Jax and gave him a strong handshake and a bear hug. "Good to see you, my friend. I heard about your accident,

I'm glad you're alright."

"Alex, old man, great to see you too! I'd like to introduce you to…"

Before Jax could get another word out Alina jumped onto her dad as she had done since she was a little girl.

"Papá!" She screamed in delight at the man she adored.

"Hola, amorcito," her dad said, hugging her tightly.

Jax stared, his mouth wide open. If he didn't close it, he was sure his chin would drop to the ground. Alina was Alex's little girl? Seriously!? It could have been as simple as visiting his friend to meet this amazing woman? She was his neighbor. Jax was almost sick to his stomach—so much time spent concocting, planning, researching, dreaming, and even getting hit by a car. Well, that wasn't planned, but he now realized the universe would have inevitably brought them together. He was sure it was meant to be. He watched the adoring interaction between father and daughter and wished all families loved each other so deeply. He also understood why she was so friendly with the chopper crew. He realized why Alina seemed so familiar to him as his mind pictured the photograph of the family in the villa in Seville when she was twelve years old. The features were similar, as they were now, but not fully developed. He remembered thinking she was a pretty young girl, but never imagined how much of a beauty she would become.

"This is the guy you hit with the car?" Alejandro whispered in his daughter's ear.

"*Sí,* Papá, he's the one."

"He's the one, eh? I see."

"You do?"

"I'm pretty sure, considering this is the first guy you ever introduced to your Papá."

Alina chuckled. "I've always loved how smart my daddy is, but no, he just lives down the road."

"Mm, well, is he the one?" Alejandro asked again, wanting to make sure. The double meaning was not lost on his daughter.

"I've only just met him," she answered.

"I approve, little one, he's a good man. I've known him for a while." He did approve, but a shiver ran down Alejandro's spine as his mind jumped to the Charles Aznavour song "A Ma Fille", To My Daughter, its poignant words every father's sentiment about their 'little' girl. He also noticed that unique glow in her eyes, just like her mother's that night at *La Tusa Pachorra*, The Sluggish Heartbreak, the bar in Colombia after their first mission. He would have to explain that special shine to Jax. Life had been wonderful without jealousy and he would want the same for his daughter and the one she loved.

"Why didn't you ever introduce us?" Alina asked.

"I don't think any of our schedules coincided, but here we all are now," her father answered. Alejandro smiled. He knew Jax was crazy about his daughter, he could tell, but Alina didn't realize what her heart already knew. He turned to Jax. "I'm glad you two finally met each other, although your circumstances are a little unusual. Are you going to the ranch?"

"I'd like to show Alina the compound and the horses," Jax answered.

"She'll like that, she adores horses."

"I really would love that. I still can't believe we never met before, Jax," Alina said.

"Yes, I know what you mean," Jax said, still mentally kicking himself.

"Papá, I'm going to get one of the cars," Alina announced.

"Go right ahead. The keys are in the office."

Alina took off and Alejandro turned to Jax. He stared at him and, simply but firmly, said: "Young man, if you break her heart I will come after you—hard." The older man's eyes were as cold as steel as he waited for the right answer.

Jax stared back with composure and sincerity: "Alex, I would rather cut out my own heart and give it to you on a platter. My plan is to make her the happiest woman in the world, like no other person could."

"Thank you, Jax, I believe you." Alejandro had the answer he wanted. He expected nothing less from the man he had come to appreciate since the CEA.

The two men were shaking hands when Alina drove up in one of the company's cars. "Have you two solved at least one of the world's problems?" She asked as she saw the two men in what seemed to have been a serious conversation. Jax walked over to the passenger side and got in.

"Absolutely," Alejandro said as he planted an adoring kiss on his daughter's forehead. He waved to them as the couple headed over to Jax's ranch.

"How long have you known my dad?"

"I've known Alex for years, since the CEA actually."

"The Campeonato Ecuestre de Andalucia?"

"Yes. Maybe you remember the one eight years ago, with the guy who got thrown from the horse and onto the bars? They made a whole fuss about it. I got banged up pretty good."

"I saw that! That was you?" Alina recalled the event quite clearly. Her father and HeliEmerg had been involved in the emergency as well. She knew exactly who this man was.

"Uh, huh."

"Oh, no, that was terrible. Ended your career, right?" She asked, picturing the incident that had shaken her. She could still see the equestrian landing forcefully on the bars and his leg brutally and unnaturally stuck between the logs. She remembered the grotesquely misshapen leg that seemed to just hang from the rest of his body when they finally freed him. The live televised event had been gruesome. She tried to remember his face and thought perhaps he was a good-looking guy, but then most of the athletes were. She still didn't quite know what he looked like.

"Yes, it did. Not only the CEA, but any kind of competitive riding," he answered. "HeliEmerg air lifted me to the hospital for my leg. It was thanks to your dad they were able to save it. The crew, and especially Alex, were amazing. After the operation he and your mom helped me with the healing, not just the physical but the emotional. I spent about ten days with them. To me they are family."

Alina thought about what Jax was saying. Why hadn't she seen him at the house? Where had she been? Then she remembered she spent some of that summer in Portugal with some friends and their parents. No wonder they hadn't met. Had they been destined to meet after all? The world was incredibly small.

Following his directions, Jax and Alina arrived in less than twenty minutes. A large sign with a beautiful logo greeted them. It depicted a caduceus with sea horses instead of serpents, their tales intertwined and wrapped all the way down to the bottom of the staff. A heart adorned the top between the wings that seemed to be flying and in motion.

WELCOME TO HIPPO-CAMP

Hippo-Health
Hippo-Heart
Hippo-Heaven

"You know," Alina said, "I've known about your place for a long time, but I've never been out here. That seems so strange to me, especially with my love of horses."

"Perhaps it just wasn't the right time. Maybe I was the one who had to show it to you."

"You're right. I think timing and schedules probably had something to do with it," Alina said, remembering her father's words.

"Welcome to the 3 H's."

"Tell me about them, Jax."

The man was melting on the spot. This woman wanted to know more about his business, and she was sitting right next to him! He focused and explained: "Okay, Hippo-Health is one of the three centers. It's led by a team of veterinarians, assistants, and staff, all specialized in equine care. They take care of horses and their well-being."

"Like a hospital."

"Exactly. At any one time we could have everything from pleasure horses to thoroughbreds, and anything in between." Jax pointed to a second building. "Then we have Hippo-Heart, a rehab center."

"Human?"

"Yes, anything from accident victims to emotional and mental health problems and phobias. Hippotherapy is also wonderful to help sensory, cognitive and neuromotor systems. I'm particularly fond of the equine therapy for people who suffer from PTSD. We do a lot with veterans. We call the program Horses for Heroes."

"Oh, that is so wonderful," Alina exclaimed. She was impressed.

"Ah, look, there is Sir Charles."

"Sir Charles?"

"Yes, former Colonel in the British Army and Olympian, recipient of several medals. He was my coach for the Games, now he helps vets who have PTSD with the horses. Look, there's a new group. He's about to talk to them. Would you like to listen?"

Alina was already captivated. "Oh, yes!"

Sir Charles stood in front of a small group and addressed them. The vets seemed to stand in formation and at ease, their leader in front of them. His voice was loud, clear, yet soothing. "Think of Hippo-Heart as your main base of operations. The horses are the cavalry, literally. In ancient times they protected you, they were part of a war machine. Remember the Mongols? They couldn't have done anything without their horses. Or the amazing Lipizzaners? Today you can watch them put on a magnificent show with their unique moves, in their home in Vienna. However, those moves were once used for warfare and to protect the rider. For example, they used the capriole where they disabled the enemy with a powerful kick of their back legs, better known as knocking the shit out of them." Although an English aristocrat, Sir Charles considered himself a military man first and always enjoyed the colorful language that came with the terrain. The group laughed. Jax and Alina smiled as well. Sir Charles continued: "The horses helped the rider win the battles. Here at the camp, they are still a cavalry, but their focus is no longer on warfare, rather it is on healing. They are just as honorable and courageous as they would be on a battlefield, but their goal is still the same—to protect their riders and make them better. They are here to help you heal and they will work hard for you. They will give you their heart. Let them. They don't expect anything in return; however, I would like you to give them your respect and your attention. They can feel it and deserve no less. They are just as loyal as the men and women who fought alongside you." Sir Charles looked at the new group of suffering veterans. "Treat the horses as comrades who are caring for you. Is that understood?"

"Yes, Sir!" they answered back. They no longer were in the military, but the atmosphere and the former Colonel brought forth the respect. Sir Charles knew how to treat and order soldiers in a dignified way. The former warriors appreciated him and would follow his instructions. They wanted to melt back into society and not worry their PTSD was the one in charge. The Hippo-Camp was helping make that possible for them and, warriors that they were and always would be, they were willing to fight.

"Sir Charles seems to be a special person," Alina said to Jax.

"That he is."

"And what is Hippo-Heaven, the third H?" Alina asked.

"Ah, that too is unique. I wanted a place where horses could 'retire', where older unwanted horses wouldn't be euthanized due to their age or their inability to produce results for their owners, such as racehorses or stallions. Or even perhaps their owners can't afford the expense to keep them around. Here, they just roam freely, graze and are well looked after. They are provided with food, grooming and medical needs until they pass away. Hence the name Heaven."

"A kind of equine nursing home and hospice."

"Exactly." Jax turned to Alina. "I'm very proud of what we built here. I hope in my small way I can help as many people, and horses, as possible."

"Without a doubt. You should be incredibly proud. You are providing such a wonderful service and I can sense how much love is involved."

"Yes, we have amazing people working here. I've had good fortune in my life, some downs of course, but that's part of the path."

"That's true."

"Our doors are open to everyone, especially those who need our help and could never get it."

"How do you mean?"

"We don't charge anything."

"Really? You must have a lot of expenses."

"Oh, we do, but we're also on the honor system."

"How does that work?"

"We trust the people that come through our doors. If someone cannot pay, that's okay. We provide the service they need and don't ask any questions. If they can pay, that's fine, and if per chance they happen to be wealthy and happy with the service they received we leave it up to them to write any amount they would like on their check."

"That's amazing. Does it balance out?"

"Sometimes it does, sometimes it doesn't, and sometimes most definitely. My accountant keeps threatening me with a nervous breakdown or his death by anxiety, no matter how many times I tell him not to worry."

"I can just see a happy family member being truly

grateful for any of the services and writing a decent amount on their check."

"It is very gratifying. I'm lucky the clothing lines are doing so well and I can keep things rolling if needed."

"You're a wonderful person, Mr. Jax Logan. I wish you only continued success." Alina was amazed by this man and his heart.

"Thank you, Alina." Jax had never been happier in his life. He was successful in all his endeavors with the ranch, the clothing lines and the people and horses he loved helping. He had a couple good friends and of course Bernardo. Most importantly if he and Alina never became a couple, he knew she would be a friend for life. Of course, he wanted more than just a friendship and would continue his quest for her love.

Jax directed Alina to the stables. She drove to the entrance and parked. They left the car and headed for the stalls. The staff greeted him and wished him a speedy recovery. He graciously thanked them.

"I would like you to meet my favorite girl," Jax said to Alina.

Did he have a girlfriend? Why hadn't it crossed her mind? She followed him.

Jax opened the door to one of the stalls.

Alina looked in and saw the magnificent horse. "Is this Almea?" She cried excitedly.

"Yes! How do you know her name?"

"Oh, I remember her from the Olympics and because it means dancer, and that's what she was doing to the music of the tango during the dressage."

"Ah, of course, the dancer and rider in you would remember that."

"I also recognized her because her markings

reminded me of jewelry."

"Yes, she is a beauty," Jax said proudly. *And so are you, lovely Alina.*

"And quite refined."

"She owes a lot of that to her breed, she's a Paso Fino."

"Ah, makes perfect sense. How is she doing?"

"Better than ever, still in competition form."

"May I touch her?" Alina asked, dying to caress the mare's neck.

"Of course." Jax had been watching Almea and noticed her ears and nostrils when Alina spoke. "Besides, she likes you."

"How do you know?" She asked as she caressed the strong neck.

"Give me your hand."

Alina did. They each felt a tingle as they touched. Jax took her palm and led it to the horse's side. He kept their fingers together and he put their hands on Almea's heart. The horse's heartbeat thumped rhythmically and then slowed a little. "Did it just get slower?" Alina asked, whispering.

Jax nodded. "That means she likes you."

"Really?" Alina was thrilled. She was quite knowledgeable when it came to horses and she connected with them very well, but this was a truly special moment for her. "It's like she's talking to me!" Alina said, still whispering.

"Exactly," Jax said, whispering as well just next to her ear. He could smell her hair. He absolutely wanted to lose himself in her essence. "This is how they connect with us, where they sing from. It is a melody from their hearts to ours. It's their heart song." *And you are mine,* Jax wanted to add.

Alina gasped. How much more special could that be for a singer? She put her cheek against the mare's body and closed her eyes. She let her tears run down her face, incredibly moved and grateful for the momentous connection.

Jax gently wiped the rivulet from the cheek closest to him as his body slightly pressed closer to hers. Alina opened her eyes and turned to him. She could smell the combination of his manly essence and hay, while trying to keep her mind away from his hard physique. She was starting to see the handsomeness of his face as the swelling was slowly disappearing. His eyes were cat-like and the piercing blue seemed to penetrate into her. She looked at his soft, beautiful lips and longed to touch and kiss them.

Jax was slightly trembling, his body's senses trying to take in every inch of the stunning woman so close to him. Their hands were still on Almea's heart and Jax slightly turned Alina toward him. They faced each other and looked into one another's eyes. "May I kiss you, Alina?" What if she said no? Would she leave? Would he ever see her again? The man was in agony until Alina answered him by putting her hand behind his neck and pulled him to her until their lips met. She had wondered about those lips and now she was finally savoring them. The kiss was soft and gentle and then it became more passionate until they both stopped and started laughing.

"You felt it too?" Jax asked.

Alina nodded, grinning.

Almea's heartbeat had speeded up while they were kissing. She had related with them.

"I think she gave us her heart song," Alina said.

"My two favorite girls are both singers." Jax chuckled.

"I'm your favorite girl, well, one of them?"

"Most definitely," Jax answered, remembering the exquisiteness of her lips. They were even more delicious that he had anticipated.

They took their hands off Almea and embraced as their mouths met. They kissed with the ardor they both desired and projected.

Almea snorted. Alina started laughing. "I think she's telling us to behave or to get a hotel room."

Jax's dopamine was overflowing and he didn't know what to do about her comment. With any other woman he probably would have made love to her right then and there. But this was Alina. He didn't want to ruin anything with a quick roll in the hay, literally. His body heat was becoming feverishly high.

Alina realized she had made Jax uncomfortable. "I'm sorry, that was…"

"No, no, that was fine," Jax said quickly. "Besides, the idea isn't bad at all," he said grinning.

Alina looked at him and smiled until her cheekbones lifted slightly and made her even more enchanting. Jax held his breath. It was the same smile from the first time he had seen her on the television screen, the one that made him fall under her spell.

"Really?"

"Definitely." He confirmed.

They were comfortable with one another, found each other easy to talk to and had several passions in common. "Well, we wouldn't have to go to a hotel, there are plenty of rooms here, or we could go for a ride," Jax said. There wasn't anything in the world he would rather do than make love to her, but he wanted more, he wanted her in his life forever. If he achieved that then they could make all the love they wanted.

"How about we start with the ride. Maybe we'll take the other one step at a time."

"Great. I'll have someone saddle us a couple of horses."

"Sounds great, but are you sure you're okay to ride?"

"That's second nature, besides it's all about movement. The horse's pelvis has the same three-dimensional planes as the human one, and the interchange provides the therapy needed and transmits healing when the horse walks."

Alina loved listening to Jax's knowledge about anything equine and always enjoyed learning new things.

One of the stable hands brought out two saddled horses. He helped both Alina and Jax mount up.

"Ready?" Jax asked.

"Absolutely. This is such a treat. I haven't ridden in quite a while. Thank you for showing me around, Jax.

"It is definitely my pleasure."

Jax and Alina rode around the property for a while until it started getting darker. Even with his discomfort which was quite tolerable with the pain pills, Jax was sure he was floating from happiness. He was with Alina, the woman who rocked his world, riding side by side on his ranch, just like in his dream. He was sure this was as close to paradise as he would ever get. "Are you hungry?" He asked.

"Starving! What did you have in mind?"

"Churrasco?"

"Really?" Alina asked excitedly. "One of my all-time favorites! Is there an Argentinian restaurant around here that I didn't know about?"

"Oh, no, better. I have the real deal. Come, you have to meet Bernardo, he's waiting for us," Jax said, steering her toward the fire pit.

"Who is Bernardo?"

"An incredible churrasco chef and an even more amazing man. The one who took over when my parents were killed and who helped me through tough times and grueling rehab after the CEA. The one who molded me when I was very young and who taught me the most about horses and my love for them. He's quite a guy and a real gaucho from the Pampas of Argentina."

"He sounds amazing."

"He truly is."

As promised Bernardo was waiting for them when they arrived. The food was cooking. Introductions were made and the gaucho appreciated the beautiful woman Jax presented to him. He removed his beret and kissed her hand. Alina smiled and greeted him. One of Jax's eyebrows went up. He had never seen Bernardo's charming side. He liked it. He could tell the older man was taken by Alina.

They enjoyed small talk and the music in the background playing from the old cassette player. "La Cumparsita", a classic tango song written by Gerardo Matos Rodriguez and recognized the world over, kept the atmosphere warm. It was also part of the tango medley Jax used in the dressage competitions and the commercials. Bernardo asked Alina to dance. She never hesitated and extended her hand. He took it and as they came together they started. She was sure the gaucho would be a good dancer. What Argentine wasn't? And she was right, the man was incredibly smooth.

Jax watched the two people he loved most in the world—the man who had raised him, taken care of him since he was a boy and the exquisite woman, the love of his life. They were magnificent together, dancing a tango he could have sworn had been rehearsed over and over. Jax remembered Bernardo when he was just six years old, when he had watched him dance with his invisible partner around the fire, and later when he showed him, the boy, how to place his feet and make his body a vehicle for the music flowing through him. His eyes followed the couple and his chest inflated with pride. Bernardo and Alina were fluid, gliding through movements with the music as if they had been performing together for years.

"You are very special, Señorita. I am not talking just about your dancing, but about your heart. I can see a new light in Jax's eyes. You make him very happy and I believe he gives you the same joy. I am sure you two will stay that way an entire lifetime."

Alina slightly raised her eyebrows. What did this wise *anciano* know? What was it Grace, her father and even Bernardo knew? She looked into his weathered eyes and saw the old man's happiness. She smiled, that signature smile that always made others beam in return. *"Sí?"*

"Sí, Señorita Alina."

Jax saw Bernardo slightly move his head and the younger man immediately took over. Alina never stopped dancing as the transition was flawless.

"That was one of the most wonderful tangos I have ever danced," Alina said. "What an amazing teacher he must have been to you."

"In many ways."

As superb as the dance had been between Bernardo and Alina, the younger version with Jax was even more impressive and incredibly sensual.

"Bernardo taught you well. You may have surpassed the master," Alina said. She truly loved dancing, any kind and from anywhere in the world, but never had she enjoyed moving and gliding with another person as she was doing at that instant with Jax. She was sure she was floating through the breeze caressing her skin as Jax guided her with his strong arms, torso and hips. He was light on his feet and an amazing leading partner. She loved the slight pressure of his body and his hands as he guided her and longed for more of his touch. Alina knew he was a very talented individual from his business and his equestrian accomplishments. She added dancer and great kisser to the list and wondered if he was as brilliant as a lover? She had a difficult time focusing and tried to stop thinking about making love with Jax.

While waiting for the food Alina regaled Bernardo with two of his favorite songs: "El Día Que Me Quieras", The Day When You Will Love Me, written by Alejandro Gardel; and "Gracias A La Vida", Thank You To Life, by Violeta Parra, made famous by incredible artists such as Mercedes Sosa, Maria Farantouri and Joan Baez.

"This has been a wonderful night and it has been a very long time, Señorita, that I have enjoyed dancing so exquisitely with such a charming, talented and beautiful lady. Thank you."

"Thank you, *Don Bernardo*. The pleasure has been all mine."

"I think when it is my time to go, I would like to fade away while dancing a tango," the Argentine said.

"That's quite a wish," Alina concurred.

"It certainly is," Jax added.

"Perfect, *si?*" Bernardo asked.

"*Sí,*" they answered back.

"Bernardo, you have been a wonderful chef and a very gracious host, thank you for the delicious food and an amazing evening."

"If I had this chiquito's age, and I had never met my Maria, the boy wouldn't stand a chance, Señorita," Bernardo said grinning and kissed her hand.

"I have no doubt, Don Bernardo, you would leave him in the dust." Alina confirmed with her signature smile and gently touched the older man's cheek. She gave him a kiss on the other one.

Bernardo put his arm around Jax's shoulder and whispered one of his favorite Argentinian expressions in his ear: *"¡Qué chica copada!"*

"Yes, she is very cool."

"You better make her yours, chiquito."

"That's my intention." *Oh, Bernardo, if you only knew.* "I guess it's true that something good always happens to me after a catastrophe, just like after the CEA. I hope this one will be just as successful."

Jax and Alina hugged the gaucho and rode back to the stables. The groomer took care of the horses and the couple walked to the house.

"I have a wonderful bottle of wine I think we should uncork before you leave."

"Alright, just a glass."

Once inside Jax invited her to sit down.

"Why don't you let me help you?"

"No, I'm good, thanks. Not much pain, either."

"I'm glad to hear that. Do you need anything before I leave?"

"No, I'll manage." Jax didn't want Alina to leave. He wanted her to stay the night. He wanted her to stay forever. He just wanted to hold her, although making love would be heaven itself. His mind wandered off, picturing them as lovers.

"Jax?"

"Yes?" He said, coming out of his reverie.

"Are you okay?"

"I'm fine. I believe in love at first sight, ever since I saw you on television," Jax blurted out. *Oh, shit, now why did I have to say that?* Had he just ruined everything between them?

"What? How do you mean?"

"You wouldn't believe the ways I dreamed up of how to meet you."

"I presume you weren't very successful, since I didn't know you until the accident."

"Not successful at all!" He cringed as he remembered his visions about reaching her on the yacht and in the Vinyl. "Yeah, from under the sea and from the sky."

"How do you mean?"

"Oh, nothing, just dreams. However, had I thought of stepping in front of your car I would have done it immediately. It would have been so worth it, and saved so much time."

"Don't be silly, that's not even funny." Alina said with emphasis, a little perturbed.

"I'm sorry. I'm not trying to be an obsessed fan, but I have to be honest. I'm very much in love with you and I just had to tell you. Nothing like this has ever happened to me. I never believed in love at first sight and I would love to be the man of your dreams, to please you like no one else in the world could. But I'm sure you have hundreds, no, thousands and thousands, lined up who feel like I do. Oh, Christ, I sound worse than a lovelorn teenager." He went to the sofa where she was sitting and handed her a glass of wine.

"Thank you," she said and took a sip.

Jax sat next to her, took her other hand and kissed it.

Alina looked at him, put her glass down on the coffee table in front of her and slightly lifted his chin. She looked at his face and carefully touched the bruised skin. "Does it hurt?"

"Not really," he answered, trembling at her touch.

"I'm so sorry," she said, the guilt crawling into her heart.

"Please stop feeling guilty. It wasn't your fault at all. I was the idiot not paying attention." Jax looked at her and grinned, "but I was thinking of you."

Alina gently pulled his face towards her. She carefully kissed the areas where there was no bruising or stitches. Her lips on his skin were as light as a feather caressing him. Jax let her continue until she arrived at his mouth. He tasted the wine on her lips and his tongue caressed the slight opening. When he pressed a little harder their tongues danced. Jax cupped her neck and pulled her toward him until her breasts sensually crushed against his chest. They continued kissing until Alina stopped. She looked into his eyes and asked: "How are you feeling?"

"If you mean physically, no pain and invincible. If you mean emotionally, I'm pretty sure my heart has grown inside my chest and has never been this happy."

Alina smiled and took his hand. "Show me your bedroom?" She asked softly, slowly getting up. She had never wanted anybody or anything so much in her life.

Jax firmly believed heaven had just descended on earth. They looked into each other's glowing eyes, blue to amber, as he guided her down the hallway. As they entered the room they faced each other. Alina touched his firm chest, undid the buttons on his shirt and put her hands behind the material on the bulging muscles before removing it off his shoulders. Jax breath caught in his throat as every nerve in his body stood at attention. He didn't move as Alina caressed his torso and gently kneaded his abdominals. She started to pull off her own shirt and Jax helped her. He kissed her neck and held her close as he undid her brassiere. He put his fingers under the straps until they fell away. His mouth still kissed her skin as he moved down from her neck to the exquisite firm breasts. He continued with his tongue, pleasuring her as she moaned in delight. He didn't stop while he undid the rest of her clothes and removed his own as well. He gently guided her to the bed behind her. He started kissing her feet, slowly moving up to her calves and thighs. He continued licking and nibbling until he reached the flower of her womanhood. Alina's back immediately arched up as she moaned in delight and abandon. Jax promised himself so many times that when they would make love it would be the most magnificent pleasure he could give her. He hoped he was fulfilling his promise.

Alina put her fingers through his hair and gently pulled his head toward her. Jax understood her need and swiftly made them one. She gasped at the smoothness and the exquisite fullness of their bodies' mutual desire. They both sighed as their rhythm guided them to their ultimate crescendo.

Jax realized that he had never made love. He, of course, had had wonderful sex with many lovely ladies, but he had never loved any of them. Tonight, for the first time, he understood what that miracle of life really meant—to be one with another human being, in body and, most importantly, in heart. He looked at the magnificent woman next to him and beamed in delight until he noticed the tears slowly rolling down her cheeks.

"What's wrong?" He whispered, momentarily frightened, hoping he hadn't hurt her in any way. Like most men, seeing a woman crying pinched his heart.

Alina lovingly caressed his face with the back of her hand. Her lips parted and formed the smile that would always melt his heart. "That was the most special and incredible experience I've ever had." She kissed his lips, slowly at first and then with more ardor.

Jax was glowing, his self-worth soaring to new heights, his intention on giving her an ultimate experience fulfilled. Their love making was even more exquisite than in any of his dreams. He returned her kiss with just as much fervor. Little Jax was just as happy, and ready for an encore.

Through the night Jax and Alina continued sensually discovering each other, learning how to give their partner a part of their heart through their bodies, making their own unique and original compositions. Every move was as smooth as a musical note, every kiss a refrain for more until they culminated into their very own exquisite symphony.

♫

CHAPTER 34

The next day Jax and Alina woke up late. She found one of Jax's shirts and put it on. She headed toward the bed and the man she wanted to share unrivaled ecstatic abandonment, love and bliss with every day of her life. Jax watched her as she took his breath away. He loved everything she wore, ranging from the most exquisite evening gowns to the sexiest bikinis, but his favorite was the way she wore his shirt. Especially since she didn't have anything on underneath. Rolled up sleeves, buttons open to just below the breast line and the curve of the bottom of the shirt where the legs started, mesmerized him. He loved the way Alina pulled off such natural sensual elegance every woman and fashion designer would kill for.

Jax and Alina took a long passionate shower together, had brunch and toured more of the estate with the horses. They both loved riding in the open range and continued until it was time for dinner with their favorite gaucho.

Bernardo sat in front of the fire pit as the glowing

embers reflected into the pastel and orange sunset. He remembered one of Claude Debussy's favorite sayings: "There is nothing more musical than a sunset." The canvas of the sky was one of the most splendid he had ever seen and he wondered if it had a special meaning. He had prepared the food and it was ready for the grill. He was happy and could hardly wait to see the young couple again. They filled his heart with such joy.

Suddenly Bernardo screamed from the intense pain in his chest, but no breath or sound came out. He was sure someone had thrown a pair of enormous bolas at him, which were continuously tightening around his torso. The pain was excruciating and the most penetrating the man had ever experienced. The pressure traveled to his left arm, his back, neck and jaw. He remembered a full-grown horse tripping and pinning him to the ground when he was younger, but that pain was only temporary as the animal stood up quickly. This was more of an elephant just sitting on him and not moving. Bernardo couldn't breathe. He couldn't expand his lungs to get air and he was getting dizzy and lightheaded. His mind told him this was the end and that it was time to be with his Maria. He would be so happy to see her. He had missed her so much throughout the years, but he wanted to say goodbye to Jax and also to Alina, the love of his chiquito's life. In one day Bernardo came to love the young woman as if she were a child of his. "I have to last just a little more, please," he whispered to the stars that had come out. "I want to see my gauchito and his *diosa*, his goddess, one more time." He hoped the Creator and his Maria were listening as he begged them for this last request.

Bernardo tenaciously held on. With the little energy left he managed to turn on his cassette player and sit in a garden chair, even with only half of his body working.

Jax and Alina rode to the fire pit where they dismounted and tied up the horses before going to see the gaucho. When Jax saw Bernardo, the younger man was shocked. His mentor looked so pale and frail. What had happened since the last time they had been together? Jax almost cried when he remembered what a vibrant man the Argentine had been his whole life. Now Bernardo seemed to be shrinking away. Something was definitely wrong.

Alina looked at the older man and knew immediately what had happened. Her medical knowledge from her parents told her he had suffered a heart attack, and when she saw his left arm slumped to his side and the slight downward angle of one side of his mouth it gave her confirmation. "Bernardo, we have to get you to the hospital right away."

Jax whirled around, terrified. "What's wrong?"

Bernardo motioned to them to come closer. They knelt in front of him. He spoke slowly, his voice barely a whisper. "My children, it is my time to go, to…"

"Bernardo, stop that." Jax chastised gently.

The older man put up his working hand, the other one was paralyzed. His voice was barely audible. "Please, listen to me. I've had a wonderful life, first in my native Argentina with my Maria and my horses, and then here with you and your parents. Jax, I love you like my own child and now I love Alina just as much. You are beautiful together, in body and in heart. You make each other better people and you both make the world a better place. Always stay like that. I want your life together to be so happy you won't know if you are living it or dreaming it. Agreed?" he asked them. They nodded. "Now, help me up. It is time for my last tango," he said with as much authority as he could muster.

"What are you saying? What do you mean your last tango?" Jax asked, frightened, as the knot in his stomach kept twisting painfully.

"Help me," Alina said, starting to lift Bernardo from his chair. She knew. They all knew.

"Of course," Jax answered. He gently raised the older man from behind until he was standing up and facing Alina. She held him up momentarily as Jax ran to start "La Cumparsita", Bernardo's favorite tango, on the trusted cassette player. Alina took the gaucho's paralyzed hand and delicately put it in hers. She held it up, looked into his eyes and smiled. Bernardo smiled back as best he could. His eyes, however, spoke for him and they related how grateful he was and how much she meant to him. Alina nodded back and kissed his cheek. Jax looked at the two people he adored and then stood behind the older man. He carefully lifted Bernardo until the gaucho's feet were on top of his and his back was leaning on his chest. Jax put his hand around Alina's who held Bernardo's. Jax's other arm circled around to her back. One of Alina's cheeks was on Bernardo's face and Jax put his own on her other cheek. He squeezed their hands and the trio danced together, a smile on their faces, a love and three bodies that were as one. Jax guided them into a traditional walk and through several steps. When the music player stopped Bernardo whispered into Alina's ear to sing "Gracias a la Vida" and told Jax to continue a few more steps and to do a dip at the end of the song. Alina knew the time had come. With all the stoicism and professional self-control she possessed, she began singing. Jax wasn't sure he could pull off the dip with three people, let alone in his frame of mind about what was happening, but he swore he would do it. He would make Bernardo's last request a reality. He owed the man so much. He dismissed the pain from his ribs as he slowly pushed his right leg back until his left knee was at a 45-degree angle where he managed to hold both Alina and Bernardo in place, until the three of them very slowly sank to the ground. They lay there, together as one, in one embrace. Alina finished the last notes of the song and she and Jax looked into each other's tearing eyes, fearing the eventual outcome had happened. They turned to Bernardo and saw a perfect, happy smile on the gaucho's face. His wish had been granted. He had left the world of the living, while enjoying one of his great passions, in the arms of the children he adored.

♬

CHAPTER 35

Randy wasn't as upset as he expected with the failed attempt against Jax at the hospital. The competitor in him chalked it up to a new challenge, but first he was going to make some changes in his life. He knew how easy goals could be achieved with money and, after his recent transaction with his father, his offshore accounts had plenty of funds. While he was in Miami, he changed his name from Randolph Newton III to Randy Rinato. He liked it. It felt light and cheerful, especially since Rinato meant reborn in Italian. He applied for new papers, including a driver's license and a passport. While waiting for his documents he stayed at one of the best hotels in the city and enjoyed all its amenities. He remembered the wealthy days and smiled, a little of the old snob in him resurfacing, but from now on his life would be different. Not only was he free, the world was at his feet. He could buy anything he wanted and could do anything his heart desired. There would, however, be a big difference—he would never be like his parents and would stay quiet and inconspicuous. He didn't want to flaunt his wealth and certainly didn't want to be well known. He rather liked the simplicity of it all.

Randy left his suite, helped himself to the restaurant's delicious morning buffet and decided to enjoy the beach and the ocean. For lunch he ordered a sandwich by the pool and by the afternoon his skin was pretty red. He stopped by one of the hotel shops and picked up some cream. As he headed back toward his room, he noticed a fine jewelry store. He looked at the window display, smiled, and went inside.

When Randy's documents were ready, he became a 'new' man. He returned to Connecticut to meet up with Darla. He thought about her constantly, realized how much he missed her and wanted to give her everything her heart desired. The man understood for the first time in his life what it meant to love someone, a person he wanted to spend every moment of every day with. Even more wonderful was that the woman loved him back. Someone actually really wanted him and loved him for himself. He thought of it as the greatest gift in the world and something money could definitely not buy.

Randy walked into the diner. It was lunch and it was packed. He spotted his favorite corner table. It was empty. He quickly sat down and waited for Darla. When she saw him, she ran up to him and hugged him. He returned the hug and kissed her longingly until some of the patrons started ribbing them. Randy let her go and smiled. He took her by the hand and led her to the middle of the diner.

"Randy, what are you doing? This is the craziest time of the day, you know, lunch… rush hour. I have to get back to work."

"Sh," he said, putting a finger to his lips.

"What's up?" Darla whispered.

Randy looked around and said in a loud voice, making sure everyone could hear him: "Ladies and gentlemen, may I have your attention, please?"

Darla was worried, and a little embarrassed. What was he up to? The people enjoying their lunch looked at the couple and didn't know if they should be annoyed yet. The manager came out, wondering if everything was alright. "Hey, what's going on?" He asked.

"Sir," Randy said to the manager, then turned and faced the patrons. "Everybody, I know you are all busy and I don't mean to disturb you, but I have an important announcement," Randy said.

All eyes were on him. He turned to the woman he loved and got down on one knee. Darla gasped, as did most of the people in the diner. The manager grinned. He loved Darla, had taken her under his wing ever since she walked in off the streets over ten years earlier and considered her just as close as his other children. And was just as protective of her. Darla had told him about Randy and watching the two of them in the middle of his diner, well, he couldn't be happier for her.

Randy produced a velvet box from his pocket and opened it. He removed a ring, with a diamond bigger than Darla had ever seen in her life and presented it to her. She worried how much it cost him. She had no idea how wealthy the man was. "Would you marry me, my sweet Dar? Would you be my wife?" The patrons, who had stopped eating and were now fully paying attention, collectively held their breaths, as did Randy. Darla fiercely held back the tears accumulating behind her lower lids, but it was in vain. They cascaded down her cheeks as she nodded in affirmation. The people in the diner erupted in applause and shouts of congratulations. Randy placed the rock on her finger and they kissed for a long moment. He turned to his audience and yelled: "She said YES! Oh, by the way, everybody's lunch is on me." The patrons were even happier and cheered some more.

"Did you hit the lottery or something?" Darla asked him.

"Or something," Randy answered.

The manager liked the young man. He had style.

♫

CHAPTER 36

2022 – ATHENS, GREECE

Jax and Alina had been together for several months when the annual Polyphony Awards, one of the most prestigious music tributes, nominated Alina for one of the honors. Cities around the world would vie to be the host for the event as it was unique, brought the biggest celebrities and always filled the coffers of the host country. Similar to the Olympics, the countries bid for the venue. This year Athens, Greece, had been granted the honor. The exclusive show would be held at the prestigious open-air Herodus Atticus Theater, one of the world's most majestic odeons.

The two-thousand-year-old venue, hewn of the rock at the foot of the Acropolis, welcomed only elite entertainers and composers such as Nana Mouskouri, Frank Sinatra, Yianni, Placido Domingo and Mikis Theodorakis. Operas, national ballets and symphonies from around the world were also highlighted in the unique marble semi-circular auditorium. The venue would host an audience of more than 4,000 people for the awards. Before entering, an immense red carpet in front of the theater would welcome the impressive list of entertainers and spectators.

Randy had been following Jax's life since the hospital in Miami. Every day he would check his sources on the man's whereabouts and his activities, either via computers or private investigators. When Alina's nomination was announced, Randy investigated some more and knew Athens would be the right place and time. One week before the awards he flew to Greece, first class of course, and planned his revenge.

Randy hired one of the best local guides in the city. He told the man he was part of a team that was researching venues to shoot a commercial, and he needed an expert who could help him. He promised his name would be included in the credits at the end of the piece. The Greek man was thrilled and went out of his way to please Randy. He explained details and answered every question. First, he took Randy to the Plaka district of Athens. They walked the ancient cobblestone streets, smelled local specialties from the restaurants lining the neighborhood and took in the little stores. Some were very touristy, others housed works of art. Randy found the area of the city magical. Darla would love it here, he was sure. One day he would bring her.

"It is the oldest district of Athens and lovingly called the 'Neighborhood of the Gods'," Vassili, Randy's guide, explained. "It extends from the foot of the Acropolis almost to Syntagma Square, also known as Constitution Square, and is said to have been continuously inhabited for about three thousand years. It is the oldest neighborhood in the world."

"It's beautiful," Randy agreed.

"You like for the commercial?" Vassili asked.

"For what? Oh, yes, this is definitely one of the spots we'll be filming."

"Excellent. Now we go to the top of the Acropolis with the Parthenon.

"Great. Lead the way."

Randy and Vassili toured the grounds of the Acropolis, climbed the ancient sanctuary and walked to the edge behind Athena's temple. They stood under the enormous Greek flag.

"Fantastic view," Randy said, taking in the entire city of Athens and its surroundings.

"Yes, straight ahead is Mount Lycabettus with St. George, its little church, at the top. On this side you can see as far as the port of Piraeus and the sea, and over here is the new Acropolis Museum which is exquisite. Below us you can see the Herodus Atticus theater."

"I hear the Polyphony Awards will take place there."

"Yes, that's correct," Vassili said excitedly and very proud his city was hosting the show.

"Can we walk around it? It looks quite spectacular."

"Oh, it is. Come, I will show you."

They left the top of the Acropolis and walked back down. When they reached the front of the theater Randy was ecstatic as it was surrounded by a forest of enormous olive and pine trees. Randy smiled as he found the spot he would take his shot and end not only Alina's life, but more importantly Jax's happiness. As with his parents he was sure that would be even more painful than a quick death.

"Vassili, you've been great. I think I have everything my company needs as far as locations for the commercial shoot."

"Yes? Ah, that is good. Anything else I can help you with?"

"As a matter fact there is."

"Tell me."

"Do you know of an Army surplus store?"

"You mean military things?" The Greek had never been asked such a question by a tourist, or anyone else for that matter.

"Yes, my nephew is in the military, American of course, and he likes to collect items from other countries. I thought I would bring him back a gift."

"Ah, I understand. Yes, I know of a shop."

"Excellent. Can we go there now?"

"Now? Oh, yes, of course. We can take a taxi."

"Good, I wouldn't want to forget a gift for my nephew. He would kill me."

The guide looked at Randy with big round eyes. "That is joke, yes?"

"Yes, Vassili, that is joke."

"Okay."

When Randy walked into the store, he knew exactly what he needed, but he didn't want Vassili there. The two men went up to an older man, who perhaps was the owner. Vassili introduced him and told him that the American gentleman wanted a souvenir for his nephew.

"Do you speak English?" Randy asked the older man.

"Yes, little. I help you."

"Wonderful, thank you very much. I'll take a look around your shop if you don't mind."

"Of course, please, anything you like. I am Costa, the owner, and make you good discount."

"Thank you," Randy said and started checking out the merchandise. He had to find something small and seemingly inconsequential. He didn't want Vassili getting any strange ideas about him. Randy went up to the old man and looked at the wall. "How much for that?"

The other two men turned and saw what Randy was pointing at.

"This is medal from my father, he fight in WWII. Very brave. This given him by Prime Minister. My father big *palikari!*"

"Palikari?" Randy asked.

"A strong, young, beautiful, very brave Greek warrior," Vassili explained.

"Palikari means all that?"

"Exactly."

"I'm sure your father was a great man," Randy said to the owner.

"Yes, thank you. But no, I'm sorry, not this one, sentimental you know. But I have other medals."

"Okay, that would be perfect. May I see them?"

"Of course."

Randy made his purchase and he and the guide left the shop.

"My nephew will be very happy, thank you Vassili. You have been an excellent guide." Randy handed him a few extra bills and the Greek man was very happy indeed.

They parted ways and Randy walked around the block and sat at a nearby café. He had a Greek coffee and a *tiropita*, a cheese pie. When he finished he went back into the store.

"Ah, you need something else?" Costa asked. He liked the American, he didn't bargain very well.

"Yes, Costa." Randy looked around the store. It was empty. The last clients had left. "I need an SRS A2."

The old man whistled. "The smallest, lightest, long range rifle, yes?"

"Yes."

"Very difficult."

Randy pulled a large wad of Euros from his pocket. "No more than two days. I'll be here one hour before you open the day after tomorrow." He started peeling bills and laying them on the counter.

"*Endaxi.* Okay."

"I also need…"

Two days later Randy walked back into the military surplus store. Costa saw him and motioned him toward the back of the shop. As they entered a room the Greek man went to a long table where items were covered by a blanket. Costa pulled it off and Randy's eyes smiled. Everything he needed and requested was right there in front of him. He checked out all the equipment and paid. There was no bargaining and Randy handed the older man a couple extra thousand. Costa's eyes grew larger. Today was a good payday.

"Perfect job, Costa. Thank you. I just need one more thing."

"What is that?"

"I need a place where I can try the rifle out."

"Yes, I know where you can do this. Not far, maybe one hour from Athens." Costa gave him directions.

"You have never seen or met me."

"Never." The older man grinned. "But if you ever need anything else you know where to find me."

"I do."

The two men shook hands and Randy left the store. He had parked his cheap rental car around the corner. He opened the trunk and put his purchases inside. He left Athens and drove for about an hour to the deserted area Costa had suggested. There wasn't anything or anyone for miles around. It was off the beaten track with hardly any road. It was perfect.

Randy parked under a large tree. It was hot and the shade was welcoming. He opened the trunk and took out the rifle and a bag of small watermelons he picked up along the way. He walked with long strides and measured about fifty yards. There were more trees and he placed several of the round fruit on different branches. Randy walked back to the car, assembled the rifle and added the scope and silencer. He placed the weapon's miniature stand on the roof of the vehicle, took a deep breath, exhaled and squeezed the trigger. He missed the melon by a foot. He adjusted the scope and tried again. Still a little off. On the third try the bullet hit dead center and the red and green fruit violently exploded into hundreds of pieces. Randy practiced until he was satisfied. He packed up his gear and headed back to Athens.

The next day Randy prepared his equipment. He carefully put the rifle pieces and cartridge in the foam compartments he had cut and placed in a camouflage colored backpack. He also added a harness, a rope, two bottles of water and a couple protein bars in the same bag. The last item he packed right on top was a lightweight camouflage suit. He also remembered the letter he had written to Darla. The contents hadn't changed but he had torn up the check and instead added his offshore account numbers. Should anything happen to him she would inherit his fortune. He couldn't think of anyone more deserving. He also knew that Darla would know how to help others if she so desired.

At four o'clock in the morning Randy left his room and went to the rental car, put the back pack on the floor next to him and drove to a street very close to the

Acropolis. It was still dark and he avoided any street lights. He still had a couple of hours before sunrise. He looked around. No one in sight. It was deserted as the city slept, at least where Randy was. He opened his backpack, removed the suit and quickly put it on over his other clothes. The man was covered from head to toe in fake pines. He could have been the Yeti's camouflaged cousin. He put the green rope through the loop at the top of the backpack. He left it on the ground next to the enormous tree he had selected from his walk with Vassili. He tied the other end of the rope to his ankle and silently climbed the immense pine. He found a spot high up, deep in the tree's dense canopy. He sat on one of the huge limbs, reached the rope on his ankle and pulled up the backpack. He assembled the harness and positioned it among the branches and the leaves. He tried it out. It was sturdy. Randy sat in it; it wasn't as comfortable as a camping chair, but it would be a help for the long hours of waiting. He looked around. All was still quiet. He assembled the pieces of the weapon, attached the scope and the silencer and hung it around his torso. The rifle was camouflaged as well. No one would ever see him in the tree.

♫

CHAPTER 37

Alina had attended other music awards before, but this was the most prestigious and she was nominated for one of the Polyphonies. As she sat in the limousine next to Jax, holding hands with him, she looked at her parents sitting across from them. They too were holding hands. She watched their tête-à-tête as they were probably saying niceties to one another, the amazing glow in their eyes relaying their mutual adoration. Alina couldn't imagine loving her parents any more than she did at this very moment. Her mind flashed back to her young life. She watched herself as if a film was being projected in front of her eyes, from the first moment she could remember as a little girl in Spain until this very instant. It had been an amazing journey she called the University of Life.

Jax was seeing his own film, mainly about Bernardo and the many teachings and amazing moments they had spent together. He missed the old gaucho and would always carry him in his heart.

Alina squeezed Jax's hand. He knew she loved him, but he wasn't sure if she was just telling him through her hand or if she needed a little reassuring support. Perhaps her nerves were just a little tight because of the awards.

"How are you doing?" He asked.

"I'm good." Alina looked deep into the eyes of the man she loved. "I was just thinking maybe Bernardo is watching us."

Jax's breath caught in his chest. How did she know he was thinking about his old mentor? How was it possible to love this woman even more than he already did? "I'm sure he and Maria are both sitting on their star, holding hands too and eating popcorn."

Alina laughed. "I think maybe not popcorn, but his favorite churrasco."

The Mercedes stretch limousine stopped at the foot of the Acropolis. An immense red carpet welcomed them. Miguel and Santiago, both very chic in their designer tuxedos, emerged from the car first. Alejandro and Stacy followed, just as distinguished in their eveningwear. Jax was next and helped Alina out. He stood out in his own tuxedo, courtesy of Siyavash and the JAX line, and thankfully his nerves were at a minimum. He was used to competitions and being in the spotlight, but this was different. This was the world of entertainment and huge celebrities. But just as with his collection, he was a quick learner about the details of the business and never missed a beat as he held Alina's arm and with confidence walked her down the carpet.

Alina didn't walk, she glided. She was everything every woman longed to be, and someone everyone wanted in their lives. The men around Alina, as well as the venue's security, resembled peacocks as they inflated their chests and spread themselves around her. They vehemently wanted to protect the stunning woman and they momentarily had goose bumps when the diva happened to touch their arms. Their body language screamed to everyone around "Look at me, I'm with the great Alina and she makes me special too. You are not as lucky as I am, so just envy me".

Alina was a major focus of the event. She was beautiful, talented, elegant and nominated for a Polyphony for the Best International Song, a song that had to include at least two languages. She had composed and written the lyrics to "Our World", and included two additional languages. There were four—English, Spanish, Portuguese and Arabic.

Alina looked stunning in her gown, a creation by a man who had become her good friend—Siyavash. There had been an immediate friendship, their international backgrounds a major factor. Jax had introduced the designer of the JAX collections to the woman he loved. He knew they would understand each other perfectly when she had mentioned she needed a new dress for the awards. Of course, her love for horses and his name only added to their mutual admiration. Although some of the world's best designers had boutiques at the Vinyl, Jax suggested his Iranian friend and his collections' creator. It was a match made in heaven. Alina and Siyavash discussed what the singer wanted and the result was unique and magnificent. He had come through brilliantly and the revelation of the gown at the awards was one of the highlights of the event. The dress was reminiscent of an ancient Hellenic toga with only one shoulder covered. The gown was made with several layers of silk, giving it a flowing cape-like allure. The band on her left shoulder held up the dress and was the beginning of the ombré effect which started with an off-white and continued with very light lemon on down to a pastel orange-red. It rivaled the Greek sunset on the horizon. Her shoes were the same orange-red hue as the bottom of her dress, as was her clutch, both made of the same silk material. There was a long slit from her right thigh down to the hem of the gown.

Alina and Stacy had gone shopping the day before, trying to stay incognito with big hats, as Santiago nonchalantly walked a few steps behind them. The ladies were impressed and ecstatic by the exquisite Greek jewelry and craftmanship. Alina purchased a lovely eighteen-carat solid gold necklace of olive leaves, with a matching bracelet from one the premier Athenian jewelry stores. She also picked up a pair of gold cufflinks for Jax which resembled antique coins. The design was of a horse and rider depicted during the ancient Olympic Games. Around the edge was the same olive leaves wreath which was the prize the athletes received. She wanted to honor him for having been an Olympian. Alina now wore the necklace and bracelet with the gown. It was not only very Greek and emphasized the dress, it was also a classy homage to the country and its people. Alina and her ensemble would have fashion critics talking and analyzing for days. Siyavash was very proud of his creation and he loved the way Alina effortlessly showed it off. Together they were a work of art.

Alina exuded a sensual elegance, a warm kindness, and was known for her charities around the globe. She was also a photojournalist's and interviewer's dream as she graciously gave them some of her time. They wanted to know everything about her and what she was up to. The cameras clicked and whirred relentlessly. The press loved her and were complimentary in their reportages. They also took pictures of her parents and of her manager with his husband.

Randy had been watching Jax and his entourage through the rifle's scope since they left the limousine. He recognized all of them as he had studied the people in Jax's life. He saw Alina and thought she was even more beautiful than the last time he had seen her at the scene of the accident. Jax even got the prettiest girl and made her his own, Randy grumbled to himself. He kept watching as the little group walked the red carpet and moved toward the theater. He moved slightly out of his harness and positioned the rifle for the shot he would deliver. He braced himself comfortably and waited for the exact moment. He looked through the scope and brought his index finger closer to the trigger. He wouldn't miss. He would kill Alina and make Jax wish he were the one who was dead. That death would be even more painful to the man who clearly adored the woman next to him.

A little girl called out to Alina. The singer heard the young voice and turned. She saw the cute face which reminded her of the girl of the Desana tribe in Brazil.

"I'll be right back," Alina said to Jax as she took a couple of steps toward the youngster. Members of the press swarmed around her as if they were hungry flies. Alina lowered herself to the child's height and opened her arms under the stanchion ribbon cordoning off the spectators from the celebrities. The little girl ran toward her favorite singer's open arms. They hugged for a long moment, longer than the press corps had anticipated, but the paparazzi found them endearing and bent down, their cameras closer to the little girl's height. They waited to see what would happen next.

Perfect! Randy thought. He would shoot her in the head as she stood back up. The shot would be effortless as she wouldn't be moving or walking. This was going to be even easier than he anticipated. His slowly lowered his index finger until it was on the trigger's curve. He waited for his moment and held his breath. As Alina stood up, he released the air in his lungs and squeezed the trigger on the rifle. The woman was smiling and at that moment Randy realized it would be the last time she would ever smile. NO! His brain screamed and his hand immediately jerked the rifle upward, but the bullet had already left the barrel. Alina Alonso wasn't to blame for Jax. Her only mistake was having fallen in love with the son of a bitch. The bullet headed straight for her head. Randy started to perspire. He fervently willed the projectile to follow an upward path which would take it above the woman speaking to the girl. He thought he had stopped in time, but he wasn't sure. He now prayed the movement might have steered the shot just far enough away, but it might have been a fraction of a second too late. The milliseconds it took for the bullet to arrive at its destination seemed an eternity to the man who had pulled the trigger. Randy willed the bullet to pass over her head. Alina caressed the girl's cheek. The move lowered her body a few millimeters. It was just enough extra little space for the shot to sail over her and land in the dirt of an enormous amphora housing a large plant, one of the many lining the red carpet. Between the slight trajectory deviation and Alina's bending down she was safe. No one noticed the mini projectile imbed itself in the roots of a small olive tree.

Randy exhaled. He was covered in sweat. He shook his head as if trying to clear his mind. As much as he wanted Jax to suffer and lose what he loved the most, he didn't think it was right that Alina should pay. She was faultless, an innocent woman whose songs he actually enjoyed. Killing her wouldn't be fair. He would still get his revenge, but only on Jax.

Alina's group and the other celebrities continued into the open-air theater, unaware of the near disconsolate catastrophe. Alina, her parents, Jax, Miguel and Santiago sat in the same row. Diego Molina, the man who was instrumental in starting Alina's career, was also nominated for an award. He greeted her with an enormous hug and kissed her cheeks. She returned the love to the man to whom she was grateful and would always cherish. Diego's wife, who was a brilliant composer, also kissed the newcomers. She and Diego had met at another award ceremony and had fallen in love. They sat in the row in front of the group.

As Stacy and Diego greeted each other she whispered in his ear: "You are the luckiest man in the world. Your wife is exquisite in every way. Always cherish her." Diego would always have a soft spot for Stacy, but his wife eclipsed any regret. She made him a very happy man, and it showed.

"I do, and always will." He whispered back.

"Good man."

The spectators enjoyed the award ceremonies with the Polyphony statuettes being handed to the deserving artists. Some of the nominees performed their songs to the pleasure of the audience and the television spectators watching worldwide. Diego received one of the Polyphonies for his latest song and he was also one of the entertainers in the show. It was his turn to perform and, as he had always done before stepping out on stage, said a quick prayer and crossed himself.

The lights opened up on Diego and his band. They started playing the song he had just won the award for and when he finished the musicians segued into one of his older songs, still one of his biggest hits. As Diego started to sing, he pointed to Alina in the crowd and insisted she come up on stage. The audience clapped and whistled as many remembered the Diego-Alina duet from the concert in Miami when Alina was just a teenager. She stood up and a member of the theater staff escorted her up on stage. She thanked him and went to Diego. As the music played in the background, they hugged each other. At the same moment a large screen behind the band showed the original duet footage from the Miami concert, from the moment a young fourteen-year-old Alina was lifted onto the stage.

"Do you know the words to the song?" Diego asked, just as he had so many years ago.

The audience laughed.

"I do."

"Can you sing?" He asked, as he had that first night.

"I think so," she answered shyly.

The crowd roared.

The questions and answers were the same as the original, and the show's sound engineer managed to coordinate the live version to the recorded one.

"Perfect," Diego said and the duo leaned into the square microphone in front of them. They sang as they had a decade earlier, one of them with a few grays in his hair and now sporting a goatee, the other a woman in the prime of her life, both physically and professionally.

The spectators noticed the change. The singers were more mature, wiser and even better at their craft. The combination of old and new was heartwarming, enlightening and entertaining. When they finished Diego's classic the audience immediately gave them a standing ovation. Their performance was one of the highlights of the evening. Diego and Alina held hands and bowed to the audience. A few moments later Diego spoke into the microphone: "Ladies and gentleman, ten years ago a pretty young girl became a part of my heart and one of the greatest gifts of my life. I love Alina like a little sister and I have no words to say how proud I was of her then, and of course all she has accomplished since. She inspired me and always will." Diego hugged Alina. She would always be his protégée. The spectators clapped profusely. He continued: "I am honored to share this next piece Alina wrote and composed, an incredible song and nominated for one of tonight's awards."

Alina thanked Diego and turned to the people in the theater. "As you might know my music is very international and my ideas come from every corner of the globe, from the depths of tropical jungles to the dwellers of great deserts, and to the whispering and roars of the seas. This composition, "Our World", is an homage to all people and to our Mother Earth who graciously lets us live in her beauty and bounty." This was Alina's signature, using sounds from nature and voices from birds. The music was a collection of indigenous sounds and warm rhythms from around the planet, from clapping bamboo to a crescendo of a full classical orchestra while still retaining an upbeat, modern and soothing tempo. Her composition reflected her powerful voice and the meaning in four different languages. She knew the words would not be understood by everyone, but certain ones were, such as love and peace. The lines of the song were short and spoke of understanding and unity among all people of the earth. The same lines were repeated, but in a different language. Alina and Diego sang together in the English and Spanish parts, and she did the Portuguese and Arabic on her own.

Alina watched the audience and understood how much they liked the song and appreciated the message.

The musicians continued as she continued and repeated one of the refrains in Greek, in tribute to the host country. She had learned the words in the last few days and was happy when one of the organizers heard it during rehearsal and asked her if she spoke Greek. That's when she knew she had nailed the accent. She also appreciated the amazing acoustics of the ancient amphitheater, and would always cherish the honor of having performed at the glorious Herodus Atticus.

Miguel didn't miss the audience's reaction, especially the Greek people who knew the song, but had never heard a piece of it in their language. The manager's creative juices exploded in his head as he envisioned the different languages and versions, and the duets recording the song with Alina. Perhaps they could gather a larger group of musicians as well and donate the proceeds to one of Alina's charities, as others had done in previous years with songs such as "We are the World".

When Alina and Diego finished singing, they returned to their seats. It was time for the last and most coveted award of the night, the Most International Song, the one Alina was nominated for and had just performed.

The last presenters came out from behind the ancient walls of the theater. The audience immediately smiled when they saw the duo. Although both at the very top of their fields and revered around the world, their look and backgrounds were complete opposites. One was a younger man, a very large rapper whose strong physique could impress professional linebackers. His white lamé jacket, white pants and multiple thick gold chains around his neck just about blinded the onlookers. The other presenter was an older, very petite woman in a simple long black silk designer gown. She was about a foot shorter and gracefully held on to his arm. She was an attractive woman and always would be, no matter her age. She wore matching diamond earrings and necklace, and a brooch.

In the background the announcer's smooth voice introduced them in fluent French, English and Greek. "Ladies and gentlemen, please welcome our last presenters this evening, opera sensation Dame Lena Everidge and rapper extraordinaire X-Lent." The spectators gave them a hearty applause. The duo stopped in front of the podium housing the microphone.

"So, you're X-Lent," Lena said. It was neither a question nor statement.

"Always, my Dame," he replied.

"It's Dame Lena, young man, no 'my'. Why don't you just call me Lena." Her voice was a little snobby and exasperated.

"You're from England, right Lena?"

"I am. And you're from the United States."

"Uh-huh, better known as the big 'hood'."

"If you say so." Lena turned her lips up a little and slightly raised an eyebrow as if in agreement.

"I dig your bling. Does it have a special meaning?" The rapper said, pointing to the brooch.

"It's a DBE."

"Disadvantaged Business Enterprise?"

The spectators laughed.

Lena's look was one of incredulity. "Dame of the British Empire."

"Cool! They give medals over in England to dames, just for being girls. Now that's gender equality!" He said excitedly.

The audience of course knew the duo was following a script they probably had written themselves. They laughed at their skit. Lena's face was one of disbelief.

Would she laugh or cry? They wondered.

"Not exactly, in this case Dame is the female of a Knight. I'm in agreement that it does sound quite plain. They could have maybe come up with something more original, perhaps even a little flattering."

"Well, night isn't much better for the guys. You just think of night and stars."

"Uh, not quite."

"Can I get one of these? You know a guy's version."

"That would a KBE."

"What's a KBE?"

"That would be Knight of the British Empire, the boy version of the DBE," Lena explained.

"Oh, right, *K*-night," he said, emphasizing the pronunciation of the K. Okay, I'll take one."

The audience laughed again.

"You can't just go to the corner store and pick one up. You have to get it from the Queen."

"What Queen?"

"Her Majesty Queen Elizabeth II."

"Oh, yeah, I know her, she's Meggie's granny-in-law."

"Who?"

"Meghan Markle, the American princess."

"Ah, yes, the Duchess of Sussex. She would, of course, be your American princess."

"You think she could ask Grandma Liz for me?"

The spectators roared.

Lena cringed. "It doesn't quite work that way. Now, how about we get on with the show?"

"Yeah, it's a cool award."

"It is. Do you have the envelope?"

"I do, right here in my pocket." X-Lent pulled it out and handed it to Lena. "Let's do this together," he said mischievously and raised his eyebrows a couple of times. X-Lent was endearing and the crowd loved him.

Lena looked up and grinned. "Of course, my big friend." She played along, never missing a beat.

"You know, our music comes from opposite pages."

"You think so?" Lena asked.

The crowd laughed some more.

X-Lent continued: "We may even look a little different…"

"Really?" Lena asked again.

"Juuuust a little, but we each make our own beautiful music." He looked into the audience and said: "See? Opposites attract and we are from different ends of the spectrum. I'm a big black guy wearing a big white jacket with shiny little petal-like things, and Lena here is a small white lady wearing a little black classic dress and she absolutely glows too. That means we're as coordinated as piano keys."

"Thank you, uh, I think, but are you saying we look like a piano?" Lena asked.

"Yeah."

Lena thought about it for a moment. "I think I do know what you're saying."

"You do?" The big man asked.

"Each person is a key and when played makes a sound, which is lovely in itself, but when many keys come together, we make a melody."

"Exactly!"

"X-Lent, if you and I, who are quite opposites…"

"Ya think?"

"…If we can produce love, because as far as I am concerned that's what music is, why can't all people be keys? If each person accepts the musical tastes of others, and of course not everyone will like the same thing, but can still respect the other's choice, why couldn't the same be said for an understanding of all people? Like a rainbow, a mixture of colors used to produce a beautiful unified symphony."

"Wouldn't that be an amazing phenomenon!" He exclaimed.

The audience clapped in agreement.

"Exactly," Lena said. "And yes, together our sounds cover the world from one end to the other, just like a rainbow."

The big man bent over and kissed Lena's cheek. She smiled and gently pulled on his thickest chain until his face was very close to hers and their noses practically touched. She looked into his eyes for a long moment. The crowd held their breath as they thought the two were getting pretty sexy. Lena moved her lips close to his mouth and at the last moment kissed his cheek. "Ready, my X-Lent young man?" She asked.

"Ready, my darling Dame Lena."

The duo opened the envelope, looked at each other and smiled. Together they announced: "OUR WORLD, by ALINA!"

The theater patrons exploded in agreement and applause.

Alina, who had been holding her breath, finally released it and smiled. That signature smile that made her so endearing. She had won the coveted Polyphony award for the song she had written and just performed.

Alina stood up, hugged her parents and kissed Jax lovingly. She sashayed toward the stage and held Jax's arm as he helped her up the stairs. Each step brought a flashback of her path on how she arrived at this moment in her life. Her mind's eye saw her first guitar lessons with Carlos, a protégé of great Spanish masters. He made the chord changes look so easy, his fast nimble fingers hardly visible. She remembered her own little fingers desperately trying to reach the same chords the same way her teacher was doing. But as she struggled she also swore she would practice hard and would be just as good as Carlos.

On the next marble step of the open-air theater, she could have sworn the same warm after summer breeze coming from the Mediterranean was caressing her body, just as it had when she rode the magnificent Arabian on the beach in Lebanon. That ride would always stay in her heart, as would the events of the kidnapping and her father being shot.

As Alina climbed the last step before the stage, she saw her little Ferrari hitting Jax and how their love for each other had bloomed. She worshiped the man with every fiber in her being and was sure the next day she would find, somewhere in her infinite fountain of love, how to adore him even more. She was also grateful for Bernardo who helped mold Jax into the man he had become and for the added bonus of the extraordinary bond the three of them shared with their last tango.

As Alina stepped on stage Jax stayed on the last step. He kissed her hand as if reading her thoughts. She bent down a little, cupped his cheek with her other hand and gave him an adoring kiss. He smiled and turned her hand over to X-Lent who had come up to them. Jax turned and went back to his seat. The big man offered Alina his arm. She laid her hand on it and kissed his cheek. He put his fist to his heart and smiled. Lena waited at the center of the stage where the podium stood with the award. The big man led Alina toward the diva. He let her go and the two women embraced.

"Brava, beautiful one, you will go far. Well deserved," Lena whispered in her ear.

"Thank you, Dame Lena, it means so much coming from you!"

"You are a favorite of mine and you are down to earth. Stay that way and your life and your music will be a triumph and legendary."

Alina held her favorite opera singer's hands and kissed the back of them. The two divas looked at each other, respect and mutual admiration in their eyes. The audience's hearts fluttered as they were moved by the unique understanding and veneration between the two amazing songstresses.

Alina accepted the statuette from X-Lent and went to the microphone on the podium for her speech.

"I would like to thank Dame Lena, one of my idols and one of the greatest divas ever. She has the amazing capability of making people listening to her lyrical singing start to cry, the same people who believed opera was just a bunch of absurd cat wailings." Approval from the audience as they clapped. Alina continued: "And of course the fabulously flashy philanthropic fellow X-Lent, an amazing musician, wonderful guy and brilliant humanitarian." The audience liked her play on words and clapped.

Alina looked into the crowd. She made eye contact with as many people as she could. "*Kalispera*," good evening, she said in Greek. The audience greeted her as well and shouted back in appreciation. "Thank you, beautiful Greece, for giving the world so much by being the birthplace of western civilization. Thank you, Athens and all the wonderful Greek people, for hosting these awards in this magnificent theater. Thank you to the Polyphony Awards committee for this incredible honor. Thank you to my amazing parents who made me into the person I am today. They introduced me to what I call the

University of Life, an exposure to many cultures with wonderful traditions, especially music." Alina blew her parents a kiss and then looked at Jax and said: "I will thank *you* later this evening, and show you how much I love you, as only I can." The spectators clapped and whistled. Jax smiled, raised an eyebrow and gave her a little nod. He could hardly wait.

Alina continued: "Diego Molina, thank you for being the beautiful instrument who guided and helped me when you knew what I needed, even before I did. I will always be grateful and the biggest fan of your incredible heart and talent." Diego blew her a kiss and made a heart with his hands. "Miguel, you are the maestro of talented managers. Thank you for everything. I wouldn't be where I am without you. And Santi, you are my other maestro and the epitome of a great musician. You represent all the amazing musical artists of the world, and you're a great 'little' bodyguard as well. Thank you." Alina smiled as she remembered their escape out of the club in Cali. The spectators laughed as they saw the size of the man. "There are many others to thank and I assure you, I will do so individually."

Alina looked at the audience and said: "When I was a little girl, I thought the world was this beautiful sphere with a pretty blue color between the continents. Then I noticed there were lines, borders, and I couldn't understand why. This globe was filled with people, all different and unique, but all the same. Each one wanted the same thing: to love and be loved, to be happy and at peace." Alina looked at the audience, her face very serious. "I still have this little girl's dream of one world with no conflicts and global unity, each nationality proudly representing their rich traditions. Why can't we all be like Dame Lena and X-Lent, different in just about every way but with the same heart. I hope the words and music of "Our World" will be a message to every individual and group, warring and not, so we can be one harmonious world."

Alina looked at the people in front of her which included famous artists, politicians and heads of enormous enterprises, each with certain powers and influence. She hoped they would heed her words and try to bring the world a little closer together with their own talents, resources and inspiration. "This Polyphony Award is a testament of the best the world has to offer. As its name states it has many voices, and music is its vessel. I am humbled and honored to be a recipient of this very international award. Thank you." Alina slightly bowed her head to the crowd.

The audience applauded and stood up. The young woman was wise beyond her years and had touched their hearts.

As Jax followed Alina's words he remembered one of Bernardo's favorite Pythagoras quotes: 'The highest goal of music is to connect one's soul to their Divine Nature, not entertainment'. Wasn't that what all entertainers, in this theater and everywhere in the world, were doing with their talent? Weren't they enabling the connection to each individual's Divine Nature through music?

♫

CHAPTER 38

Randy waited for the sun to completely disappear. He would let the night give him the cover he needed. He estimated the awards would be over soon as he listened to the show and could hear the announcer. When he was surrounded by darkness, he quickly climbed out of the tree and removed the camouflage suit. He packed it in his bag and went to the rental car. He was parked in a spot where he could see the limousines leaving the venue. He waited for Jax and his entourage to exit the theater. When he decided not to kill Alina, he still wanted Jax to die. He knew there would be an opportunity to get rid of the man that had caused him so much grief. Killing Alina would have been a worse death for Jax, but he liked the woman and she was a brilliant entertainer. She still had a lifetime of talent to offer the world. She was just stupid for falling for Jax. Ah, no one could be perfect.

Alina and her group left the theater under the Acropolis. They rode in the limousine taking them toward Piraeus, about twenty minutes outside of Athens, and arrived at the lovely port of Microlimano. The stars in the blue-black sky reflected on the water as the luxury yachts bobbed about. The *Adonis*, the yacht Alina rented for a week's holiday, waited for them in the serenity of the harbor. The group took in the postcard-worthy surroundings and headed toward the vessel.

The captain and his crew of five of the modern, sleek one-hundred-foot yacht saw them arriving and welcomed them aboard. They appreciated the contemporary warm décor and the large windows from all the interior rooms. The guests were shown to their staterooms with the en-suite facilities. They changed out of their formal attire and into casual clothes. Once ready, they headed to the upper deck and the buffet of local delicacies awaiting them.

"This has been one of the best days of my life," Alina said as she caressed Jax's cheek in their suite.

"I agree, and what an amazing way to start a vacation," Jax said as he picked her up and kissed her. She wrapped her legs around his body. He took a few steps back and found the edge of the bed. He sat down with Alina in his arms. He leaned back, still kissing her. She lay on top of him until their ardor moved them to sensually discover each other. Jax and Alina took a little longer than the other passengers as the diva fulfilled her promise in proving how grateful she was for her man, as mentioned in her speech at the Awards.

Randy had followed the limousine in the inconspicuous rental. When the passengers boarded the Adonis he parked in a dark area, attached a knife and its sheath to his ankle and tucked a gun in the back of his shorts. He donned a mask and snorkel and lowered himself into the water. He swam toward the yacht. When he arrived, he looked around. All was quiet, with just a few voices conversing in the distance on one of the upper decks. He silently pulled himself up the swim platform in the back. He removed the wet suit he wore over shorts and a t-shirt. Randy soundlessly climbed the stairs to the deck and did a quick reconnoitering of the vessel and the crew. Two of the sailors were in the engine room, another was on the bridge and the others, including the captain, were tending to the guests in the large open-air seating area. This is where they would all gather. A couple of them were present and he was sure the others would join them. Randy hid behind the lifeboat at the back of the deck. His view was perfect. He could watch for Jax and keep an eye on the crew and the passengers.

It was late and the group was hungry. It had been a long day. The crew had prepared a buffet of Greek amuses-bouche instead of a formal sit-down dinner. Each guest could go to the long table and let their eyes enjoy the feast in front of them and then choose anything from the dozens of platters filled with the delicacies. They included mini filo-wrapped triangles of cheese and spinach; *keftedakia*, small meatballs, and bite-size souvlaki skewers. Dips of *taramosalata*, *melitzanosalata*, roe, eggplant and tzatziki abounded. Other dishes included different raw and cooked vegetables, some of them stuffed; bite size balls of lemon roasted potatoes; a variety of local cheeses including feta smothered in oil and oregano; pita bread, several salads, and from the sea grilled fish, shrimp and octopus. All decorated with lemons as the Greeks firmly believe it is the 'other blood' in their veins. Dessert included small baklava pieces and mini *loukoumades*, Greek beignets with nuts and honey. Baskets of watermelon held cut fruit, and between the dishes several chocolate Polyphony statuettes made by the chef decorated the table.

The crew members waited for each guest to choose their selection and asked them for their beverage preference. The passengers sat in comfortable lounge chairs and enjoyed their food. Randy watched and realized he was hungry. He hadn't eaten in over twenty-hours, the adrenaline of his mission making him forget any kind of hunger. He would wait until Jax was dead.

The sailors waited for the passengers to finish their food and quickly removed their plates. The vacationers relaxed, enjoying the lights of the city, the port and the tranquility. Soft Greek and international music played from the yacht's speakers. Randy watched. Only one crew member was present, should any of the passengers want anything. The others were busy with their duties. One of the guests ordered a drink and the sailor went inside. That was Randy's cue. He slowly removed the knife from its sheath around his ankle and then jumped out of his hiding place. He ran toward Jax who was seated in one of the loungers. Randy lunged at him, the knife coming down fast toward his torso. Out of the corner of his eye Jax saw the blur and instinctively fell off his chair, the weapon missing him by just inches.

"Randy!" Jax exclaimed, recognizing the man and surprised by his presence.

"Yeah, it's me, back from the dead."

Jax quickly jumped up from the floor of the deck. The two men faced each other, Randy wielding the knife, Jax trying not to get stabbed.

"Please stop!" Alina shouted as she watched Randy pull out a gun from the back of his shorts. Why did his face seem familiar to her? Randy aimed the pistol at Santiago who was getting closer. He figured the big man was probably the biggest threat and also the easiest target to hit.

The sailor came back with the drink. When he saw Randy and the gun he gasped and dropped the glass.

Randy spotted the radio on the crew member's hip. "Get on that walkie-talkie and tell the crew to get over here! Right now! And say it in English!" He screamed. "And tell them to leave any weapons and to not even think of calling the police or someone will surely die. That's not my intention, but I won't hesitate if you don't follow my orders." He looked at the group as shouted: "That goes for you as well. Stay exactly where you are."

The young sailor did exactly as he was told. The others, including the captain, were immediately on deck.

"You're all here, that's good." Randy looked at the captain and shouted to him: "You, take the rope from the lifeboat and tie your crew up. All hands together. Don't try anything stupid because I'll check it. And add the big guy."

"No, please, not Santi," Miguel pleaded.

"Shooting him would be easier, and save some time," Randy retorted.

Miguel nodded and raised his hands. "Okay."

"Now shut up and stay in your chair."

"Randy, why are you doing this?" Jax asked.

Of course! It was Randy Newton, from the equestrian team. Alina remembered him from the Olympics in Beijing and from the CEA. Jax had told her what he had done, although she remembered seeing the scandal on the news. Why was he doing this? Why did he want to harm the man she loved?

Randy whirled around and faced Jax, keeping the pistol on Santiago. "I just want you!" He shouted.

"But why? Did I do something to you?" Why do you want to…"

"You ruined my life, you bastard!"

"What? How?"

"Do you know what kind of living hell I've gone

through since that CEA?"

"I heard you were in jail, but were released a few days later."

"I was there long enough to have my life become an inferno and to collect scars inflicted by bored inmates."

The group cringed. They didn't need to have a great imagination to understand the horrors Randy had probably endured. "It's your turn to know what hell is."

"But why? I just don't understand this vendetta."

"Because of you I spent twelve years of my life in prison, you idiot!" Randy screamed.

"What are you saying? You were released after only a few days."

"I'm not talking about Spain, but in the States. Twelve long fucking years! All because of you!" Randy lunged at Jax but he moved just in time.

"Enlighten me, asshole!" Jax shouted, getting angrier by the moment. Jax was usually a calm guy and it took a lot to get him riled up. The man was now really pissed off. "You were the one who tried to kill me back then, but you were caught. I had nothing to do with it. You did it to yourself, man. And speaking of hell, do you have any idea of what *I* went through? Not just physically, but emotionally? Months and months of therapy, you bastard!"

"Aw, poor baby," Randy moaned sarcastically. "And for your information, you moron, you were just supposed to fall. I had no intention to kill you."

"And as far as competing, you took that away. I can't do it anymore."

Randy hadn't known about that, and always wondered when he watched the big competitions why he never saw Jax. As livid as he was, the equestrian in him regretted that. Jax had been a magnificent rider with a gift, but he still wanted the man to suffer as much as he had.

"All set," the captain said, having tied his crew together.

"Do I need to check it?" Randy asked.

"No, I can assure you."

"I'll take your word for it but if you're fucking with me your young sailor gets the first bullet. Understood?"

"Please, it really is fine."

Randy turned to Santiago and the group tied together and screamed: "Go close to the side and get on your knees. Face the water!"

They did as he asked.

"Tie them to the banister," Randy said to the captain.

The skipper followed directions.

Stacy knew Alejandro was concocting a million scenarios, as she was sure they all were. Her husband had been a military man and that's just the way his mind would always work. He looked at his wife and gave her a wink that told her how much he loved her and not to worry. He had something in mind. She knew it. She slightly nodded, giving him a look that relayed she was ready for anything and whatever he needed.

"Randy, stop this, man. It's not worth it," Jax said, trying to reason with him.

"Oh, it's very worth it! I've been dreaming about this for years. You're just as good as dead."

"Please, take me instead," Alejandro said.

"Ah, and you are Alina's daddy, Alejandro Alonso," Randy said.

"You know me?"

"I know of you, yes, and everyone else here. I have studied each one of you."

"Please, you must stop. No one will win, if anything

it will be a loss, especially for you," Stacy chimed in.

"Ah, the wife and mother of the singer. Shut up," Randy said, dismissing her.

Stacy started walking to the man holding the knife and the gun. "I don't think so."

As much as Alina would always think of her mother as Wonder Woman, she wasn't impervious to bullets or knives. Alina was worried. What was she up to? She better not get hurt, Alina's heart screamed.

The interruption was just enough to sidetrack Randy. Alejandro and Jax dove for the gun and the knife at the same time. The Spaniard managed to disarm him and threw the pistol in the water. Jax knocked the blade out of Randy's hand. He landed a few feet away and lunged to grab the blade but Alejandro reached it first. Randy was a split-second late, but managed to grab his opponent's arm. The Spaniard punched him with his other hand and Randy fell back just enough for the older man to thrust the weapon. Randy moved just in time to avoid being stabbed in the stomach, but the knife landed deep into the upper part of his leg. He screamed in pain, fell backward, the blood from the wound in his thigh forming a slow widening dark crimson circle on his shorts. Jax and Miguel held Randy down. The captain untied his crew and Santiago. Alina helped Alejandro to his feet.

"I'm fine, amorcito," the Spaniard said.

"Get me a first aid kit!" Stacy, always in healing mode, shouted to one of the crew members. As she ran toward Randy, she grabbed several of the linen napkins from the buffet table. When she reached the injured man, she quickly placed the cloth around the knife on the bleeding wound. She didn't remove the blade as she didn't know the depth or extent of its damage. If she did, he could possibly bleed out.

Jax held the man who once had been his buddy, his teammate, the guy he still somehow wanted in his life, even after all the pain Randy wanted to inflict on him. Since the day they met, Jax held a place in his heart for him. He firmly believed that if a person crossed his path there was a reason for it and should be a cherished acquirement. He still had hopes for Randy and wanted to believe the man could find peace in his life. The two men had a unique connection. Maybe it was the equestrian bond, maybe because Jax somehow understood Randy had been dealt a bad hand along the way.

"Randy, right?" Stacy asked the bleeding man.

"Yeah, that's his name," Jax answered.

"Don't move an inch or you'll bleed out."

Randy stared at her.

"Did you hear me, asshole?" Stacy was just as angry as anyone there.

Randy nodded.

"Don't you fucking die on me, you son of a bitch!" Jax screamed at his former teammate.

"Why would you care?" Randy hissed.

"Because I do."

Randy looked at the other man's eyes. He could tell Jax meant it, but couldn't understand why.

Jax watched Stacy working on his old teammate. "Randy, listen to me, man. You're going to be fine, thanks to Stacy, and we're not going to press charges."

"But I attacked you, tried to kill…"

"I know. Everyone is okay, other than you of course, you idiot, but you'll heal."

"Why Jax? Why aren't you pressing charges? Why don't you want to kill me yourself, or at least get me thrown back in jail?" Randy couldn't understand and needed to know.

"I don't believe in an eye for an eye. I do believe that problems can be worked out, with communication, with knowledge, with understanding. With second chances. Get it?"

"I think so. But why aren't you bitter?"

"I am and what I went through wasn't easy, but I had help and a lot of support. I think that's what you need too. I lived with the pain and maybe that made me stronger. However, what you did to Almea will take longer to forgive, although I think you're paying for it with your injury."

"I knew she would be alright, and I really apologize for hurting her. I didn't think the pain would be so bad. I want you to know that I more than paid for her pain… back in the prison in Spain. It took me months to recover from what those bastards did to me."

"Listen, Randy, when this injury is healed, I want you to come find me." Jax put his hand out.

Randy just stared and shook the other man's hand. He didn't know what to say and just nodded. Maybe it was karma giving him a second chance because he didn't kill Alina, or even his parents.

"Jax, hold his back up a little," Stacy asked.

Jax lifted Randy and sat on the deck behind him, holding him as a father would a boy who had just scraped his knees. "I'll be waiting for you. We're a team, man, always," Jax said to him.

Randy thought of the first time Jax had taken care of him when they were in Beijing and had gotten so drunk off the local liquor. The muscle memory in Randy's body remembered Jax's strong caring arms supporting him, and wondering at the time why he had been so considerate. He also flashed back to the very early hugs he received as a child, which faded away the older he became. This was the first time he had been affectionately hugged since he was a youngster, other than Darla, but that was a different kind of embrace. He shuddered as he was sure his body was shedding one soul for a better one. Randy started to cry, looked at Jax and said: "I'm sorry, man, please forgive me. I promise I'll come find you and I'll fight like hell to become an honorable person."

"I know you will. Now just relax, the ambulance is on its way."

"Thank you, Jax. You always believed in me."

"And still do."

When the EMTs arrived, they quickly checked Randy's injury, nodded in approval at the care he had been given, picked the man up and put him on a stretcher before taking him to the ambulance. As Randy stared blankly at the inside of the medical vehicle, he thought about Jax, the man who had just taught him a great lesson. For the first time in his life, he didn't feel a mountain of pressure and looked forward to learning more from his friend. He was a friend, right? He had never had a real friend and he swore he would do everything possible to be an upstanding member of society. He knew Jax would help him, as would Darla, and he looked forward to this new chapter in his life. As Randy lay on the stretcher in the ambulance he analyzed the last decade of his life. He realized that Jax wasn't at fault, rather, it was his parents' doing. He spent some of his best years in prison, but he was happy with the life as it was at this moment. Physically he would heal, financially he was set for many lifetimes. He was in love with a wonderful down to earth woman who made him happy in every way, and he knew he now had an incredible friend. His life had been bittersweet. Now it would only get sweeter. He understood that his thirst for revenge and his bitterness only withered his soul, and was never a real solution. Randy told Darla the day he proposed to her he still had one more thing to do before they could get married. She had been understanding and patient, although she didn't like being kept in the dark or worrying. She didn't know how dangerous this 'thing' he had to do would be, remembering he had been in prison. She agreed under one condition—that when it was over, they would never lie or keep any secrets from each other again. Randy had agreed. He could hardly wait to get back to her. He would take her on a vacation around the world, after they chose and bought a private plane to travel in. They would make a stop in Florida and find his *friend*—that sounded so good—and would help Jax and Hippo-Camp any way needed. He would also contribute handsomely to Alina's charities. Randy finally understood that by giving he was receiving even more. He couldn't wait to help try to make the world a better place. He was happy the huge amount of money he possessed would prove useful in the endeavor.

EPILOGUE

After the ambulance left for the hospital with Randy, the group sat down and quickly recuperated. Thankfully there were no paparazzi as Miguel had been overly secretive. Members of the press who knew Alina was going on vacation were promised an exclusive, with photos, when it was over. They could live with that, although following one of their favorite celebrities was always fun and brought them joy and money.

The group was finally relaxing with a drink and talking about the day's events.

"I heard you say to that man you couldn't compete anymore, is that true?" Alejandro asked.

"Is it because of the fall at the CEA?" Stacy asked.

"I went through a tough time with the therapy and the aftermath for quite a while. To be honest I think I actually could compete and Almea is still in top shape, but I don't feel the passion I once had. Without that it's no fun and you need that drive, or you don't stand a chance of giving your best performance or of winning. And Almea would sense it as well. Also, Bernardo is not around," Jax added as a shadow lowered over his eyes.

"You know, Jax," Alina said, "I think Bernardo and even Maria would be very happy and proud if you tried."

"Maybe you should reconsider," Miguel said. "The Paris Olympics are in 2024 and I think it would be a great coup if you and Alina performed at the same venue."

"Oh, there's that manager's mind, always envisioning the future. Nice segue, Miguelito," Santiago chuckled.

"You want me to enter an equestrian event?" Alina asked.

"Hey, I hadn't thought of that. That would be brilliant too!" Miguel said excitedly. He knew her prowess as a rider. This was getting better by the minute, the man thought.

"You know, that actually sounds really special," Jax said, looking at the love of his life. "I think I'm starting to get my passion back, and really fast!" Jax lifted Alina up and whirled her around. "You and me competing together! That would be really nice."

"Miguel," Santiago said, "I think you better straighten this out and tell them the news."

"Yes, Santi, you're right."

"What news?" Alina asked.

"I was informed, just after the Awards, that you are invited to perform at the opening of the Games." Miguel let a moment pass by so the full impact of the information would sink in. "But in addition, just imagine, and of course this has never been done before by any athlete or celebrity, singing *and* competing at the games by the same person!" Miguel started thinking out loud. "The publicity, the interviews, the late shows… History will be made!"

"The man is on a roll, don't pay any attention to him. When he gets like this, I just leave him alone," Santiago chortled.

"He's a genius," Alina said. "He has the world's most organized and creative mind."

"Amorcito, remember when you were younger you asked if we could one day go to the Games?" Alejandro asked his daughter."

"I do, Papá."

"Well, here's the opportunity. A little different than you originally thought, but perhaps even better."

"Well, sweetheart, are you going to take part in the Olympics?" Stacy asked.

"Oh, yes, I would love to open at the Games. And I wouldn't dream of bursting Miguel's bubble. Look at him!"

The group did and laughed. Miguel's mind had teleported to 2024 Paris and his gaze was watching the future events as he imagined they would unfold.

"You know, Mom, I think I would like to try. It would be so exciting, and a once-in-a-lifetime opportunity. Of course, I would need to be good enough and qualify." Alina looked at the man she loved. "I would need to find a coach, perhaps someone who has been on that path before."

"That would be me." Jax said with a gleam in his eye.

"Perfect."

"And I know Sir Charles will be thrilled to participate at the Olympics again, and with coaching not just one, but two riders."

"I'll follow your lead," Alina answered.

Stacy laughed good heartedly.

"What's so funny?" Alina asked.

"I meant singing at the opening," she giggled. "But I think competing as well would be extraordinary, my darling."

"Yes, Mom, definitely the opening, and I would love

to try making the equestrian team."

When the group first boarded Alejandro asked one of the crew members to start recording when he was given the signal. It was time, even with Randy crashing the party. Yes, he was sure it would be fine. He looked at Jax who smiled back and confirmed by slightly nodding. Alejandro discreetly signaled to the sailor waiting. The young man slightly dipped his head and inconspicuously started the camera.

"You know, Alina," Jax said, "we could seal the deal and go as husband and wife." Jax knelt down on one knee and produced a little red box from his pocket. "Your Daddy gave me a green light when I asked him for your hand. Alina, love of my life, would you make me the happiest man in the world and become my wife?" Jax took the ring out of the box and held it in front of him. It was a large heart-shaped extremely rare red diamond surrounded by smaller orange, yellow, green, blue and violet diamonds. He had it designed to remind her that the ring was surrounded by the rainbow between her heart and his. He intended to make her smile and happy every day of her life with him.

Alina's mind flashed back to Grace at the hospital in Miami, her father's comments when they landed at the Florida compound and Bernardo's words. They had all known because the glow in her eyes confirmed what her heart already knew.

Miguel, whose mind had been multi-tasking, put his vision and his breath on hold as Santiago was squeezing his husband's shoulder. Alejandro and Stacy were holding hands and waiting for Alina's answer. The crew was practically at attention. They had never had such celebrities on board and the beginning of their vacation had already been an adventure. Now they were witnessing a proposal between a beautiful couple and they held their breaths as well.

"Yes, my love, with my entire soul," Alina answered. "May I always make your heart sing as you make mine." She gave Jax the most enchanting smile he had ever seen. It was a new one. The man understood it was one reserved especially for him and could swear his heart was expanding.

Jax stood up, put the ring on her finger and kissed the lips of the woman he adored. Alina hugged her future husband and wouldn't let go. Jax would never get enough of her smiles, her sensual caring and her amazing heart. He remembered the first time he saw her on his television and his fanatical obsession to make her his own. He was glad he hadn't given up. His soul must have known that together they were whole.

The group clapped and shouted their congratulations. The sailor was still filming, making sure he shot the amazing ring that made its very own rainbow under the lights. Alejandro thought Miguel might get another idea for some publicity stunt and would maybe want to use the footage, but he was more interested in giving the recording to Jax and Alina as a special moment in their lives. He was sure they would figure out what they would to do with it.

Alejandro and Stacy reached them first and gave them an enormous hug. Miguel and Santiago did the same, and the crew and staff congratulated them as well. Alina would never forget this day. She suddenly saw an image of Bernardo beaming with pride. She remembered some of the gaucho's last words: 'I want your life together to be so happy you won't know if you are living it, or dreaming it.' He was right, as life at this moment was as wonderful as the best dreams.

Jax pulled his future wife close to his chest and held her in his arms. He kissed her lovingly, took one of her hands and interlaced their fingers. He put it on his heart, as he had done when Alina met Almea. He whispered in her ear: "You are my heart song."

♫♫♫

About the Author

My very first memory of life was the sound of my mother's glorious voice singing to me, most likely a Brahms lullaby. I'm convinced that is why music always has a delicious way of creeping into my writing and becomes an integral part of my novels. I lived in Europe for over twenty years while my father was a diplomat with the U.S. State Department. This provided the basis for many of my story themes and settings, and my love for languages, five of which I speak fluently and use quite often when recording audiobooks (my own as well as other authors').

I write different genres: Romance, Adventure, Metaphysical, Military and Historical fiction. My non-fiction work includes a photo book, 'Around the World in 80 Quotes on Photos', and 'Travel Tales', short adventure stories from different places around the globe. 'Violet's Voyages', is a Children's Books series I created for my granddaughter.
I believe there is no stronger bond than sharing a book. My desire is that my work entertains and informs, and that my readers, from 3 to 103 years young, cherish the time reading and discovering together.

I am a proud mother of a gallant Marine Veteran, and among the members of our household you will find Louie the cat (aka King Louie XIX), so named because of his clawing love of Louis XV and XVI furniture, and surely thinks he was a king in one of his former lives.

Acknowledgments

Pamela Carter, *thank you!* for being such an aficionado of my work. It means so much. Your friendship is truly cherished and I always look forward to your, always spot-on, detailed suggestions.

Margarita González Giraldo, my lovely 'Colombian insider', *mi parce,* you are one of Colombia's greatest examples of what it means to have a big heart and a helping hand at all times. Working together has always been a pleasure, including on details of this book. *¡Gracias!*

Frossene and Larry King, thank you for your wonderful and caring friendship. Your talents in design and the culinary arts are amazing.

And to my family—you are my Heart Song.

A Note from the Author

The Beijing 2008 Olympic equestrian event takes place in Beijing, although it was held in Hong Kong.

HeliEmerg, the Vinyl building, the Campeonato Ecuestre de Andalucia (CEA), La Tusa Pachorra (the bar in Colombia) and the Polyphony Awards are fictitious and were created for the sole purpose of this story.

On my website you will find photos of locations in 'Heart Song' (and my other books as well). Please enjoy. denisekahnbooks.com/photomusic-gallery/

If you would like information on new releases and events make sure you sign up for my newsletter.
You will automatically receive a FREE PDF of **'Around the World in 80 Quotes on Photos'**.

I love hearing from my readers and I answer all my mail personally. Thank you for your interest and for reading!
e-mail: Denise@DeniseKahnBooks.com

DeniseKahnBooks.com / DeniseKahnVoices.com

Denise's books

Peace of Music

A once lost magnificent antique vase from China's 13th Century Song Dynasty reappears from the depths of the Mediterranean Sea where it comes to dwell on a piano in a doctor's home. It becomes the impetus in steering the lives of this doctor and his descendants through their heartbreaks, romances and ultimately successes. An assassination, a sabotage on a Greek island and amazing musical performances are but some of the events that strike their lives. Spanning from 13th Century China to the present, the story takes place on four continents, with talented individuals of different nationalities and backgrounds, always interrelated by music.

Obsession of the Heart

Set against an international backdrop of jet setters, music, romance, murder, terrorism and true friendship is Davina Walters, an international singer. Davina meets Jean, a young woman almost paralyzed with fear, as her sadistic ex-husband is bent on killing her. On the spur of the moment Davina decides to take her along on tour and the murderer plans his ultimate revenge in a deadly showdown.

Warrior Music

Max knew the drugs and alcohol would eventually kill him, and sooner rather than later. So he enlisted in the Marines. His timing is unfortunate, as the events of 9/11 find him at the beginning of his military service, and he is sent to Iraq. The journey he embarks on is unlike anything he could ever imagine.

From Washington, Boston and New Orleans to the ancient sands of Iraq, Max and his entourage endure the toils of war with gallantry, patriotism, courage, heartache and passion.

Only one weapon gets them through the anguish they come face to face with... Music.

The Music Trilogy

The Music Trilogy, a family saga, is a compilation of three books: **Peace of Music, Obsession of the Heart** and **Warrior Music**, a combination of **historical fiction, thriller, romance, military prowess and music**. The Music Trilogy can be read or listened to in sequence or each book as a stand-alone.

Enchanted Football

A football story with humor. A promising new NFL team with unconventional yet winning methods.

The New Mexico Natives are a new NFL football team with an unexpected promising future, until an accident leaves them without enough players. Their determination won't let them quit and they manage to find world class athletes, albeit somewhat unpredictable, to take their places. The players include a quarterback on the run, an Olympic sprinter who can't catch, a spiritual Navajo man, a Greek dancer, an Italian goalie, a French rugby player, and a beautiful English Lady who winds up on the sidelines.

With laugh-out-loud moments, uplifting events and even romance you will root for the characters with each turn of the page.

Whether you are a football professional, couch or otherwise, or someone with very little knowledge of the game, you are bound to enjoy a humorous and heartwarming story.

A perfect way to celebrate 100 years of the NFL!

Split-Second Lifetime

On a business trip from the U.S. to Paris, Jebby meets Dodi on a flight. Jebby is an ethnomusicologist, and Dodi is an international photographer. They are immediately attracted to each other, but from the very first moment Dodi triggers what seems like past life memories for Jebby of a poignant and passionate time they shared together. As Jebby tries to figure out if she is "losing it" or if past lives really do exist, they embark on a path of adventure and romance where lifetimes and cultures interweave in modern day Paris, Uzbekistan, and in the old Southwest. Jebby and Dodi live their unusually diverse and rich adventure and romance, surrounded by an international cast and superb musicians. At the same time Jebby discovers where the Hopi originated from, that death is not a finality, love transcends lifetimes, and music is eternal.

Hot Air

A thriller filled with passion, romance, survival and courage. Sean Sandoval, half Navajo, half Irish, has bravery in his blood and passion in his heart. From boyhood to one of the Air Force's elite Pararescuemen, his path in life is always connected to air. As a hot air balloon pilot Sean communes with that air. As a Pararescuer he flies into danger to saves lives.

An enemy combatant from the mountains of Afghanistan, presumed killed, arrives in Albuquerque, New Mexico and is bent on such revenge that he puts thousands of people at the annual International Balloon Fiesta in lethal danger. Will Sean stop him in time?

Guitar Woman (novella)

Filled with romance, suspense, passion, and set in beautiful Greek locations.

Alex Kouros's passions are making exquisite guitars and producing Greece's premier beer. At a prestigious art gallery he meets artist Cassandra Beckham. A whirlwind romance ensues, but is cut short when malicious kidnappers board the yacht they are sailing on in the turquoise waters of the Aegean. As they struggle with the malefactors Alex is shot and Cassie falls into the sea with a blow to her head. They are left for dead, and although they survive they both think the other died.

Alex blames himself and tries to drown his sorrows with his brew. Cassie washes up on a deserted beach of a tiny island.Will they be destined to find each other again?

Around the World in 80 Quotes on Photos

A photograph portrays a thousand words. A quote is but a few more powerful ones. Together they are food for the senses. They make us think, wonder, and engulf us. They represent traditions, civilizations, cultures, and offer us splendor, progress, grand vistas and minute details, all in a planet rich in majestic beauty. Embark on this journey of quotes and photographs, from ancient sands to calm seas, from sky to pebbles, from natural magnificence to man-made luxury.
Photographs were taken in countries around the world.

Travel Tales

Travel Tales is a series of short travel stories, journeys spiced with humor and interesting international characters in famous or little known places.
True stories of the author finding herself in adventures in foreign lands while discovering different cultures, local folklore, food, music, and sometimes danger.

We were 12 at 12:12 on 12/12/12 (Mexico)
Entertained by the Gods (Greece)
Sai Baba's Ashram Rendezvous (India)
Gstaad Grace (Switzerland)
Thanksgiving in 24 Hours (Mexico)
Olympic Honor (Italy)

Violet's Voyages
(Children's Series)
Switzerland: The St. Bernard Adventure (Book 1)
Greece: The Dolphin Adventure (Book 2)

Violet always starts her adventures by catching a ride on a shooting star!
To what area of the world will it bring her? She hangs on tight until her destination, where she is welcomed by a special local animal who is on a mission. Violet always helps them with their quest.

KKO *Keeping Kids Occupied (and adults too)*

....

**All books are available as e-books.
Most are available as paperbacks and audiobooks.
Violet's Voyages available in hardcover as well.
For more information please visit:**

DeniseKahnBooks.com
DeniseKahnVoices.com